The Road to Ramallah

The Road to Ramallah

Alan W. Horton

Madison Spring Press
2015

Dedication

For Joan

Over all the years, my principal inspiration and guide
has been my late wife,
Dorothy Joan Ryder Horton

Acknowledgements

Many people and places have contributed to this fictional narrative. My late wife and I spent many years in Cairo and occasional years in Gaza, Beirut, and Aleppo. I am profoundly grateful to the people we met and learned from during those thirty or more years, for the knowledge they imparted and for allowing a foreigner to become a friend – in many instances, a close family friend.

I began writing this story about fifteen years ago, wrote a draft, then placed it in a "finish later" file. About a year ago, I revisited the file and was inspired to revise. For help with the earlier draft, I am particularly grateful to the distinguished editor Alan Rinzler, and for incomparable commentary on the revision I am deeply indebted to writer and editor William Craig.

My children, grandchildren, nieces, nephews and in-laws have also made truly invaluable comments. They have my thanks.

The Road to Ramallah

ONE

Cairo, March 1990

The first time I saw the man in the pinstripe suit was shortly after midday at the Nile Hilton. My friend Sam Paul and I were just finishing a poolside lunch on the terrace, a luxurious expanse of blue-and-white tile and casual arrangements of white chairs, tables and umbrellas. The tables were occupied by well-to-do Egyptians and foreigners. The terrace was an upper-class enclave surrounded by high walls and overlooked only by tall palm trees. Migrating rainbow-green bee-eaters swooped gracefully over our heads. A few stray cats competed with sparrows for crumbs that fell to the tiles. Three or four middle-aged swimmers stroked sedately across the pool. Sam and I never swam. Our offices were close by, and we often met on the terrace just to eat and talk. The sun felt good on the shoulders, and the walls allowed us to forget the dust, noise and poverty of the city just outside.

Sam nodded in the direction of a table on the other side of the pool. "There," he said, "sits an example of the young educated Arab who has no job because he refuses to work with his hands." Sam, a businessman from Detroit who came up the hard way, spoke contemptuously. Sneaking a quick look, I saw a slender man seated by himself, a lemonade in front of him. A strikingly handsome face, thin mustache, well-cut pinstripe suit of Oxford gray, no necktie. In the context of Egypt's mix of peoples, his ancestors could have been Turkish, or perhaps Circassian, conquerors from the Caucasus Mountains of Southwest Asia. He was at

3

ease, aristocratic, a cut above the Hilton's usual crowd of affluent youth. He neither stared at others nor worried about being stared at.

"Very common type in these parts," said Sam. So I looked at the fellow again, disagreeing with Sam's assessment, but I didn't bother to mention it. We still had business matters to discuss, though it did fleetingly cross my mind his assessment was a bit odd. Sam had been around the Eastern Mediterranean a long time and would ordinarily have been more perceptive. Business matters took over and I forgot the fellow.

But that evening I saw him again outside our apartment in Zamalek, the upscale residential area of central Cairo's Gezira Island. The sun had set, and without turning on the living room lights, I had slipped out to sit in the gathering darkness of our small balcony, watching the light's last reflections from the Nile, following the endless patterning of the eddies. From my secluded second-story perch I saw him sitting on the wall along the top of the riverbank. The street lamps had just come on, and in the lamplight the good looks, the graceful carriage, the well-tailored pinstripe suit were unmistakable. He sat beside a shorter, older man whose face I could not see, two friends chatting in the cool air coming upstream from the Mediterranean. I thought idly about coincidences.

But both men suddenly looked up, and the notion of coincidence began to crumble. My wife or one of the children had just turned out some lights in the back of the apartment after the evening's homework session, and the swift response left no doubt that our apartment was the focus of their interest. Now the two talked purposefully, scanning our apartment's windows, chatting no longer. As night moved in, I sat absorbed, senses alert, motionless lest they discern some flicker of movement from the unlit balcony. Then the man in the pinstripe suit took the hand of the other in a formal gesture of farewell and strode off down the street. The second man settled down on the wall, moving to the part with least light. At his post.

For a while I sat in the darkness, utterly astonished. I wanted it to be a coincidence, but the evidence refused to cooperate. Yes, I was being watched. Or perhaps it was my whole family. The changing of the guard, which I had just witnessed, crushed all doubts, like a bolt sliding home and locking out other possibilities. I realized I had been holding my breath, and I struggled to assemble my thoughts. The basic question, of course, was why.

I reached quickly for the simplest explanation. Just one more problem of Cairo living to be coped with. Like most Cairo problems, it needed reflection, then a few visits to the right people. Certainly my existence – the straightforward story of Bill Hampton, an American businessman in Egypt – held no mysteries or secrets that could interest Egyptian officialdom. No need to anticipate any difficulty in sorting things out. Americans like me, unlike the Egyptian poor, had the clout to set things straight, to explain and be listened to.

Nonetheless I felt odd. Something unordinary had suddenly invaded my conventional life, and I felt some kind of Anglo-Saxon guilt. If the police had a man watching me, I must have done something wrong. Because surely it was a police matter, an event in keeping with routines of Egyptian life I knew about from others. If only to keep their burgeoning bureaucracy occupied, the police had an insatiable curiosity, and while no Westerners I knew had lately reported any police activity, a few Egyptian business friends spoke offhandedly about being watched. One of them, sixtyish and successful, claimed with joking pride he'd lived through the surveillance of four regimes – Farouk, Nasser, Sadat, now Mubarak – and appreciated the attention. Having a man outside, he said, gave his wife a feeling of security and made him reluctant to initiate the fuss that would interrupt a police routine. So he made casual friends of those on duty, giving them small tips on feast days. Would an expatriate like me receive the same treatment? Had the government decided to harass the foreign business community as if it were an opposition group, as it might have done in Nasser's day?

Cath remained busy with the children. Slipping from the darkness of the balcony into the living room, I picked up a book and sank into my chair. The book would serve as cover when Cath emerged. Hasan, our extraordinary servant who seemed to be available whenever wanted, came to ask if I needed something before dinner but I said I didn't.

Perhaps it was routine police behavior. The trouble was, it didn't make sense.

I led a humdrum life. If some friends thought otherwise, it was because they found it exotic that I'd been born and brought up in Palestine, the son of the Ramallah School's Quaker headmaster, and that I knew Arabic the way I knew English. But Cath once called me un-exotic in an argument we had about the "ordinariness" of our existence. "I enjoy being ordinary," I had said. I exaggerated, of course. Everyone has moments when they see themselves as adventurous. But such moments in Bill Hampton's life were hard to find. And in the business world of Cairo, my life as Middle Eastern representative of Starr Johnson, a major American electronics firm based in San Francisco, contained no adventure, nothing exciting enough to attract the attention I was now getting.

And outside the business community? Did I have friends who were anything less than respectable? Cath, I thought, would call many of them less than exciting: a smattering of Egyptians, some other Arabs from my semi-missionary boyhood, a few diplomats and AID officials, several academics at the American University, some fellow members of the board of the suburban American School that educated our two children. And what about Cath herself, my wife of eighteen years? Was she anything less than respectable? She was, in fact, absurdly free of taint. In any community she'd quickly gain the reputation of "good wife and mother," a woman beyond reproach, with the wholesome air of a field hockey player at a proper girls' school in Philadelphia, exuding forthrightness and cheer, treating our children (and others) with happy, hearty firmness, like a head nurse. Moreover, she was known and admired as a writer of short stories, member of a coterie of American and European writers. Yet despite her beauty and her success, other women liked her, even when their husbands surrounded her at cocktail parties.

I knew she had arrived in the living room because I felt her watching me from her chair. I looked up to face the direct gaze of her very blue eyes.

"Kids in bed?"

"Yes. Only needing a goodnight from you," she said. The gaze did not waver. "What are you worried about?"

"Nothing. Just wondering who to see tomorrow." She knew I was avoiding a straight answer; she waited for more, applying her special smile.

I'd fallen in love with that smile; it was an invitation to communicate, personal, almost conspiratorial, an insistence on honesty, on a response as direct as the gaze.

I almost succumbed. "I was just trying to organize myself for tomorrow. Looks complicated." I wasn't lying. Not exactly.

The gaze and the smile continued, combining beauty and energy as always. Yes, energy. It drew both men and women to her. Somehow it made her too honest to be devious. She patted my knee and allowed me to stop explaining. As I went along to see the kids, I resolutely put the matter out of my mind. Sleep on it, my schoolmaster father used to say. Tomorrow, not tonight, make a plan. Get on the phone, learn the reasons, talk to the people involved. The Cairo tradition.

I went first to Sarah's room. At age nine, she was fighting to stay awake for my evening visit. Her beauty was eye-catching. Her blue eyes were like Cath's.

"Hi, Daddy." Her smile was both sleepy and affectionate.

"So how are things?" I meant, *How are things at school?* This was my usual bedtime question, to which she responded with each day's information, as if saved for me specially. Only on a few social occasions or when I was traveling did we miss each evening's small ritual.

"We have a new French teacher," she said with a smile, "but she's not really French. She wears lots of lipstick and stuff." She giggled, then her arms went round my neck in a tight hug. I stroked her blonde hair and said good night. She smiled again, almost asleep, and managed to blow me a final kiss.

Larry's room was only one door away, but the ritual was different. At age thirteen, his later bedtime hour permitted a longer exchange, often based on a book he happened to be reading, usually one that had nothing to do with studies at school.

"I can't believe the scientists are right about time," he said, looking up.

"What are you reading about?"

"About the beginnings of the universe. First chapter in this book about human history. Big bang and all that." Usually at this hour he read novels about the life he was missing in America, and after a minute or two on human history we shifted to his customary interest in the United States. Any information about it evoked his immediate attention.

This time it was soccer. "Why don't they call it football the way they do everyplace else?" he asked. Then he grinned. To call it football was a family joke. At Maadi's American School, he played halfback on a junior team, and I had watched him play many times. So we talked sports in America for a few minutes. When I got up to go, he raised his hand.

"See you tomorrow," he said. He went back to his book on human history.

*   *   *

In the morning the matter of being followed seemed less important, needing attention but not urgent. I had not slept particularly well, but it felt good to stride through the riverside park on my way to the office. Gardeners grubbed in the flower beds, pruned flowering shrubs. Acacias and palms reached up toward the sun. It seemed to be one of those mornings when little could go wrong.

But my buoyancy lessened abruptly when I reached the Kasr el-Nil Bridge and saw the fellow in the pinstripe suit halfway across, leaning on the rail as if watching the river and the feluccas beating upwind. Passing by on the other side, I resisted an impulse to turn and check on him. I didn't want him to know that I knew he was following me.

My big office building was close by, just off Liberation Square and at the edge of Garden City. Without looking back, I took the elevator to the ninth floor. As the ancient elevator moved slowly upward, I tried to focus on next moves. The usual clutter of papers awaited me on my desk, and with less than half my mind I began wading through them. What I urgently needed, of course, was a plan. What should be my next move? In Egypt one should not upset official applecarts. The delicate way of handling difficulties is always recommended. A word to the right person, who says a word to another right person, ruffles no egos and makes no enemies. Sometimes a little cash, though it should never be more than the going rate, helps higher-ups soothe some of the lower-downs.

I phoned a few business acquaintances, including Sam Paul, to ask if they had noticed a change of atmosphere. They expressed no surprise at the query, which was a standard way of asking for political information of mutual interest, but they had noticed nothing. I said I was checking on latest developments prior to writing a report to my home office. We all knew that political atmospheres can change quickly in Cairo; the business community was always anxious to keep abreast of changes that might be brewing. But according to my several acquaintances, no changes seemed on the way at the moment. One of them even voiced gratitude for the current stability of things, as opposed to the uncertainties we both remembered from Nasser's day. The inpouring of United States dollars, particularly for development projects, had given the Egyptian economy an important stabilizing boost and had done wonders for Western business.

I did not have a good morning at my desk. My competent young secretary at Starr Johnson, a big-breasted Coptic woman named Laila, brought in two sandwiches made from cheese she kept in the office refrigerator. Looking at the few scraps in my outbox, she smiled anxiously. As always, she seemed to know when my state of mind was hindering my progress. I wasn't making my usual quick decisions. What, I kept asking myself, had I done? I kept reminding myself that I lived in an authoritarian country where certain sectors of government can move swiftly and silently. Though I did better in the afternoon, doggedly pushing out paper, I couldn't consider it a good day. Laila, competent and courteous as always, returned a major order of software for "review"; I'd made a gross error in the calculating of costs, and as so often I became aware how much I had come to depend on her.

That evening I waited for darkness again and slipped out onto our balcony in time to witness the changing of the guard. After the two shook hands and the tall man's graceful figure disappeared beyond the lamplight, a fact thrust upward and asserted itself. The tall man in elegant pinstripe was no policeman. Nor was he a member of the internal security apparatus known as the *mukhabarat*. Conceivably he could fit either's description of an officer, but officers do not do guard duty. I knew of no other government organizations engaged in surveillance, though perhaps they existed.

Would any of them put on guard duty a well-dressed fellow like the one in the pinstripe suit? It didn't fit his bearing, the cut of his clothes. He would never accept small presents on feast days.

Later that evening the phone rang. I recognized the gravelly voice of Jim Harris, the principal of the American School. I was a member of his school board, and we had always been on good terms. "Bill," he said, "I thought I ought to tell you about something. Something odd. You know that food stand outside the main gate out here at the school?"

"Sure. What about it?"

"Well, there are these two guys hanging around and chatting with students who know Arabic. Between classes. Nothing serious, just chatter and jokes."

He paused a moment, as if finding it difficult to proceed. "Listen, Bill, what I wanted to say was this. You know the kind of suburb it is out here in Maadi. These two guys stick out like sore thumbs. Medium height, light skinned, shabby suits. I went up to talk to them, but they only speak Arabic and mine's not good enough. They kept smiling at me and just wandered away. But I saw them later, hanging around again near the gate. They were chatting with the Sorenson kid who speaks good Arabic. He came to me afterward. He said they were mostly joking around, but he said they were also trying to get information."

"What kind of information?"

"Well, that's it, that's what's odd. He says they wanted to know about you, where you worked, what your job was, which kids were yours. It was all very casual, he said. No direct questions."

"What did the Sorenson kid tell them?"

"He says he told them nothing at all."

"Christ."

"Listen, Bill, maybe it wasn't that serious. Just casual chatter. Probably nothing to worry about. Just thought you ought to know." Neither of the two at the school resembled the man in pinstripe. For a moment I thought of telling Jim Harris a bit more. But only for a moment. It was not his problem.

"Have you talked to the Maadi police?" I asked.

"Yes, and they sent a couple of sergeants right over, but the two guys disappeared. Of course, they came back five minutes after the police left." He paused. "Tomorrow I thought I'd go chat again with Captain Tabrizi at the police station, have him assign someone for a couple of days. I'd rather not take chances. These Muslim fundamentalists are all over the place these days, and some could be crazy enough to take things out on an American school."

"Thanks, Jim, for letting me know about all this," I said. "By all means, go see Captain Tabrizi."

He hung up determinedly. Clearly he wanted no part of someone else's problem. Nothing to worry about, he said. Maybe not in Scranton, where he was from. But he'd lived in Cairo long enough to know the difference. Which meant he also smelled something seriously wrong. I slumped into a chair. Precious children named Larry and Sarah went to the American School in Maadi, children of a man being followed for no apparent reason. Perhaps the two matters had no connection. Perhaps. But as Jim Harris said, he couldn't take chances. Neither could I.

*   *   *

From the office in the morning I phoned Jim Harris again. The Armenian gym teacher had just reported hearing the two strangers talking by the gate. It was the gym teacher's opinion that their accent sounded Palestinian. When I asked Jim if he'd talked to the Maadi police yet, he said Captain Tabrizi had promised to come by at lunchtime. Though by this time I'd come to understand that the suburban police could not be much help.

I made another phone call, then put on my jacket and told Laila I'd be out for a while. Her young face showed curiosity; I usually told her where I was going. My nearby destination was Egypt's Ministry of the Interior, a massive three-story hulk of dirty gray stone that dwells among its own kind, larger than the other nineteenth-century ministry buildings in its neighborhood, but otherwise indistinguishable. It was not a walk I often took; it was short, easy, and full of contrast. Starting from modish

Garden City I skirted Liberation Square, strode past the American University compound, then crossed the tracks into poorer, less tidy streets. In the last century these streets had filled up with handsome French-style government buildings but they had been allowed to become grubby, to deteriorate along with the rest of their neighborhood. Today the streets were filled with human waste – cigarette wrappers, random sections of newspaper, chunks of watermelon rind – and jammed with people moving in every direction, their voices discordant and inventive: hawkers and vendors in traditional dress, a Southern Sudanese at his peanut stand, four young men in black trousers and soiled white shirts desperate to sell razor blades and ball-point pens. A Coptic priest dragged a small boy by the hand, cursing a roadblock of three donkey-drawn carts piled with tomatoes and zucchini. On the fractured sidewalk a family of landless peasants, its children in rags, bargained for bean sandwiches from a gray-bearded Nubian with a white pushcart besieged by flies. Other pushcarts, their owners leaning against dingy cement walls or once-handsome street lights, sold cheap clothes and tin pans. A grossly fat woman, a large basket of bread loaves on her covered head, dodged through the throng.

The crowd thickened in front of the ministry itself. Seated on low stools, petition writers in soiled western suits were extracting piasters from the illiterate poor; some of the latter were women enveloped in black from native quarters of Cairo, others were peasants in town for the day. As always I marveled at Cairo's colorful mix: young women with shawled heads but in fashionable skirts and spike heels, old women in black tatters begging, other younger women in the toe-length nun-like dress of fundamentalists, government servants in shirts and ties strolling away from their desks, sheikhs from the Azhar in turbans and white robes. Near the steps of the ministry, a taxi driver with the trimmed beard of the Muslim Brotherhood was honking his way gently through; he smiled when he saw me, making me aware that I was outside my usual part of town. Yet it was somehow soothing. Of this mass of standing, squatting, gesturing, assertive humanity, I felt myself a part, a rightful part, of its variety. If nothing else, my Palestinian and Lebanese boyhood somehow allowed me to feel as if I belonged. Cath, a much purer product of North America, would feel out of place.

The sergeant at the door delegated a policeman in rumpled uniform to show me to the office of Dr. Abdul Latif el-Turki, a name that produced instant respect and action. Preceding me along dreary but assiduously swept dark corridors, my guide strode ahead as if on a vital mission, glancing back at intervals to make certain I knew he was concerned. When I thanked him, he gave me a salute reserved for the highly born and then a shy smile, displaying light brown teeth. He accepted a small tip.

I sat for a moment in an outer office, carpeted and upholstered in deep red and peopled by two males, one an upper-class Egyptian in burgundy tie who greeted me in excellent English, the other a lesser being, thin and hardworking, punching an Arabic typewriter. Abdul Latif's exact rank and position I did not know; until this moment it hadn't mattered. Ours was a special friendship, an accident of Cairo life, based on bridge and golf and social evenings. Why the friendship grew as it did, I can't say with certainty. Our wives had become friends. In the summer, with wives away, he and I would sometimes spend an evening at one of the clubs, dawdling over grilled steak and cool beer. I called him Abdu. Not that we had become close friends in the Egyptian sense that he knew my cousins and I knew his, but we became companions in the special context of Egypt's overcrowded capital, where our separate worlds overlapped. The worlds did not overlap by much. For him, at least at first, I may have been a respite, an escape from an intricate network of obligations he found cloying, a door to someplace else. But I could not fail to understand that he was influential, especially in government circles. He was ranked third or fourth in a major ministry. Egyptian acquaintances, in a position to know, reacted attentively to the mention of his name, visibly impressed by my easy relationship with him. His air of assurance sprang not only from good looks and upper-class status but from success. Though sought after by many, he had few friends. He kept his personal life to himself. Yet he was willing to speak impersonally about any matter of intellectual interest. Cath once said he was a lonely man.

When he appeared at the door of the inner office, his face showed no surprise, though I had never come to his office before. With a charming smile, acting as if it were normal to make an appointment at short notice, he ushered me through, sat me down in a comfortable chair by a low table, and ordered Turkish coffee. Like the outer office, his was done up in deep red, but the paneling was luxurious mahogany. Ritually he began on a golf story that lasted until the servant had brought coffee and departed. We fell silent as we took the first sips. He spoke first. "What has happened?" he asked speaking in English, our usual language together. His face was grave, his glance sharp. I told my story, feeling foolish. Was it a fuss about something minor? I had to know. I said I wanted his advice on what to do next, if it should turn out the Egyptian government was involved. Abdu, listening attentively, showed no sign of tolerant amusement at the ignorance of foreigners. When I finished, he sat for a moment, looking at his hands, face impassive. "Yes, well, let us see where we are," he said. "If you permit, I should ask you some questions. Which may be impolite questions. But then we know each other almost well enough for that, and I may be better able to help when I finish. Is that all right?"

He smiled unexpectedly. "You know, I don't know enough about you. The important things I know. But what exactly do you do? I know it's electronics, computers, things like that. Sales and service."

"Exactly. On behalf of a company based in San Francisco."

"And where do you sell? All over the Middle East?"

"The company consults and sells everywhere. I cover the Arabs. We have a Greek agent who covers Israel."

"Are these electronic instruments you sell hard to come by?" he asked.

I understood the question and followed his lead. "No, I doubt if there's a smuggling angle. At least I can't work out the mechanics of it. How would information about me help a smuggler? All the stuff I sell is available. Even in Beirut." Especially Beirut, I thought. Even now, in the chaos besetting once-lovely Lebanon, a smart buyer could find almost anything and in bulk. "I've also thought about mistaken identity. I don't think it's that either."

The professional cross-examination that followed was more like interrogating a prisoner than helping a friend. He pressed for flaws in my story. Was the man I saw at the Hilton pool the man outside my apartment? How could I tell in the dark of the evening? What led me to believe it was not just a coincidence? Might the two men have been watching another apartment altogether? The questions came quickly; he gave me no time to think about answers or qualify them.

"And even supposing it wasn't a coincidence, how could you know the man was not a policeman or one of the *mukhabarat*?"

"You could tell. He didn't act like a cop. Didn't dress like one."

And so on. The grilling lasted ten minutes. Then with a gesture of his hand, he stopped, walked to the window, and stared down at the top of a plane tree. "Let me think out loud," he said. Unsmiling, he chose his words with care. "We are friends, and so I know you well enough to know the kind of witness you are. For the sake of self-esteem or to prop up a story you felt was feeble, you would not distort your own evidence. Also, you were born in Palestine and grew up speaking Arabic. Palestine is different, but after a decade here the language has given you a sense of things Egyptian that most foreigners don't have."

He paused, looked out the window. "Given all this, plus some intuitions of my own, we can say for certain this is no coincidence. And not mistaken identity. So we are left with the big questions: why and who. I don't know the answers. So far the two men at the school sound the most dangerous, but until everyone is identified we won't really know."

He smiled faintly. "The weak link in your chain of evidence? You assume that the man you saw, let us call him Pinstripe, is *not* an employee of the Egyptian government. You have made perceptive, uh, sartorial comments about him, and without those comments I would have bet heavily he was from this ministry."

"And your guess now?"

He looked out the window again. "I need more information. Certainly that's our next job. But we must move carefully."

His words came across like a glass of cool water after a dry day in the desert. Or was I reading too much into that small word 'we'? Where I had been on my own, now I had an ally, almost a kinsman, who would stick with me and help. So I felt. On this day he could have coped with me like a bureaucrat: nice words, little or no action, an assertion that the problem would go away or could be handled by someone else. Friendships are seldom tested, but this one had passed a test of a kind.

"Oddly enough," he said, "I may have more difficulty with the police of my own ministry than with the *mukhabarat*, who are connected with the presidency – where I have a cousin who can find things out." He shook his head in mock despair. "I like to think things were different when the pharaohs ran the country. Perhaps they could be less devious."

He took a new tack. "What about Cath? What have you told her?"

"Almost nothing. Just enough. She knows something's on my mind."

He nodded, either in acknowledgment or approval. "One step at a time," he said. "This must be handled delicately. If no government inquiry exists, we don't want to initiate one."

He saw the questioning look on my face and smiled thinly, not bitterly, a bureaucrat commenting silently on the realities of power. "Yes, the politics of this ministry are intricate and devious, perhaps more than any except Defense. Crazy things happen. The police would jump at the chance to open a new file involving foreigners."

"Listen, Abdu, I …" I searched for the right words. "I'd be, well, mortified if you got into anything difficult on my account. Perhaps …"

He cut in quickly. "Don't worry, I won't get into difficulty. I've had twenty-five years' experience inside these depressing walls. You'd do the same."

His tone veered away from any suggestion of sentiment. "So where are we?" he proceeded. "I do some research. We shall hope Pinstripe is an Egyptian employee. But almost certainly we are dealing with some other organization, which will be harder to handle."

"What's your hunch?"

"Pessimistic. I know you, I know my government. I can't imagine why either of you would be interested in the other. Nor can I believe there isn't a connection between Pinstripe and the two men hanging around the school. I'm guessing the gym teacher is right, they're Palestinian. So the interest in you and your family is disturbing."

"Could Pinstripe be a fundamentalist?" I remembered the conversation with the school principal.

He ignored my question and pursued an inquiry of his own. "I understand you're known among some circles in America as someone who knows a lot about Palestine, someone the so-called experts can check things out with. Have you actually kept in touch with old Palestinian friends?"

"Quite a few, a lot of them on the outside. I haven't been back for twenty years."

"But I understand you keep carefully in touch with what's happening inside Israel and Palestine. Is that really true?"

He wanted a straightforward answer. It was true that I had a casual network of old friends who kept me informed, especially about Palestine and the people I grew up with. And recently I'd noticed a number of seemingly casual questions about Palestine from American officials of various kinds. Almost as if the word was getting around that Bill Hampton was a good source. As if Bill Hampton, an American, was a better source than the Palestinians from whom he got his information.

"Yes, you could say I keep in touch. After all, I grew up there."

"And Americans who ask you about Palestine, I suppose you tell them what Palestinian friends tell you."

"Well, not everything. And nothing personal, of course."

"What I'm guessing," he said, "is that your brains have been picked often. As if casually. Especially since '87 and the start of the uprising." He was referring to the so-called *intifada*, the violent Palestinian protests that were now spreading to places with Palestinian refugees and sympathizers. Such as Lebanon, which was now split into two. "The whole thing," he said, "smells of Palestine."

On the way back to the cleaner fashionable streets of Garden City I remembered to turn around, pretending to search for a taxi. There came Pinstripe, fifty yards behind, mingling easily with the many humans and the colors, but somehow aloof.

If the Egyptian government were involved, I thought, Abdu could handle it. But the involvement of the dark side of Palestine, which was an assumption I now had to make, would thrust me into a world whose rules and subtleties I did not know well enough.

*   *   *

Laila came in to say the American Embassy had confirmed an appointment for twelve noon. To see Jim Spence, the political counselor. I was covering all bases, including embassy support for the Hampton family if matters should deteriorate in a way I could not foresee. Pinstripe was not in sight during the short walk to the embassy, though I had little doubt he was somewhere nearby. As I strode past a few modern apartment buildings on clean streets and small shops geared to the affluence of Garden City, I thought about Spence, whom I did not know well, though I knew him well enough. We had joined forces from time to time on the board of the American School in Maadi; in one not-quite-bitter fight among board members he and I had stood together against the appointment of an ultra-modern principal. Whenever we met, he made a point of showing respect for my knowledge of Palestinian and other Arab affairs. In Foreign Service parlance he was called an "Arabist" and had held several posts in the area. Many called him a comer.

The marine guard behind the bullet-proof glass waved me through the metal detector into the compound, a security-conscious patch of American territory not unlike a middle-income enclave in Los Angeles. In the large courtyard, Americans, and Egyptians dressed like Americans, moved here and there among the buildings, some purposefully, some on trips to the cafeteria or the PX, pausing to chat. Tunnels and passageways led to other buildings behind. On the right stood the chancery inside which loomed another bullet-proofed enclosure with another marine guard. Spence's secretary came down to escort me to his office. Jim Spence greeted me warmly, as always. Cath, out-of-date on men's styles, once called him one of the new breed because his hair came down mod-fashion over his ears, but his manner and build and face reminded me of what British diplomats were reputed to be fifty years ago. His office, the size occupied by my company's president in San Francisco, had a worked-in look. Books and journals lined two walls; the desk was piled high. He offered me American coffee but I declined.

"Jim, I'm really sorry to bother you with a small personal matter. But it would help a lot to have your input." So I told Spence what I had told Abdu, though I made light of it, as if I were routinely keeping the embassy informed. "I've also been in touch, by the way, with an Egyptian friend at

Interior. He's looking into it all." Without voicing the near certainty that Pinstripe, his colleague, and the men out at the school were not Egyptians, I said I wanted Spence's advice on what I should do, what precautions I should take, what he would do in my place.

Spence listened with care. Then, like Abdu, he asked questions. "What does the fellow outside your apartment look like?"

"He's a tall youngish man, well-dressed. Some would call him handsome."

"What about the man who replaces him at night? Can you describe him?"

"Not very well," I said. "Older, heavier."

"And what about the two men at the school?"

"As I said, I didn't see them. The headmaster said they were medium height, light skin. Shabbily dressed. Didn't speak English, seemingly."

He smiled courteously, automatically. "What else can you tell me that would help identify these people?" Clearly he was less concerned with my personal problem, more concerned with what I knew about the problem. Between questions he smiled courteously, automatically. Without speculating about why I would be followed or why two unknowns would be inquiring about me out at the school gate, he pushed me, in his studiedly casual way, to be precise. Like Abdu he kept at me to describe Pinstripe in detail.

"Listen, Bill," he said, producing his automatic smile again, "it doesn't sound like a serious matter. Not real trouble. I'm glad you've got Egyptian friends in on it. With your expertise, of course ..." He paused, implying that my expertise, such as it was, was somehow important to the problem's solution. "Not something to worry about, that's what my intuition tells me. My hunch is simply keep an eye on things. I'm guessing the surveillance will stop when the government realizes there's nothing in it for them."

The words left me uneasy. Not only because they were pap.

"And if anything gets annoying, Bill, I'll initiate a move of some appropriate kind. Probably your Egyptian friend will be able to bring the whole affair to an end. Let me know what happens, and above all don't worry."

Thus he wrapped things up. Unlike the Egyptian I'd seen earlier, the American bureaucrat behaved the way the species is supposed to behave; he coped with the meeting and left the outcome in his pending tray. I suppressed an urge to push questions at him, to have him explain the inconsistencies of what he had said or implied. Some instinct held me back. The soothing nature of his wrap-up set off alarm bells. The dish seemed digestible until the teeth crunched on the hard facts. I had withheld the probable fact that Pinstripe and the men at the school were not Egyptian, but my description of them, offered at the diplomat's own urging, had to give an Arabist like Spence a solid clue. Yet he asked no questions leading in that direction. Nor did he ask for the identity of my Egyptian friend. And as we proceeded, his phrases, I thought, had changed flavor, becoming overly comforting. The Palestinians of my youth called this "bread without salt."

When I thanked him for his time, the automatic smile appeared again. "Sounds to me like there's not much to worry about," he said. Yet I imagined I saw a worry in his eyes. Did his final phrases not have the effect he hoped for? I felt abandoned by my own kind, and I guess I'd half known I'd get little help from Spence and his ilk. I clutched at the thought that if the Hamptons had to leave Egypt fast, it would be Abdu who would get us safely to the airport and into the air. As I left the compound, I saw Pinstripe in the upscale flower shop across the street scrutinizing the birds of paradise.

* * *

I decided to have lunch at home rather than one of Laila's cheese sandwiches from the office refrigerator. When I rang the apartment, it was our fabulous do-all Nubian servant who answered.

"Hasan, I'm coming for lunch. Can you fix me something?" No need to tell him what I'd like. In his Nubian accent from Egypt's far south, he said he'd have one of my usual sandwiches ready for me. Cath, I knew, was out lunching with women friends.

I walked home over the Kasr el-Nil Bridge and along the river in Zamalek.

I needed time to think. But now I had time to feel scared. I took a deep breath. Pinstripe, I felt sure, was behind me but I didn't look around. I remembered my mother years ago saying, "Bill, it seems you always need to know what to expect." That was the problem. I didn't have the least inkling of what to expect. Why were they interested? Who were they after? Who were *they*? These unknown Palestinians watching me and my family, trying to identify Larry and Sarah out at the Maadi school? Spence had made no attempt to explain them. Though I kept telling myself there was no need to be scared, deep down I knew better. Any Palestinian – and at this moment I felt myself almost a Palestinian – would know enough to be scared.

Hasan had a lunch waiting for me. I watched the river as I bit into a specially constructed and delicious egg-salad sandwich. I knew that if I went on to the porch, I would see Pinstripe on watch. Where was Cath? She had told me where she was going, but I couldn't remember. What I kept remembering was that two men wanted to identify our kids out at the school. I had to make a move. But what move?

Someone was turning a key at the front door. It was Cath coming home early from her ladies' lunch. "I left because the conversation was not all that interesting," she said. "Anyway, I wanted to work on my manuscript. Why are you home for lunch?"

"Just thought I'd relax a bit." I felt her looking at me a bit carefully. "How's your story coming?"

"So-so. Not yet ready for anyone to read it. Including you." She smiled as she sat down at the table. "Especially you, perhaps."

"What does that mean?"

"Well, as you know, sometimes my fiction spins out of control. This story is getting a bit too personal. It needs editing." Hasan came silently in from the kitchen and put a cup of coffee near her right hand. "Why do you need to relax?"

Her question was a good one, but not one I was prepared to answer. I steered the conversation in the direction of Larry and Sarah. As subjects of conversation our kids could usually preempt other topics.

"I've been thinking about Larry. I still think he should be learning a lot more Arabic. He may speak colloquial okay but now he needs lessons in classical, reading and writing." We had had this discussion before. At thirteen, Larry spoke the Egyptian colloquial dialect well. But he was already past the age when on Fridays or Sundays Egyptian friends of ours were supplementing their children's French or English educations with special lessons in the classical language. I had already identified the local imam who could do the teaching.

"As you know, I'd much rather both kids learned good French." Her face had a resigned look, this being an argument she expected to lose.

"They're learning beginning French at school, and they can improve it any time when they get older. But the chance to learn decent Arabic probably won't come again." I thought the subject of why I was lunching at home had been sidetracked. I should have known better.

"We can talk about this some other time," she said. "I know it's important to you. But something else is bugging you. Please let me know what it is as soon as you can." She gave me her special smile, kissed my cheek, looked at me hard with her blue eyes, and went off to work on her manuscript, coffee in hand.

I slumped down in my chair. What could I tell her? Without scaring her, perhaps needlessly. What I needed was to talk to someone who knew a bit about Palestine, who would know what I was talking about, know the implications, make better guesses than I was making about what was happening and why. I phoned Sam Paul at his office. Cath was out of earshot down the hall in her workroom. When Sam came on the phone, I said I could use a sounding board for a personal problem. What he took that to mean, I do not know. In his undemonstrative way, he said he'd cancel an appointment and meet me in an hour at the Hilton for a cup of coffee.

*　　　　　*　　　　　*

Sam sat stolidly near the pool, glasses pushed up on top of his head. No trace of Pinstripe. I waved to a group of journalists at another table. Having ordered coffee for us both, Sam was studying the menu because he had nothing else to read. I put on good cheer I did not feel.

"Something new on that menu?"

He gave a small smile, pulled his glasses into place, looked me over. "There's always hope," he said. Then he turned to the hovering waiter, who knew us well, and asked him, dead-pan, in absurdly Lebanese Arabic if the diet never changed at the Hilton. Sam's Arabic, some of it, came from his Lebanese parents in Detroit, and he'd picked up colorful idioms from his business years in Beirut. Language, in fact, constituted a bond between Sam and me, not just Arabic but its "Shami" dialect, the dialect of the Arab Levant we had both spoken as children. Its flavors, nostalgically distinctive, evoked memories of green countryside in Lebanon and Palestine.

The waiter grinned at Sam and waited for our orders. As he finally went off, Sam reverted to English and said, "Someday, maybe next week, I'll order something, something he doesn't expect. Like snails." The words came out terse and expressionless. Only the glint behind the spectacles signaled humor. For Sam, the lapse into tongue-in-cheek Shami Arabic constituted high slapstick. Yes, I needed to talk to Sam. Not just because he knew a lot about Palestine. More because he and I went back some ten years, and I respected his judgments. At first we were "business friends," those we did not invite to dinner. We started with lunches and found the interchange was profitable. He sold office-systems equipment, I sold electronic products, and we threw business to each other. Our sales records flourished; time saved could be measured in weeks, not days. We both had enormous areas to cover, a time-devouring spread between Libya and the emirates of the Persian Gulf. So our lunches at the Hilton became an institution, and the resulting friendship was unexpected in some ways. Cath thought so at first. Though Sam and I had arrived in Cairo about the same time and same age, we came from different social places, had traveled different roads. In Detroit he had worked nights to take a business course at a community college. His father, he told me once, came from Lebanon, worked as a stone mason, and switched names from Boulos to Paul. I knew little else; Sam seldom alluded to his past, and I did not pry.

"And how is James?" I asked. His son was James, not Jim or Jimmy. Sometime in the last year I had come to understand that wife and son were the focus of his life, not the business he ran so successfully.

He asked what I was worried about. So I told him the story, starting with our previous lunch. As I spoke, I glanced around occasionally, but Pinstripe was absent. Listening intently, Sam interrupted only once, wanting more on Jim Spence's reaction. When I finished, he sat looking at the remains of his cheese sandwich.

"Tricky," he said. "Now you wait."

"Wait for what?"

"Wait, say, until your friend Abdu reports back to you. First you've got to be certain they're not Egyptians. So wait until the thing develops, whatever the hell it is. There's nothing else to do right now."

I sat in the sun, absorbing his words, then let my breath out audibly. "But damn it, what about Larry and Sarah out there at the school?" Every instinct told me I had to act. This was not Philadelphia. His eyes scanned my face, like an analyst searching for clues.

"Listen, Bill, this is probably no big deal."

"Come on, Sam."

"I mean it. Look, you're right to take precautions, to make all the moves you've made. Now take it easy."

"Take it easy? How can I take it easy? I can't just sit here."

Sam cut in. "I know. It's no fun being followed in a police state. All that."

"You sound like this is just routine, perfectly normal. Those two guys at the school can't be Egyptians, they're Palestinians. There's an *intifada* going on. I've got kids to worry about."

"You can't be certain yet who they are." He paused, then went on. "You know, you're a fellow who's used to having things come easy. Because of your luck – how many others were born and brought up like you? – you've had nothing but success, as if success was easy to come by. I had to do risky things, you never had to. Now along comes something that threatens your success routine by a fraction. Christ, just a fraction. And you get all upset."

"Listen, I can't take chances."

The waiter was hovering. Sam waved him away. "Look, so far you've had a nice happy conventional life. You're known for being knowledgeable about the Arab world, especially Palestine. Newspapermen have even quoted you. A lot of people think you're great. Now suddenly you realize you're not in control; society or fate or whatever is taking potshots. So you think there must be some mistake and you go tearing around talking to the right people, so things get fixed up." I detected a touch of resentment in his voice. It didn't bother me. On other occasions I'd also seen flashes of something like envy. His eyes kept examining my face. "Listen, Bill, you're acting like this is a setback. Like suddenly the world's not cooperating with you anymore. What we're talking about is just an ordinary difficulty, to be handled and dealt with. Routine. Sure, stay alert, and if it comes to a crunch, you've got lots of friends who'll help. But like I say, no big deal."

"Okay, but who do you really think those guys are?" I asked. This was the key question.

He looked at me for a long moment. "I don't know," he said. "Probably some screwball thing, maybe fundamentalists like the school principal said. Plenty of them in Palestine as well as Egypt."

He had to know it was unlikely they were fundamentalists. Fundamentalists had special objectives. Why would they target me and my children? If I had felt better a moment ago, now I had to suspect Sam knew more than he was telling me.

"What about Cath?" he asked.

"What about her?"

"What are you going to tell her?"

"Nothing for now, I guess."

"Yeah, better not," he said.

*   *   *

Again I sat on the darkened terrace nursing a drink, waiting for Cath to finish with the kids. The street lights had come on ten minutes before. The lights from the other side of the river glinted unevenly on the water. Below me on the wall sat the man on night shift, putting on a sweater to fend off the evening breeze, settling down at his post.

I made no move that might catch his eye, just sat there. Sam's words came at me. Relax and wait, probably nothing to worry about. Bullshit, there was plenty to worry about. How could Sam think I would think Pinstripe might be a fundamentalist? And at the school, two men hanging about the place wanting to know which children were mine …

What about Sam anyway? Was he devious? I couldn't be sure. Faced with some nameless pressure, would he stay cool, follow his own advice? Perhaps. Even probably. Despite his mild appearance he possessed a tough core, something unyielding I glimpsed every now and then, but where he was willing to yield and where he hung tough, I did not know. Politically an Arab nationalist and a tiresome Israel-hater, he could sell anybody almost anything. And that meant accommodation, stroking the egos of clients.

At the mention of his wife his manner would change. If you knew him well, and not many did, you could see the pride steal onto his face. He had met Mary a scant three years ago, a newly arrived secretary at the American Embassy, one Mary Hashwa, also Lebanese-American from Detroit. Strangely, I believe it was his first serious affair. Determined to marry her, he conducted the courtship that one would expect of Sam: undemonstrative, a bit formal, stubbornly persistent. Whatever Mary first thought of him (his unglamorous middle age and shortish build seemed an odd match for her statuesque good looks) she decided in a few months that he was what she wanted. Our friendship evolved after he asked me to be best man at the wedding, though it remained essentially between him and me, not a family affair involving Cath. But Cath came into the act her own way. She and Mary spun a separate web of friendship, which included phone calls, late afternoon tennis, and shopping outings when Mary's embassy job did not interfere. When Mary got pregnant, the number of phone calls shot up; from my chair in the living room I would hear Cath pouring out baby lore, what to do in the first weeks, tips on pampers, how to find a second-hand crib. Cath took charge of finding a local nanny whose trustworthiness and competence would permit Mary to continue working; this, apparently, the embassy wanted her to do. After baby James arrived, I arranged for the christening at the American church in Maadi. Cath was a godmother.

Now you wait, Sam had said. He had to know he was wrong. Perhaps in Philadelphia I could wait. In Philadelphia, the elements of security were clear-cut: concerned neighbors, local constables, an FBI number. In Cairo, security was supplied principally by oneself, by one's friends and relatives, by social clout. Sure, Abdu had clout, but he'd be the first to know he could do little to protect me from a Palestinian underground that seemed to appear and disappear at will. But Sam? He was playing some game. So, for that matter, was Jim Spence.

TWO

Cairo, March 1990

Later that evening the matter became more disquieting. Cath and I had been invited to a dinner party, a big affair at the Maadi villa of the number two at the American Embassy. We'd been invited two weeks before. In the light of what was happening, I toyed with finding an excuse to stay home but couldn't bring myself to deny Cath the pleasure. That morning an embassy secretary had telephoned the guests to say the party would be held in the garden, the first outdoor event of the season. Cath loved the embassy garden parties, especially in Maadi, Cairo's suburb to the south. Under ordinary circumstances, these parties produced a pleasant feeling of easy affluence among one's own international kind.

Before we left, I checked the locks on the windows, not letting Cath see me do it, and gave the kids a longer-than-usual evening visit. Unexpectedly I found my eyes welling with tears as Sarah gave me her special goodnight hug, but I don't think she noticed. I had recovered by the time I chatted with Larry for a few minutes.

Then I spoke to Hasan, who also served as our babysitter. "Odd things have been happening in Cairo," I said carefully. "Don't open the door to anyone unless you know exactly who they are." He nodded, and with his special Nubian accent he said he would do exactly that. As if he did not always do exactly that.

Driving south along the corniche, I realized it was good we were going. For two days I had been preoccupied, my mind crammed with personal and family worries. I wanted to talk about golf or someone else's children, to drink good wine from the embassy stores. I needed a respite. Cath, knowing something was wrong, turned to study my face, as if it could signal the nature of the trouble.

"Bill, you should tell me what's eating at you." She shifted in her seat and faced me, the blue eyes fastened on me, but it was too serious for the special smile. I had to answer.

"It's a business worry. No sense burdening you with it. What I'd like is to tell you about it when it's over."

The Nile flowed by on our right. I braced myself. "That," she said finally, "doesn't make me very happy. You've always told me about things to do with business. Or other things."

We were moving onto tricky territory. Glancing over, I saw in her eyes a thin covering of tears glistening in the headlights of oncoming cars. My fingers tightened on the wheel. When she spoke again, it came after a full minute. "Is it something to do with" – a long pause – "you and me?"

Without thinking I pulled the car over across from the gate of the military hospital. The traffic rushed by in both directions. Switching off the ignition and turning toward her, I put my hands on her shoulders and leaned forward to put my cheek against hers. It was a way we had. "What's most important to me is you. That's a fact." I meant what I said. "What we have together, the kids, everything. That day when we talked by the fountain, when we were freshmen, that was the luckiest thing for me. From then on, it was always you. Nothing could ever change that." I heard myself reciting phrases I had used before.

She pulled her head back and looked at me hard. Her hands came up and framed my face. Then a deep sigh and a release of tension. Kissing me lightly on the lips, she looked at me again. "If it weren't for the make up, I'd kiss you properly." She took a deep breath. "All right, I feel okay now. Sorry for the fuss."

She powdered her face as if scrubbing away the hurt. I suppose some of it lingered because I had told her nothing. But now it was bearable. "Tell me about the business thing," she said, "when it's over."

I nuzzled her cheek again, telling her I loved her. Which was true, though on some days our marriage seemed dominated by its routines. Across the corniche, through the traffic, I caught glimpses of the hospital guard on duty staring in our direction. Egyptians in Cairo are used to seeing foreigners carrying on in cars, but the less sophisticated consider it fornication and are offended. I switched on the ignition and drove off toward Maadi.

∗ ∗ ∗

By the time we arrived, some guests had already finished their first drinks. The garden, with lanterns shining on flowers of every color, looked like a fairy tale. White-gowned Nubian servants with red sashes moved back and forth on a meticulously groomed and spacious lawn. The women, expensively dressed, hair-dos dating from that morning, had shawls for the evening air; the men wore dark suits. Mostly diplomats and spouses, a more formal affair than usual, place cards at linen-covered tables. Cath, looking beautiful, was soon surrounded by friends, her healthy blondness and infectious laugh pulling at others like a magnet. Moving toward a couple of acquaintances, I made small talk about school board problems until it was time to sit down.

I found my place card at a table in a far corner. I was joined by two women I knew, wives of American diplomats, and by Gavin Middleton, a good friend. Gav was, in fact, my only really good friend at the American Embassy. A tall man in his mid-forties, massive but in good shape, enormous hands, dark hair thinning on top and receding fast. He had arrived in Cairo on assignment seven years back, and after chatting with him on many social occasions we became conversational pals. Though he and I never mentioned it to each other, I came to understand he was a spook, the label not unaffectionately conferred by the Foreign Service on employees of the Central Intelligence Agency. Publicly Gav Middleton described himself as part of the embassy's political section. Because of his secretive and undoubtedly important connections, and perhaps in order to avoid embarrassing him by invading the secrecy that I was not supposed to know about, I had so far shied away from consulting him about my small problem.

Gav was not just a golf partner; he provided companionship of a special sort, based on common interests in Arab peoples and politics. And he and his wife, always good company, did things with Cath and me and our kids, such as desert picnics, trips to archaeological sites, boat rides on the river. When he and I finished a round of Saturday golf, we would meet our wives at the Yacht Club for hilarious lunches that included *kufta*, *tahina*, and Gianaclis wine. I found him trustworthy as well as personable. And he did know, I was certain, that I would never threaten the privacy of his professional life.

This evening, with a delicious meal effortlessly served, the talk at our table flowed soothingly. Both women, social experts, would one day make competent ambassadors' wives. After ice cream from the embassy commissary and a choice of sauces, the red-sashed servants brought cups of Turkish coffee. Guests began moving from table to table to chat; the two women, coffee in hand, got up to do the same. Thinking Gav and I might do likewise, I made as if to rise, but he put his hand lightly on my arm.

"Got a minute?"

"Sure," I said, settling back comfortably. I soon realized we were seated together for a reason. The women had left us by prearrangement. Over in our corner, away from the larger tables, our conversation could proceed privately.

"Well, maybe more than a minute." He took a deep breath. "I've got to lay something on you, and I don't like it. On the other hand, it's in a good cause. At least I think it is."

He reached forward and pulled a daisy out of the vase in the center of the table. "You know, of course, I'm with the Agency. I'm called station chief. I don't apologize. Most days I'm proud of the outfit. We do the best we can." He stared at the daisy. "So I'm a real spook, not knee-jerk but a spook just the same." He paused, and I nodded. Eventually he would tell me what this had to do with Bill Hampton. He soldiered on.

"Anyway, many of us, including our top people, are convinced neither State nor Defense nor ourselves really understand the Palestinian community. We don't know enough. All those tricky little differences, tricky family connections that appear when you least expect them. We swim around; we dream up policies and hope they fit, but we don't *know* whether they fit or not. They just sound good. Quite apart from whether they're politically possible, which, God help us, is another ballgame."

Palestine, surfacing again. I did not know why I was not surprised. He twirled the daisy in his big hand. As long as I'd known him, he'd always tried to keep his hands busy at something. He expelled breath as if finding the going hard and pushed on. "About the Agency, probably I'm talking more than I'm supposed to. We like to think we're good. Sometimes we are. But about Palestinians we could make a disastrous error without knowing it. One of the troubles is personnel. We train people in particular countries; our people are supposed to go and learn, operating out of the embassies. But Palestine isn't a country. It's just an idea."

"Yes," I said, interrupting the flow, "an intense nationalism in search of territory." I mouthed the cliché dutifully, if impatiently, hoping to provide a helpful shortcut. He looked up and flushed slightly.

"Look, I'm only making the point we don't have the talent pool of Agency officers we need for Palestine. I mean, we haven't got the officers we need to supervise the Palestinians we recruit, to keep our hired Palestinians from playing their own little games, to know if they're telling us the truth or not."

The daisy was twirling faster now.

"And the talent pools at State and Defense are no better." He looked at me earnestly. "I know you'd agree the Palestinian community is crucial to what happens out here. The *intifada* has been under way for a couple of years or so, and we don't really know how to handle it. Even though some of our people think they know. So our ignorance is bad, dangerous. The community is compact as hell, talented as hell. Wherever he is, any Palestinian knows where everybody else is: Kuwait, America, Egypt, Gaza, you name it. The diaspora's small, not like the Jewish one. Four million Palestinians total, that's all. Which means they can coordinate, act, do things. They're a force, a political force."

I nodded as he proceeded, as much from courtesy as anything else, to let him know I was listening. He knew I knew all this. I saw Cath glance our way from one of the livelier tables. From the dogged look on his face, Gav was reciting from a prepared pitch. "So," he said, "what several of us hope is you'd be willing to have your brains picked. About Palestinians, who they really are, how they think, who connects with whom, who hates whom, and so on. I'm not conning you, there's no American knows as much as you do. No American has old friends from school days the way you do."

Embarrassed, I laughed and shifted in my seat. "Come on, Gav, what I know is from growing up in Ramallah. I'm really not in touch. I've been back only once since college. Everything's changed, especially politics. I wouldn't be a help." I stopped a long moment, not wanting to help. "Listen, I'm flattered to be asked but it'd be a waste of time for all of us. Lots of professors have studied the Palestinian community. They're the ones to talk to."

"Bill, those professors only know what we know. They know the political events, they've done surveys, they know a few Palestinians personally. But even the few they know, they don't know really well. They may think they know them well, but they don't." He looked at me carefully. "You say you're out of touch. That's not true, and you know it. You may not get to Israel these days, but you get to Amman and Damascus and Beirut. You talk to Palestinians all the time. You're probably the American who knows most about Palestinians. Last year in Washington you spoke at the Middle East Institute. On Palestinian society. They asked you because you grew up there. You really know what you're talking about."

I said nothing for a while, remembering that Washington speech about a part of the world woven into my life like the design of a tightly knotted carpet. To simplify was to distort, yet this is what I had done, putting things as if Middle Eastern events fit the patterns of American life. The faces in the audience had shown gratitude. I was warmly congratulated for clarity, but I knew I'd been misleading.

We gazed at the other guests elsewhere on the enormous lawn. I didn't want to get involved, but I feared I was already involved. My chest felt tighter than before. Somewhere in the murk there had to be connections with all that had been happening in my life the last two days. I had to learn more. I had to keep the conversation going.

"What do you need to know about Palestinians that you don't already know?"

He continued to gaze at the other guests. "Well, for instance, we don't know which Palestinians to get to the negotiating table with the Israelis. We don't know which Palestinians could do both things: get the agreement of the Israelis *and* carry the Palestinian community with them. For instance."

He spoke solemnly like a man reading tea leaves. The daisy had stopped twirling. I stared at him for a moment.

"You know the answer to that, Gav. What have you guys been doing all these years? Just sitting there watching the Israelis stall the talks?"

"Listen," he said, "the PLO as negotiating partner is not the answer. Sure, after the Camp David Accord between Begin and Anwar Sadat, we all thought it was Yasir Arafat and his PLO or nothing. But Arafat's PLO is politically impossible. The Israelis won't touch them – and the Israelis have to agree on which Palestinians they talk to. So we have to move ahead without the goddamned PLO."

"If they'd wanted to," I said, "the Israelis could have talked. There've been plenty of ways to talk, plenty of ways to pretend they're not talking to the PLO."

He cut in impatiently. "Sure, sure, they're stalling. We all know that. And sure, they need time to get their settlements in place. That's exactly why we've got to come up with somebody new to talk to. For our purposes the PLO is no help. The Israelis say they're all terrorists. That's the end of it."

"Gav, the U.S. government is off its rocker if it thinks the PLO can be circumvented. Maybe you can't start with Yasir Arafat, but in the final analysis Arafat's PLO is the only game in town."

Adamant, he shook his head.

"Listen, Bill, there's more to this than meets the eye. I'm not just blowing off. Your help could make a difference." He paused. "We don't know the Palestinians well enough. You really have to know people from way back, way way back."

What was this all about? He went on. "Who are the people one knows really well? I mean the people you could be close friends with in five minutes after being apart, say, for ten or twenty years? In my case, I can tell you, it would be the guys I went to high school with in Pasadena and guys I knew in college. How many friends like that have you made after college?"

Where was he headed? Staring at the daisy, which began twirling again, he kept going. "With me, since I left college, maybe a couple from graduate school. Two or three in eighteen years of government service. Outside the service, well, maybe none. You come closest, and we might be close friends one of these days, but the Agency gets in the way. I mean, we're good friends but we're not old buddies. Hell, you know what I mean."

He broke off, embarrassed. I knew what he meant, but I didn't know what he was getting at. He saw the question on my face, perhaps sensed my impatience. A white-gowned Nubian was coming toward our table with a tray of liqueurs. "So," he said, "you're the kind of person we need to talk to, the kind who has old Palestinian buddies whose loves and hates you know instinctively."

I saw flaws in this argument but I switched to something else. The waiter arrived and poured me a slug of amaro in a slender glass. "Why," I asked, "should I be so unwise as to involve myself with the CIA? Who needs that kiss of death? For chrissake, I'm suspect already because I know the language. I'm careful as hell. My friends know I'm *clean*."

I said this last with a smile. Middleton, of course, knew what I meant. It doesn't take much to get oneself suspected, to be almost irretrievably labeled as CIA.

"I don't see what I suggest as involvement," he said quickly. "Nothing like that. Simply a stopover in New York. Aren't you making a business trip to San Francisco in a couple of weeks? You could stop off in New York, talk to some of our people, let your brains get picked. Nothing secret." He paused, saw my reluctance. "Listen, think about it. I'll be in touch in a couple of days. I have to say I'd reckon it a personal favor if you'd say yes."

His eyes dropped to the daisy, and the thick fingers began pulling off every third petal. Was he under so much pressure, he had to make it personal?

"Would there be money involved?"

He caught the drift of my question without trouble. "Not even expenses if you prefer."

"I prefer no money at all. I'll let you know." I took a deep breath. On our way over to join the others, partly to cover a slight awkwardness, we talked about meeting for golf the following week. The awkwardness, springing from a new dimension to our friendship, signaled no impairment. Only a change, a small one. In Gav's terms, if we'd been "old buddies" we'd have felt no awkwardness at all.

Cath sat close to me on the way home, chatting impishly and happily about some of the guests. She even had me laughing. Hasan our babysitter reported there had been nothing unusual and took off immediately for his tiny room on the roof. I told Cath I'd check the kids, a job she usually did. Their bedrooms were neat and clean, as they always were when Hasan was in charge. In sleep they looked innocent and defenseless, even if the books at their bedside tables suggested an adult knowledge of human behavior. Larry had been reading about the impurities of the sports world in the U.S. In Sarah's very feminine room there were three bedside books that Cath had described as somewhat racy. To me they seemed mild. As always I loved these kids more than I could ever explain. Larry, I thought proudly, was a man in the making. Sarah, just nine, would eventually be as gorgeous as her mother.

Would they survive whatever it was that threatened our family? Could I, a Quaker by inheritance, bring myself to kill in order to protect them? My father and mother had been dedicated Quakers whose revulsion at the idea of killing had been passed on unalterably to their son. For me, was that simply a psychological quirk? Or was I a sort of a Quaker myself?

When Cath came out of the bathroom, I was in bed. She stood for a moment, looked at me, then in a swift motion pulled her nightdress off. Despite my nagging anxieties, it was a coupling to remember. When it was over, we dripped with sweat. She held me close and said "you passionless bastard," a term of endearment. I kissed her gently and went to take a shower.

The water of the shower pulled me away from the beauty of what had just transpired and dragged me reluctantly back to reality. After ten quiet years in Cairo, could three unconnected Palestinian matters suddenly break the surface? There had to be a link. Pinstripe, two men at the school, now the CIA. What next? Cath was already fast asleep. I slipped in beside her but it took me a while to doze off.

THREE

Cairo, March 1990

The next morning, I phoned the school principal as soon as I could. "How's it going?" I asked.

"How is what going?"

"Did the police come by again?

"Oh that. Yeah, they sent the two sergeants again. No good. The two men disappeared again."

"False alarm?"

"Got to keep our eyes peeled. It seems one of the teachers spoke to them, late yesterday afternoon. I'd already gone."

"Why was the teacher talking to them?"

"I understand they told him they were interested in the school for their kids. Asking if they could see some of the literature."

"What did they see?"

"Nothing much. Some stuff hanging around the office. I guess he gave them our regular brochure, a copy of the directory, stuff like that."

"Which directory?"

"The one with the addresses. You know. Parents, home and office. Nothing wrong with that." Christ almighty.

"What do you mean, nothing wrong with that?"

"All in the public domain. More or less." He sounded defensive.

"Palestinians?"

"No doubt about that, I guess. The Sorensen kid says they were. He said they seemed educated. I told the police."

Like a board member doing his duty, I said it was good he was alert. My stomach muscles had gone tense.

"They seem interested in me and Larry and Sarah," I said. "Will you for God's sake tell your people to have them talk to you and no one else?"

"Sure," he said, "I'll get the word around."

I hung up. It was too late. They had the information they needed. Or did they?

I looked in the bookcase behind my desk for the school address booklet the two men now had. The chaotic Cairo phone books, in Arabic or Latin letters, would not help them; the tiny booklet would. I checked my name, then let my breath out in relief, remembering Cath's annoyance that an incompetent secretary had left out our home address and phone number. So I was still one step ahead. The two men at the school now knew where I worked, not where my wife and kids lived. A bit of luck, maybe life-saving. Pinstripe and his nighttime partner, on the other hand, seemed to know more, to be operating separately. Pinstripe, of course, already knew where I lived.

*   *   *

I sat on in my office for a lonely hour, dry-throated, weighing options one after the other. Laila knew something was wrong but kept herself busy with backlog filing. I had a Palestinian card to play, and the time had clearly come. I should have played it a lot sooner. The elevator rumbled and creaked on its way down to the dingy lobby. I crossed the lobby, opened the door into the courtyard, and glanced about quickly. Yes, there they were. Unmistakably. Two men dressed in brown suits and dark ties over by the newsstand. I did not have time for a good look, though I remember thinking they did not look Egyptian. Nor did I know if they would recognize me. I did not see Pinstripe but I spent no time glancing around.

Keeping my gaze straight ahead, I strode toward the nearby *midan* known as Liberation Square and clambered up onto the high pedestrian catwalk that encircles the huge, traffic-crammed square, providing easy passage on foot over the arteries vomiting cars and trucks and buses and carts into the chaos. As I hurried around the catwalk, I glimpsed the two making their way through the crowd at a distance of seventy-five yards. When they saw me take the stairs down to the American University, they hurried a bit. Quickly, I headed for the area behind the University, once a neighborhood of fashionable apartments for Europeans, now a warren of narrow dingy streets. I remembered a corner near a tiny grocery where I could throw off my pursuers by doubling back and waiting in a deep doorway.

I got back to our apartment forty minutes later, by way of the Zamalek bridge. No one followed me. Without going upstairs, I took the elevator to the basement and backed the car out from the garage, which fronts not on the Nile but on the street behind.

I had left the two men behind somewhere near the office. Now I had to cope with Pinstripe, who knew where I lived. I did not know where he was at the moment, but in the unlikely event he spotted me driving away from the back of our apartment, he could not have followed in time even if he had a car at his disposal. To make absolutely certain, I waited, motor running, for five minutes at the other side of a blind corner four streets away.

$*$ $*$ $*$

The big suburb of Heliopolis lies on the other side of the city, on the way to the airport. Heliopolis is a huge tangle of European-style three-story apartment buildings inhabited by well-to-do Egyptians and foreigners. Fashionable shops on the main roads. Quarters for the less well-to-do hidden behind. During most of the day and parts of the night the main road is crammed. In the daytime, even on the flyway that goes over the city, the trip takes an hour; below the flyway, traffic jams are so long and tight that drivers become desperate, edging up onto the sidewalks to find ways to move ahead. I would do the same if it helped.

This particular afternoon, though the traffic was dense, my usual resentments bothered me little. I inched along unaggressively as I sought explanations, taking deep breaths from time to time. What kinds of Palestinians was I dealing with? Sure, Pinstripe and the two men hanging around the school came from different factions, but any hope of knowing more was shattered by sheer numbers. There were factions of all sorts, some big, some small, some vicious, some inside and some outside the PLO. Most with outside funding.

When I came off the flyway, I plunged into a denser automotive mass. The air, laden with exhaust fumes, pressed down poisonously. Reaching the campus of Ein Shams, I pulled over onto the sidewalk and went to a telephone near the pedestrian overpass. A familiar voice answered. "A little coffee?" I asked in Arabic. No need to identify myself.

"Where are you?"

"Twenty minutes away."

"Meet you here."

I grunted, left the booth, squeezed the car back into the polluting traffic. Gav Middleton had spoken of "old buddies," and in about twenty minutes I would see one. The slightest awkwardness between us was difficult to imagine.

*   *   *

Mohamed Hasan Abu Saleh. As was the custom, his nickname – Abu Taleb – indicated family connections. The name Taleb was not only the name of his father but also the name of the son he was later expected to have. And he had disappointed no one; his oldest son was named Taleb.

He and I were laced together by the bonds of secondary school in Palestine, years together living in the same room at the Ramallah School in the heart of Ramallah town, north of Jerusalem. He and I and two others. Do friendships like this one happen in America? The four of us were known at school as a closed group, friendly to others but basically exclusive. We had been, and still were, a group of four that would last forever. Yet even though Abu Taleb and I had both washed up on the banks of the Nile, we saw each other only a half-dozen times a year, partly because Heliopolis had become a long way off in traffic-ridden Cairo, mostly because his life and mine were different.

When Cath and I first arrived in Egypt from eight years in Dhahran, she didn't understand how it was between Abu Taleb and me. In Dhahran I had used Arabic successfully as a way to get ahead in the Aramco world, but almost all of our social time was spent with fellow Westerners. Cath had had little opportunity to meet people of Abu Taleb's caliber. And I had made little attempt to explain him, making only vague references to the school in Ramallah and to Abu Taleb's Bedouin background. Before meeting him, she may have imagined him as one of the ragged Bedouin lounging around when we lived in Dhahran. Or a less noble tribesman from the sands of Gaza, a "native" friend I enjoyed seeing because he was "interesting" – not someone I really wanted to see. But she had come to understand that Abu Taleb was a part of my past she had never sufficiently explored. After meeting him, she once said I seemed to share his allegiances and attitudes but disguised them with an American covering. I had strongly disagreed.

Even in his Cairo exile Abu Taleb did live something like a Bedouin, though of a different breed. His nomadic ancestors, Beersheba Bedouin of Palestine, had herded sheep and goats between Beersheba and the sea. During the British mandate his father, who had been an influential tribal sheikh, acquired good land near Gaza that he put to work profitably by planting orange trees. He kept a couple of camels for show and stabled a few stallions of Bedouin stock to be ridden by Abu Taleb and his brothers on school holidays and other special occasions. The brothers all went to the best schools, such as the Quaker school at Ramallah, as expected of Palestine's male elite. Because that is what Abu Taleb's family was, elite, a kind of Bedouin royalty. And all the mixing they did with elite sons of townsfolk and landed gentry never erased something Bedouin about them, something courtly, the flavor of a world gone by, graceful images when they spoke. Om Taleb, his wife, wore Bedouin dress and cooked Bedouin food. She looked after him in a walk-up apartment he selected after the '67 war, near other exiled households, a few of them Bedouin, most of them peopled by educated and unemployable refugees committed, as he was, to the Palestinian cause. From relatives in the Gaza strip who managed his two orange groves, he received enough money to live modestly, including the costs of maintaining and educating six children.

He read widely in English, wrote poetry in Arabic, spent many hours with friends at his café within walking distance of home.

The opening moments of Cath's and my initial visit to the Heliopolis apartment had not gone well. After three flights of dreary stairs, Abu Taleb's wife ushered us into a reception room with cheap upholstered furniture and machine-made oriental carpets. Our host had not returned; our hostess spoke only Arabic. Her chin was covered with traditional blue tattoos. Cath adopted a patient expression, prepared to spend an awkward two hours over lukewarm tea and sticky cakes. Our host arrived five minutes later, sticky cakes in hand. His lean body was clothed Western-style, jacket and trousers of light gray. His wife, gratefully abandoning an effort to converse with Cath, departed for the kitchen. Abu Taleb shook hands with Cath, embraced me warmly, and then, in a graceful gesture that transformed the atmosphere, sat down not on an upholstered chair but on the carpet, Bedouin-style, his back against the divan facing Cath.

Magically the room became a place for good talk, for personal reminiscence, for words of value. In his literate English, his slender face alight with pleasure at seeing me for the first time in a decade, he talked on about Cairo, about the old days at Ramallah, what mutual friends were doing. I saw Cath lean forward to catch the nuances of what he said. For her his charm may have been partly good looks (she called him "devastatingly handsome"), but it was more than that; his charm involved a quality of mind, an intellect at once urbane and poetic, yet founded on a rock of Bedouin warmth and integrity. On that day the conversation touched on Shelley, on John Dewey, and on Palestinian politics; Cath had always found Palestinian politics a major bore, but not that day with Abu Taleb. For myself, in a rush of remembrance, I felt as if I had come home, as if some unseen but overpowering presence had put an arm around me and welcomed me back to boyhood. The passage of time had not diminished the pull of Palestine; the cords that bound Abu Taleb to me and me to him had not frayed.

Om Taleb brought tea and put it on the floor in front of her husband. Two of their teenage boys, bright and charming lads named Taleb and Hussain, came in to be introduced and sat on the floor listening respectfully to the words of elders in a language they only vaguely understood.

When I caught their eyes, they would smile. With the second cup of tea, Abu Taleb and Cath began talking about Shelley, and so I switched to Arabic and talked with Om Taleb and the boys about the Palestine she remembered and the boys had never known. Gripped by a special happiness, I chatted on in Palestinian Arabic about what it had been like, there in the hills near Jerusalem. The boys asked questions, always wanting to know details about how it was in Ramallah itself. Then I became aware Abu Taleb and Cath were listening in, that Cath noticed the eagerness in my face and was looking at Om Taleb with new eyes, discerning the quiet beauty and dignity behind the tattoos.

Despite the ultimate success of that visit, the women had little in common and no language they could use comfortably. Om Taleb never came to our Zamalek apartment – it was somehow inappropriate – and Abu Taleb dropped by perhaps twice a year in the early evening when in town on other business. One evening he fixed a meeting with Cath to talk about the romantics; he wanted comparisons for an article he was doing on nineteenth-century Arab poets. Cath was enchanted. On rare occasions I stopped at his apartment or his café after taking a client to the airport. Yet the rarity of seeing each other made no difference to our friendship. We could always be sure it was there, close and unalterable.

*   *   *

He was waiting downstairs at the door. His eyes searched my face. "Let's go to the café," he said. "A lot less noise."

"Just so we can talk."

"Talk, talk. All I do these days is talk." He smiled. We strolled to his nearby café. Tables and folding chairs were strewn on the sidewalk of a reasonably quiet side street. Abu Taleb gave the assembled regulars a quick glance, nodding in a few directions. Most were undoubtedly Palestinian, gathering for late morning coffee and political discussion. Waiters, who seemed to know everyone by name, stayed to chat a bit at each table when they brought the basic brew. Abu Taleb led me to a corner table, dropping a word to the head waiter on the way. His usual coterie would be told to leave us alone. I told him the whole story, omitting nothing. His questions were focused because the field of inquiry had shrunk. Now it was Palestine. Only Palestine. I described Pinstripe sketchily. He asked for more details, then stared at his coffee cup.

"Half a second." He went on staring at the coffee, then talked to himself. "Well, it could be. Seems to fit. Well, well." Then he spoke directly. "Listen, a long shot, but possible. I'm thinking of a man I know, a little younger than us." He thought a bit, then proceeded. "Yes, just possible. Palestine's a small world." He looked blankly at a point ten yards away. "Tall, as you say, and wears elegant *franji* clothes. Of course plenty of people wear fancy European stuff. What makes this one different is the way he does things, a grand air as if he were special. In the old days he could have been a prince. The women in my family called him handsome. The trouble was he was Christian and they couldn't marry him." He looked at me intently.

"Yes, it could be him," I said eagerly. "What about him?"

"If I'm right, his name is Nabil Farah. Family's from Jaffa. After the troubles of '48 they moved to Jerusalem. He and my cousin Adnan, Om Taleb's brother, came over from Jerusalem to Khan Younis twice. For school holidays. The way you and I did." We smiled in remembrance. Before '67, the eastern part of Palestine was governed by Jordan. In the west the Gaza strip, where Abu Taleb's family lived, was administered by Egypt. To get from one to the other one had to cross the unfriendly third part, which had been Israel since '48. For members of Abu Taleb's tribe the night-time trip, fairly safe despite Israeli patrols, cost little, perhaps a special gift to Bedouin guides at the next feast day, maybe a sheep.

"Those were the days. To think it's now only a cheap taxi ride from Gaza to Jerusalem. Ah, the benefits of being occupied by the Jews." He was pleased to switch his mind away from exile. More people were drifting into the café for late morning talk.

"So what about now?" I craved to know more. And right away.

"Take it easy. There's no rush. Don't *look* so excited." The words came out clipped and cautionary, but the handsome face came across bland, relaxed, boyish. "What you're involved in, we don't know, but make as if we're talking family. For instance, I'm talking to you about my son

Taleb's education in America, perhaps you can help him get there." I sat back, seeking to match the look on his face, the body posture. His lips stretched into a gentle smile. "That's better. Yes, much better. You've simply got to get with it, friend. Like a politician. That's it, casual." He grinned suddenly. "The way you never were at school. Who knows who's hanging around?"

He finally got back to Pinstripe. "When I last heard of him, he was in Beirut working for that splendid faction-ridden ineffective organization known as the Palestine Liberation Organization. Which is indeed Palestinian, but scarcely organized and certainly we have not yet been liberated."

"What faction is he with?" I wanted him away from political commentary and back on track.

He spoke the next words with relish. He had waited for me to ask. I saw the merriment in his eyes. "Well, I seem to remember he was closely connected with a certain Abu Kerim." And he began to laugh. Softly at first, then from the gut, overcome by the irony of life. Not to laugh with him was impossible, and it felt good, and once started, hard to stop.

"God," I said. The laughter had special magic; I felt less tense.

"Yes," he said, wiping his eyes.

"Well, shit," I began to laugh again, trying to cope with this extraordinary information. Abu Kerim was one of us, one of the four, from that room at school, a part of both our lives, part of a closed schoolboy corporation. Abu Taleb, delighted with the surprise he'd administered, tried to stop laughing. Acquaintances of his were now sitting near us.

"We must look as if we shouldn't be interrupted," he said, forcing his face muscles and body back to a sober position. I did the same.

"*Ihki*," I barked, using the Arabic word that ordered him to speak, to tell me what he knew.

"I only know what I hear. I understand he's paid by Fatah and is responsible to Abu Kerim. At least he was. A sort of hatchet man. Does some killing now and then."

"Is Abu Kerim still top man in Beirut?"

"Yes, but as you know, top man for Fatah, not the whole PLO. He has enemies." He paused. "We can't be sure our friend Nabil Farah is still with him. Things change."

"Yes, things change," I murmured. I thought back to the dormitory room in Ramallah. Where were the four of us now? Myself in Cairo, cut off from Palestine by the accidents of personal history. Abu Taleb in exile in the same city. Abu Hisham, a lawyer in Jerusalem, famous, prestigious. And Abu Kerim in Beirut, the only bachelor, boss of the PLO's dominant faction in Lebanon. If his real name was Hasan Abdul Hayy, few bothered to use it. Known by Palestinians everywhere as Abu Kerim, he stayed behind in Beirut after the Israelis invaded in '82. Now admired and hunted, he shifted beds and usually women each night.

I forced myself to sit back, to ask one question at a time. "Why would Nabil Farah follow me?"

"I don't know. We have to think carefully. If Pinstripe is Farah, and we can't be certain yet, somebody in Beirut knows why. Something to do with Fatah, of course, though as I say maybe Pinstripe is no longer with Abu Kerim. Maybe he's switched. Maybe he ..." His voice trailed off.

"Anything to do with the *intifada*?" I was avid for any combination of fact, opinion, or speculation. But the Palestinian uprising, or *intifada*, was not exported.

Abu Taleb looked at me impatiently, changed directions. "What about the others?"

I tried to describe them but didn't do well. Pinstripe's partner had nothing to distinguish him, except ordinariness. Nor had I done more than glance at the two men outside the office. Abu Taleb shook his head. "I remember little about Farah. Only from those visits to Khan Younis. Adnan admired him, said he was a leader at school, led some big student demonstrations in Jerusalem. I'd say he was probably a leader, competent, persuasive, a dedicated sort. Maybe dedicated as much to himself as to our cause, but hell that's a common failing. And what I say is based on impressions from when he was a teenager."

He glanced around the café. "Enough speculation about Pinstripe. Not much help at the moment." His tone, not his posture, turned business-like. "Probably more dangerous are those two others. Even if they're from some other outfit, there has to be a connection. When is that trip you're supposed to take to America?"

"In a couple of weeks."

"Can you find a reasonable way to go sooner? Without making it seem unnatural? The sooner the better on finding out what the embassy people have in mind. Which is clearly an important part of the puzzle. We've got to know what they're trying to do, and that would put us ahead of the game. Anyway, I don't trust your impatience. Too much Palestine in your life."

"What about Cath and Larry and Sarah?"

"That's the real problem. I suppose you can't leave without being sure they're safe. At least," he said quickly, "almost sure they're safe. Nothing in this world is completely sure. The simple answer is it looks like you're the problem, not them. But someone should keep an eye on them. Haven't you got Egyptian friends who can help? Listen, probably they'll be all right. Easy to say, of course."

He glanced at the other tables. Some were occupied by Palestinians I knew slightly. Near us was a cousin of Abu Taleb, seated with a group of fellow refugees. I waved a greeting. "We'd better be less exclusive," said Abu Taleb. "When there's something I don't understand, I want people to be sure it has nothing to do with me."

We got up and strolled toward the door, Abu Taleb greeting friends on the way, smiling a lot. I shook a few hands as well. As we started back toward his flat, he looked reflective.

"Listen," he said, "let's not get our signals crossed. This morning we talked about my son Taleb's education and the possibility of his going to America. I'll find a chance to mention this later today. In the meantime, I'm here if needed. But until we know more, let's take great care. Avoid walking around by yourself at night." Then after a short pause, he said, "Those two from the school, you'll have to keep them away from your apartment while you're away in America. My instincts are giving me trouble. Some denizens of that café have Damascus connections."

At the door of his flat he again hesitated before he spoke. "Bill," he said in Arabic, his eyes intent, "it's time you became a Palestinian again. I want you to survive."

We embraced Arab-style. As always, I thought, his company was somehow reassuring. What had been true in our schooldays was true now. Abu Taleb, Bill Hampton, and the other two formed a cabal, unaffected by the passage of time. My departure to America for four college years had not made a difference. And indeed my college classmates seemed to know that my personal loyalties and attitudes were of a different order, removed in some way from theirs. I understood what went on in their world, more or less. But what I understood instinctively was Palestine.

Small boys played bare-foot soccer in the dusty street. Abu Taleb, shifting to a big smile, told me to be careful in America, and I went off to find my car, which had a new dent on the right rear fender. I spotted no one following me back to central Cairo.

*   *   *

I took the car back to the garage in Zamalek, took a taxi to Groppi's downtown, and walked to the office, changing my direction of arrival. I saw neither Pinstripe nor the two others, though I did not peer around. Upstairs, Laila looked up brightly and smiled. As always, her cheerful face made up for the cavernous gloom of the building's entrance hall ten floors below, its unkempt stairways, its rickety elevator. "Everyone's after you today," she said. "Here are your calls. Some things to sign on your desk."

I went into my office and dialed our Zamalek apartment. "I sort of knew it was you," said Cath. Some echo in her voice brought back memories of being inside her the night before. I felt a sudden surge of love. We chatted a few moments, inconsequentially, sending silent messages of affection and remembrance over the phone wires.

"Listen," I said finally, "it looks as if I have to get to the U.S. a bit sooner. Some things need doing in New York, then they'll expect me in San Francisco a bit earlier." I held my breath, hoping for no queries about New York. I said nothing untrue, but I meant to deceive. Our marriage had not been built on such stuff.

"Oh hell," she said. I heard a deep breath. "It's always hard for me when you leave, and earlier is worse. I should be used to it by now. Would you get back sooner?"

"By about a week, I hope."

"Well, that's good news, I guess." She fell silent a moment. "Last night was special," she said.

"Yes, it was," I said. "Very special." When I hung up I thought for a while about the previous night, remembering its special moments. Then I worked on a fax to San Francisco, saying I needed time in New York for personal reasons, asking if I could schedule company consultations a week earlier. I knew it made little difference to the company but I had to ask. Now, at least, I had a plan of action, though part of the plan was avoidance of action. Leave the Palestinians behind, allow things in Cairo to evolve without me. Smoke the Americans out in New York, ferret out the link to Pinstripe and the others.

But the reason for everything was Cath and the kids. Would they for God's sake be safe if I took off for the States? I was running out of time. I wished to high heaven I had the three of them tucked away in some small Midwestern town, a community of good citizens to help fight the indignity and danger of unwanted attention. Especially the attention of the two men who had been hanging around the school.

Stay flexible, I told myself. A friend at TWA – Cyril Hughes was his name, he was director of the Cairo office – could get them to Pennsylvania at the last minute. My instincts (or was it my optimism) told me they would be all right in Cairo, but if danger from a Palestinian faction was logically remote, logic was not the strong suit of those who felt cheated out of a nation.

What further precautions could I take?

If Abu Taleb was right about the identity of Pinstripe, the embassy or at least the CIA, whether they knew it or not, had a link with the PLO. The PLO? What link with the Palestine Liberation Organization could the United States have, given the current American refusal to recognize and deal with it? Or what kind of activity could each be engaged in that would lead to the Zamalek apartment of an American businessman? I caught a glimpse ahead of life-bending complications. I sat at my desk staring out the window. Laila came in with more papers and looked at me carefully. She asked if I felt all right. I said I felt fine and moved a few papers around until she left the room.

Later Laila brought in some sandwiches for a tardy lunch. Afterwards I did a little work but for the most part sat at my desk looking straight ahead, focusing on nothing. My mind slipped away into fantasy and I began to imagine heroic ways in which I could win through – win through what?

I finally admitted to myself I had no alternative. I had to take the trip to the U.S. The information I needed was available only in New York. I dialed the embassy. Gav Middleton's phone rang several times before anyone answered; apparently his secretary had left her desk.

"Yes?" said a voice. "Political section." I knew the voice. Mary Paul, Sam' s wife.

"Mary?" I said. "This is Bill. I was trying to get Gav. How are you? How's James?"

"Well, surprise, surprise. Things are chaotic today, meetings everywhere. I happened to be passing this desk and saw the secretary was away. How are you doing?"

"Okay, okay. I may have to leave on my usual business trip a bit early, so I'm running out of time. Otherwise fine. I wanted to talk to Gav about a final golf game. Could you leave him a note?"

"Why sure. Expect I'll see you before you go. Special love to Cath, tell her to set time aside for me while you're away. James will want to have long talks with his godmother."

I was taken by surprise, having always assumed Mary worked for Jim Spence. Apparently she was part of Gav's shop, the embassy's CIA enclave. Gav rang back in a few minutes. We made a plan to meet.

*　　　　　*　　　　　*

Leaving the office I saw none of my followers but took no chances. So it took me a while to get to the first tee. We did not play. Nor did it take long to say what had to be said. I told Gav I'd scheduled two days for the Eastern seaboard.

"I'm very grateful, Bill." The blunt voice betrayed relief.

"I still don't see what good I can do you."

"Let me be the judge of that. What about money, expenses?"

"Not a whiff, thank you." We discussed dates and times and meetings. Then in wordless agreement we went to the clubhouse. Like almost every part of the Gezira Club, it was packed; these days the aristocracy called the club a public picnic ground and seldom showed up. Gav ordered beers, the chair creaking under the weight of the heavy body. The big hands kept wiping the frost off his glass. At no time did the subject of being followed arise. Did they think at the embassy I was no longer worried? Did they think I thought it was an Egyptian?

"I didn't know," I said at one point, "that Mary Paul worked in your shop."

"She doesn't work in my shop." He looked me straight in the eye. CIA people are supposed to do that: deny with sincerity what is clearly true. In Gav's defense, on most matters he avoided fake sincerity. As we parted, for instance, he grinned broadly as he asked a question.

"How about me sending an embassy car to get you to the airport?"

With a matching grin, I declined with thanks. We both knew I wanted as much distance as possible between the American government and me.

∗   ∗   ∗

When does fear begin? It steals into the heart, tightens the chest, and finally one recognizes it is there. One can discount it by reasoning things out, persuading oneself that fear is unnecessary at a particular time and place. Yet it persists. Unreasonably. I recognized I was afraid. Perhaps more for Cath and Larry and Sarah, who were caught in a crossfire of my making, but also for myself. A Palestinian crossfire that I did not understand, except I knew enough about Palestine and its desperate impulses to know it could be lethal. The likelihood of violence was high. If my shortcomings, whatever they were in some Palestinian eyes, were serious enough to have me followed, they were serious enough to have me killed. But what had I done? Once again, round and round, I reviewed everything I could think of.

It could not be my business life. Without difficulties, political or otherwise, I sold electronic equipment and arranged maintenance for all sorts of people and governments ranging from the wildly free markets of Lebanon and some Persian Gulf states to tighter economies such as Egypt. Nor could it be my personal life. My marriage was a happy one, or so I thought. At any rate Cath seemed happy, particularly after our move from the Gulf to Cairo and her successful launch into a writing career. Her short stories were now eagerly awaited by an agent in New York. True, I had always sensed her impatience with what she called my devotion to living in the Middle East. I think she dreamed that one day she might live on Manhattan's Upper East Side. I guess Cairo was our compromise. And the kids? They seemed content. Neither I nor Cath had sensed any difficulties at the American School in suburban Maadi. Cath, of course, did not know about the two men who had inquired about us at the school, but as Abu Taleb said, I seemed to be the problem, not Larry and Sarah.

But the basic question of family would not go away. I kept deciding and then undeciding. Should I leave them in Cairo unprotected or persuade Cath to take the other two to the States?. If I told her what was happening, would she really wish to go? What would Abu Taleb do? He would elect to leave his family in place and if any were killed, take revenge. Those who contemplated the killing would know that tribal revenge would eventually occur. But I had no tribe. Nor would my parents' Quaker beliefs allow me to kill.

For some reason I felt better on my next trip to the Gezira Club later that afternoon. I had made an out-of-the-office appointment to meet my Egyptian friend Abdu to ask a big favor. Perhaps, I thought, one gets used to fear, to the feeling in the gut. Once again I made certain my pursuers were not following. We met at one of the tables on the small balcony near the entrance to the main building and exchanged pleasantries a few minutes. From other tables people were glancing at Abdu's well-known face, wondering why he was there. I told him my plan to leave in a few days on a business trip. With aristocratic distaste he looked at the crowd and suggested some exercise. So we walked over to the race track and marched briskly along it, far from other ears.

"I can report," he said with his reserved smile, "that there is no connection between you and the Egyptian government, unless there is some super-secret organization created recently without my knowledge."

"That was quick."

"Well, I knew you were planning a trip to America, and I had some good luck, which I will not bore you with. It allowed me to proceed nicely on the police front. As for the *mukhabarat*, my cousin at the presidency is a very bright fellow, which is, I suppose, why he is at the presidency." He smiled, though I caught a suggestion of disapproval. "I also checked some other organizations you don't know about and I'm not mentioning to you."

"What do you think now?"

"I don't have any new thoughts. The disturbing fact is there seems to be no connection with Egypt. But one thing you should know. When I spoke to an old friend at one of those organizations I'm not telling you about, and this is a friend with whom I could be frank, he had more than a casual interest. Actually asked about how Pinstripe carried himself, his bearing. I couldn't get anything more out of him, just that, a kind of special interest."

He was quiet a moment, looked at me carefully. "His organization is one that keeps an eye on unwelcome persons from abroad. I believe you call them undesirable aliens. Such as Palestinians. The people you were brought up with."

I said nothing, just went on walking by his side, eyes ahead. I knew he'd asked a question; my silence, I guess, was an answer. "So you must be careful. I cannot help by starting major surveillance because the cure would be worse than the disease, and the disease may, after all, be a mild one."

I hesitated several moments, then took a deep breath. I had to ask for help. "Abdu, I think I should tell you I'm scared. For my family. What's happening, I don't really know. Your guess about Palestine is probably right. I have to take this trip to the U.S. for a whole variety of reasons, but my family needs protecting while I'm gone." I did not tell him the major reason I was taking the trip was to get more information about why I needed protecting. Probably he understood this. He heard the appeal in my voice.

"I think I understand the situation." His voice was almost formal. "Yes, I do understand. And I will make some arrangements. It had, in fact, occurred to me that you might need help while you are away. So I will keep an eye on your family. I have a few special people I can count on, and no one will know. Leave me your addresses and how to get in touch. If you hear no word, you have nothing to worry about." Perhaps it was limited comfort, but my cup of gratitude filled and for a moment I couldn't speak. I was more wound up than I thought. Courteously he shifted his gaze away.

"If anything did threaten," he said, "I could get them to the airport immediately. What airline do you use?"

"TWA. A friend there named Cyril Hughes could arrange things. I'll tip him off, ask him to say nothing."

"Good. Again, my view is that none of this will be necessary. But if it were, I would phone you. Then you could phone Cath to explain."

I nodded, not knowing how to thank him, what to say. His friendship had suddenly become a bulwark. I took another deep breath.

"No trouble at all," he said quickly, putting his hand on my shoulder an instant, then withdrawing it in embarrassment. "Let's have a drink and talk about something more interesting, such as our children's many talents." Once again, the reserved smile.

∗   ∗   ∗

With the care that was becoming second nature, I again took a cab to Groppi's and made the short walk to the office, prepared to tackle the mountain of paper I had to deal with before my trip. Though it was time for Laila to leave, she stayed on to help. Finally I told her to go. I said I'd leave a pile of stuff on her desk. She would have stayed if I'd asked. I phoned Cath to say I was in for a siege and would have bread and white cheese when I got home. The work went better than expected. About sundown the phone rang, but when I picked it up, I heard no voice at the other end, simply the silent sound that comes when someone says nothing and just listens. I said hello a few times, then hung up.

When I phoned Cath to say I was on my way, she said she'd meet me with glass in hand. She sounded in good spirits. Switching off the lights, I made my way into the corridor, pressed the hall light, and called the ancient elevator. As it rose to get me, I noted that its single electric bulb, an uncertain feature at best, was not working. And as it creaked slowly down, the hall lights went out. At the ground floor, I reached for the light button, but nothing happened when I pressed it. I stood for a moment in the dark, orienting myself, planning my route through the large lobby to the street light whose glimmer I could barely see through the murky glass of the main door. I had about thirty yards to cover before I could see where to put my feet.

Suddenly I knew something was wrong. I knew it as well as I knew my name. I moved noiselessly to my right in the darkness, which was absolute except for the dim light from the distant door. A short sharp cough and the splat of something against the elevator cut the silence. My stomach knotted as I realized a bullet had come to the place I'd just been.

Then not a sound for twenty seconds. I did not move. Against the light from the door I could dimly make out two human shapes. They could not see me but I could discern the outline of them. Like me they stayed motionless, straining to hear.

"*Marhabba*," said a voice from the darkness, using a universal greeting but giving it a Palestinian accent. They were making an inquiry. Was I dead? Had they missed? The next events happened fast, but my memory of them has not faded. Suddenly the human shapes loomed large, running at me to find me in the darkness; a third shape appeared from the front door, moving with incredible speed. I sensed a quick movement, then felt a tremendous blow under the ribs. I desperately sucked air into my lungs, trying to breathe. Gasping for air, I slumped to the ground, upper body against a wall, covering my stomach with my arms, waiting for the next blow. Against the light the third shape, taller than the others, acted lightning fast. I could see the glint of knives and hear the grunts of struggle. Then a sound of pain like the wailing of a cat, and then a sob, and then one of the shorter men fell. The other short man broke for the door. As I struggled for air, the third man, the tall one protecting me, dragged the fallen man away quickly. The fallen man's shoes made a scraping noise on the concrete floor. As the tall man maneuvered his burden through the door, I could see by the silhouette it was Pinstripe. It was the way he

carried himself. I didn't know if the body he dragged was dead or uncon-
scious, or what he did with it. I sat there, eyes straining into the dark,
breath returning to normal, gut aching badly around the liver. Then Pinstripe hurried back into the entrance hall and ran catlike over to where I
was.

I closed my eyes; I did not want him to know I knew about him. I
wanted to give the impression I would easily recover but was for the moment knocked out. I tried to breathe easily, visibly, not knowing what
people do when they are knocked out. A flashlight flicked on, stayed on
my face a long moment. A hand felt my wrist and then the side of my
neck. I heard him leave. After five minutes, perhaps it was ten, I picked
myself up slowly and finally got to standing position, supporting myself
against the wall. I stood there awhile experimentally, gauging my strength.
Had I eaten anything recently, I'd have thrown it up, though the ache in
the gut was now less intense. Automatically I made an attempt to brush
off my clothes but stopped because it hurt and because it used too much
energy. I concentrated on getting to the door.

Stopping to recoup every few steps, I stumbled toward the light,
down the steps, and onto the street. Steadying myself against a lamppost,
I stood there, wondering about my next move. After some long minutes
a taxi passed by, and I was able to signal it. The cabbie looked at me
strangely, but when he saw I was a foreigner, he said nothing. My guess is
he thought I was drunk. I forgot to worry about being followed home.

One thing I knew, the two men had attacked to kill. But for Pinstripe
I'd be dead.

*   *   *

I slept badly that night. Every time I turned over, which was often, I
felt a sharp pain just under the ribs. I kept hearing the splat of the bullet.
The area around the liver ached unpleasantly. I told Cath I had stumbled
in the entrance of the office building. The lights suddenly went out, I said,
and when I fell, I bruised my side against an outcropping of wall. She
insisted on seeing the bruise, then I heard her suck her breath in. My right

side was blue and yellow, the size of a platter. I said it looked worse than it felt.

"Please don't play games," she said. "That was no accident."

For a short interval I stayed silent, considering my next move. "I just can't tell you about it right now, I'll tell you as soon as I can."

"You've got to tell me what's happening. It can't go on this way. It's too serious for games."

"No, it's not serious. Really. And it's over now, the worst of it anyway. Something to do with Palestine. Old friends have asked for help. I'm honor-bound not to say anything. Please."

She looked at me, weighed my appeal a long moment. I should have had a better story.

"What kind of help can you give that turns you black and blue? You could have been killed." She paused, then with angry reluctance went on. "All right, no more questions. I don't want you to lie." But I had lied all along.

In the morning the pain and stiffness had increased. I took a shower, as hot as I could manage. As always the four of us had breakfast together, and because the kids were there, Cath acted cheerful as if things were normal. But Larry knew something was wrong.

"Did you hurt yourself, Dad?"

"Yes, I fell in the hallway at the office. It'll feel better soon."

"Have you taken a pain killer?" He already had medical training in mind for later in life. His look was quizzical and he had more questions. But Cath interrupted to tell the kids it was time to go down and catch the school bus. They gathered their backpacks with the usual rush. Sarah came round the table before leaving and contrary to her usual habit gave me a warm silent kiss on the cheek. Cath watched with an almost wistful smile. After they left for the bus, she sat quietly, saying only what had to be said.

I decided to walk to the office, partly to persuade Cath I was all right. When I came out the main door, Mohamed, our dark-skinned Nubian *bawwab*, stood at his post. A professional doorman for forty years, a stately man of infinite patience and grace, beloved by our children. He usually greeted me with a gentle smile. This time his greeting was different, had different overtones. I looked at him sharply. He gazed up the street toward the small park along the river, the bit of greenery through which I usually strolled to work. A knot of people had gathered on the grass near the road. Nearby stood a police car.

"What happened?"

"Someone apparently died," said the Nubian, avoiding my eye. Someone he must have seen on the wall the last few nights. As I drew even with the police car, I slowed my steps. There, propped up with his back against a tree as if he had decided to have a sandwich, sat the other Palestinian, not Pinstripe but his co-watcher. Blood drenched the front of his shirt; its color was dark. He had been dead for a while. I kept walking, proceeding to the office as if it were ordinary to find a body in the park. I did not see Pinstripe among those crowding around, nor did I spot him between the Kasr-el-Nil Bridge and Garden City.

Suppose I hadn't moved to the right. The bullet would have hit near the heart. Though I tried to slow it down, my mind shifted into overdrive. No thought stayed in place long enough to be worked through; others came along unbidden like rush-hour traffic. And my bruised side seemed to ache more. As I crossed the park I tried to appear normal. As if my body did not hurt.

Thwack – a metallic sound, not the sound of a bullet going into wood.

In later editions of the papers, the body in the park was identified as that of a certain Mousa Hashem Sabri born in Jerusalem, traveling on a Jordanian passport that showed no entry stamp for Egypt. Whatever game we were playing, within the last day it had reached the killing stage.

I had to assume my family would be safe. I told myself Abdu would stand by Cath and the kids whether I was in Egypt or the U.S. I had to keep moving. To the office, to New York and San Francisco, to someplace I could find someone to talk to and negotiate with.

Thwack …

*   *   *

Abdu phoned to suggest an afternoon walk. We met at the Gezira Club and trudged again around the race course. My gut was better, though the pain was lingering on.

"That fellow phoned me back," he said, "the one who heads the outfit on undesirable aliens."

"Oh?"

"Yes," he said. We trudged a few steps, then he went on. "I think things are okay. My friend was more forthcoming this time. Mousa Hashem Sabri, the man killed near your flat, turns out to be connected with our Mr. Pinstripe. My friend said the killer is unknown but is presumed to be Palestinian." He paused, then looked over at me. "I gather you were not surprised to learn from the papers that Mr. Sabri was Palestinian. Any more than I was."

"No," I said. Abdu, I thought, needed no details about recent assassination attempts.

"My friend who handles undesirable aliens," he said, "says it looks like a factional squabble, perhaps not much to worry about. Another Palestinian, not our friend Pinstripe, was also found dead, somewhere in Garden City. Near your office. When I said you'd be leaving for a business trip, he thought that was a good idea."

After a moment, he went on. I held my breath when he talked about family.

"When I asked my friend about the safety of your wife and children, he said that while nothing is clear in Palestinian politics, his experience led him to believe they do not ordinarily kill families or involve them in other ways. When I asked why you should be part of all this, he said if you told me, I should tell him."

He stopped walking and fixed me with a friendly stare. "I knew what he meant. So I told him I was totally certain you were not a part of the CIA. He then asked how it was you spoke good Arabic. He asked why had you bothered to learn the language. I explained about your boyhood."

"How do you know I'm not part of the CIA?" I asked with a slight smile. I was getting used to hearing the bullet hit the elevator cage.

"Well, I've had experience in police work and related matters, one might say. You're not the kind they hire."

Before we parted company, I handed him addresses and phone numbers for my trip. I'm certain he knew I had a lot more I could tell him. He told me again to let *him* worry about my family while I was gone.

"I've got to tell Cath something sometime," I said.

"If you can tell her later, it might be better. She shouldn't have to worry."

But Cath was a worry. A preoccupation. Larry and Sarah, my wonderful children, worried me also, but I had not been lying to them.

      *   *   *

The last two days in Cairo became special family days. On one of them the four of us drove to a favorite ruin, a Pharaonic temple, on the Fayoum road. Far away from crowds. Lately I had watched crowds with care and avoided them when possible. The temple watchman, delighted to see us again and anticipating an oversize tip, protected us from staring peasant children, who somehow manage to appear, even in the desert. We played sardines among the ruins, a kind of reverse hide-and-seek, and then Cath dug into the picnic basket, bringing out the cards for a game of hearts with vicious rules we invented ourselves. The sun and shade and sky and laughter came together for a few golden moments of acute happiness, acute because I knew it had to pass. Larry was winning, determinedly putting down the rest of us. Sarah struggled to stay in second place, seemed to accept her brother as the eventual winner, and was delighted to put down either of her parents whenever possible. The kids were absorbed by the game; Cath leaned over and laid her cheek against mine. I did not want the game to end.

On our last night she held me very close. Usually she would act determinedly cheerful when I left on a trip, but this time I tasted tears on her cheeks, not crying, just an involuntary welling as if a delicate mechanism of control were worn out.

"What makes it all right, really all right, is I know you love me," she said.

      *   *   *

The next day I set off. As if apologizing for something, Sam Paul insisted on coming by early to take me to the airport. "Have to meet a client, Athens plane, mid-morning," he had said. "Might as well take you out. Be a pleasure anyway, morning air's nice, less traffic."

I thrust my bag in the back seat of his Ford.

"Tickets, passport, money, office papers?"

"All here," I said. He fell silent, concentrating on his driving. We were running late. It felt good to relax against the seat of the car, a soothing moment of no responsibility. For the moment Pinstripe had disappeared. His co-watcher had been killed. And the two other men had disappeared, one because he was dead, though there had been no mention in the press. Grateful for Sam's skillful driving, I began once again going over my options. My mind wandered off irrationally.

The car gave a sudden screech. Sam had braked and swerved to avoid hitting a donkey cart in Nasser City. The driver of the cart shouted at us angrily.

"Sorry. Wasn't concentrating enough."

"You handled that well."

"Oh really? Nice of you to say so. Still got your front teeth?"

"Yep," I said, unconsciously imitating his accent, which has traces of inner-city Detroit. So do his table manners, I thought, letting my mind wander again. Cath once tried a couple of dinner parties for the Pauls, but Sam was clearly uneasy. He tried hard, energetically determined to fit in, but then foundered and fell almost silent, leaving the talking to Mary.

He glanced over at me. "Don't worry about your family," he said. "Nothing will happen while you're gone."

"How do you know that?"

"Feel it in my bones. Whole thing will sort itself out." He slowed down for another donkey cart. "Anyway, with your record you could pack up and move. Latin America, maybe."

The idea had never occurred to me. Well, maybe it had, but not seriously. Yes, it was an alternative to consider, logically speaking. But to give up half my heritage, living like a refugee in Brazil? Wrenched away from all the memories? Starting a new language? And what about a promotion to San Francisco, a move into the big time at headquarters? It had already been suggested by my superiors. To be sure, it was not New York – which Cath would love – but certainly it was a great center of artistic achievement. And much more beautiful than Manhattan. Cath would thrive. She was already in touch with several writers from the San Francisco area. I could get used to it, I thought, but the idea was somehow repellent. I didn't want to live in San Francisco, dreaming about decent coffee, imagining chats with old friends in Egypt, Lebanon, Palestine. Those places in the Eastern Mediterranean were my special heritage, where I had lived most of my life, where I felt at home, truly comfortable, happy to mingle. Yes, my formal and legal attachment to America provided status and a few economic advantages, but I did not think it had created a deep allegiance. I had never had the chance to be a patriot. If, from long ago, I had had connections with the Philadelphia area, these had never been more than indistinct: my brother and a few friends from college days with whom I was now barely in touch, the sketchy memories of my parents' Quaker community in the suburbs, Cath's unexciting family remnants in another suburb.

On the other hand, suppose staying in Cairo meant losing Cath, by death or by separation. What then?

Sam glanced at me again. His face had a look I did not remember. "Listen," he said, a touch stubbornly, "I'm sure everything will be okay at this end." His certainty, puzzling but reassuring, reminded me that Sam was a good friend, though, as so often, I recognized there was much about him I did not know.

FOUR

New York, April 1990

They had a man at Kennedy to meet me: tall, my age, standing high above the crowd at the TWA exit gate. His manner was linked to the dark hat he wore, almost a homburg, an important covering that matched a confident expression on the face. But the eyes moved about restlessly, as if rebelling against an instruction to be steady. A driver held open the door of a comfortable Buick and moved us into the afternoon traffic toward Manhattan. "Bill," said the man, "we all appreciate your willingness to stop over and talk about this Arab problem. Knowing what's happening in the field is crucial to good decisions." He mouthed the maxim with relish, not unlike the bureaucrats of my San Francisco office. He said to expect a session in the morning after I recovered from jet lag, and he asked if we might have "a drink and quick dinner" before he caught his train for Greenwich.

I murmured about my fatigue. This public-relations man would not know what I urgently needed to know. Weariness, more than usual, hovered over me, pushing me gently against the car's soft seat. I felt secure. Safe in New York.

He spoke again. The restless eyes took in the silent driver in front, signaling that no discretion was required. "Let me fill you in. On tomorrow morning. There'll be three of you. Two fellows from Washington plus yourself. The big man is Curtis Blake, one of our very top people. I'm sure you've heard of him. The other man, David Rosberg, is on the research

64

side. Non-Zionist Jew, very bright." I nodded, trying to keep alert. Like most people who hear Washington gossip from time to time, I'd heard of Curtis Blake. I also knew something about Rosberg.

"I should learn a lot."

"We're the ones should learn a lot," he said, with modesty born of courtesy, presumably on behalf of his organization. "Arabs are crucial to what we do. Gav Middleton, by the way, says you have a special insight into the Palestinian community." Was that what the Washington officials wanted to talk about?

*   *   *

The meeting place was furnished for comfort, a suite of rooms at 46th and Madison. The door to the suite declared that inside were the offices of American Research Inc. The receptionist, a good-looking woman with horn-rimmed glasses and a sterile smile, showed me into a conference room, on one side a long table surrounded by straight chairs and on the other a restful arrangement of armchairs and coffee tables with large ashtrays. Against the wall, which was papered dark green and studded with prints of English country life, stood a mahogany-colored sideboard with coffee and doughnuts at the ready. In back, through a partially open door, sparkled the white tile of a large washroom.

I had no difficulty identifying Curtis Blake and David Rosberg. Blake came forward first. Medium-height, fifty-five or more, blond hair mixed with gray. The face square, the body compact. Something about him, perhaps the marble-like blue eyes, suggested authority. His stomach was flatter than that of most men twenty years younger.

Rosberg waited one step behind and one step over. I'd gone through a couple of his books, scholarly stuff about the politics and economics of Arabs. I had not known he was CIA. His prose boasted dispassion and academic balance. Though the same height as Blake, he seemed smaller, a spare balding man with steady brown eyes that offered friendship. Neither tough nor evil, I thought. His soul showed on his face. Blake's soul, by contrast, was not standing parade. It resided somewhere behind the armor-plating of the blue eyes.

Rosberg said it was good to meet me. I sensed he would like a meandering conversation about people, Arab places, Middle East gossip, mutual friends. But Blake, with a gesture toward the coffee table, led us to the armchairs. Cups in hand, we wasted less than a minute on small talk. If I had a sense of urgency, so apparently did the "big man" up from Washington.

"How to begin?" he said, though I felt he knew exactly how to begin. He exuded confidence. "Perhaps with a profound apology. We've brought you here under false pretenses, telling you we wanted to know more about the Palestinian community. That is true, as far as it goes. But eventually we want to make a patriotic appeal for help." Eyes riveted on my face, he and Rosberg searched for reactions to this abrupt opening. "Nothing about this," Blake went on, "will get you enmeshed with *us* or with any government. What we have in mind is something you might do that would help everybody. I mean everybody." He paused for effect. "I'm talking about nothing less than a just settlement between Israelis and Palestinians."

Again the four eyes fastened onto my face. I stared at Blake for a moment, then looked at Rosberg. Then I stared back at Blake. Both were dead serious. For an instant I had thought it a joke of some kind, or some tricky test. Few knowledgeable persons known to me expected a settlement, let alone a just one, within two decades. They kept gazing at me intently, insisting on their presumptuousness, the presumption that a just peace could happen soon, could depend on what we said here, could depend on the likes of me. And why so abrupt? I sensed I was expected to respond.

"I doubt I could help in that sphere." But I knew I had to stay. The air around the armchairs smacked suddenly of sticky politics. "Exactly what did you have in mind?"

Blake put up a hand. "Having apologized, and it is a very genuine apology, I'd like to ask if you'd be willing to delay that question. Without a preamble, the answer would seem simplistic. But in fact, pretentious as it may seem, we may be on to something beyond the importance of anything since 1948. I should also say your own knowledge and inputs are crucial to clarifying our understanding of the background." Another pause. "Would you, then, be willing to wait a bit for the answer to your question?"

He asked this disarmingly and with great gravity, as if much were at stake. Did he think I would be too intrigued to walk out? Too flattered at being drawn into high-level consultations to be angry about being deceived? A minor deception, I thought, a sin of omission. He'd asked me to come and talk about Palestine; I was under no obligation to respond affirmatively to a "patriotic appeal" missing from the agreed agenda.

"Yes, please go on."

He gave a detached smile. "Good. First I want to be sure we agree on basics. I'm assuming we are all patriots. I'm assuming our goal in the Near East is a settlement between Jews and Arabs, or if you will, between Israelis and Palestinians. I'm assuming it doesn't matter what we call things or peoples providing we know our hearts are in the right place. David Rosberg is Jewish, I'm a lapsed Presbyterian, you're a sort of Quaker. Any trouble with any of that?"

"I guess sort of a Quaker is all right."

"Change the definition if you like."

"No, that's all right."

"One more assumption. No, a confirmation rather. Your views might be called well-known in certain ex-pat circles in Cairo and Beirut. But viewpoints change. Middleton reports from Cairo you share ideas with which we're well acquainted. That there'll be no settlement until an Israeli government negotiates with the PLO, that no Israeli government right now could even suggest such a notion and survive, that negotiations will get more difficult to launch as younger hardliners move into power. Or Muslim fundamentalists, who get stronger every day."

He searched my face for the confirmation he sought. Once again, the detached smile, which may once have been a youthful try at courtesy, now a reflex as impersonal as granite.

"Yes, that's roughly my position."

"And what would be the time frame for something like that?"

"Maybe ten years. Maybe twenty. Hard to know. We need a new generation that's sick of the hate and the killing."

"Since '77, when Sadat made his visit to the Knesset and Carter brought about the Camp David accords, have you noticed much progress in negotiations between Jews and Arabs?"

"No, not much."

"You mean the Israelis have spent their time stalling the talks on autonomy for the occupied territories?" If I was startled at the way he was leading his witness, plainly it bothered him not at all.

"Well, that certainly," I said. "But the talks have been pointless anyway. Without Palestinians to talk to, what's the difference?"

"Do you see anything hopeful for the immediate future?"

"Not much. People of good will, people who really want peace, exist on both sides. But they don't have political clout. The *intifada*, I suppose, has made a difference, but the Israelis are learning how to cope."

He nodded in acknowledgment, looked down at his coffee cup. Clearly he was used to controlling discourse. Rosberg sat motionless as if awaiting a grand entrance. When Blake looked up, the flat eyes were fixed on mine. I sensed something unyielding, willful.

"That's the way it seemed to David and me," he said weightily, "until quite recently."

He sounded like a non-believer reluctantly accepting the importance of a new revelation. A way to turn dilemma into opportunity. He continued to look at me, perhaps expecting a response. I sat gazing at him, not moving, trying to guess what was coming, trying to figure what lay behind the marble-blue eyes and the compelling manner.

"This is what we want to consult you about," said Rosberg finally, his manner diffident, the brown eyes looking hopefully at a future I did not yet know about. "We believe we're on to something that could change the face of Arab-Israeli politics. Nothing less."

I had to say something. "Very interesting," I said. I was impatient but wanted to appear unhurried. "My Quaker father used to say both sides were intent on living unhappy lives. If that's no longer true, I'd like to know about it."

As if preparing for a long siege, Blake got up to visit the washroom. Rosberg and I followed. As we stood at the urinals I noted that Blake seemed taller than he actually was. We washed our hands ritually. Back in the main room, Blake resumed his chair as if claiming a throne. He cleared his throat. His voice was solemn.

"It would be difficult to overstress the significance of our meeting today. We're on to something historic." He paused. With his next words came a change of tempo and timbre. He became a chairman anxious to proceed with an agenda. "Before we go further, it would help us, I think, to get more of a line on you, so that we know where your advice and counsel can help us most. Is that acceptable?"

A bend in the road. A program to be worked through before I got the information I had to have. I nodded reluctantly, gesturing for him to proceed.

"Let me give you the outlines of what we know about you, most of it from Gav Middleton. I gather you stayed for your secondary years at the Ramallah Friends Boys School where your father was headmaster. You spent your summers in the mountains of Lebanon, at Shemlan, with your parents and your brother. Then at eighteen you went off to Swarthmore, studied physics and chemistry, met the girl you're still married to. Correct so far?"

"Yes," I said. I found myself almost smiling, interested in hearing about myself from this man. Like a television show I had seen once or twice.

"Later you went to work for Aramco and spent eight years in Saudi Arabia, mostly in Dhahran working in Aramco's programs to help new Saudi enterprises get off the ground. One of the Saudi companies was an electronics firm, and with your help it became more successful than most. Which interested Starr Johnson in hiring you for their Middle East manager job. Which you accepted. And you chose to live in Cairo."

"That's roughly it. My wife was particularly pleased about moving out of Dhahran."

Blake went on. "A few things have piqued my curiosity about your earlier life … For instance, why secondary school in Ramallah? Didn't most children from families like yours come back and go to some prep school in the States? Wouldn't it have been better to go to Deerfield, like your older brother?" Had I told Middleton my brother John went to Deerfield?

I felt guilty about John; my life had turned out better than his. At Deerfield he doubtless received a fine education, but I remember my aunt reporting he was unhappy, and this he confirmed the following summer when he came to Lebanon. The nearer the time for returning to Massachusetts, the more withdrawn he became. I overheard my worried parents discussing it. A matter of adjustment, my father said. But for John things never went well at Deerfield. Despite the fact that other missionary and quasi-missionary families had placed their sons at this prestigious school. Nor did things go well at Haverford. They simply dragged on. Despite his summers in Shemlan, he found himself isolated, cut off from his boyhood, trying to make his way in an America that made him feel foreign, a country he couldn't claim fully as his own.

"Because of John," I said, "my parents thought I'd be better off at the Ramallah School." Because of John's unhappiness, they wanted me nearby.

More than two decades later, with no family and few friends, John lived in Philadelphia, teaching math at a private school. On Sundays he attended Quaker meeting. When we spoke on the telephone, which was not very often, he had no interest in recalling the Palestine years.

"My parents were prepared to be unconventional, Quakers and all that. Yes, I had a hard time getting into Swarthmore, but I think family connections helped. It worked out all right."

"In Ramallah, didn't you miss contact with Americans your own age? You must have realized you were missing out on your American heritage, cheated of something." Like a psychiatrist he sought the source of something nonconformist.

"Well, I knew it was different for me. My father made me proud of the difference, I think. Also, he was proud of me himself. He'd say to visitors his boy spoke perfect Arabic, his boy was truly part of the life of Palestine. Stuff like that." Something pushed me to explain. "Of course I knew from summer friends in Shemlan, American kids my own age, what I was missing. Some of it sounded good, particularly having dates with girls from American families like mine. But when I got back to Ramallah, I forgot all about it. We had good times there."

"Wasn't it pretty tough when you actually got to Swarthmore? Didn't you feel out of things? Out of place?"

"Maybe at first, but things went well. My parents had friends in Philadelphia, and I went to their homes on Sundays, even Saturday evenings, and I always felt I was part of a community. Well, sort of a community. Of course, I met Cath — that's my wife — when we were freshmen, and that made things easier. I never really needed any other girl."

I imagined I saw an amused look on Blake's face, but perhaps not. Yes, I looked at other girls after I met Cath and had a few sex-oriented encounters, one on a sofa in a dormitory basement and a couple of others in the fields near the campus. But Cath was the one I wanted to talk to, to walk with, to be seen with. In our junior year, she, not I, made the decision we should sleep together. We made careful plans; she arranged for birth control. For both of us the experience was overwhelming, for me an unbelievable intimacy.

"But what happened about girls when you were at Ramallah?" asked Blake. Then he smiled, almost genuinely, and shook his head at himself. "What a question! I apologize."

I stared at one of the pictures of country life on the green wall. Horses, hounds, riders in red jackets. I wanted to answer his question. "Well, my roommates and I used to have escapades, you might say, trips into Jerusalem my father never knew about. At the time lots of fun. Looking at the women and the city sights. Four of us shared the same big room in a dorm, and we did things together." Yes, my God, we did things together. Not so much what the four of us did (there were slightly bawdy "escapades," there was everything else) but the persistent togetherness of it. A group closed to outsiders, though friendly to them. We never imagined the possibility of taking a fifth member into our dormitory room. The other boarders understood this, even if my father and mother over in the headmaster's house did not. We weren't considered stand-offish, just that what we did, we did together. For five years.

Other memories came along. What days those were, growing up in the clean sunlight of the hills. Olive groves, red earth, white rock, tile roofs, good friends. Friends? Not just the other three. Ramallah itself, six miles north of Jerusalem, was my lifetime friend. I knew almost everybody, so it seemed. In those days the town was smaller, perhaps fifteen thousand people. My friends were shopkeepers and their shops, merchants and gentry, beggars and back alleys, stopping on my bike at age eight to chat. I was part of the scenery, a foreigner who was born and grew up there, almost one of their own, a person whose true home was Ramallah. If some other Americans resided there for periods of their adulthood, it was not for crucial childhood and teenage years. I tried to explain this to Cath; I think she understood. But it's a long leap from a "hometown" in Pennsylvania to a market town in Palestine.

Blake's voice cut into my thoughts. He spoke gently, as if he felt the nostalgia himself. "So it was a happy time for you, as you look back?"

"Yes, Palestine was special then. Before the '67 war, from the mid-fifties on. Jordan was supposed to be our country but the West Bank was really Palestine. We went on picnics with Palestinian families, often to a special olive grove we liked, where we helped with the harvest; my mother always invited the other three if they hadn't gone home for the weekend. Or I visited one of the three for the weekend, to Jerusalem or Gaza or very occasionally to Nablus, which was fifty miles away. Some of the families that we did things with had daughters my age, but of course it was always in groups. We never, what you call, dated anybody." I was conscious of using a jarring word, alien to the life I was remembering.

"What did you talk about with your three friends?" Blake's tone remained gentle, inviting me to stay on in Palestine a while.

"Oh," I said, happy to linger, "I guess we talked about everything. Everything. People we knew, girls, social problems, family problems. And of course there was always politics. That took a lot of time. I remember defending my father's Quaker positions."

"How did those arguments go?"

"Oh, you know. Bearing arms won't help get Palestine back. Understanding between peoples is the only way to peace. Neither Israelis nor Palestinians are evil, just misguided. Violence begets violence. And so on. But the others remembered what their families had lost. Only one of them would side with me and argue the merits of different approaches. The others felt violence, or at least confrontation, was the only path to take."

"And are you a Quaker like your father and mother?"

"When I visit Philadelphia, I'm a Quaker whether I like it or not. I mean socially; I don't go to meeting." I remembered Cath saying there was a lot of Quaker in me, especially my feelings about non-violence, my revulsion to killing, but she may also have meant puritanism.

Blake had apparently run out of personal questions. I marveled at how much I'd talked about the past, to a person I hardly knew. How had Blake done it, how had he created the mood for it? Palestine was in the room with us. The three of us sat silently, comfortably.

Then Blake began again. His tone of voice had changed slightly. "When you were at school, who was the one who could see your Quaker point of view? Was it a man named Yusuf Hisham Al-Khalil?"

I stared at Blake. The tide of early-sixties memories ebbed abruptly, the nostalgia shattering like dropped china. I remembered they wanted something from me but hadn't said what it was. I turned wary, a bit cross. Everyone knew about Yusuf Al-Khalil, the distinguished Jerusalem lawyer, the man known to me as Abu Hisham, but few were aware or cared that in his teens a roommate at the Ramallah School had been an American named Bill Hampton. I spoke up sharply. Perhaps my voice had an angry edge. "Why have you taken the trouble to learn about my school days? In fact, what is all this? What else do you know about me?"

Blake uttered no soothing words. The marble-blue eyes were unrevealing. He spoke intently, as if each word was crucial, his gaze fixed unwaveringly on my face. The very energy of his voice made it impossible not to listen carefully. "I didn't mean to startle you. You'll see that it all fits in. There are matters of great moment we must now tell you about." Rosberg's expression appealed for my attention. As Blake continued, I leaned back in my armchair in a futile attempt to break contact with the steady eyes.

"We have only this conversation to help us settle matters and to make plans," he said, "that is, if you finally agree on the importance of the new information we have. Time is short, in terms of our chance to talk and take action. At the same time," he went on, almost as if responding to a show of impatience on my part, "none of our talk this morning has been wasted. We needed to know about you, to take in what you know that will help us plan. Also to know what would be best for you to *do*. I'm now convinced you're precisely the person we need. Your attitudes and your balance are of paramount importance to how we might proceed." I found the flattery agreeable, calming. Even though I understood its purpose.

"At the moment the only group the Israelis could consider as a negotiating partner is the PLO." Blake's intentness took on a somber quality. "In spite of some wishful Israeli views to the contrary, the PLO commands the support of most West Bank and Gaza Palestinians. We've tried to strengthen the PLO factions and the parties within Israel that might one day have the political courage to negotiate. And we've also had to cope with the friends of Israel in Washington, not just Jews by any means. Thankless tasks all around. "

Blake leaned forward in his chair, hand on one knee, the gaze unremitting. His face had the look of a cross-country runner who has broken from the pack on his way to certain victory. "So here it is. Over the last few months we've come to understand there is a Palestinian who might turn matters around. Only one. The only one with enough prestige and reputation for personal integrity. The only one who could buck the PLO and sit down with the Israelis to negotiate, as per the Camp David accords."

"Christ almighty," I said.

"Yes," said Blake, understanding what I said, "he might get killed, it can happen to anybody, but probably not. Once he got started, there'd be a groundswell of support for him in the West Bank and Gaza, and even in PLO ranks, especially in Arafat's Fatah where the power really lies." I had no doubt whom he meant. A leading West Bank personage, the foremost lawyer, a Palestinian of prestige and distinction. Known to me as Abu Hisham.

"Jesus H. Christ," I said. "This is crazy. Crazy. He wouldn't have a prayer."

"We believe he would. Once Abu Hisham, as you call him, began to negotiate, Israeli public opinion would swing as well. Concessions we haven't been able to dream of would become possible. They're all sick of the killing, sick of living in a garrison, sick of threats to children. They're ready to deal with someone they think they could trust. Such as Yusuf Al-

Khalil. He's the only one, other than the PLO itself, who could negotiate credibly. That is, who could come to an agreement, then carry the Palestinian community with him."

Middleton had used the same phrases. "Listen," I said, "Abu Hisham is a Palestinian nationalist. He could be called a PLO sympathizer. A move to the left inside Fatah and he'd be right in the middle. The Israelis know this, he hasn't kept his opinions to himself. Say what you like about his moderation, at heart he's a nationalist. I haven't seen him for twenty years, but nothing can change that fact. So why would the Israelis even *consider* having him at the negotiating table? For God's sake, he couldn't agree to anything less than a Palestinian state."

"Yes, very true. And exactly our analysis up to a few months ago." Blake stopped, glanced at Rosberg. We were nearing the heart of the matter. Rosberg's brown eyes, excited by the drama, shone with hope.

"The crucial fact is this," said Blake as if he had just found the grail, "we now have nothing less than an Israeli agreement to negotiate with Abu Hisham. If Abu Hisham is willing, the Israelis are willing to have him. I know you understand this will change the entire face of Arab-Israeli politics. Arafat would be forced to go along because the ground swell would be overwhelming and would give all branches of the Palestinian community the special hope that has been missing all these years. Your old friend Abu Kerim in Beirut would join in with galvanizing enthusiasm."

I wanted to cut in but I doubt he would have heard me. His face had a mystical look. When he went on, his tone had become almost reverent. "After nearly half a century our breakthrough is within reach. Now it's up to you."

*　　　　　*　　　　　*

He went on for a while. While he spoke, I sat bemused, wondering what kind of man this was, wondering if he knew what he was doing. Something felt wrong. A few months back, he said, at the end of a routine meeting in Jerusalem with a counterpart in the prime minister's office, the fellow leaned forward and said formally that Al-Khalil would now be acceptable as the negotiator in the Camp David peace process. When Blake, recovering from surprise, asked why Abu Hisham, the Israeli answered, "Because he's honest and could compromise."

Proceeding with greatest caution, Blake said, he then asked various staff members at the American Embassy to bring the matter up with Israeli counterparts. While some responses were circumspect, the weight of evidence showed a consensus among "Israeli decision-makers." Blake said he made two more trips to sew up the commitment. If Abu Hisham would play, he said, so would the Israelis.

"But that's playing Israel's game," I said, conceding nothing. "They let you know who they'd be pleased to have negotiate, and you deliver him. They wouldn't agree if they didn't see an advantage. And then you get him killed, probably. Why should he take a risk like that?"

"For the same reason as everyone else." His voice took on theatrical intensity. "Is it really worth living now in either Israel or the occupied territories? One group arrogant and scared, the other oppressed and frustrated. From what you say, isn't Abu Hisham the kind who'd think the risk worth taking? What's more, I don't think he'd get killed, though no one could be categorical about it. He lives in Jerusalem. He'd negotiate on Israeli-controlled territory, say in Jerusalem itself, where the security is excellent."

Again I wanted to cut in but Rosberg quickly steered us away from Jerusalem.

"Let's back up a minute," he said. "If I were Bill, I'd ask why bother with Abu Hisham at all? Why not put pressure on Israel to negotiate with the PLO? Just make them negotiate. Right now. All it would take is firmness on our part. They're almost totally dependent on us, yet they do what they please, including embarrassing us."

Blake took the cue, used my name for the first time. "Bill knows the answer. We all do. Getting tough with Israel is a non-starter. We've tried it. The fact is, no U.S. government is finally going to permit Israel to be pushed around by the U.S. government." He paused. An exasperated note crept into his voice. "The spoiled Jewish kid has got to be protected while he bullies the Arab kids on the block."

Rosberg, looking anxious, intervened with something positive. "You see, we've talked about this issue for as long as I can remember. The same words, the same arguments. As Curt says, whenever we've tried out the notion of U.S. pressure on Israel and persuaded the top boys to adopt it, the top boys never stay the course. We have to pull, not push. If the Israelis talked with a man like Yusuf Al-Khalil, they could begin to see possibilities, have hopes, change their minds about PLO evil." He sounded the way my father used to sound.

"Those are nice thoughts," I said. "But why not have the U.S. recognize the PLO? Your top men don't have to stay any course to do that, they do it one Friday afternoon and, once it's done, the lobbies can't reverse it."

"Bill," said Rosberg, earnestly, "formal recognition may be less important than we think. Suppose the PLO said the right things and made it possible for us to recognize them. It could happen. Perhaps sooner than any of us expect. But it wouldn't change things all that much. What's truly important is to have the Israelis eager, really eager, to talk to Palestinians. The PLO has too much of an anti-Israeli past and has too many factions. What we need is someone the Israelis themselves choose to talk to. If we insist they talk to the PLO, they might talk but in the end nothing would be accomplished. Just talk."

He may be right, I thought. So much had happened. So many new political wrinkles. So many Palestinian factions, their attitudes ranging from willingness to seek peace to total obstinacy – with new factions appearing at crucial moments, as if to prevent a united front. Most were loyal in their way to Arafat's PLO, some a lot less than loyal. After the Jordanians expelled them in 1970, the PLO headquarters had moved to Beirut, and when the Israelis began their six-month invasion of Lebanon in 1982, they moved again, this time to Tunis. When the uprising of '87, the *intifada,* suddenly erupted with its vigorous protests against Israeli occupation, the now-distant PLO was almost taken by surprise and Arafat's influence in the Palestinian community receded. But gradually he reasserted the PLO mystique. He said he now supported Israel's right to exist within its pre-1967 borders and he declared the existence of a Palestinian state in the West Bank and Gaza. For its part, the U.S. began to allow diplomatic contacts with PLO officials. Some friends in the State Department had even told me they thought this was the year when effective two-way talks involving the PLO could begin. Plans were already afoot, they said.

But the two bureaucrats up from Washington clearly disagreed. Blake got up from his upholstered chair, walked to the end of the room and back, hands in pockets. He turned, sat on the edge of the conference table, and regarded me carefully. The missionary look had returned. "I don't want to put this too melodramatically, though it is melodramatic, the whole thing. Let me say it straight out. You, personally, may have it in your power to change the course of history. No less. You can help bring peace to Israel and Palestine. No less. You can reestablish those days when happy lives could be led, when family picnics were possible, when ownership of a plot of land meant you could keep it." I glanced at Rosberg, but the brown eyes revealed nothing but anxiety. Perhaps he thought that Blake's pandering words would not help persuade me, were off-key.

"Bill," said Blake, "I'm not asking you to persuade Abu Hisham. And I don't underestimate his political savvy. I'd never make that mistake. I'm simply asking you, for the sake of peace, to get in touch with him and lay the situation out. The facts can do the persuading."

"And what are the facts?"

"We can," he said, emphasizing each word, "deliver an Israeli agreement to talk seriously. The U.S. can arrange for Abu Hisham's presence at the negotiating table, with full ceremony. If he comes, we have every reason to think the Jordanians will come too. These are big stakes."

Again I wanted to break contact but the marble-blue eyes had me skewered.

"Bill," he said, "can you, in fact, think of any other realistic way to get things moving? Can you think of any other way to get a settlement, to let Israelis sleep soundly, to give Palestinians a fair deal and a stable future? We've tried everything else. Your friend Al-Khalil, your friend Abu Hisham, has to know that time is running out. If there's no settlement soon, there'll be no Palestine left to deal for. The Israelis tighten their grip every day. They scare or force a few Palestinians out, then build a new house on Palestinian land. Every day Sharon breaks ground for new Jewish settlements in the occupied territories. Is it fair to deprive your friend of the chance to decide for himself whether this is a good idea? What if he thought this might work but never knew about it till too late?"

Suddenly it had become my fault. "For God's sake," I said, my voice rising, "if you think this is such a great opportunity, by all means get in touch with Abu Hisham. Send a letter, see him at a social gathering, mention the possibilities. You don't need me to mediate."

But I knew the answers before they came. Rosberg, at least, knew I knew. We were discussing a part of the world where few secrets exist for long, yet the atmosphere exudes secretiveness and intrigue, with plots, real or imagined, surfacing and disappearing each day. Not just politics, whose separateness from other matters is a Western notion, but all of living, the relations of one family to another, one friend to another, the real stuff of life, all inextricably mixed with each day's scramble for influence and each person's yen for power.

"Bill," said Rosberg, "you know better than I that we couldn't send just anybody to pass the message. An American of almost any kind would guarantee failure, or a Palestinian, however discreet. These things always seep out. A wife tells her closest friend, who tells only a few friends, then it becomes known to a few more. To protect himself Abu Hisham would have to make a big splash and denounce the whole thing in the most public way he could."

I knew all this. If Abu Hisham ever came forward to negotiate, providing he was not assassinated in the meantime, it would be known it was at the urging of the United States. Especially at a time when the rumor mills in Washington were hinting that the Secretary of State was trying to legitimize Arafat, who was off in Tunis, as the negotiator for Palestine. Abu Hisham's credibility in the Palestinian community would self-destruct. Amidst laughter and scorn, jokes about him would circulate throughout the occupied zones and the diaspora.

Blake was watching me intently. "But what if the messenger were his longtime friend Bill Hampton?" His voice was solemn. "A perfect cover? No, not perfect; nothing's perfect. But as an old school chum, you could pass a message at almost no risk – over a cup of tea, say, on a sunny afternoon in Jerusalem."

"Sorry," I said. "I see the need for someone like me. I just don't want to get involved." I groped for words. "It would be a kind of betrayal."

"Betrayal?" Blake pounced on the word, shaking his head unbelievingly. "But of what, of whom? Betrayal of a chance for peace? Betrayal of a man's opportunity to decide something for himself? All he needs to know from you is the Israelis would agree. And you are the only person who can safely take the message, who happens to be part of a four-man solidarity front from school days, one of those historical accidents that may never come our way again."

In the throes of impassioned reason, Blake could not understand my reluctance. Betrayal, for me, had nothing to do with what he was talking about, but I myself could not have explained what I meant; the word had spilled out uninvited. Something about the sanctity of our circle of four, something threatening to its memory. About using the circle for an unsavory purpose. And was Abu Kerim somehow involved in their thinking? Rosberg may have understood some of this; I felt sympathy coming my way in waves.

"Bill," he said, "we're not asking you to do anything you don't feel right about. I understand the family feeling you have for your three friends. But turn the thing around. Suppose Abu Hisham had a message for you that would redound to your benefit, make you famous, provide you with a fortune, or whatever, what should he do?"

"He should tell me, of course." I did not like my inner feelings to be on display. "But the message would not be from the CIA and it would come without a recommendation. Sending me is a recommendation, a message that I endorse your plan."

Blake's impatience showed on his face. Rosberg cut in. "Do you really think," he asked, "that Abu Hisham would think you were recommending us, that you could not make clear this was only message-bearing? Is Abu Hisham not a man of balance and perception? Is your empathy with him not such that you could explain exactly what was going on?"

Thus Rosberg, compassionately, pushed me against the wall.

*   *   *

Blake put a sympathetic look on his face. "Bill, I'm sorry to spring this on you so suddenly, and you've handled it with, I have to say, remarkable equanimity." The misstatement came out like truth, and I accepted it. "Of course you need time to think it over."

The impersonal smile came and went.

"What we need to do now," he said, glancing at his watch, moving for the first time to the agreed agenda, "is pick your brains about Palestine. David and I get lots of information, but it's the context that eludes us. We don't really know the social picture, and your knowledge is unique."

He overdid the flattery but I did not mind. Whether Blake decided to have a session on Palestine as a way of working on my self-esteem, I do not know. The probing questions and discussion that followed were, I can only say, exhilarating. When I looked back later, they were also revealing.

So for an hour we talked about Palestine, and I was able to forget my troubles. The other two milked details from my mind, matters long forgotten. Again I explained how it was before '67, but this time I was not allowed to bask in nostalgia. At one juncture we went into the nuances of the relations of one family to another, one clan to another. How did they band together, when did they become enemies?

"It's a system," I said. "Extended families usually have traditional friends, traditional enemies. When there's a disagreement, a family expects to get its usual support from its traditional friends. Or it may seek out an arbiter. If that doesn't work, or if the system breaks down in other ways and traditional supporters change sides, then violence can happen. Especially in villages and among the least westernized sections of the towns. Usually the expected support is there and somehow things work out. But on rare occasions nothing helps, and even for small unimportant reasons, killing or violence can begin."

I was simplifying matters, but the other two seemed to find it useful. After more talk about village disputes, I switched to another social level. "But the kind of families my parents knew, upper-class folk really, were never involved in violence. I remember, though, when two well-to-do Nablus families did not converse with each other, and I understood it had been that way for several generations. Only rarely were members of the two families found at the same social occasion, and if they had to be there, they stayed on opposite sides of the room. If their kids were at the same school, the kids soon learned the arts of family dislike."

Later Rosberg brought up the subject of Beersheba Bedouin, the nomads or former nomads of Palestine and Jordan. "How do they fit into the social picture?" he asked. "Didn't you go to school with one of them?"

"Yes, I did," I said, thinking of Abu Taleb and pleased with the topic. "Well, for the Bedouin things are changing pretty fast. It has a lot to do with the closed borders. Because of Jordan's and Israel's concerns about border control, the annual treks are pretty much over with. The tribes that want to continue their nomadic ways have found it difficult. But viewpoints are changing also. Living near villages and towns has become attractive. Now some of the wealthy tribal leaders have nice town houses, and some have become landowners with political influence. Just as if they were upper-crust townsmen. Some Bedouin kids are going to good schools, even the women. Lots of lesser-class men have abandoned the idea of caring full-time for sheep and goats, have taken jobs as manual laborers. Some of the younger and better educated males have secretarial or even administrative jobs."

We went on about Bedouin longer than their political importance merited. Rosberg was clearly interested in information for its own sake, but both men, I thought, were fascinated when I told them about the 'Obeid, the black sub-tribes and perhaps ex-slaves, that were still connected to most Beersheba tribes. But I begged off on extensive questions. For additional data I would need Abu Taleb at my side.

Inevitably I found myself studying Blake. Whenever he made an assertion or asked a question, he made as if he were interested in facts, projecting an image of scholarly balance. His face seemed always to reflect careful thought about what I had just said. Though occasionally, I thought, the facts he really wanted were those that would fit snugly into theories he had adopted long ago. He seemed to want confirmation, not information. At one juncture he wanted me to agree that the *intifada* had strengthened the hand of the traditional "inside" leadership of the PLO, and though I presented evidence that a new kind of "inside" leadership was emerging within the occupied territories, he was able to ignore my disagreement and proceed almost as if I had agreed. At another juncture,

I almost lost the thread of conversation when I found myself admiring the manipulative skills with which he conducted our meeting, and if for other reasons I had not felt uncomfortable about him, I might have been swept along. As it was, his ideas of right and wrong policy, though shrouded by diplomatic ploys and the impersonal smile, kept thrusting upward, angular formations under a blanket of flattery.

Rosberg was something else. Likable, decent. He had plunged with visible academic enthusiasm into the Palestinian world, speculating about it, looking at it close up. Off in a corner of my brain I remember thinking he expected the best of his fellow humans. Could such a man be an effective spy and intriguer? Would the honesty in his eyes not always betray him?

Many people they asked about I didn't know or couldn't remember. They never asked directly about Abu Hisham and his family. But I made no attempt to disguise the fact that some of the time I had in mind the East Jerusalem of Abu Hisham, the Nablus of Abu Kerim and his Palestinian enclave in Beirut, the orange groves near Gaza where Abu Taleb grew up. The receptionist brought in sandwiches and we ate away in silence for several moments. Leaning back, I realized I could fall asleep, less because of jet lag than because I felt drained by the effort to remember. Yet I couldn't stop the memories. I had to force myself not to talk on.

When it was time to leave for the airport, Blake and Rosberg stood up. Blake now looked older, the folds under the eyes more pronounced, the flesh no longer taut across the face. "It was a long morning," he said, "but worthwhile. You performed just as we'd hoped, brilliantly I'd say. Like other Palestinians of the diaspora, and in some ways that's what you almost are, you've kept closely in touch with home."

He stopped, sat heavily on the arm of an overstuffed chair. We all knew we were not yet finished. "Bill," he said, "you need time to think. Of course. Remember, it's a question of presenting him with new information, then he'll decide what he has to do. Surely a gesture of friendship on your part. But you'll do what you think best." He paused, then asked if I could come back from San Francisco by way of Washington. He wanted to have me talk with "some of our people." And it would, he said, give me a week to reflect.

I did need a week to reflect. Now I knew the American plan, but I also knew it had major flaws. I had crucial reasons for seeing Blake again.

*   *   *

On the way back to Kennedy I stared from the cab at the traffic and the ugly buildings, but my mind flitted elsewhere, half in Palestine, half in the room where I had spent the morning. The two men had opened a door on the past. Walking through it left me abstracted, tugged at by small things gone by. Like reading old letters. Blake had arranged it. He took me back to the old days because he wanted to know where my heart was, what stops to pull to get me to do what they wanted.

Now I knew. They wanted me to carry a message because they thought a visit by me would be considered innocent. An innocent visit by an American Quaker businessman with no history of governmental involvement. No one, they thought, would connect my visit with Abu Hisham's later agreement to negotiate. The American involvement would remain unknown. Except to me. And a few others. Then a few more, ho ho. Then Pinstripe. Then…

The radio in the front of the cab spewed news. Four Israeli soldiers had been ambushed and killed the night before in the Lebanese buffer zone south of Tyre. "Fuckin' Arabs," said the driver, "At it again." The accent was Brooklyn, the cab license gave the name as Levine. Others of my acquaintance would say "fuckin' Jews." Or maybe "fuckin' Israelis," if they felt like making the distinction. Everyone screwing everyone else, mindlessly torpedoing each other's dreams. In the name of what? Justice? Happiness?

My Quaker father had looked on for years in helpless sorrow. Was I helpless now? Was there something I could do, something positive in the cause of peace? Would my father be pleased? Oh for chrissake, I muttered, and jerked my mind savagely away from Blake's vision of me as one who might "change the course of history." Listen, Walter Mitty, I told myself, first get out of trouble. Be sure your family is safe. Disengage. But how and from whom?

FIVE

Washington, April 1990

Washington makes me uneasy. The untidy pattern of the streets is disorienting; in Manhattan I know where I am. Perhaps it's the people that make me feel alien. As I made my way through gentle rain and early morning crowds, dodging umbrella spokes, I heard casual chatter full of names I did not know. Bureaucrats, I supposed, on their way to work. They surged around me in various shapes and colors, all doubtless plugged into overlapping networks of gossip and power, each one at home, each one in place, his own place.

Where was my place? I had one, but it was elsewhere. Not San Francisco, where I had just spent seven days focusing on the electronics business. Certainly not this capital city and its alien ambience. And what was happening in my possibly death-dealing place, my real home? I had heard nothing from Abdu. I reminded myself that not hearing from him was a good thing, but I felt a sudden urge to pray for the safety of Cath and Larry and Sarah. To someone – to God, I think – I said silently, "Please take care of them." In this city I could turn to no one else.

They had arranged the meeting downtown, not out in Virginia. After querying impatient pedestrians I arrived at an office building, gray and dreary, crammed with companies and agencies I had never heard of. Charter Inc. was listed for the fourth floor. Again a good-looking woman with sterile smile showed me to a conference room with green walls, over-stuffed chairs on one side, long table on the other. This time washrooms for both sexes were advertised in the corridor outside.

Five people awaited me. One was a woman. Though it was only nine in the morning, they had already conferred. Used cups and ashtrays were strewn on the coffee tables. The air-conditioners struggled to make in-roads on the smoke. Through the windows I saw other gray buildings.

Blake, cordiality itself, introduced me as if I were a visiting prince. He and I stood in a reception line as the others came forward. David Rosberg, likable as before, decency and dispassion on call. Then two other men. And then Barbara Corum. I will not forget that first impression. Her face, not beautiful in the accepted fashionable sense, seemed to me to be beautiful; the blue-green eyes were delicately molded, full of knowledge, long dark lashes without mascara. Framed in dark hair, the face was that of a woman in her late thirties, or so I guessed, for the face would look much the same in twenty years. Tall, slender, simply dressed. When we shook hands, her smile was personal, not public, not a matter of form.

Blake placed himself at the head of the conference table and held up a pencil like a conductor beginning a symphony. "I don't want to waste time," he began, "but let me begin by telling you about an extraordinary meeting David and I had with Bill Hampton last week. On our way back the two of us agreed that seldom had we learned so much in so little time. As you all know from David's memo, Bill's knowledge of the Arab world, especially of Palestinian affairs, goes back ..." He went on in a laudatory vein for several crisp sentences, then glanced at his watch. "We have," he said, "one hour and thirty-five minutes. If we get on old ground, matters we covered in the previous session, I'll blow the whistle. First, let me give you a one-paragraph wrap-up on that session."

His summary, though a long paragraph, would serve anywhere as a model of its kind. Neat distillations of the previous week's verbiage in the form of social and political principles, with concrete examples I had provided. Brilliantly done. Yet he returned to an honored place several notions Rosberg and I had sought to discredit, as if he had not heard what we said. The *intifada*, he said, greatly strengthened the hand of the traditional PLO leaders. Rosberg glanced my way, his face showing a trace of apology. Brilliance, he seemed to say, has its blind spots.

A man named Singleton propelled us forward, speaking from notes written on three-by-five cards, an agenda of unanswered questions about Palestine. He lacked Blake's commanding style, but he'd done his homework. Indeed, not just Singleton, all of them had prepared for the meeting. Each kept referring to "David's memo"; the questions and comments, clearly honed by office discussions, were concise.

Another man, Wilmot by name, asked about "decision makers." He wanted to know about the Palestinian upper crust. "What," he asked, "is the process by which the natural leaders take power? Who chooses them? On what grounds?"

At one point Rosberg attempted to return to his new interest in Beersheba Bedouin, but Blake, as promised, held up his pencil and moved us on to what he considered more relevant matters. For the most part Blake sat silently at the head of the table, allowing the talk to wash over him. Whenever I thought he'd gone off on his own, he'd snap in a razor-keen comment, his face taut. Such as how public opinion was formed among the upper classes. When the discussion permitted him to sit quietly, he looked older, heavier. He closed the meeting on schedule, wrapping up what he wanted them all to retain. I was tired but pleased with myself, my mind pulled away from family, from danger and reality, by the medication of remembrance. Blake's wrap-up brought things into sharp focus. Singleton and the other man came up to say goodbye, but Barbara Corum, it seemed, would stay on for the smaller session that was to follow. For no reason it crossed my mind that she, like Rosberg, would be disturbed by the notion that humans are usually self-serving. We moved toward the washrooms in the corridor. I gathered the real meeting was about to begin.

When the three men – Blake, Rosberg, and myself – returned, Barbara Corum was seated in an armchair. Her legs were long and beautifully shaped. We poured coffee and settled down. Had the chairs been upright, we could have played bridge on the coffee table. I faced the window, looking at Blake against the light.

"Bill," he said, "that was a splendid session. Again we're in your debt, yes, in your debt. I kept wondering how you managed to be so courteous to us all." He smiled slightly. Rosberg and Barbara Corum also smiled. We all waited expectantly. In a window of the grey building across the street I saw a man leaning back from his desk talking earnestly into a telephone. "We come now to the other matter." Blake paused like a minister asking for the greater attention of the congregation. "To begin with, I should say Barbara has been completely in our confidence all along. The others here this morning know nothing about this part of our discussion, which I have cleared with the director and his deputy but no one else. I say again, no one else. Barbara is what we call case officer. Our people in the field will be informed only on a need-to-know basis, and none of them will be fully informed."

He looked at each of us in a solemn way. "I stress these security aspects now, before we begin on Bill's thinking. No matter what you decide, Bill, the importance of secrecy cannot be exaggerated. I know you know this, but I have to say it. Any notion wandering around that the U.S. had a hand in our project would be the kiss of death. Of course." Did I imagine that for an instant Blake's gaze rested on me speculatively? I nodded, as if I had never seen Pinstripe. "Now Bill, tell us your thoughts since we last spoke."

All eyes shifted to me as I sought the right words. What were my thoughts, my fears? During free moments in San Francisco, when I should have fixed my mind on computer sales, Blake's "project" and Palestinian politics had absorbed me. My mind kept moving off to Cairo. Whenever the phone rang, I feared Abdu was reporting a disaster. On calls to Cairo, Cath's voice, the special one she uses for the telephone, provided only limited relief. Local colleagues in San Francisco had invited me to dinner, but with only two exceptions I'd begged off, pleading other engagements or work. I believed I needed time alone to think, but once again I learned that preoccupation is not the same as thought. In my hotel room, I sat mindlessly in front of a television set, watching Westerns when available, otherwise so-called comedies with canned laughter.

All the same my mind must have been on duty. A few things clicked into place. Whether I said yes or no to Blake mattered little to the Palestinians who were following me. They *thought* I was involved whether I was involved or not. Yes or no, the danger remained the same.

One day there came a moment of self-inspection. My mind, which had been roaming around, focused on Bill Hampton. Had I begun to change my approaches to things? Had I become more devious, less honorable, perhaps tougher, more prone to think ends could justify means? Whatever the changes, Cath would not approve. Nor did I, though I accepted them as personality traits I might need in the days ahead. Something else pulled at me. A chance to be center-stage? To play a pivotal role in a great modern drama? In San Francisco I sometimes cursed Blake for his remark about "changing the course of history." At other times I allowed myself to daydream. I became Bill Hampton, master of political compromise and the art of conciliation, putting himself at the service of childhood friends whose lives would be transformed. Bill Hampton, somehow in the company of his father whose face was suffused with pride, receiving the thanks of Abu Hisham and other notables of Jerusalem ...

Might Blake's scheme work? Part of me yearned for it to work. If... If one could skirt the fact that some Palestinians seemed to know about it already. Despite what Blake said, my job would go beyond transmittal. The messenger had to be someone Abu Hisham trusted. At least someone who could be trusted to tell the truth insofar as he knew the truth. But I couldn't guarantee the sincerity of the United States. Three officials of the United States waited for me to speak. I had a small agenda of my own, aimed at smoking them out. "You may know," I said, watching Blake's face, "that in Cairo I had people following me."

Blake did as he had done in New York; for ten seconds he gazed at me without expression. I did not see the reactions of Rosberg or Barbara Corum. When Blake spoke, I imagined I heard an awareness that potholes lay in the road immediately ahead. "Tell us about that," he said. His gaze held mine. I wanted to look at the others but could not do so.

"I thought Gav Middleton might have told you something about it," I said. "He did mention a minor problem with the Egyptians but said you had things under control." Yes, Spence had told Middleton. Not that I'd doubted it.

"What he didn't tell you," I said, "was something he didn't know because I didn't mention it. Though I think he should have known. The people following me weren't Egyptians, they were Palestinians."

Blake's gaze did not falter, but this time I leaned back in my armchair and could glance around. Rosberg also gazed at me expressionlessly, though I had the impression he held his breath. Barbara Corum stared intently. "How do you know that?" asked Blake.

"Friends of mine have identified one of them." Had I begun acting like a Palestinian myself, doling out information bit by bit, no more than necessary at any given moment, to a meddlesome scheming world? Why not tell them about the body propped against the tree, about the attempt to kill me in the office building? No, said my Palestinian self, I'll save those bits for trading purposes or shock tactics.

"Have they continued to follow you or was it only for a short time?"

So that was the line. No connection, Blake would say, between being followed and his own project.

"I was followed for about a week," I said, "then they stopped." So Blake would not call the whole thing off. On the contrary, he would brush aside minor matters of personal risk and press on, flying the banner of peace and conciliation.

"And did you consult local friends about it?"

"They didn't know who it was or why. Neither do I. That's why I'm bringing it up."

Blake leaned forward, suddenly aggressive. "You mean you think there might be a connection between what happened in Cairo and what we've talked about? Out of the question. I'd put it out of your mind immediately. It is impossible, yes impossible, that anyone else knows about the help you might give us. Gav Middleton is the only person in Cairo who knows anything, and he knows only part of the story."

He stopped. Barbara Corum sat motionless, her eyes now fixed on Blake. Rosberg flipped through the pages of a small notebook, as if looking for a relevant entry, but if so, he never found it because soon he put the notebook back in his pocket and looked hard at the floor.

"I understand your wondering about a connection," Blake resumed, "but despite the logic of it it's impossible. Therefore, it has to be one of those things that can happen anywhere, and especially Cairo. An unusual coincidence. A couple of men stay only a few days, then leave because you are of no further interest. The kind of mistake that can happen anywhere."

All of them watched me as I thought what to say next. Nothing broke the stillness, no shuffling of papers, no crossing the legs, no looking for a more comfortable position in the chair. I decided to dole out another news item. "You see, one of the men watching me was killed outside my apartment. I have children living there. The fellow was shot in the chest. The press said he had a Jordanian passport that showed no entry mark for Egypt."

Blake moved in his chair and threw out an odd-sounding chuckle that seemed inconsistent with his style. The others took the cue and smiled, and Rosberg put a tolerant look on his face as if the worries of an amateur were old hat to a professional. Barbara Corum's smile did not linger long.

"Look, Bill," said Blake, "in our peculiar world, in the intelligence community, these things happen all the time. Just because someone watching you got killed near your house means only that, that someone watching you got killed near your house." I examined the expression on his face carefully. Clearly he expected me to take him seriously. He went on. "Nothing to do with what we're talking about, which is simply getting in touch with an old friend and passing on information that affects *him*, not you. Peace, a possible Palestinian state, those are your friend Abu Hisham's final goals, not yours. Peace and conciliation" – I knew this word would sometime reappear as a weapon – "these are for him to decide about, not you. Whoever it was in Cairo cannot know about this and cannot care about it. Who cares if you carry a message to an old friend?" He sat back in his chair. "Bill, the two things cannot be related." He made the assertion as if it were a cornerstone of the universe. The bulldog would not be budged. Thus he instructed me to accept a proposition I knew had to be false. Did he know I knew it had to be false, or was he himself convinced? Anyone brought up in Palestine would know a connection of the two things had to exist. In Palestine a connection always exists, and if it is a hidden connection, it is known as a plot. And in the view of most Palestinians, a plot always exists. Which is almost always the reality, because, by instinct, Palestinians keep connections hidden when they can. Blake's cozy Washington world might find this difficult to understand. His world believed itself sophisticated, and doubtless it was, with rules, one supposed, that reflected the impersonal ambience of Western cities. But sophistication has many definitions; Washington's version of it applies poorly to the passionate and personal interlockings of a nationalist community smaller than many Western capitals. In Palestine, which is a living organism striving to survive, the pain from a cut finger hurts everywhere, connects everywhere.

It would waste information, I thought, to tell them now about the attack at my office. The response would be the same, simply another coincidence that must not be allowed to obstruct peace and conciliation. They waited for me to speak. What to say? I had to proceed. How else to arrange a non-violent exit from the morass? Did Blake, in fact, know there was a connection between the happenings in Cairo and the message-bearing that he proposed? Did he think, as I did, that to call off his project would make no difference to those already convinced I was involved? In San Francisco I had played with the idea of persuading Blake to help me, but I knew now that I couldn't trust my own government. I was on my own. I decided to make Blake sweat.

"I'll think about it," I said "I'll tell Middleton what I've decided when I get back to Cairo." My audience listened intently. I may have discerned a look of relief on Barbara Corum's face, but I can't trust my memory about Barbara. Perhaps I could get more information out of Gav than out of Blake. And Blake's plot might work. This I longed for.

"I guess I should say," I went on, "I'm uneasy about what you call a coincidence, but getting a settlement in Israel and Palestine is important to me. As you know. I just have to think a bit. Lots of people involved besides me. My family, Abu Hisham, others ..."

I couldn't read Blake's expression, but I think he was content for the moment. When I mentioned the involvement of others, a muscle moved along his jaw line. For a fleeting moment I saw the missionary look flash over his face. "Whatever you decide, Bill, let me say how important it is to say nothing to anybody, even your wife."

I said he need have no fear about security. I didn't mention Abdu or Sam Paul or Abu Taleb. We all stood up.

*   *   *

On the way out Barbara Corum asked if I was free for lunch, and I said I was. I didn't know whether the invitation was part of a plan, but I wanted to avoid being alone. I thought also that Barbara Corum might let something slip out without the others around. More flexible than Blake. More straightforward, or did I mean more transparent? The other two hopped a cab to their offices in Virginia. She and I made our way through the lunchtime crowd to an expensive place she said served bearable food. Quiet enough for good talk, tables available. The decor, an odd modern colonial with white columns painted onto light pink walls, was matched by waiters dressed in white with pink trim. We sat down at a small table, and she smiled in that personal way.

"I thought you did extremely well this morning." The smile became broader. "Including the way you handled Curtis Blake, who is something of a mystery to me. As he said, you do know what you're talking about. Incidentally, does anyone else know about the possible connection between you and the man killed outside your apartment?" She placed the question lightly at the end of a paragraph of praise, like a slice of lemon after a scoop of peppermint ice cream.

"No," I replied. The lie came easily. For a fraction of a second she may have considered another question, then seemed to change her mind.

"Why is Blake a mystery to you?" I asked.

"Just that, a mystery. I never know what he really has in mind." She smiled. "But his heart's in the right place. He wants a settlement more than anything else. And he wants to be the one to engineer it."

"Does he say that?"

She hesitated. She had the air of having said more than she intended. "Yes, he did once, when he was telling me about your old friend in Jerusalem. The final feather in his cap, that's the impression I got. He's pushing hard. We hear that people over in State are trying to bring it off too. In a different way."

"Do you think he knows how unlikely this all is?"

She looked at me earnestly. "Only optimists can succeed. I hope you'll help."

I found myself nodding agreement and saying I hoped I could. She moved us deftly to another subject and asked about my family. So I talked about Cath and Larry and Sarah in what must have been a boring recital. If I said relatively little about Cath, beyond the basic facts of where we had met and lived, I found myself suddenly eager to tell her about the children, their exploits, their virtues. As I spoke, her attention didn't waver, and our eyes met easily. Finally I stopped.

"I'm overdoing it."

"No, no. I enjoyed hearing about them. Sounds like you're one of the lucky ones." We gave orders to a hovering waiter with longish blond hair. The pink trim clashed with his pasty complexion.

"You mean you've not been quite so lucky?" I asked. She had invited the question.

"It depends how you look at it. I've had one marriage go on the rocks, now I'm resisting getting involved again."

"Children?"

"No." She picked up her fork, put it down again. "Which makes me sorry for myself some days. Other days I'm glad because I wouldn't do well by them, I'd always be wanting to be a success in a man's world. I'm suddenly doing well now, prospects good, all the rest of it."

"What happened to your marriage?"

She looked at me, puzzled but not annoyed. "You know, all of a sudden we're talking terribly seriously. Maybe reading someone's file makes a special bond." The pasty-faced waiter arrived with food and we ate a few mouthfuls. "Yes, that must be it. I don't often talk about my marriage ..."

She could have changed the subject.

"I guess," she said, eyes on her plate, "the marriage was meant to be a flop from the beginning. He was, is, a nice man, I think. Well-meaning. Maybe not very bright. Big and handsome. Born and brought up in Ohio, got his engineering degree at Ohio State. When we met, we both worked in New York, and we went out a lot, and it seemed the thing to do to get married. We were pretty young." She looked up with a smile. "Yes, so were you. But with you it was different, I know from your file. I grew up in New Rochelle, a nice Jewish girl who knew lots of nice Jewish boys. And then I married the most un-Jewish boy you can imagine, unassertive, placid even, very gentle."

She laughed suddenly. "You know, all those stereotypes for the *goyim*. And here I was, basically a New Yorker wanting to meet interesting people, have bright conversations, see the latest plays. My parents liked Don, no pressure there, we just never wanted the same things. Nothing to do with being Jewish. Maybe if we'd married later, it might have been different. Or if we'd had children."

So she was Jewish. I realized I was not surprised, though at first it seemed strange the CIA would assign a Jew to an Arab project like Blake's. Or was it not an issue? After all, Rosberg, also Jewish, had been assigned, and this did not seem strange. So it had to be because she was a woman, and even to be in line for the job, she'd need an extra flair, an extra competence. I gazed at her intently. I knew, suddenly, that her face had to be, now that I was asked to perceive it that way, either Jewish or Greek or somehow connected with the Eastern Mediterranean. A lovely face. My mind registered something else, nothing to do with being Jew or Gentile. It was the sudden presence of the special bond she mentioned, an easy comradeship established quickly and astonishingly. As if we were former lovers who had parted without rancor years ago, now catching up on each other's lives. Not that I had had lovers, or any great affairs, before Cath; it came to mind as something I could imagine happening.

"You didn't know I was Jewish." Her eyes looked straight into mine. Neither of us looked away.

"No."

"How much does it matter?"

"It really doesn't."

"What does that mean? *Really* doesn't. Is that a qualification?" Her tone, neither tart nor angry, said she wanted to know. How to explain to an American? Once at Swarthmore a friend accused me of anti-Semitism because I wanted to know who was Jewish; he had not noticed that I also wanted to know who was Greek, Italian, Maltese, Cypriot, Armenian, Christian, Muslim. The mosaic of peoples I grew up with.

"When I say *really* doesn't, I mean just that. I'm not an anti-Semite. People keep trying to pull me into the system but I'm outside it. Or I was when I grew up."

Her gaze held mine. "Sorry about that. Perhaps I was being defensive. All the same, and because I think we're friends, you said you were outside the system. What system?"

"Well, for instance, if a Westerner says someone is Armenian or Greek, that's casual talk. To say someone is Jewish is not. In Palestine, we just want to know which community people belong to. There's no special hate for Jews."

"Why do you want to know someone's community?"

"Because there are rules. You ask about someone's community so you don't make the mistake of, say, falling in love with someone from another community. We're all proud of our differences from each other but we get along."

"Why is it so bad to fall in love with a person from outside? Aren't we all human beings?"

"I'm just trying to say there are other systems," I said.

She was silent a moment. "You said you were outside our system when you were growing up. Are you less so now?"

I chose my words carefully. I wanted to be honest but I knew America planted mines in such fields. "I've lived like an American for quite a while. You get pulled in. Remarks about Jews puzzled me at first, then exasperated me, now I let them pass and change the subject. It seems to be an issue with some American friends of mine. A few of them find it hard to handle. So I live with the system ... But I'm still outside it." I paused, then went on. "You see, I don't *need* to think Jews are different, and I don't *need* to bend over backwards to be friendly."

The waiter came to ask if everything was all right. We said it was. She propped her chin on her hand and looked at me.

"Listen," I said, "I'm pleased to know you're Jewish. I don't have to react. I'm just pleased to know. If you hadn't mentioned it, I'd probably have asked. I always like to know what people are."

"But I'm not a 'what.'"

"No, you're not. But that's the way I was brought up. Maybe for me people are 'whats' first, then 'whos.'" I stopped, shook my head. "I'm not saying this well."

"Have another try."

"Maybe having respect for *what* you are makes you part of living, gives you a legitimate place, protects you." I shook my head again. "Let's change the subject."

"No, I want to go on. My father used to say the same, only different words, arguing with my mother. You're talking about something Jews go on about among themselves. I suppose you know that."

"No, I really don't." My mind leapt to something further I wanted to say. "Then there's Israel," I said. "That changes things in a way."

"What way?"

"It changes the atmosphere. Now that I'm an American, if you know what I mean. I get indignant about America's lack of sympathy for Palestine, the blind support of some for Israel. Which means I often react against American Jews, not Israelis. Especially hard-nosed Zionists. Especially if I know they know about my background." I paused, wanting to explain further. "Once I know someone's Jewish, I'm careful with him. I want to know where he stands. As a Jew. I guess this makes me more of an American." I concentrated a moment on my food. "The fact of Israel is trying to pull me into the system. Makes me a candidate for membership."

"Do I pull you into the system?"

"No, you don't." I smiled. "In fact, I don't remember talking about this with anyone before." She looked at me steadily, saying nothing. Finally I continued. "You see, it's the way so many American Jews treat Israel. For me it's something political, not social, but it's making me treat Jews with special care, like walking on eggs. Is that anti-Semitic?"

The waiter brought our coffee. She made a slow business of putting in cream and sugar, stared at her cup as she stirred. "The short answer of most Jews," she said, "would be yes. Because you're saying that when you know someone's a Jew, you give him special treatment. A Jew, not a German, not an Italian ... You're not really an American, or at least you're very different, and I can't put my finger on it. You come at things from someplace else. You say things were different when you were growing up, and I guess they were." She gazed at me. "I can only judge by you, by William Hampton. Finally it's a matter of what's in the heart. Knowing you only a short time, I feel" – she hesitated – "I feel you're not an anti-Semite, in the usual sense. You're being pushed toward it perhaps. By events, by Zionism here. But the difference is, there's nothing deep-seated about it. It's not what I'm used to. That's what I think now. An anti-Semitic remark doesn't strike a chord in your subconscious. That's how my father used to phrase it."

The bill arrived, and she reached for it, saying it would all go on her expense account. "Pretty serious conversation," I said, seeking to lighten the burden of unexpected and sudden sharing.

"And it was honest," she said, "which is unusual. We must continue sometime because there's more to be said. One irony is so many Jews think it's good for their community here to have a Jewish state over there, and your, uh, testimony seems to say the opposite."

"My testimony may not be relevant."

"That's the other irony," she said. "If Americans generally felt like you, probably we'd have no anti-Semitism in America."

We moved toward the door. I reached to open it but she stood where she was, as if undecided about something. "Bill, I'm having a few friends in for drinks at my place tonight, about 6:30 or so. Could you come? Nothing exciting, just a handful of people. I know you leave in the morning and probably have plans for tonight already."

I accepted with pleasure. I had nothing to do that evening beyond worry and television and being alone in my hotel room. Outside the restaurant we shook hands, and I wondered again at how fast we'd become friends, at the easy way we'd plunged into delicate, personal topics. I felt uncomfortable about it, as one does after such closeness, but not depressed.

*   *   *

I am acquainted with the downtown beginnings of Connecticut Avenue, but soon my cab reached an unfamiliar residential part: ten-story apartment buildings looming on either side, a town house with garden behind high fences, a cluster of neighborhood shops. The morning's gentle rain had persisted, blurring the outlines of late afternoon.

The cab pulled up at a plush-looking apartment house, set back from the street by a large courtyard whose flower beds were separated by narrow concrete walkways. Inside one of several main doors, behind a counter that needed only a brass rail to be a bar, sat an African-American woman, stunningly dressed in green, who looked at me impersonally, then returned to her paperback. I asked twice to get the number of Barbara's apartment. Through Barbara's door came a civilized murmur. The door itself was opened by a man in his late forties who introduced himself as Myron Kitchen, one of the guests. He smiled and said I must be Bill Hampton. Barbara appeared from the kitchenette carrying a plate of cheese and crackers.

"Bill, how very nice. You've met Myron, I gather." The way she said it implied a special link to Myron. She wore a long black dress, the color of her eyes matched by a turquoise pendant. "I'll get you a drink while Myron introduces you. He's so good at it."

She moved toward a table in the corner, and Myron clapped his hands for attention. He said a few words about me, then took me around. Ten people smiled. Two guests were introduced as "servants of the government," producing mild amusement. "Same as Barbara," said Myron. I remember only a few of the names. Everyone appeared to know everyone else. Clearly it was a gathering of long-time friends and acquaintances from all corners of Washington. What struck me was a matter of style; men and women alike were elegantly turned out, quietly self-assured. Most of them looked important, and I was to find they talked that way, as if they knew what they said was worth hearing, as if assertiveness were gauche and unnecessary.

Myron Kitchen, it seemed, represented someplace near San Francisco in the House of Representatives, and a heavy-set woman with hair in a fashionable bun was a Representative from Boston. A man with thick glasses and a quiet air worked at the Supreme Court. I recognized the name of a well-known columnist, a gray-haired woman in her mid-fifties. She and Kitchen took me over immediately to ask about "the political situation in the Middle East," partly out of courtesy (I was introduced as "an expert"), partly because they wanted to know. Well-informed and incisive, both urbanely picked my brains. They wanted to know about Israeli settlements in the occupied territories. How could the U.S. allow this "creation of facts"?

Soon we were joined by a competent-looking woman with horn-rimmed glasses and sleek blond hair who had heard the last comment on settlements.

"Why not create facts? Americans did the same with the American Indian," she said.

"For beginners," said the columnist, with charming but steely smile, "Begin gave an undertaking to Carter and Vance at Camp David that there would be a freeze on settlements."

The blond woman responded as if the discussion was among good friends. But first she told me she was Jewish. Then she said, "You know, of course, that Begin has denied giving such an undertaking. So did Dayan before he died, and there's nothing in writing."

"If the principal objective is to make peace," I said, hoping to steer the conversation into more productive areas, "each new settlement alienates the very Palestinians needed to reach a peace agreement. The hardliners win out."

"And each new settlement needs new land for itself," said Kitchen, "and control of land is the crucial factor. An Israeli newspaper reported last week that Israelis now own forty per cent of the West Bank by purchase or outright takeover." The discussion continued with no one getting upset, as if only by intelligent disagreement could one arrive at the truth. Others came up to talk. Barbara glanced my way occasionally to make sure I was enjoying myself. I was. By some magic my fears for Cath and the kids had for the moment gone elsewhere in my mind. I felt safe, savoring the last hours before returning to a danger zone. The vestibule below would be safe, so would the lobby of my hotel. And more than that, the general atmosphere was somehow diverting, geared to important consultation, crucial decisions, momentous deals. When our minor discussion lapsed, the Jewish woman kissed Myron and said to me, "I always forgive Myron for not being Jewish. Poor lad, not his fault." Everyone smiled.

People began to leave. At one point Barbara turned to Myron Kitchen and said she'd phone him in the morning, at which moment, but not before, he made his goodbyes and moved toward the door. The Jewish woman gave me a hug, said she'd enjoyed talking to me. When I made as if to go, Barbara put her hand on my arm and asked me to stay on for a minute. I went over to put more whiskey in my drink; I didn't need more but I needed something to do while the farewells were said. Everyone came to shake my hand and finally everyone left.

"I'm guessing," she said, the black gown accentuating the curves of her body, "you have nothing else to do tonight. I'd like it if you'd join me for a tiny bit of supper."

"That would be great." I smiled at her and at the world in general. How good, I thought, to have supper with a good friend (because that is what she had become) and (here I was honest with myself) an attractive woman. Though for a moment I felt awkward.

"Come help me in the kitchen." She sensed the awkwardness. "I need help with the salad." So we made ourselves a supper of steak and salad and went on talking, both having much to say: the people at her party, more thoughts on our lunchtime discussion, a reaching out in new directions. It seemed natural, like brother and sister, though not like that because a special kind of magic was at work.

"At lunch," I said, "you mentioned you were resisting another marriage. Was it Myron Kitchen?"

She looked at me gravely. "Was it that obvious?" Only a lover would heed that indirect order to leave. The look on her face was demure, as if she were a younger version of herself and vexed at giving away a secret. The steak was almost ready, and she kept her gaze on it. "I'm fond of him," she said. "It would be what people call a good marriage. We'd do well together. He has three nice children from his previous marriage, and they like me. So marrying him would be easy, no strain. I'd simply move into his apartment, which is larger than this. His kids come and go, two of them are in college. I'd go on working." She paused as if seeking the right words. "But more days than not, I don't want to marry him. Not sure it has anything to do with *him*. Probably more to do with *me*. I like my life this way, I like seeing him not all the time. Some evenings I want to be by myself in this little place. He knows all this, at least I think he does." She studied the steak. I wanted to suggest it was ready, but I didn't want to interrupt. "Why am I telling you all this? ... I really ought to be telling him, not you. Maybe I'm looking for something I don't find. Sounds like high school."

She took the steak out, placed it carefully on a platter, spent more time arranging it than necessary.

"What do you think?" she asked. Very quietly. She glanced at me quickly, then lightened the question by laughing as if it were something of a joke. I did not know how serious my response ought to be, but I was glad, irrationally glad, that she was unsure about Kitchen.

"I'd have to be judged inexperienced on such matters. Given my history, which you know almost as well as I, how could I make a good judgment?" I kept my tone at a level I thought she preferred, not jovial, not serious either. "I fell in love once in my life and married the girl. Very ordinary."

"You're not ordinary." She handed me a corkscrew for the bottle of red wine. "Though you may be square."

We sat across from each other at a small table in the living room. Conversation flowed swiftly, for a while on less personal topics, though I couldn't say, at this remove, what they were. But the ambience was special. If what we talked about seemed important, more important was a sense of being together, a feeling of things to come, a touch of excitement. We talked on. My coffee had gone cold, and so I joked about my long-windedness and said we must do the dishes. It was late. I jammed things into the dishwasher as she put food away. We became less talkative, but smiles came easily when we got in each other's way in the small kitchen. Soon it was time to go.

"I'm sorry to have stayed so long. I had no idea how late it was. A wonderful evening and thank you for the supper." I moved toward the door. The thought of staying did not occur to me, and I think she realized this. As I stood by the hall table, looking down at two beautifully painted earthenware bowls, she came and stood near me, also looking down at them.

"They're lovely things," she said. "Italian, from Pesaro." She turned her head to look up at me, and her face was suddenly close to mine. She looked at me steadily, not moving away. I put my arms around her as if this were the kind of infidelity I committed every day. The kiss was long and gentle and sweet, her hands at the back of my head. She pulled her lips away from mine and looked at me.

"Bill," she said. She stroked my cheek, then my brow, smoothed my hair. "Bill," she said again. I said nothing, just looked at her lovely face. Her belly came against mine, and the excitement I felt was intense. We kissed again, locked together, my hands caressing her hips. I knew I would stay, and so did she. Again she looked me straight in the eye, an odd small smile on her face, a throaty quality to her voice when she spoke.

"God, this is so complicating, so unprofessional, so crazy." Her cheek came against mine for a long moment as I waited for the next words. "And so very nice."

*   *   *

On the way back to Cairo I had lots of time to think. Barbara came into my thoughts more than Palestine. I was overcome by wonder. And by guilt. Wonder at what had transpired, its beauty, its tenderness. Guilt at the thought of Cath, because I'd never been unfaithful before. Nor had I wanted to be, beyond vague surges of distant desire for some unattainable actress or diva. Would the relationship between Cath and me, built up over so many years and through bouts of physical and psychological adversity, now crumble? Would she, instantly and intuitively, know I'd slept with another woman? I remembered a phrase from college: what so-and-so doesn't know won't hurt her. Cath, however, would know. And be hurt.

As for myself, was there a way of blunting the memory, of desensitizing the mind, so that casual infidelity was, in thirteen-year-old Larry's words, "no big deal"? Would the next time be easier? Was that the way things worked? Some machine in the brain switched me to another time, another place. I was fifteen, and I went over from the dorm to the head-master's house because my father said he wanted to see me. He wanted, he said, to have a long chat about family matters. What he meant was, he wanted to be sure I knew about growing up, about sex, about masturba-tion. He struggled valiantly through an agenda of facts he thought I should know, things I already knew about, and I admired him for doing his duty by me, for persisting in the face of embarrassment. Instead of talking about masturbation, he spoke of over-stimulation of the sex organs; he called the vagina a woman's receptacle. When he came to pre-marital sex, he hesitated a long moment, then said:

"The finest thing one can say to a woman is what I said to your mother when I asked her to marry me; I said I'm so glad I saved my lips for you." I asked if that was the first time he had kissed a woman. Yes, he said, it was. Then he went on to speak about the sanctity of the marriage bed.

While the night with Barbara could not be called sanctified, for me it was not casual. Nor was it for her, I thought. I still sensed the sweetness, the softness of her touch, the gentleness of her lips, and somewhere, per-haps on my hands, lingered the scent of her perfume. Might last night have been casual for some men, a routine roll in the hay? Perhaps. I had to believe such men must be consummate actors, professional lovers of skill and experience, artful enough to deceive Barbara into thinking it was *not* another roll in the hay, even if for them it was. But I was less of an actor, and she must have known how it was with me, an inexperienced lover who would not easily have an affair, a man whose conventionality, if Cath was right, tied him into knots. Would Barbara have led me on for a lark, treating me like a nice-looking country bumpkin good for a bit of fun? This, I knew with a lover's certainty, she did not do. Some special chemistry had been at work. Why else had we become friends so quickly, discussing matters I'd buried or never thought about? Why else the onrush of confidence in each other, the sure knowledge that the other was hon-orable, decent, caring?

Yet was I building a pleasant one-night affair into something Barbara did not mean it to be? Justifying lust by dressing it up in the robes of love? An Aramco friend once described a meeting with a girl in New York as "just a friendly fuck." Stripping away the glamor and the self-deception, was this the right description of my night in Washington?

The stewardess came with dinner, smiled brightly, and went away. I ate mechanically, my mind on a small room on Connecticut Avenue. Once, during a wakeful moment, she told me I was a wonderful lover. Another time she held me fiercely close and asked me to be careful, to watch where I went and what I did. I told her about being attacked in the darkness of the office hallway in Cairo; I had felt no need to keep that from her now. She responded with a quick intake of breath, pulling me to her again. Later the stewardess asked if I wanted a liqueur. I shook my head and settled back in my seat, tired but knowing I would be wakeful for a while. I knew I should put my thoughts in order, see where I stood personally, politically, every way. How should I protect my family? What action should I take? But the disordered fragments of thought that floated by refused to make straight lines. Images of Barbara arrived unwanted. Fear lurked somewhere nearby, ready to take over.

I had to go ahead with Blake's scheme, and I'd tell Gav Middleton when I got home. We'd work out details. For some reason I had more confidence in Middleton than in Blake, whom I didn't trust. His doctrinaire personality repelled me. The others – Rosberg and Barbara Corum – seemed honorable, likeable. And trustworthy, I thought. Yes, from the beginning, Barbara had been trustworthy. I could not rid myself of the memory of her body. In retrospect, at that moment I would not have backed out even if there had been a way to disengage. Blake's poison had taken hold.

SIX

Cairo and Jerusalem, May 1990

The reunion with Cath could have been called joyful. On the surface nothing had changed. So I thought. I felt a surge of love for my kids as I sat at supper and listened to excited chatter about school and friends, marveling at what fine-looking children they were, how decent, how bright. They wanted to know about America, especially California. So did Cath.

"Do the women wear bras all the time?" This from Sarah.

"Well, I was in northern California. It's cooler there. But anywhere in America, when it's hot, they wear cool clothes. Bras and other things."

"Why don't they do that in Cairo?" asked Larry, then he started to laugh. "What a sight that would be in the market place."

"Don't the girls your age wear bras at the Maadi School?" I asked Sarah

"Yes," she said, "they do. But there isn't much behind them." We exploded into laughter.

"Mom," said Larry, "wouldn't you like to live in San Francisco?"

"Someday, perhaps," said Cath, glancing at me with the suggestion of a smile. "Or maybe in New York. But not right now. We have to live where your father does."

"Yes," said Larry. "He's the bread winner."

I reached ostentatiously for the bread. We all smiled. The smile on Sarah's face reminded me that she had recently acquired braces. One day,

I knew, she'd be a most attractive woman; I imagined her fleetingly as a movie star. Jet lag, I realized, was at work, and I struggled to stay focused on family matters, on the ritual of reporting after a business trip. Cath put in a sentence or two now and then, but the kids did most of the talking. I think Larry noticed my jet lag because he asked about how the trip had affected me. As if it were of scientific interest. I said I was looking forward to a good sleep. Cath smiled. Hasan came in to clear the table.

But it was almost a tradition to stay on at the table on my first night home. After Hasan finished with the table and left for the roof, we went on chatting about the time I'd been away.

"There's a new teacher at school," reported Larry, "and I don't like her very much. She seems to notice me more than she does the others. Always notices what I'm doing."

"Maybe she likes you a lot," said Sarah. After general laughter, the rest of us agreed that noticing Larry was not necessarily a bad thing.

"Tell us what San Francisco looks like," said Larry. So I talked about San Francisco and its special beauty. They all listened attentively as if they needed to know. Cath reported that she had finished the first draft of her latest short story and sent it off to her agent in New York.

"What does the agent do?" asked Sarah

"He decides if it is good enough to publish, and if he thinks it is, he decides where to send it." Cath smiled as if in apology for simplifying matters. Then she smiled at me, also in apology, for not telling me this on one of our numerous phone conversations while I was away.

"I wouldn't mind living in America," Sarah said. "Might we move to California some time?"

"Probably not," Cath said quickly. She had a look on her face I had seen before. I knew that the possibility of living in New York or San Francisco came into her thoughts from time to time. I steered the conversation back to the school in Maadi and asked Larry about the soccer team.

Later on, after the kids had left, it crossed my mind it would be dishonorable to sleep with Cath, not just to share our double bed but to invade her body, but the thought was put with other matters in a new pending file I had developed. I was excited when I later slipped in beside her. Cath was demanding, and my response, despite jet lag, was eager. The routines of life, ardent lovemaking included, reestablished themselves easily. So I thought.

Only later did I realize that I was probably deceiving myself. Things were not really the same. The next evening, when she sat in her chair with a book, I looked up to see her gazing either at me or at a place on the wall. The gaze was reflective, as if she were seeking a word for a crossword puzzle.

*   *   *

As far as I could tell, no one was following me, but fear was never far away. I phoned the school principal a couple of times, but he had nothing to report. In an indirect way that deceived him not at all, I asked Mohamed the *bawwab* if any strangers had been hanging around. When he said no, it was clear he had not forgotten the small man leaning dead against the tree. Gav Middleton and I spent time on the golf course discussing options. Only in a general way. While I wanted the benefit of his experience, the record showed I could trust neither him nor his organization not to leak information. Like Blake he rejected the idea of a connection between Blake's scheme and the appearance of Pinstripe. Exasperated, I told him about the attack in the lobby of my office building. Just another coincidence, he said, lots of violence in Cairo these days. For him, quite clearly, this was not new information, and I had to assume his response came readily because Barbara Corum would have reported the incident, despite the intimate circumstances under which she'd been informed. Though he denied the connection, he acted as if it existed.

"The long and the short of it," he said one day at the sixth tee, "is you have to see Abu Hisham without anyone knowing you've seen him or plan to see him and so far we haven't thought of a way to do it." The secrecy became crucial only if one accepted the proposition of a connection. Otherwise a chat in my old friend's garden would suffice. No, I said, we haven't thought of a way. But, in fact, I had one in mind, not to be mentioned to him or any colleague.

Trying to get information out of Middleton came hard. I reminded him he'd asked me to stop in New York as a personal favor. I did not, I said, expect to learn state secrets in return, but I needed to know what kind of person Blake really was. An assessment might just save my life on the trip I was about to take. I'd know what I could and could not count on. "Bill, I can't see anything tricky like that arising on your trip." But the appeal for a return favor had an effect. He studied his golf ball. "I guess I'd say he was rock hard. He gets what he wants and doesn't change his mind. You don't want to be his enemy."

I tried more questions to find out what else they knew in Washington, anything else, but got nowhere.

I also spent time covering my tracks, turning off the concern of friends in whom I had confided. I needed to hold Cairo steady while I worked on Palestine. Sam Paul and I had lunch by the Hilton pool, and after talking business I said my troubles, whatever they were, seemed to have disappeared. I would not, I said, worry about them further, at least until the next time, and I thanked him for his moral support. He listened and nodded; his expression said for friendship's sake he would believe me. I don't think my aristocratic Egyptian friend Abdu believed me either. He said gracefully that if I should again need someone to find out what Egyptians knew about Palestinians in Egypt (or visiting Egypt, he added with a trace of a smile) I should let him know. When I thanked him for looking after my family while I was gone, I'm certain he believed me when I said I was deeply grateful. For the moment, he said, he'd continue assigning a few carefully chosen men until I was absolutely sure all danger had passed. Cath told me Abdu or his wife had phoned once a day during my absence. So did Mary Paul, she said.

Abu Taleb, of my Palestinian world, was another story. I phoned to say I'd be out to Heliopolis to bring him the medicine he ordered from America. One day, in the heat of early afternoon when his café was deserted, we sat and sifted what we knew, coming up with strategies that would protect me and also "do good." I was able to guarantee no one had followed me to the café.

It was a long afternoon, long and dusty and sweaty. Except for the episode with Barbara, and mentioning no Washington names, I told him the whole story. I did not consider I broke a trust; the CIA, if I needed a justification, had proved itself unworthy. My salvation lay with old friendships, not governments. Abu Taleb would stand with me no matter what. If he disagreed, he would treat me as he would his brother, staying out of it but backing me when trouble arrived. Blake, on the other hand, showed a capacity for self-deception or deviousness. Nor did I think he would be loyal to individuals like Bill Hampton if his ambitions got in the way. I'd be sacrificed to a cause such as "peace in the Middle East" or "the American interest." Though Blake and I might be working together for the moment, we were not on the same team.

When I finished, Abu Taleb sat quietly, staring at the grubby Heliopolis street. Three schoolboys in yellowish-brown smocks, strolling home late, were kicking a tin can, keeping it moving through the dust. The waiter dozed in a far corner. My friend shook his head, grinned slightly, let out his breath.

"Christ almighty, as you Christians say."

He gestured with his hand, thinking to say something else. Then he changed his mind, said nothing for a short while.

"I suppose it would be nice," he said finally, "to leave this dust and corruption and get back to where things are green. One of your poets talked about a 'green and pleasant land,' and that's the way I think about Palestine. I'd be pleased to be there before I die."

His slender fingers fiddled with the coffee cup, rotating the cup in its saucer, round and round.

"Of course we all want a just settlement. You do, I do, perhaps even the fellow in Washington, I give him that. Even some Israelis, within their own context of thought, want a just settlement. But that's the catch. What is *just*?" His eyes stayed on the revolving coffee cup. "The question really is justice for whom? Perfect compromise is a notion for babies. The way things stand, we started with everything, we'll get nothing."

"You can't give up."

"Who's giving up? Sure, get as much justice as possible. But if it ever by some remote chance came off, how much would that CIA scheme get us? Would it be justice for us or only for the CIA and the Israelis?" He clapped his hands to wake the waiter and ordered beer. It tasted cool, delicious. "Hell," he said, "we've all changed, you, all of us, but maybe

Abu Hisham least of all. He was always the leader. He still is. But at a negotiating table, what would he do without the PLO? What leverage would he have? All he can do is agree or disagree." He looked away with an exasperated sigh. "And the Americans, my God. Whoever's at the negotiating table, the only way we'll get our half-loaf is with outside clout, which means your country. There's nothing in the record, not a fucking thing, to suggest the Americans would buck Israel in order to get half-justice for Palestine."

"So you choose to stay in Cairo the rest of your life?" I asked. "Why not try this? What's there to lose? Abu Hisham, at least, could *talk* with the Israelis, he doesn't have to agree, just see what they're prepared to give. Listen, he could disagree effectively, make a public relations act out of it, pose as a moderate Palestinian in the face of Israeli intransigence." I leaned forward. "Granted, this scheme is not great, a lot of risks, but it's the only scheme around. Have you got another? Has the PLO been able to talk to the Israelis? Remember the times Arafat sent messages about a deal, about recognition, all that. Have the Israelis given in to U.S. pressure to stop expanding? Have they been willing to talk? Shit no!"

The slender Bedouin face had a sardonic look.

"If negotiations got going with Abu Hisham," I said, quoting Rosberg, "the Israelis might even be persuaded to talk to the PLO itself." His gaze became thoughtful, then he drained his glass.

"Got to pee." He stood up and headed toward the cafe's smelly toilet. It was late May, summer had moved in. No humans were visible except the waiter. A few sparrows hopped from table to table. When he came back, we ordered coffee. Neither of us spoke. A short interval of comfortable silence.

"Well, it's a long shot. But possible," I said. "And by this time the Israelis know the PLO isn't going to go away."

"Yes, I keep telling myself to be encouraged. We're doing all right." He sought to sound hopeful. "We're back in Lebanon, even friendly with Jordan and its devious king these days, we've got money from the Gulf and from that horse's ass Qaddafi. The *intifada* may be losing steam but it's still attracting attention. Now if *your* friendly little country will one of these days recognize us ..."

We sat a moment longer.

"I think I need a nap," he said, "and anyway we should be out of here by the time people start arriving. What were we talking about?"

"Your son's education in America."

"That's it, that's it. We may hate America but we love her educational facilities. Great snob appeal." We got up, paid the bill, and wandered back toward his flat. Cars were squeezed tight along the curbs, baking in the sun. "All right," he said, "it can't hurt and might just help get recognition for Arafat. And more interesting than writing poetry. A long shot, as you say. Anyway, for you it's the only way out."

And then, in Arabic, he paraphrased a joke we had at school. "Don't forget the old saying, when you're standing up to the neck in shit, it's hard to scrape it off."

He had me laughing, mostly from relief he was willing to help. As we walked along, he put his hand under my elbow.

"What about Cath and the children?" I asked.

"I think they'll be okay. We can't be certain about anything yet, but you couldn't do much better than the support you're getting from your aristocratic friend Abdu. The next step is get to Beirut and see Abu Kerim. Find out about Pinstripe and those others. We know what the Americans *think* they're doing, bless their hearts, but we don't know what some Palestinians are doing about it. Trust nobody. Including Abu Kerim. If you tell him too much, he'll be honor-bound to report. He may guess a lot, but he doesn't want to *know* a lot."

"The key question …"

"Yes, I know," he said. "Your friends in Washington, who are definitely not friends of mine, have screwed things up nicely. They tell you to get in touch with Abu Hisham, then they let everyone know."

"We don't know it was them."

"Who else could it be? Listen, somebody is still anxious to see you dead. Somebody is regrouping, making a new plan."

"I've had an idea about how to get in touch," I said.

He cut in quickly. "Don't change the subject. I said someone is anxious to see you dead, someone could be hanging around anywhere."

"I heard you. I'm being careful."

He nodded, satisfied his message had been received. "So you've had an idea," he said.

I winced as I said it, knowing I was playing with lives.

"Yes," he said. "I've thought about that. Carefully. Trouble is, Bedouin families are big, you can't control everyone. But my two full brothers and my sister Ni'meh know you, we can keep our plot to see Abu Hisham inside that small circle. Anyway, that's the place to start ..."

*　　　　*　　　　*

The place to start, he said. Israel, Gaza, the West Bank. Much of it known to me as Palestine. It was now a lot more than a few years since I had visited what Cath sometimes called my homeland. But I had kept closely in touch by way of the diaspora, by way of friends everywhere. In fact I was almost unaware that I had been away. When I told Cath I had suggested to my home office in San Francisco that I might be able to develop new business by visiting Israel, she was clearly intrigued. She asked if one day Larry and Sarah might make a visit to Ramallah and Jerusalem, my home territory to which I had taken her shortly after we were married. For their part, the people at the home office in San Francisco were also intrigued, reacting quickly and enthusiastically, a warm response to the possibility of greater profits.

Thus ten days later I set off for Israel, changing planes in Cyprus, a normal business practice for foreign businessmen stationed in Egypt. As expected, the Ben Gurion International airport at Lydda (the Israelis call it Lod) was crammed with people of all descriptions, foreigners, Israelis, some Palestinians. I finally found a taxi to take me across the plain and up the long hill to Jerusalem.

I was excited by what I saw, by changes everywhere apparent, by things remembered. We started by crossing through large fields of wheat and vegetables. In May the wheat was turning gold, and irrigated plots of tomatoes, squash, melon, and beans formed rectangles of deep green. Then the road wound up higher onto rocky terrain, through groves of ancient olive trees nurtured long before the coming of the Western disease, which is what Abu Taleb calls nationalism. Among the trees grazed a few cattle and sheep, and in the middle distance, off to right and left, appeared Arab villages or modern farm buildings. Near the road, in clumps of grass and weeds, lay relics younger than the olive trees: corpses of machines used in the name of the Western disease, the twisted rusted remains of tanks and troop carriers from 1948.

The cab driver pointed at them, smiling affably, groping for a word in English.

"War," he said.

"Yes, war." I looked at the eyes in the mirror, at the back of the neck. He might remember 1948. "Were you there?"

He understood, but explaining in English proved too difficult. Giving his attention to the road, he peered uphill, shifted gear, zoomed past two trailer trucks. A big man with a Sicilian face, the eyes shrewd and friendly as they checked me out in the mirror.

I wanted to chat to give my mind a rest. We finally realized we had a language in common, not popular among Israelis but useful. From his accent I knew his Arabic had been learned in Iraq, though like many Jews from Arab lands he turned the hard 'h' into something liquid and guttural. We dealt carefully with each other at first, sniffing out elements of each other's lives. I asked the obvious question. "Where did you learn Arabic?"

A broad smile in return. "You know already, I think," he said. "My father came from northern Iraq, from Kirkuk, when I was ten. My mother cried but he said it was for the good of the children. That was mandate times, the English were here. You are English or American?"

"American." Perhaps the answer pleased him, but he needed to know more before broaching more personal matters. Political matters.

"Where did you learn Arabic? You are not Jewish. You are not an Arab." He launched his assumptions like clay pigeons.

"I lived in Ramallah when I was growing up. My father was headmaster at the Ramallah school." I hesitated, then took the plunge. "I had many Palestinian friends."

"Ah, then you know our country well." He concentrated on his driving a few minutes, searching for an opening to the next stage. "What do you think of the present situation? The cost of living is difficult for us." He latched on to economics, its neutrality unassailable. My move.

I proceeded carefully. We exchanged harmless information. Eventually I gave him the information he was jockeying for. I worked for an electronics company, I said, and lived not in America but in Cairo.

"Ah," he said, "our new friends, the Egyptians. Is your company an Egyptian company?"

"No. American."

"Do the Egyptians like it when you come here?"

"They don't mind."

"But you came by way of Cyprus." He had observed the passengers I arrived with. Why, he was asking, didn't you take one of the direct flights inaugurated by Israel after the peace treaty was signed in 1967.

"More convenient," I said, cutting off this line of inquiry. Like others of my kind I was traveling by way of Cyprus to avoid reminding Egyptians and anybody else I was going to Israel. A politically advisable business technique, like having my Israeli visa on a separate piece of paper, not stamped into my passport for all the world to see.

"I have a cousin who had a holiday last year in Cairo. He went on a bus tour that crossed the Sinai." Again the glance in the mirror. "He said the everyday people were friendly. Not like the Palestinians."

A major move. Palestinians. Under ordinary business circumstances I would have changed the subject. "Aren't they friendly?"

"Sir, you know of course they are not friendly." When I did not respond, he waited, then went on. "They hate us, and we hate them. But we hate them for good reasons. They want to drive us into the sea, they kill our children."

I remembered the discussion in that far-off apartment on Connecticut Avenue, but that had been a cocktail game. "Do you kill any of *their* children?" I asked. For a few moments he concentrated on his driving. His body posture said he wanted to shift the level of discourse to one that required less public relations, less care.

"Yes, we killed some of their children. Not on purpose. And only after they killed ours. That's the only language they understand, the only way they'll stop. We know them well, we have lived with them, don't forget, for many years. They will never like us. We must protect ourselves." His voice rose a bit, his eyes stabbing at the mirror to see if I understood.

"Why will they never like you?" Something was pushing me. Perhaps I feared being left without a reason to go on talking. Without talk my mind would revert to Hampton, his family, his problems.

"Because that's the way it is." He said it as if the end of the conversation had arrived, the only valid conclusion reached. The road straightened momentarily and he changed gear, zooming past another of the endless stream of trailer trucks. Now we heard only traffic sounds. He must have used the time to decide that his answer was unsatisfactory. To himself.

"They will never like us, because *wallahi*" – Arabic for "by God" – "their minds are poisoned against us, by rich leaders who live in fancy houses in Amman, by all those Arab politicians, by the terrorists who hide like cowards in Syria and Lebanon. Any Palestinian friendly to us gets killed, or his family gets hurt, we all know that."

"What do they say to them to poison their minds?"

"They fill them with lies, lies. They tell them we took their land. What we took we made into good land, and we bought it from them, and if they'd kept it, it would be worthless. They don't know what to do with land, how to make things grow. They have good jobs because we created the jobs. We worked hard, they profited."

"Do the poisoners tell them about Jewish settlements in the occupied zones?" I heard my voice becoming sharper. "Do they tell them about East Jerusalem? Did you pay for that land?"

"That was later, after they hated us, after they started listening to Abu Ammar, that terrorist pig Arafat." Abu Ammar, the name for Arafat, headquartered in Tunis, headlined on visits to world capitals. With the mention of his name, the driver stared stolidly at the road, head immobile, face flushed.

"Do you have Arab friends?" I asked. I softened my voice, wanting to defuse what might get out of hand. Hands gripping the wheel, he took a deep breath, visibly controlling himself, remembering I was a customer, not … not what? An enemy? An old friend?

"Yes, once I had friends. I used to go to their houses, play cards, then …"

"Then what?"

"Then they moved away."

We fell silent. I already knew the end of the story. I searched for a question. "Did you say goodbye when they left?"

"No." He stopped, then went on. "My children did, they were very unhappy. The Arabs wouldn't say goodbye to me. I went around but they wouldn't speak. They thought it was my fault. That they had to move. And I went around to the authorities, to say they should stay, but the government said it was necessary."

"Why was it necessary?"

"They didn't say." He stared straight ahead. "The bastards are all alike. I told them I went to the government to help, my wife told his wife, but they wouldn't speak. They just left, not a word, no thanks, no goodbye, nothing."

We fell silent again. Perhaps like me he mused on lost friendships, on hate, on the seemingly unbreakable circle of hate. "After that, they killed my sister up north. Their boy, he used to play with mine, he joined the PLO. They're all murderers."

"Was it their boy who killed your sister?"

"He was one of them, one of them." His voice started to rise again. "I tell you, we know them well, we know what they do. The only thing they understand is force."

"Will force stop the *intifada*?"

"Listen, we are willing to talk, any time, but they won't talk. Except for business, that's all. We say come talk, we will be fair, but they don't come, just stay in their houses. Or throw stones at soldiers. Or go to Lebanon."

We had entered the Jewish side of Jerusalem. Rows of orderly apartment houses had been built since my boyhood. After crossing into East Jerusalem our trip would come to an end. In a sudden urge to speak directly, the driver swung the car to the curb, yanked on the handbrake, took a deep breath, turned to face me. "Listen, you want the truth? The truth about them?" His eyes looked into mine. "The truth is they hate us, but they are wrong to hate us. If they would talk to us, they would find we were friendly. Friendly. If they would leave us in peace, not listen to that prick Arafat, they would be surprised. Surprised how much we would do for them."

His eyes filmed over, but he paid no attention.

"Just remember what I say," he said, "remember what I say. Some day they will come talk to us and they will be surprised what kind of people we are. Instead they don't talk, just listen to that prick Arafat and those others."

Without apology he brushed away two or three trickling tears, turned back to the wheel, and drove off. In silence we crossed the city and pulled up in front of the American Colony, a hotel on the Arab side of town. In a moment of guilt for badgering him I offered him too large a tip, but he shook his head, accepted a minimum amount. "I'm glad we talked," I said awkwardly.

"*Maa salama.*" Then, reminding us both I was not an Arab, he gave the translation himself. "Goodbye," he said.

*   *   *

The American Colony, now a fashionable and expensive hotel inside East Jerusalem near the Damascus Gate, was the first stop on a trip into the past. My parents had known the parents of the owner. Ramallah was not far away, and we used to drive in for lunch on sunny Sundays.

I walked through the archway and stood looking at the familiar patio: flowering shrubs and gravel paths and tables for tea, all surrounded by two stories of the old villa that had housed the original colony. Built with blocks of pink granite, its beauty enhanced by graceful archways here and there, the villa blended into its surroundings to form a picture of a different era. More than a century before, a group of foreigners, Americans and Scandinavians, had come to Jerusalem to await the second coming of Christ. Where once maiden ladies of uncertain years had worked and prayed, now tourists happily cashed traveler's checks. My father had enjoyed telling the story. After arriving in the Holy Land, the members of the colony had settled down to await the second coming, but because they were raised to be industrious, they found it hard to be idle, and so some of them established enterprises, including a hotel that became uncommonly successful. In recent years a descendant of the first owner had even built an elegant annex across the street. Such, I thought, were the merciless transformations of a century. I gave thanks for what had endured; the tranquility of the patio and the sunny patches of color among the blooms, these I remembered from earliest boyhood.

A hundred yards from the hotel, the main road led north to Ramallah, less than seven miles away. Even on the main road, the quiet persisted, traffic was sparse, the pace of life slow. Speed and bustle were reserved for the other side of town or for occasional agricultural settlements, where Jews dealt energetically with Jews and looked with scorn or gentle amusement at the indolence of East Jerusalem. Since '67, crossing to the other side of Jerusalem had become easy; no physical or bureaucratic barrier got in the way. But except for a few who wanted an ethnic meal or something in the bazaar, Jews seldom came over, and in the other direction Palestinians crossed only to work. At any moment of any day each resident of Jerusalem knew exactly where he was: either with, or not with, his own kind.

When he saw my name, the young Palestinian at the desk smiled. He said they expected me. The owner, who had known my father, would want to say hello. "I, too, went to the Ramallah School," he said, almost shyly, "but only recently."

I knew suddenly I was close to home, to my place. My family, built into the woodwork, was part of the lore. The young man and I exchanged a few sentences about what had happened at Ramallah, and I felt pleased and spoke as if I kept up with things, though I did not recognize the name of the Palestinian headmaster. I asked if any messages had come for me. He hesitated a moment, then said he thought two phone calls had come in from persons who did not leave their names. Over the last few days, he said.

An aging porter, who doubled as gardener, took my bag, and we crossed the lobby. The pink Jerusalem stone had the same scrubbed look. From the courtyard we climbed the stairs to the second floor. Cath and I had stayed in the same room seventeen years before, stopping by on our way to Saudi Arabia. I had not been in Jerusalem since. Though I had expected to remain a while, it turned out our stay was less than a success. My enthusiastic nostalgia was overdone. I wanted not only to show her my boyhood territory but also to introduce her to old acquaintances and have her see the beauty of it all, the hills, the clear sky, the intimacy. But the intimacy, the closeness I felt, resided in *my* mind, not hers.

We drove to Ramallah several times, wandering about the town, stopping at a few shops not to buy but to remind the owners of young Bill Hampton, to whom they had waved when he pedaled by. Some owners were dead; others, perhaps pretending to remember, talked happily about the old days. So did the Quaker community clustered around the school, over cups of tea and brown cookies. Everyone welcomed us, but Cath must have felt excluded in small ways. Too cozy and much of it in Arabic. I translated and tried to make her part of it, and those who knew English would switch, but I finally understood Cath's magnetism would soon give out. I had forced the pace. So we shortened our visit and went to take in something of Jordan while we had the chance. If Abu Hisham had been there, things might have gone better. But he had been exiled to Lebanon. A month before, the Israelis had taken him to the border and expelled him for "political activities." I was bitterly disappointed. Cath and I visited his wife and saw his infant son, but his wife's disquiet, clearly displayed, made the visit little more than a courtesy call. She called in two women cousins to share the visit's burden and risk; I think she feared a more intimate meeting would become known, might prejudice Abu Hisham's return. At the door she said quietly she hoped next time would be better. "Perhaps two months," she murmured. I heard later he was readmitted in three months, thanks to interventions from moderate Palestinians the authorities were anxious to please.

The hotel room had changed little, a pleasant room with coarse Gaza rugs and two old-fashioned dressers against the wall. But the view from the window had changed drastically; what were fields had become small villas and three-story apartment houses. Where peasants had worked, small boys went by on bicycles, and someone had obliterated the cluster of peasant huts that had enchanted Cath. For her, toward the end of our stay, the room had become a refuge from insistent courtesies coming our way from Ramallah.

When the old porter left, I took off my traveling clothes and stretched out, business agenda beside me, phone in hand. I had made careful plans and had a long list of possible clients. Though many of them involved Tel Aviv, I'd collected enough "good bets" in Jerusalem to justify staying up in the capital. San Francisco was in favor of new business wherever I could find it. I had not, of course, mentioned the real reason for my interest in new territory. Palestinian politics was not considered good business practice. But business success would justify almost any plan — including a ten-day trip to Beirut that would occur (as I put it to San Francisco) during the lull between my first contacts in Israel and the follow-up when I could "get down to brass tacks." The Beirut trip also made business sense, though for me the bottom line was survival.

*   *   *

The place to start, as Abu Taleb had said. Gaza and Jerusalem. To which I had added Beirut. Now I was close to confronting head-on some possibly harebrained scheme to right the world, or at least the Eastern Mediterranean, and in the process – what? How many people would get maimed or killed?

From the hotel room I saw the greens of early summer, suggesting the beauty farther afield, beyond the apartment houses. The desert dust and grime of Heliopolis where Abu Taleb existed came suddenly to mind; no wonder he yearned for Palestine. And his children? Brought up in Egypt, did they too yearn for this place? Later, at the time we had agreed on, I phoned Cath in Cairo. I knew the kids were away at a school function. She picked up the phone and said, "Hi!"

"Hi," I said. "You'll never believe which room they gave me at the hotel."

"Oh that lovely room. I remember it so well. How was the trip? How are you?" I said I was fine, even though that was not an exact statement. But it was the customary response. I could not tell her that fear was now an ever-present part of my life. Nor had the self-inflicted wound of my secret infidelity healed over, and if it ever did, I did not know how long the scab would remain.

"I've had some good news." She sounded upbeat. "Paul phoned and is really enthusiastic about my latest" – Paul Taylor was the New York literary agent for her short stories – "and says he'll place it easily. Maybe in the New Yorker."

"Now that is good news. Hooray. Looks like you're on the way! How is Paul?"

"He sounds good. He asked if I could manage a trip to New York one of these days. He wants me to talk to some people there. Thinks it would be very helpful. What he really has in mind is for me to revise my stories, add a few more, then publish a book of them. What do you think?"

"That all sounds great. Just great."

"I don't really see how I could get away for a trip like that. Maybe in the summer."

"We'll have to work something out. Your going to New York is very important." Yes, it was important, I thought. She deserved something in her life more exciting than her current routines. Her voice had betrayed an expectation of new and interesting things to come.

∗   ∗   ∗

I slept heavily that night but not well, and I welcomed the moment of waking up. As so often, images of a bullet piercing an elevator cage had appeared. And other dreams had been frustrating. I kept working at some problem. When I struggled to a solution, the problem changed and it was all to do again. I was left unsatisfied, a non-achiever, denied the pleasure of real slumber. But in the morning the sky was blue, the air like the first sip of fine white wine, and through the open window came the noises of every day, striking my ear like a symphony I suddenly remembered – the braying of a donkey, a woman calling out from her garden, the sound of a truck changing gear on the main road, the song of a blackbird. Through a gap between apartment houses I saw orange trees and olives, red tile roofs, and the unmistakable gold of wheat. From somewhere near came the smell of baking bread.

The girl in the breakfast room smiled at me as if we were cousins and brought me a flat round loaf, white cheese, Turkish coffee. Perhaps the room upstairs and its reminders of seventeen years ago had brought on the dreams. Which I did not remember, but the leitmotif was Cath. For her I explained things throughout the night, tried to work out difficulties, justify my existence. Since my infidelity, she had hovered at the edge of my conscience, standing there waiting to be recognized, like an unwelcome visitor one hopes will leave before one has to say hello. I took a sip of coffee and picked up the Jerusalem Post, putting my guilt away for later consideration, in my new pending file.

Back in my room, I began phoning again, laying more groundwork for business conversations in Israel. Then one more call. A woman answered. I asked for Ni'meh Taleb Abu Khayyal.

"It is I," she said in English. "I've been expecting you. When will you pass by?"

"Within an hour?"

"Yes, do."

*   *   *

The taxi dropped me outside the Damascus Gate. Lingering for a moment at a kiosk that sold maps of Jerusalem, I saw another taxi pull up fifty yards away. Yes, there he was, the man who had been sitting in the lobby. I had already spotted him at breakfast. His dowdy gray suit and open shirt gave no clue; he could have been Israeli or Palestinian.

Above all I had to avoid leading him, or anyone else, to Abu Taleb's sister, whose life was at stake. I sauntered through the Gate as if on a stroll to enjoy the sights and sounds of the Old City. When he lost me, I wanted it to appear accidental, not wanting him to be more careful next time around.

Inside the old walls I took another short journey into the past. Despite Israeli occupation and annexation, little had changed. The narrow streets, devoid of cars, were packed: tourists, villagers in traditional dress, townsmen in Western dress, other villagers trying to look like townsmen, Israeli soldiers in pairs carrying machine pistols and nightsticks, a few Israelis over to shop, an occasional Bedouin. The inescapable smells of food, herbs, and spices triggered memories. Shopkeepers made welcoming gestures, hoping for a mid-morning sale, but they did not pester. I stopped a few times to look at merchandise.

I anticipated no difficulty in eluding my pursuer. In my boyhood I had played a special hide-and-seek with my brother John in the Old City. We came to know the back alleys, the narrow passages, and the tricky exits from dead ends. As I strolled, the places and strategies we had used came flooding back. Leading my follower casually for fifteen minutes, I lost him in an alley off Barquq Road. Changing direction, I moved quickly through Herod's Gate, stopped behind a corner to make sure I was alone, then walked north and east along shabby streets of the Arab Quarter.

The shops still sold what they sold when I was growing up, and I thought I recognized an old man in the English-language bookstore I used to browse in. The same restaurants still served kebab, though their names had changed. Street names were now posted in Hebrew as well as Arabic and English. I turned right on Zahara Street and walked to an old villa set back in a garden filled with geraniums and rose bushes in bloom. Separating the garden from the street were a briar hedge and a small wooden gate painted green. The villa itself, genteel and cost-conscious in washed-out stucco, stood sturdily among the flowers, green shutters straight, curtains clean, roof tiles in place. At one side, in Arabic and English, a bronze plaque announced "The Institute for Palestinian Handicrafts."

The door opened as I mounted the steps. A handsome slender woman in early middle age looked out calmly, curious to see what I had become. She herself was not dressed as I remembered but Western-style, a long dark dress, long sleeves, wearing no make-up and no jewelry other than Bedouin bracelets at the wrists. Her face, slender and fine-boned, reminded me instantly of Abu Taleb. Curling eyelashes, graceful slender neck, shining black hair with traces of gray, gathered in a bun. The slim delicacy of her body attested, I thought, to Bedouin nobility. In the old days we did not shake hands, nor greet each other formally. Perhaps, with a glance but not a gesture, we would acknowledge the presence of the other across a family room near Gaza or in a reception room when, dressed in Bedouin garb, she brought tea for the men. That was long ago. Now she extended her hand, a Western gesture to fit her clothes, for a chaste clasp, smiling the lovely half-smile her brother had told me to expect.

"It has been a long time," she said. She spoke in English, correctly and carefully.

"Yes, a long time." I groped for more words. "Much more than twenty years, I think, since you gossiped in the corner with the younger girls. As I remember, we never spoke to each other." With a nod she acknowledged that things change, but I sensed talking about the old days was too intimate, as if I were a stranger breaking into a family circle. She led the way into a dark hall with a large mirror and massive coat-and-hat rack from Mandate days. To the left a workroom was occupied by sewing machines and women in village dress. Farther along another busy room focused on looms and weaving. We turned right into what had once been the family room, light and airy with red Palestinian *kaleem* rugs on a parquet floor, straight-back chairs upholstered in pale-green against the walls. In the center of the room a white metal table held brochures describing her Institute. We sat formally, turning two of the chairs to face each other, near a large window looking onto the garden.

"Really you have changed little," she said. "How is my brother?"

"Abu Taleb is well and sends you his special greetings. Of course he asks about the children and how you are getting along." I looked away, looked at the rose bushes in order not to see the melancholy in her eyes. "Naturally I know about Mustafa and all that happened."

At seventeen Ni'meh married her cousin Mustafa. That was 1974. In 1976, Mustafa, one year older than Ni'meh, was killed by Israelis on the main road south of Gaza, near Deir el Balah, during a skirmish provoked by the throwing of "Gaza cocktails" at Israeli patrols. For a few years she could only sob when his name was mentioned. After the mourning period, she gave their house to Mustafa's younger brother and with her two infant sons moved back to live with her mother. Money had not posed a problem. Nor did protection; the clan was a big one. The problem was loneliness. No matter how many brothers and half-brothers and sisters inhabited the compound, the pain of losing her man never left her. Always there, acute, in her eyes.

"Abu Taleb," I said, "hopes you will marry again."

"Yes, he and his brothers want my happiness, and they want me to know I can choose, and whoever it is, they will approve. They think the matter is social. But it is personal. I could not marry again." She looked up at me, with that sad half-smile. Abu Taleb said sadness was her preferred state of being.

"You understand?" she asked, but this time she spoke in Arabic, admitting me a few steps into the family. I found myself, like Abu Taleb, hoping she'd change her mind. I knew enough about Bedouin life to know it would never be easy. If one day she could bring herself to abandon the memory of Mustafa, the social question remained. Who would want her, another man's widow? Only a social inferior if he was from her own world, which was Gaza or the tribes of Beersheba. But Ni'meh was born an Abu Khayyal, not just anybody, not just a good investment for domestic labor; she was a widowed princess, her father had been an important tribal leader.

"How are the boys?" I asked, proceeding in Arabic.

"They are off for the summer to Gaza, to stay with their uncles. They are really men now. Fine boys, like their father." She spoke gently and proudly. "Abu Taleb says you are married with children."

So I told her about Cath and the family and where we lived and what I had done. She listened attentively, head slightly bowed, nodding as she registered what I recounted. An extraordinary woman, I thought, steadfast and proud. Abu Taleb had it right. She might marry again but only outside her old world. She'd learned English and become a townswoman known for achievements, mistress of a well-known establishment that did social work as they would in England. Officials from international organizations sought her out, asked her guidance, gave her subsidies to continue her work. Where was her place? She left the room and returned with two photographs framed in silver. One in faded sepia showed a young man in military uniform posed stiffly against a backdrop of the Palestinian flag. The uniform was Palestine Liberation Army. I did not remember him from among the many cousins I had met long ago, but it had to be Mustafa. Despite the photographer's efforts to make him a soldier, he remained an Abu Khayyal, the same slender face, the same bones.

"What a handsome, fine-looking man," I said, anxious to comfort her. Somberly, she gazed at the picture for an instant more, in a ritual of fidelity, then without a word turned to the other one. A recent picture of two more Abu Khayyals, boys in Western dress in their middle teens, staring solemnly at the camera. I felt I wanted to see them smile or laugh. "They usually laugh," she said as if in response, "they are not like me, they are like their uncles."

A heavy-breasted village girl in an intricately embroidered peasant dress brought in the coffee. In English Ni'meh asked me to admire the needlework, which the girl had done herself. The girl turned around to show us. I made noises of admiration. The girl, her round young face flushed, swung her peasant hips as she left the room. Ni'meh's manner, I thought, reflected her upbringing: an easy dignity, kind but in command.

"Later," said Ni'meh, switching back to Arabic, "I must show you around. The women would never forgive me if I didn't, especially an American. Then morale will be good for a few days." She paused, sitting primly, feet close together, hands in lap. Then she went on. "Abu Taleb said you had family business to talk about." Family business? Yes, of course. Business to be kept within the family.

"It's about arranging to see Abu Hisham," I said, "without others knowing about it. With the help of your older brother in Gaza. Abu Hisham and I are very old friends, as you know, but I'm an American. I don't want to embarrass him."

"Yusuf el-Khalil? Why would it embarrass him? He lives right here, his law offices are three blocks away." The dark eyes looked at me steadily.

I invoked the name of her oldest brother. "Abu Taleb thinks it would be wise, for Abu Hisham's sake, to keep it secret. He says Abu Hisham is right now in a delicate position, highly regarded by all, of course, but it would not be good if he were seen with Americans."

"But you are an old friend." She sought to understand. How to explain that I was indeed an old friend, but one who was suspect, spotted, followed. Any other ordinary American, but not me. She watched as I groped for a response.

"I cannot take the risk of embarrassing an old friend. Abu Taleb and I agreed."

She looked at me a long moment, then sighed. She had understood. The melancholy, which had diminished when she spoke of her work, returned to her eyes. "I see," she said. We sat a moment without speaking. "So you are one of them," she said, her hands clasped tightly, "one of the men playing at politics. I did not expect you would do that. When you were young, you were very clean, very straightforward. The women are not supposed to know about the games. They do what they are told, then wait until someone is killed." With a restless movement she stood up and went to the window. I sat there, waiting. She looked at the roses for a while. "I am still a daughter of Sheikh Taleb. I will do what I'm asked to do. But it occurs to me now it may be the last time. My sons are happy, healthy. I want them to survive. One day they might have Jewish friends. You understand how I feel?" She fell silent, arms folded, staring at the roses. An old gardener worked among the geraniums.

"Yes," I said, "I know how you feel. I know. But what I'm doing is in the cause of peace, of less killing. I would like you to trust me. Is it possible?"

"Perhaps. A bit. You all say what you are doing is in the cause of peace, but then people die. I'll trust you for the moment only. We'll have to see. But I will do what you ask." She turned back toward me, eyes down, face set against the world. "If anything should happen to my sons, I will not kill but I will never forgive, Abu Taleb or my other brothers or you or Abu Hisham."

"There is no danger of that kind." I, too, got up to stand at the window. "Nothing like that. The whole thing is to arrange a quiet meeting with an old friend. That's all."

SEVEN

Beirut, May 1990

Lebanon is several long taxi rides away from Jerusalem. A business day's worth of travel more or less, by way of relatively relaxed political frontiers. East across the Jordan River to Amman, then north to Damascus in Syria, then west over spectacular mountains and down into Lebanon. I changed taxis twice, each time buying two front seats in a *servis*, which is a large station wagon selling individual seats.

I saw Beirut in the far distance when the *servis* came through the pass. There it was, miles below, the brilliant blue of the Mediterranean behind it, looking in 1990 almost as it did when the four of us used to arrive in the family sedan some thirty years before.

At those moments John and I felt great excitement, turning to gaze from each window, pointing out remembered landmarks, making plans for the next day. We could look forward to two glorious months, not only because the mountains of Lebanon were cool and beautiful, more because the time had come to consort with our own kind, American or British teenagers whose parents gathered at the mountain resorts of Shemlan and 'Ein Nab in the summers. For me, the season had come to shift social gears, to change from one happy life to another. For John, back from Deerfield for the holidays, no other place remained where he felt at home. A summer society that bloomed for two months, then faded as the winds of autumn hit the mountainside. Since '75, the summer flower no longer bloomed. The tennis courts and orchards where we played and talked,

129

where even John laughed, had become ethnic battlegrounds: Druse, Christian, Shiite, Sunni, Palestinian. Bloodletting had become Lebanon's pandemic. When Palestinian fighters were driven out in '82, most Lebanese rejoiced. Many thought the cause of chaos had been removed, that peace would return. But patterns of living had undergone irreversible change; families went on killing people from other families. Revenge was still sweet. When the young Palestinian men began trickling back to see their mothers and wives and often to fight again, they resumed their adoptive place in the national dance of hate and retaliation. A dance marathon that persevered. And persevered.

Every once in a while the fires of violence burned low and deaths were fewer, but here Lebanon, I knew, deceived its friends. As with a fire that has burned hard, the hot embers persist. They can flare up and burn wildly yet again.

The *servis* headed off down the long mountainside toward the foothills. The Lebanese driver, a Sunni Muslim from Ras Beirut, drove like a good skier showing off. In Damascus when I bought the two seats next to the driver, the wagon failed to fill up quickly, and so I also bought two of the three jump seats in order to hurry our departure. The driver, looking me over, had asked if I was sure I wanted to go to Ras Beirut. It was, he said cautiously, the same as West Beirut. When I said yes, he shrugged. Because I spoke Arabic, he thought I knew what I was doing. Business had gone well. In other circumstances I would have felt a sense of accomplishment. I had stopped in Amman for a day where I sold over half a million worth of electronic equipment. I even stayed in Damascus a few hours to call on an untrustworthy acquaintance, a wily Syrian Greek-Orthodox agent-for-anything. He could not buy from me directly, but I made sure he had the name of an agent in Beirut whose knowledge of illegal channels matched his own.

After a descent of ten kilometers the driver began watching the road intently. So did the passenger in one of the jump seats. The chatter of three persons in the back seat died down. At each hairpin turn, as the tires squealed, a new vista was examined. We had entered a combat zone, an ethnic borderland where once peoples had lived in peace. During the day the Lebanese Army, mostly Christian with desultory boosts from Syrian forces, controlled the main highways, but ethnic militias could appear abruptly and attack from country roads and villages along the mountainside. No one controlled Lebanese highways at night. The sudden forays, said a friend in Amman addicted to psychology, expressed rage, the rage of Lebanese at what they thought the outside world had done to them, at what they were doing to themselves, at the hopelessness of trying to sew their petty fiefs back into a nation.

The driver braked suddenly. Ahead of us stood a road block, seven empty tar barrels rolled out onto the highway. In front, five youthful militiamen pointed rifles uphill at our taxi. The driver cursed the Lebanese, the Syrians, the government, the impotent army, his own bad luck. Then he glanced at his passengers to see what hatreds they represented. He seemed satisfied by what he saw. In Damascus he had sold seats for Ras Beirut, a Sunni Muslim part of the city. With any luck, his passengers would not botch things up by being Shiites or Druse, who were currently killing each other from time to time. In the very back sat two women and a man, all middle-aged, who looked lower-middle-class; the man wore poorly cut Western clothes, had a large mustache, an enormous paunch, a prominent gold tooth. The other passenger, I thought, might be trouble; he sat directly behind me in the jump seat, a tall well-built man in his mid-thirties, dressed by expensive tailors. I had not heard him speak.

As we approached the barrier, moving slowly, the driver glanced at me. An American threatened inconvenience but not real trouble.

"No Arabic," he said. I nodded. No Arabic like mine from someone looking like me, no unexpected linguistic purity to confuse those in authority, such as the militiamen now pointing guns at us. They were dressed in the baggy black of country Druse.

The leader of the group approached the driver's window, and the others moved to surround the station wagon. They kept looking over their shoulders as if expecting trouble from downhill. The swarthy leader, a tall man in his early twenties, asked the driver where he was going.

"Ras Beirut."

"And who is with you?"

"Passengers for Ras Beirut." The driver turned, asked for our papers. He put my passport on top of the pile of brownish pocket-worn identity cards from the back.

"Is that the American in the front seat with you?"

"Yes."

"Does he speak Arabic?"

"I don't know." The driver took no chances. The Druse leader spoke to me in halting English.

"You speak Arabic?"

"A little." I said it in Arabic with a heavy American accent. I smiled. The Druse turned impatiently to the driver, assuming a driver on the Beirut-Damascus run knew English.

"Ask him what he does."

The driver translated into basic English, so basic I would have had difficulty had I not heard the Arabic. I responded in basic English, selecting words, such as "computer" and "business," that needed no translation. Like the other militiamen, the leader kept his eyes moving across the near landscape: a couple of abandoned villas, some small field huts, an olive grove, a café with boarded windows.

"Ask him where he lives."

"Cairo."

"Ask him where he will stay in Beirut."

"Commodore Hotel." I was careful to use words the driver would understand.

"To do what?"

"Business."

He did not ask where I had come from. Israel, hated Israel. Which had given me a visa and an exit stamp on a separate bit of paper. He put the passport under the pile and began questioning the others.

The well-dressed man on the jump seat behind me was a Syrian named Madkour. The militiaman's tone, which had been peremptory, became respectful. He sensed rather than knew that the Syrian was important, and he began using polite forms of address. Mohamed Madkour, it seemed, was journeying to Beirut for a few days to see friends.

The young Druse turned his attention back to me. Perhaps he wished to impress the Syrian. Perhaps in some political way he had to justify the highway barricade he and his young friends had erected.

"Ask the American why the Americans are supporting an unjust government in Lebanon."

For a tiny instant the driver looked at the heavens for help. Fearing the unmasking of our linguistic charade, he launched into a total garble that Cath might have called delightfully inventive. Now it was dangerous. The Druse stared at the driver and at me. Then he pointed his rifle at the driver's head, his finger on the trigger. To gain time I said I had not understood. For a moment the driver considered his next move. From the jump seat came the voice of the Syrian.

"Would you mind if I helped with the translating? Let me rephrase what the driver has said, if I may."

The Druse nodded agreement, pleased to have his Syrian ally enter the lists on the side of justice. The Syrian put the question into competent English.

"I am not in politics," I said, "I am only a businessman. If my country is supporting injustice in beautiful Lebanon, I am against it and apologize for my country's short-sightedness."

"The American has said the truth and said it well," said the Syrian. "He says he is against injustice and that his country has behaved badly. He hopes matters will get better soon. He says modestly he is a man of little influence in political matters but when he gets to Beirut and back to Cairo, he will let friends of his know about the injustice occurring in this beautiful country."

The Syrian produced a pack of cigarettes and offered one to the Druse. "Lieutenant, this American is not typical. He seems to be a very good man. I'm certain my good friend Waleed Jumblatt" – this was Lebanon's Druse chieftain – "would approve of him. And I do hope the next time you see Waleed, you will give him the warm regards of Mohamed Madkour." He looked steadily at the young Druse. His manner displayed a seamless mix of admiration for the militiaman's role, respect for his position, and the inbred condescension of one who would ordinarily be giving the orders. His gaze said he expected the car to be cleared through the road block immediately.

A rifle shot sounded from below the olive grove on the right. Half a kilometer away, I saw a dozen men in uniforms of the Lebanese army moving uphill unevenly to clear the road block. One of the Druze ran behind the boarded-up café and began firing downhill, compulsively and indiscriminately. The Druse leader shouted at him to stop and signaled another militiaman to move one of the empty oil barrels. Our taxi shot through the gap. As we passed, I looked at the man who had opened the road block. A boy less than fifteen years old, he gave me a delighted grin and waved his rifle.

*   *   *

The driver glanced at me a couple of times, wanting to start a conversation, but I gave him no opening. In a *servis* the selling of separate seats means that the threat of unwanted chatter looms large. Yet most travelers, wealthy or not, prefer this mode of travel. It's not only a customary mode but sometimes safer – more people, registered drivers. The greatest drawback is that one proceeds through frontiers (or roadblocks) no faster than the most awkward fellow passenger.

At the Syrian border the officials had filled out forms and stamped passports as if it mattered, but in chaotic Lebanon no one cared. At the frontier post, with the Cedar-of-Lebanon flag whipping in the breeze, a few dispirited functionaries had gone through the motions required of them, just as if there were a central government to which they reported, rather than a patchwork of local governments and warlords fighting for control, jockeying for position on mountain roads and seacoast in what used to be Lebanon — and on some days still was.

We slowed down going through 'Aleh, the resort town that used to represent "fleshpots" to me and my teenage friends. We would come for tea to the terrace of the major hotel, looking down luxuriously at the Mediterranean and at the teenage girls, dressed in Paris fashions and layered in make-up, up for the summer from Beirut's *haut monde*. The enormity of the change hammered at me, threatening memories I wanted to keep.

Now I stared not at girls but at social breakdown and devastation; no building was in decent repair, only tacky white villas and cafés and dress shops, all with broken windows boarded up, like roadside flowers gone by. The driver wheeled deftly through areas of broken glass, piles of refuse, stacks of empty vegetable and fruit crates. A rural policeman stood at one corner, a tiny convenience store had two customers. Otherwise no one. Soon we turned left off the Damascus Road to go the back way into West Beirut.

I turned to the Syrian. "I'm grateful for your help at the barricade," I said in English.

"You are most welcome. I did it for all of us. It was getting late." He gave a polite smile.

"Are you from Damascus?" I asked.

Not responding immediately, he watched the wreck of 'Aleh flash by outside, as if deciding whether to get involved. He finally settled on a guarded exchange of information, a harmless pastime. He came from Kameshli, a booming city in remote Syria, the center of Syria's agricultural success. Vast areas of wheat, cotton, and fruit trees.

So we chatted about business. The harvest, he said, should be good this year. He owned and managed five hundred hectares of pears and apples, which helped explain his well-tailored clothes.

"How do you ship your stuff?"

"Through Latakia," he said. "We used to ship through Tripoli and Beirut, of course, until '76 or so. But the stupid Lebanese decided to destroy themselves." The three passengers in back, understanding nothing, watched attentively as we conversed. The Syrian looked out the window a few moments, then became suddenly expansive, speaking as if confidentially. "You know, when I was a boy I used to think these people here were very clever, very sophisticated, they knew languages, they went to universities, and all the rich families traveled to Paris. And in Beirut, my God, they had the best restaurants, the best nightclubs, the latest cinema. And they had freedom to speak out, no censorship. Now look at them." He looked out the window again, then went on. "We have a stupid government in Syria, but with little help from them we do fairly well. We leave politics to people in Damascus. Let them play."

He moved his shoulders scornfully. "And our army. Donkeys. They too are politicians. Like the Iraqis. They all have dreams about power and influence. So our army controls this section of Lebanon. The expense is enormous. And useless."

The *servis* was now descending the hill on older roads. Suburbs appeared. Housewives in shawls and men in work clothes wandered in the streets, enough to suggest normal life. Except for the buildings. Many had been blown open, forming cement-strewn courtyards full of shanties made of corrugated iron, with laundry hanging from makeshift lines. Boys in ragged clothes played soccer in the side streets. The driver had not relaxed his vigilance. His eyes kept moving, sweeping the view ahead.

"Around here," he said, "it used to be the worst."

I turned again to the Syrian. He said he would stay a night in Beirut, then go to Paris for several weeks. Both business and pleasure, he said. He hesitated a moment.

"You know about the kidnappings, of course," he said.

"Yes, but I do not think I need to worry."

"Did you consider staying on the other side?" He meant the Christian side.

"I always stay at the Commodore. I'm of no interest to anyone."

"Perhaps not. I've heard some of the Shiites are at it again." He had done his duty, given a warning.

*   *   *

The lobby of the Commodore exudes shabby comfort and friendliness. The very smell is friendly, always the same, a mix of cigarette smoke and the special dust that lodges in the baggy upholstery of the easy chairs. Lack of pretense is the leitmotif. In recent years, when killing and chaos were just outside, the place had served me well, a psychological fortress where I could wait things out. Only once had the killing and chaos come into the lobby itself.

The desk clerk recognized me, gave me a big welcome. With one hand he pushed forward the registration form, with the other he handed me messages and a key.

"Same room as last time, Mr. Hampton." He was proud to recall such details; last time had been four months before. Checking my U.S.-approved visa for Lebanon, he glanced around and leaned forward. "Please be careful, Mr. Hampton. Next time you should stay on the other side. It's started up again. Two more foreigners kidnapped last week."

I thanked him and said I did not think I was the kind of foreigner anyone was after. He watched my face a moment.

"Also, they say there's trouble again with the PLO."

"What kind of trouble?"

"Maybe fighting each other." He turned to answer the phone, spoke a few words, then put the phone down. "Two calls came in yesterday asking when you were arriving."

"Who were they?"

"They didn't give their names," he said. "Please be careful, Mr. Hampton."

When the bellhop left my room, I looked out the window. The bank across the street had reopened, putting itself together again under a coating of blue wash. On the ruins of an apartment building next door a supermarket had sprung into being. The rubble from the last round of fighting had been cleaned up. As I looked, street lights came on at the top of newly installed lampposts. Four months earlier, without street lights, danger had waited at each doorway. In another four months the danger might return, but now the view sent tidings of cautious hope.

I flopped onto the bed, messages in hand. Three came from business contacts, clients whose hunger for small computers was insatiable, not to mention printers, software in French or English, whatever I sold that was technologically sophisticated. Lebanon's entrepreneurs, no matter the pleasure with which they focused on vengeance, absorbed new technology as easily as they switched languages.

Another message was scrawled by Mohamed Dajani, a professor of sociology at the American University of Beirut, a former classmate of mine at the Ramallah School. I remembered him as a serious student. I had not known him well. Like many of my Palestinian classmates he went on to AUB; then he went to graduate school at Chicago. When I started making trips to Beirut after moving to Cairo, I ran into him by chance.

He invited me to dinner to get acquainted, to meet his American wife, to see his two children. We all became good friends. I was particularly fond of the children.

Would Mohamed also have been one of the callers reported by the desk clerk? As usual on my regular visits to Beirut, I had let him know I was coming. He would, in any case, have left his name. His message said I must come to their apartment tomorrow night for a "major get-to-gether." Moreover, he scrawled, this event was *mush mahsub*, not to be counted as the family invitation I always received. At the family evening four months before, Abu Kerim came also; the reunion, despite the violence outside, had been filled with laughter and friendship.

The final message came from Abu Kerim. In a plain brown envelope, no signature, very short. Printed in English in capital letters. "Perhaps we can get a few words together at the Dajani house tomorrow pm. Walk from the hotel, starting at 7:30."

Yes, he was part of it. I had not expected otherwise. Mohamed or some other person of his network would have told him of my visit. Before '82, Abu Kerim and I had seen each other publicly, sitting in restaurants, once in an outdoor café on Rue Hamra. His two bodyguards, pleasant young men in leather jackets with pistols barely concealed, would sit at a nearby table, which was normal routine for highly-placed PLO officials. After the Israeli invasion, we still saw each other, though no longer publicly or with bodyguards. But now time had passed, and our old and close friendship had changed shape yet again. The note shouted a message: be indirect in our dealings, be friends in secret, just "a few words together at the Dajani house." Perhaps, he said.

On impulse I got up, turned out the light, and looked down at the street. Nothing moved. Then from the left a heavy-set man came into view strolling along Rue Hamra. I could not get a good view of his face. Clearly he was in no hurry. He stopped for a minute to look into the window of the supermarket. Then, strangely, he turned and strolled back the way he had come. I closed the shutters, turned on the light again. What I expected to see I do not know. I had the feeling of being watched, of someone hovering.

Would Abu Kerim have phoned the desk clerk? Probably not, though if he had, he would not have left his name. He had to be careful in order to stay alive. Had he changed in ways I was not aware of? At school he had reveled in the antics of our pack. His political activism, his skill at intrigue, his excitability, his willingness to take risks, these things clashed with the cautious nature I had always been saddled with. His escapades in Jerusalem, doubtless visits to shoddy whorehouses but promoted in the telling to the palaces of ravishing widows, put him at a level of worldliness I could never contemplate. And our political inclinations differed like fire and water, his scorn for my ideas about non-violence leaving us always in hopeless disagreement. If we were the least closely linked of the group of four, the links were closer than most friends ever experience. Our differences never bred disloyalty. He never spoke disparagingly about me to others. Indeed, the notion of loyalty helped explain him. His loyalty to Arafat never wavered, despite the latter's provocations and stupidities. His loyalty to me would outlast our lifetimes. Was he loyal to abstractions? To peace and prosperity? To democracy? Perhaps, but finally it was people who mattered; people were his specialty, his focus, his target, his fascination and even his passion, his way of identifying with great and small causes. Palestine held his loyalty because Palestine was a person, maybe a woman, the love of his life.

Thus he was the loyalist chosen to stay behind when Arafat's contingents had to leave, the man left in Beirut to watch over Fatah and PLO interests, a stopgap ambassador whose survival in the anti-Palestinian atmosphere depended on make-believe – and a low profile. Even rabidly anti-Palestinian groups accepted the fiction that he was a journalist, not a Fatah official. He had a small staff with similar "covers." None of them had safe retreats. Killers, presumably from hardline factions whose identities were only a guess, had made two attempts to get him within the past year, but the attempts failed thanks to his own alertness and the beds offered by women friends. Two of his staff had been killed in recent months, both when asleep.

A "major get-together"? What was Mohamed trying to say? If Abu Kerim was to be there, the authorities, those who now controlled Ras Beirut, knew about the gathering, which had to have a political purpose.

If Mohamed wanted a low profile, he would not invite Abu Kerim. For that matter, if I myself was involved in Palestinian politics, and apparently many people thought so, why invite William Hampton?

Impatiently, I reached for the phone and called Mohamed to say hello, to accept the invitation for the next night. We chatted a few minutes, avoiding direct talk.

"It's a big party," he said, as if a third party were listening in on the conversation, "for all kinds of people."

"Okay, I'll be there." I suppressed my urges for more information and asked family questions. "How are Frances and the children?"

"Fine, just fine." Something in his voice told me he too thought Hampton was "involved in Palestinian politics."

I knew that Mohamed had close PLO connections, or at least he had had close connections before '82, when the PLO was responsible for security in West Beirut. In those days a principal figure in the intellectual world of Palestine, he wrote commentary in English and Arabic for the international press, justified PLO decisions, explained terrorism, traveled to academic conferences as unofficial spokesman for the cause. But a year before the Israeli invasion he pulled back from "political involvement" lest he lose "scholarly objectivity." So he told me. But he must also have feared for his American wife and his children; political killings and kidnappings had become commonplace.

His problems did not go away. Politics, like love and death, lurks everywhere, searching out those who renounce it. At the American University of Beirut, many Palestinian faculty, resisting a silent Lebanese campaign to oust them, had clung fast, some of them disguising their origins. Mohamed Dajani, of course, could not be disguised; he was too well-known, had too much of a political past. He told me he didn't want to leave, but I knew he'd inquired about university jobs in the United States.

I gathered my business papers and went down to the dining room for dinner. In the lobby sat a young man in a leather jacket who looked familiar, one of the bodyguards who had watched Abu Kerim in the far-off days when we could openly be friends. He gave me an impersonal stare and went back to his magazine. I made no sign of recognition.

The next evening was overcast. As instructed, I left the hotel on foot at precisely 7:30 p.m. Two young men in leather jackets got up from chairs in the lobby to follow. This was no surprise. One had followed me all day on my business rounds, except when I crossed through the control posts to the Christian side for a brief visit in the afternoon. But he'd followed me as far as the Museum crossing and waited until I came back. Clearly he had a car and driver at his disposal.

Now I was on foot and headed toward a devastated section uphill from Rue Hamra, not far from the Commodore, picking my way along narrow unlit streets, skirting large pieces of fractured building block and pools of water. I felt tight and was glad the young men in leather jackets were following behind. The only cars on the streets had been trapped for months by debris. Lantern light flickered in the doorways of what had once been middle-class apartment houses; ground-floor windows were boarded up, flat surfaces chalked with political slogans.

Finally, I heard party sounds ahead, an announcement of a "major get-together," coming from the building where the Dajanis lived. Four soldiers of the Lebanese Army and two rifle-carriers from one of the militias stood guard outside. I glanced back but my two escorts had disappeared. Parked near the building were five expensive cars, which had somehow made their way into the ruined area. Drivers lounged close by.

Despite the years of random destruction since '75, the Dajani apartment had miraculously escaped. The building, like a surviving tooth crushed at the crown but still used, stood in isolation in an open area created by bombs and heavy guns. Its top floors had been wrecked by shell fire during the Israeli attack in '82. The buildings to either side had been totally destroyed in '85 and were now burial mounds at which relatives left flowers on special days. Mohamed had tried to persuade Frances to take the children and live for a while with her mother in Chicago, but she refused to leave.

A Lebanese Army captain at the outer door checked my passport and waved me up the stairs. Why, I asked myself, were troops of the Lebanese Army on duty in an area controlled by Shiite militias? With militiamen who were not Shiite? Yes, Abu Kerim could "perhaps get a few words" with me here, camouflaged by a battery of important Lebanese, the kind with official cars and drivers. On the second floor I was admitted by a waiter in a white jacket, and inside the flat two other youths in white served drinks and canapés to two roomfuls of guests. The guests stood close to each other, a few women in expensive dresses but mostly men, all sorts of men. Some wore uniforms and seemed to be generals. Gathered in groups, some postured importance, others listened respectfully. Voices rumbled steadily, the hum of men talking to men.

Mohamed stood inside the door, Frances at his side, greeting arrivals. Though my age, he looked older, an intense man whose face was heavily lined, whose hair was iron gray. The eyes had pouches of dead skin below them. When he smiled, as he now did, one almost forgot the lines on the face; they gave way suddenly to the smile's boyish quality that I remembered from years back.

Frances also wore a bright smile, her patrician face and trim figure set off by a stylish red gown. Long brown hair was piled fashionably on her head. Plainly she was playing her hostess role to the hilt. Her eyes looked tired, and she seemed tense and apprehensive. Though I myself felt tense, I was used to the feeling, as perhaps she was not. I wondered how Cath would do here, bringing up children in an atmosphere of casual violence, in constant fear of their mutilation or death.

The social smiles on both faces turned warm. Frances saw me looking at her, and after a kiss on the cheek, she gave my hand a reassuring pat. Watching the byplay, Mohamed nodded almost imperceptibly in confirmation. He drew me back a few steps and turned so that his lips could not be seen by others.

"Come by my office tomorrow at three," he murmured.

I nodded, keeping a public smile on my face, though I did not feel like smiling. The telephone call had clued me correctly; he was part of it. I was glad because I could trust him, but I was also sorry. My intuition told me he needed fewer problems.

"Best go easy on the Arabic," he said. He kept smiling but his eyes were somber. I nodded again. No Arabic unless it had a foreign accent. "Now," he said, louder, "how's your French?"

"Inadequate, by all reports."

"In that case let me introduce you to a group over here." He moved his shoulder in the direction of the dining room, as if the party were neatly bifurcated between the French and English languages. I told him I'd make my own way.

The expensively dressed women, clearly in the Gallic camp, were insisting on French rather than Arabic, on a bright self-advertising style of social chatter. I moved to the other side, toward a group near the dining room, all of them men. One was a Lebanese general. Three of them had the look of AUB faculty, one of whom, a tall Palestinian professor of economics, I had met before. They wore academic clothes – dark grey slacks, casual shoes, light jackets – and they were speaking English, partly because the language of the AUB community is largely English.

But they were also flattering the general, whose command of the language was mediocre. Indeed, they flattered the general, a short tubby man with large ears, whenever possible, and I joined in because I thought it was expected of me. We hung on the general's words and laughed at his clumsy witticisms. No one told me the name of the game we were playing but the sense of comradeship wafting my way from the professors was palpable.

One of the young men in white coats passed by with a tray, and I lifted off a glass of scotch. I didn't see Abu Kerim. Perhaps he had not yet arrived. Then something in my gut gave a lurch. For an instant I held my breath. In a far corner of the dining room, leaning over a table laden with food, was Pinstripe, plate in hand, helping himself to *wara' 'einab*. Even in the choosing of food, he proclaimed his elegance, his manner putting him above the crowd. This time his faultlessly tailored gabardine suit was without pinstripe.

The general had directed a question at me, and I wrenched my attention away from the dining room. What had he asked? I looked at him as if pondering the matter, trying to transform the sounds I had heard into a coherent query. Something about AUB? The tall economist knew I was floundering.

"Ah," he said, "we'd like Bill on the faculty but he's chosen to be in business."

"Yes," I said, picking up the cue, "I'd like to be here, I love Lebanon in spite of the troubles, but at the moment I live in Cairo. I'm just a businessman who happens to be in town."

The general would have liked to know more. How did I fit the gathering's political agenda? If I didn't know that agenda with precision, it took no genius to determine that it involved the Palestinian cause. His face expressionless, the tall economist, who knew more about me than the general needed to know, intervened deftly and changed the subject.

"General," he said, "what is your view on the French involvement?"

The general purred and began a labored monologue.

*   *   *

I glanced at Pinstripe from time to time. He remained in the dining room, chatting with other guests who came to nibble at the food. The general purred on, and my mind wandered. Now that Arafat's hated armies had gone, was it possible for Maronite generals and their allies to come to terms with the Palestinian cause? Perhaps in the Dajani apartment, though surely not yet in the streets below.

All at once I noted an air of expectancy. Guests crowded into the living room. Cocktail chatter continued, but people were now glancing toward the back of the apartment, toward the bedroom area. Pinstripe had come from the dining area and stood nearby with another group; I saw him look our way but he gave no sign of recognition.

The general stopped suddenly. The room became quiet; those with sentences to finish did so in a whisper. In the back a bedroom door opened. A hush hung in the air, as when house lights go down before curtain time. The door swung wide and three men emerged. First came a many-starred general, then a familiar-looking Lebanese civilian, then Abu Kerim. The crowd watched, engrossed in the drama. The three, conscious they had to report to the assemblage, smiled broadly at each other and made a show of shaking hands. The crowd relaxed, began murmuring. The Lebanese civilian, whom I recognized as a leader of the Maronite community, put his arm around Abu Kerim and spoke quietly to him.

Turning with a smile, Abu Kerim embraced him. The negotiations in the bedroom, whatever they had been, were pronounced a success.

Abu Kerim held up his arms and spoke to the crowd. "I have been asked by new friends to say that some old friends from Tunis will be welcomed back to this beautiful country." He could say no more because the crowd burst into loud applause.

Though distinctly an outsider, I understood the implications of what I was hearing and seeing. The identity of the three negotiators from the bedroom provided a solid clue. Who were they? Of the more than several factions on Lebanon's chaotic stage, two major ones – the powerful political wing of the Maronite Christian community and the equally powerful army officer corps – had clearly been talking not only to each other but had now finalized, through their leaders, an understanding of some kind with Abu Kerim, an important Palestinian with close ties to Palestinians in Tunis and elsewhere, Palestinians who were anxious to reside once again in Lebanon. And presumably not yet to be referred to as the PLO. Just a first step, I thought, but a very big one. As the other negotiators spoke to the crowd, once again the crowded room broke into loud applause.

Abu Kerim looked older, though I could not pinpoint why. The stocky figure had the same girth, the graying hair was still abundant, the ample moustache in good trim. Perhaps the flesh of the ruddy-cheeked face had sagged. Perhaps the dark eyes were more intense. Yet Abu Kerim had always been intense. My mother had found our friendship a strange one, and though she tried to hide it, I knew she favored the other two, the judiciousness of Abu Hisham and the contemplative bent of Abu Taleb. The four-way alliance of our dormitory room was subtle, circuitous. If Abu Hisham was the one the rest of us admired unreservedly, the one whose approval we sought, it was Abu Kerim who most wanted that approval. Approval bestowed for evidence of balance: balanced thought, deed, judgment. As I watched and joined in the applause, it occurred to me, not without a pinprick of envy, that the two most tightly bound to each other were Abu Kerim and Abu Hisham. Passion knotted to wisdom, a younger brother for whose fortunes the older would always feel accountable.

The three stood a few moments and surveyed the crowd, nodding at acquaintances, greeting those who had arrived after the negotiations had started in Mohamed's bedroom. When his eyes met mine, Abu Kerim gave a distant nod, but a twitch of the lips, familiar from school days, said a charade was under way. The eyes sent a different message; they had a look I remembered, a hunted look, as if he were encircled by persons he did not trust.

Then, like the other two negotiators, he began the rounds of the various clusters of guests. A word here, a word there, and a ratification by the assemblage as hands shook hands and congratulations were ritually presented. The hands of those uninvolved were shaken as a courtesy. When the senior general came to our group, our own lesser general introduced me as a friend of the host, a businessman from Cairo. When Abu Kerim came by, the Palestinian economist made the introductions. "Perhaps you already know Mr. Hampton," he said.

"Ah yes. Nice to see you again. Are you still living in Cairo?"

"Yes, I am. You have a good memory."

"My politician's memory seldom fails me." He smiled, so did the rest of us. Then, turning away and facing our lesser general, he signaled he'd spent enough time with an outsider and gave his undivided attention, for two minutes, to what the general had to say. When he drifted off to the next cluster, the general smiled at the tall economist, as if they had achieved a joint victory. Guests moved toward the food, and our general jovially signaled us to follow him, single file, into the packed dining room.

I soon found myself in a corner of the dining room, with a plate of *kebab* and stuffed zucchini onto which I had spooned gobs of the sauces of my youth, all of which I planned to wipe up and wolf down with pieces of bread torn from round loaves. I was hungry. But crowded into a corner, without a place to rest my plate, I needed three hands.

"Difficult to get a good mouthful, don't you think?"

I looked up. Smiling at me was Pinstripe, watching my efforts to eat, wedged beside me against the wall. "Yes, yes it is," I said. He appeared to have sociability in mind, nothing else. As if striking up a friendly conversation with a stranger.

"Are you on the AUB faculty?" he asked. Did he know I knew he was faking things?

"No, just a businessman from Cairo, an acquaintance of the Dajanis. I happened to be in town. And you?"

"Just a Palestinian. Just a Palestinian." Lest he sound too serious, he smiled disarmingly, as if it were a joke.

"Do you live here in Ras Beirut?" A normal sociable inquiry.

"Yes, here in this little enclave of peace and quiet, this is where I live. Hardly any murders here. Almost no mayhem. Only a few kidnappings of AUB faculty." Again the disarming smile. His English, literary and unusually good, and his ironic tone, gentle but incisive, blended into social charm. In a relative way, he had neatly depicted Ras Beirut. Aside from the kidnappings, Ras Beirut had indeed become a miracle of less violence in a city whose other streets spawned violence like fungus on rotting wood. Hardly any murders, as he said.

"Yes," I said, "quite remarkable." But delicate irony was beyond my reach. I groped for something more my style. "This seems to be an unusual kind of gathering."

He looked at the crowd, or perhaps above it. I could not see his face, but his words came out unfriendly. "Palestinians and Lebanese generals, the latter more murderous than the former. Plus a few persons, such as wives and AUB hangers-on, who hope problems will go away by dint of hoping."

Again the same smile, lifting the weight from what he said, but when he turned toward me, I saw his eyes. Hard, unyielding.

"If you were an American, would you go on living in Ras Beirut?" I asked.

"I don't know what it is like to be an American, to think like an American. For practical reasons, the few Americans left at AUB should leave soon; some stay out of loyalty or because they are romantics. Some who stay will get killed. Others kidnapped. What would *you* do?" He gave me an amused look as he manipulated more bread and sauce.

"I hope I'd stay, I suppose because it would seem cowardly to leave."

The hand putting food into his mouth stopped moving a moment, then proceeded. The eyes took in my face, a direct look.

"Ah, an honest answer." He chewed his food. The mob thinned, oozing back into the living room, and we could have moved to another part of the apartment, but we stayed where we were.

"You know," he said, "if I were selecting a place to have a private, rather serious conversation, I would select a party just like this. Here we are, possibly embarking on a conversation that will bare our souls, in the utmost privacy, dozens within earshot, yet no one of them hears a word. Isolated, by God, in a sea of humanity."

"Yes," he said, "I think I would leave if I were an American. Why risk death, especially if it really were me. I would be convinced, given my special self-esteem, that I could do a lot elsewhere if I were alive. But friends tell me I have an enormous ego. Perhaps my estimates of myself are wrong."

His English, I thought, might outclass my own. Yet this man spent his time doing odd jobs for the PLO, such as tailing, crossing borders illegally, killing.

"How does it happen your English is so good?" Ordinarily I reserved such questions for business prospects who needed flattery, but this time I wanted to know.

"Ah, my English, yes. People often ask, especially when I quote a few lines from Shakespeare. Of course, I know only a few lines. Well, a German mother did it for me. She insisted on speaking English at home when I was growing up, then insisted on English schools. Apparently she admired the English, her country having been defeated by them when she was young." He paused a moment, no smile now but a purposely fake grin to tell me not everything is amusing. He selected two olives with care. "She's dead now, having been defeated once again, this time by the Jews." He looked at me and reverted to irony. "And your English is quite good too. Where on earth did you learn it?"

For reasons I would find hard to set forth we had become friends. A curious friendship, to be sure, but real nonetheless. Or so I thought. I think we admired each other. For my part I had an impression of integrity; he would do what had to be done, and he'd do it without self-deception, understanding the good and the evil of it. A sort of ruthless inner strength.

We chatted on, touching on many topics. I remember the topics less than I do the style, which was his style, not mine. In some measure I adopted his ironies, his postures, even his smile. Eventually we introduced ourselves; he was, as Abu Taleb had guessed, Nabil Farah. He asked if I had children, as if we were seeing each other for the first time.

"Where did you grow up, by the way?" He knew, of course, but he had to pretend.

"Not the United States," I said. "In fact, I grew up in Ramallah."

"Ramallah, Palestine?"

I nodded.

"So your father was Carey Hampton of the Ramallah School?"

"Yes. And I went there. To school, I mean."

"Did you know Mohamed Dajani there? Or Hasan Abdul Hayy?"

"Not well, but they were in my class." It was true I had not known Mohamed well. As for Abu Kerim, known formally as Hasan Abdul Hayy, if Pinstripe knew about our friendship, little harm was done. If not, no harm at all. Abu Kerim had signaled a charade, but until I identified the audience – was it just the Lebanese generals? – I had to move with care.

Pinstripe looked at the table, where the food was now less bountiful. His face showed no expression. I thought again. If he knew about my friendship with Abu Kerim, he now knew, if he hadn't before, that I lied. He turned to me with a pleasant smile.

"Perhaps you knew my cousin Yusuf Ghashmawi?"

"Yes, indeed. Again not well. What has happened to him?"

And so we proceeded, people and places, in almost the same style as before, less ironic, more direct. He set the style; I followed.

The dining room had almost emptied. One of the Lebanese wives, big-bosomed and wide-hipped, moved by us and jostled Pinstripe's arm. Her clumsy lurch sent the fork resting on his empty plate hurtling toward the floor. The speed of his reflexes strained belief. Moving his body in such a way that he avoided jostling her in return, he bent and caught the fork before it hit the ground; in almost the same motion he bowed slightly and in answer to her apologies said in French it was nothing, really nothing. Intrigued by his looks and manners, she hesitated a moment, tempted to stay and chat, but his careful politeness moved her on to the other room, where in any case the Maronite contingent was about to depart.

He looked after her and at the departing generals. What I saw in his face matched his words.

"It is my honor to be a so-called Christian, and these are my Christian cousins in Lebanon. How charming they are, all fat and intent on money." The last words came out in academic mode, dispassionate and analytical, but the context was hate. I wondered how he had grown up. Nothing usual about him. After those quick reflexes, I was drawn to notice the body signs of physical conditioning, the tautness and muscularity of the flesh above the collar, the ruggedness of the wrists, the flatness of the stomach, the catlike stance.

"All fat and intent on money," I repeated. "Are fatness and avarice always linked?"

"Touché. You must forgive me my prejudices, as I forgive you yours. What are yours, by the way?"

"Too numerous to mention."

We talked on a bit. Soon we were the only ones left in the dining room.

*   *   *

In the other room a hard core of Palestinians, perhaps ten, stood in a circle speaking intently in Arabic. One was the tall economist. Otherwise, aside from Frances, who rested quietly in an easy chair in the entrance hall, and the three young waiters in white jackets, everyone had gone. The waiters, clearly Palestinians also, were clearing up and listening hard at the edge of the circle. I saw the bulge of guns under the white jackets.

With nods to each other, Pinstripe and I parted company, he to join the circle, I to join Frances in the entrance hall. I took a chair next to her. She looked tired, perhaps near tears, though I saw relief in her face.

"Well, Bill," she said, putting her hand for an instant on mine. "How nice."

"Same here." I sat there, liking her. "Quite an effort. And I gather a success."

"Mohamed thinks it's just a step. But a necessary one." She lowered her voice, glancing into the living room, and gave a deep uncertain sigh. "He'll tell you tomorrow. And I'm to tell you Abu Kerim will see you then. I'll be glad when it's over."

"When what's over?"

"Tomorrow we'll ..." She stopped. The voices in the living room had risen. I knew I should leave as soon as possible. I could not help hearing snatches of discussion, tactical talk about next steps, how to keep a PLO-loyalist presence in West Beirut. Nothing to do with me. Suddenly a voice said: "What about Cairo? What does Abu Jameel say?"

I had begun to tell Frances I'd slip out and phone tomorrow when the voice of Abu Kerim broke in quickly. He spoke in English.

"Ah, our American friend is leaving. My memory is he speaks Arabic like I do." He laughed like a politician, left the circle, came quickly into the entrance hall. "I hope we see each other again." The Palestinians received the message to say nothing more. I received a message also: leave now. I shook hands all round, thanked Mohamed for having me, expressed the hope, rather formally, that I would see him and Frances before I left or on my next trip. I felt Pinstripe watching my performance. When I shook hands with him, he said he had enjoyed our conversation. Abu Kerim pressed my hand in the manner of one saying goodbye to a long-time but unvalued acquaintance.

What was it someone had asked? "What about Cairo? What does Abu Jameel say?" Who was Abu Jameel?

*   *   *

I made my way down the stairs into the dark street to find that the soldiers and cars had gone. My gut tightened as if on signal. I stood a moment planning the best route through the darkness to the lights of the main streets downhill. Then I remembered I was not alone, and when I started through the first section of ruts and rubble, my two leather-jacketed escorts fell into place behind me.

When we moved into narrower streets, the darkness made the footing harder to handle. We began making slower headway. My escorts gradually closed in until they were less than three yards behind me. We picked our way along, almost companionably, moving like a night patrol in enemy territory, ready for trouble, exchanging no words.

Trouble arrived at twenty yards from the wide well-lit street that held the Commodore. Moving toward the light as fast as footing allowed, through the rocky jumble of a narrow lane, we saw a car on the wide street draw up and block the lane's exit. I had time to see a driver and two others, then one of my escorts hit me hard with his body, pushed me over and down to the side. Guns fired in both directions. I scuttled behind a chunk of cement and lay flat. The firing continued, then the car drove off with a flapping noise as from a flat tire.

My escorts came over and pulled me to my feet. One of them had been hit in the right arm, was bleeding freely. Still wordless, we used my tie to fashion a sling for him, and I showed him where to press to stop the flow of blood. They reloaded their guns, put them back into the pockets of their leather jackets. We set out toward the Commodore. I took a deep breath.

"Hezbollah?" I asked. I named a splinter group of pro-Iranian Shiites who had kidnapped a few foreigners.

"No," said the wounded one in Arabic. "Not kidnappers. Killers. Palestinians. They wanted to kill the three of us."

I looked at the other man. He was smiling, like a boy who has just won a race. "I killed one," he said, exultant. At the hotel door the wounded one said he'd return my tie in the morning. I told him to keep it and said he should come in to find a doctor. He shook his head. "The best thing is for you to get inside the hotel quickly," he said.

The one who was not wounded came in with me and sat down in the lobby. When I looked back from the elevator, the flush of success had not left his face.

EIGHT

Beirut, May 1990

That night I slept fitfully but better than expected, perhaps because sleep permitted retreat from thinking about consequences if my escort had been a second slower. I felt knots in my stomach when I got out of bed.

In the breakfast room sat the usual collection of journalists who use the Commodore as a communications center. I'd known one of them, a Britisher named Reginald Hughes, for six years. He had me on his list of people to check with whenever he came to Cairo, and so I saw him every four months on routine visits or when special events were occurring. In his mind I think I was labeled "American business community, Cairo branch." Like many journalists who cover Israel and the Arabs, he operated out of the Greek side of divided Cyprus. He was called by his full name, not "Reg" or "Reggie." I never failed to enjoy his company.

I sat at his table and watched him adjust. To him I was momentarily out of context. Hoping for some useful long-distance coverage, he asked me about Egypt and what was happening "in your part of it." He finally gave up; my mind was rejecting Egypt. We shifted to general chatter about the Levant. He said he'd decided to stay on the Christian side in the future, make only quick trips to Ras Beirut. I said I'd probably do the same. He entertained me with stories he'd been on recently. He had me almost laughing.

Given what was happening in my life, especially the previous evening's grim conclusion, how could I almost laugh? Yet I did, almost. Deep down, I think, the tense feeling was switching to resentment and anger. Anger at being fired at, anger at whoever was responsible for pushing me around. The anger was satisfying, relaxing, liberating. It put me closer to laughter.

"With your contacts around here," said Reginald, "you may have run into some rumors I want to get more on, though I must say I'm having a hard time." He put two heaping spoonfuls of sugar in his coffee. "A couple of weeks ago, in Nicosia, a Palestinian friend told me the pro-Arafat loyalists had internal problems, serious disagreements on whether to begin private conversations again with the U.S. Almost a repeat of '82. Recognition of Israel by the PLO in return for U.S. recognition of the PLO."

"You mean the same deal is brewing again?"

"So this fellow thinks in Nicosia. Anything ring a bell?"

For a moment, only a moment, I flirted with the notion of giving this nice fellow a hint about other goings-on. But it could not help and might hurt.

"That rumor surfaces every six months," I said, offhandedly. Was Hughes, I wondered, what he seemed to be? Had our meeting that morning been more than a coincidence? I shrugged the thought away; I was developing a spy's mentality. Not everyone was part of a plot. He had to be what he seemed, a bright amusing British newsman, fortyish, dressed in British blazer and striped tie, dark hair covering half the ears, slender enough to take two sugars in his coffee.

Hughes stared into his cup a moment, as if deciding something.

"Listen, Bill," he said, "I'd like to tell you something in confidence, I promised this fellow I'd tell absolutely no one, but you're the kind who just might know something."

"Sure, try me." I glanced at my watch.

"It'll only take a minute. This fellow says a hardline faction of Fatah has easy access into the CIA. That someone very highly placed is telling them if they'll agree to this old deal again, the Americans will not only recognize them but can also deliver an Israeli agreement to negotiate."

"Come on, Reginald."

"I'm just telling you what this fellow said. Bill, I can tell you for a fact he *believes* he's telling me the straight story and he's in a good position to know."

"If I had a dollar for every crazy story out of Nicosia, I'd be a rich man." I wanted to know a bit more. "Who was this man connected with? What makes you think he knows what he's talking about?"

He shook his head. "No more information. If it got out they were playing with the CIA, there'd be hell to pay. Listen, this is somebody who's never let me down. What do you think?"

"Afraid I can't help with sources," I said. "I wouldn't know how to start. Best of luck. Sounds interesting."

His face showed disappointment, as if he expected me to bring up a gold nugget from the muck of people I knew. To how many people, I wondered, had the CIA said it could "deliver an Israeli agreement"? Had the CIA promised conflicting Israeli agreements-to-negotiate, one to a hardline faction of the PLO's Fatah and one to Bill Hampton's friend from school days? To soften the impact of my casual response, I sought to change the subject.

"Are you still covering Israel?"

"Yes, I'm off to Jerusalem in a couple of days."

"I'll be there in a few days myself."

"You're going *there*?" He sounded surprised. "I thought Israel was outside your territory."

I remembered Hughes had a prodigious memory for trivia. I regretted mentioning Jerusalem. "The company wants to develop the market a bit. Apparently it's lying fallow."

He absorbed this information thoughtfully, spooning out sugar from the bottom of his cup.

"The British always like sugar and chocolate. Our parents did without both during the second war, passed on their cravings through their genes." He made a satisfied noise as he licked his spoon. "By the way, don't I remember you spent time around Jerusalem when you were growing up?"

"Yes, a little." I felt he was pushing me, about to ask for help I didn't want to provide.

"And you did your secondary work at the Ramallah School. Or do I remember wrong?

"No, you're right." I smiled, trying not to look sheepish. Hughes grinned. He was ahead of me.

"Don't panic," he said. "I'm not going to ask you to introduce me to old friends. But I'll see you in Jerusalem, maybe try out some ideas on you. How about it?"

I had to smile, partly out of relief, partly because Hughes' grin was infectious.

"Sure," I said.

We wandered toward the door of the Commodore. A new man sat in the lobby but the bulge in the leather jacket attested to his job. Hughes had appointments in Ras Beirut, mine were set up for the other side. He wished me good business fortune and strode off.

*   *   *

I looked around for my cab driver and heard a honk as his Ford came neatly to the curb where I stood. The driver, small and compact with a bristling moustache, opened the door and bounced out like a gymnast. He answered to the name Ahmad. Everything he did, he did with bounce. I always asked for him, and I tipped him well because he got me around the city without being killed. On an up-to-the-minute basis he knew how to avoid gunfire and debris, how to cope with whatever militia controlled a given neighborhood, whom to see or threaten to call in case of trouble.

We sped off toward the Museum crossing, where we would cross the so-called Green Line that divided the city. I had appointments with Christians. As Ahmad drove, skillfully skirting potholes and rock piles, he kept up a running report on conditions, including the previous night's fractional shifts in loyalty and territorial control. He thought today would be easy, he said. He'd heard a rumor the Lebanese Army planned to take over two small areas of West Beirut; if so, fighting more severe than usual would break out soon. With an unsatisfied expression, glancing at me in the mirror, he told me the blue Chevrolet that had followed us yesterday was following us today. I did not turn round to look, but I was glad to know that at least one of my two friends from the Commodore lobby was on the job.

At the western end of the Museum crossing a Syrian sergeant and a militiaman from the Shiite Amal looked at my passport perfunctorily. The Amal militiaman wore a Lebanese Army uniform, frayed, with key buttons replaced by nondescript substitutes, meaning he had deserted the Army in February '84 when the Amal called for all good Shiites to change sides. They nodded greetings at Ahmad, who smiled amiably. He began the crossing in low gear. All around us stood grotesque cement shapes, buildings at every stage of decay and destruction, like row on row of giant gravestones fractured haphazardly. Occasional piles of sand, once used to bar traffic, had been excavated into soft tracks. When I looked back, I caught a glimpse of my Palestinian watchdog, seated beside the driver of the blue Chevrolet, settling in to await my return.

Three blocks farther along, we came to the Damascus Road, the heart of no-man's land, grass growing from cracks in the pavement. Three blocks later, at the eastern end, a Lebanese Army sergeant and a Falange militiaman waved us through, and as we moved into the heart of Christian Beirut, signs of unrandom behavior began to appear again. Buildings were patched up, store fronts glassed in and painted, streets cleared and some of them cleaned.

Georges Mounir, a business acquaintance of long standing, lived and had his office in a partially restored building. I climbed three flights of stairs to reach the two cluttered rooms from which he ran his sales empire. One room contained a slovenly secretary, a blowzy woman with stringy hair who sat at a small desk with a telephone but no typewriter; the other room had a larger desk, three straight chairs, a telephone, and a lamp with a torn shade. In both rooms mountains of paper were stacked on expensive parquet floors. Otherwise the rooms had nothing, no filing cabinets, no pictures or posters on the white plaster walls. Yet Georges can sell anything I provide, some of which I know goes to Syria. The window in Georges' office, where I took a seat, looked out on other buildings and shells of buildings.

After our review of business affairs, I got up to go. I had a busy morning ahead of me.

"Sit for a minute more," he said, wanting me to understand he did not mean longer than that. "I have something to tell you."

But he did not tell me right away. Balancing his heavy body on his chair's rear legs, he leaned back slightly. His stomach hung out grossly over his belt. What gray hair remained was carefully combed to cover some of the baldness. The blue eyes, set deeply into a fleshy florid face, surveyed me thoughtfully.

"We have had," he said finally, "a good business relationship. Is this not true?"

"Yes, indeed." I forced extra enthusiasm into my voice. But it was true. Georges understood how to sell, and with some arm-twisting at the San Francisco end, I managed to get extra merchandise to him. He did what I wanted other agents to do, develop a network of part-time technicians to handle maintenance problems among his clients. Though a staunch Maronite and crammed with Falangist prejudices against Muslims, Druse, Palestinians, and such fellow Christians as Greek Orthodox and Armenians, Georges allowed none of these to interfere with his dogged pursuit of a hefty Swiss bank account that would one day permit a pleasant life for himself and his family somewhere else in the world. He had two sons doing graduate work in the United States; I assumed he hoped devoutly they would marry Americans in order to simplify immigration for the rest of the Mounirs. He told me once he wanted to get out before the Christians started killing each other "as if they were Muslims or Druse."

"I hope," he said, "our relationship will continue that way. I have invested much effort into promoting the name of Starr Johnson in the, uh, Eastern Mediterranean, and despite the troubles my effort has been quite successful. Would you agree?"

"Yes, certainly."

"But if you should be transferred to another post or for some reason should no longer be the Starr Johnson representative for this area, my effort would be less successful. For instance, I would have to develop a new relationship with a new representative. Valuable time would be lost at a time when the market for Starr Johnson products has never been better."

"Well, I have no plans to change posts at the moment, and certainly any successor would be well-disposed toward you. I would see to that." I meant extra amounts of merchandise would continue to come his way.

"I'm pleased to hear it. A nice compliment." His smile was warm, a reorganization of the jowls that provided a glimpse of what a younger Georges must have looked like. He hesitated a moment. "Does your San Francisco office agree with you? This is all in writing somewhere?" His chair creaked as he shifted his weight and brought the chair down onto all fours. "Please, it is simply a matter of personal security, just in case something should happen to you."

He did not sound like someone taking a routine precaution. Nor did he intend I should think so. The blue eyes regarded me steadily.

"*What* might happen to me?"

"Yes, that is the question. What might happen to you?" The chair rocked back onto two legs. "As you know, I have many connections, friends of all kinds. Business friends. Sometimes little bits that are not business get dropped. I do not believe all I hear, I simply pass this on because we are friends, because you should know what people are saying. They are saying you are involved in Palestinian politics." The last two words were uttered as if they were obscene.

"Whom did you hear this from?" I tried on an amused look.

"From a friend. A friend I trust. He has connections with Fatah." He kept his eyes on me, assessing my postures of disbelief, of tolerant amusement. "Please do not be amused," he went on. "Please take what I say seriously. Business" – this was the clincher – "will suffer. You'll be excluded from business dealings by the enemies of Palestinians, and there are now many such people."

"I'm grateful to you, Georges, for letting me know about this."

"So be careful. Very careful. I know little of such matters, but my friend said you should be careful about your life." His eyes scanned my face. "Yes, your life. He did not say, I doubt if he knew, why worry about your life. He was just repeating what he heard."

My throat was suddenly dry. He saw me swallow. I let my breath out slowly, remembering the sound of gunfire in the dark side street.

"When did your friend tell you this?"

"Two or three weeks ago. He said you were taking sides. Working with one group of Palestinians against others. Probably there is little to fear. A rumor could have been planted to frighten you away from something. Who knows? But it is a signal, a signal to be watchful."

"Did your friend say anything more I should know about?"

"No, nothing else." He paused. "Well, one other thing but I discount it, because I've heard it so often about Americans, or at least Americans who appear to know about Arabs."

"You mean, working for the CIA?"

Again his face reorganized itself into a smile. "Yes, the old story. And what a silly one."

He turned to look at me. The bright light from the window was on my face. For a moment I tried to look like a non-spy, then decided to smile. I said I'd make sure our successful business relationship was on record in San Francisco. He thanked me warmly for my willingness to help his "family's future," a phrase that struck me as particularly honest. Before I started down the three flights of stairs, we shook hands.

"Be watchful," he said. He made it sound like a blessing.

*   *   *

Ahmad took me back through no-man's land and left me at the campus gate, where I showed my passport to the guard. The campus, I thought, seemed untouched by the chaos around it. Things were in order at the American University. A gardener mowed the lawns, another adjusted the sprinkler system. Moving back and forth on well-swept walks, students and teachers paused to chat. I heard snatches of conversation, about campus events, not the violence outside.

The campus, a friend once told me, would remain an oasis of peace no matter who controlled Ras Beirut and the western part of the city, because the slope of the campus descended so sharply toward the sea. The fighting specialized in weapons with flat trajectories, and so the grounds, he said wishfully, would remain bullet-free. I looked down the hill at the blue of the Mediterranean. My father always insisted that AUB and Robert College in Stamboul had the most beautiful campuses in the world.

Nearby, up the hill around the Commodore, lived a lot of the faculty, an area less quiet than the campus, though quieter than other parts of the city. Bouts of fighting took place there, but murders, symbolic rather than vengeful, occurred only occasionally. What garnered big headlines were kidnappings of prominent people, especially Europeans and Americans, including an acting president of the university in '82.

Down here on campus, despite my friend's theories, bullets had intruded from time to time — with the likelihood of other bullets always hovering nearby. When the Shiite Amal moved to take control of Ras Beirut in '84, its Christian defenders inadvertently hit a few university buildings, lobbing some misdirected shells. The same occurred in '85. Each time a campus atmosphere reasserted itself, and it became almost the same as before. A carefully cultivated, almost conspiratorial illusion of serenity kept academic life bearable.

Another campus event, also in '84, came close to shattering the illusion. An unidentified group, grown somewhere in Lebanon's rich soil of hate, murdered the new president in broad daylight in the main administration building. The assassins shot with pin-point accuracy, and they left the campus and disappeared as easily as they had come. Perhaps a kind of serenity returned, but despair had come one step closer.

In my teens I had wanted to go to the American University of Beirut but my father dissuaded me. So did Abu Hisham and the other two, though with regret. "No matter what happens," my father said, "you'll always be an American, so you must learn about America, do what other Americans do." Yet he admired AUB, calling it "a great center of freedom and reason." I looked about me. Seated on some steps at my left a group of students chatted and postured as if carefree, but the set of the shoulders and the sag of the mouths, I thought, showed defeat. Life in Lebanon offered them nothing. Only a melancholy pride in "freedom and reason" – and emigration.

Entering the administration building, I ducked out the back and went to the building next door where Mohamed Dajani had his office. The tiny subterfuge would fool no one, and why I did it I do not know. Perhaps an impulse linked to my escape the evening before or to the conversation that morning with Georges Mounir. I acknowledged to myself my state of mind had entered yet another phase. Anger aimed at my enemies, who-ever they were, now brought an odd satisfaction. An intense alertness gripped me, even more than before. Any sound, normal or unusual, inter-ested me. A friend of my father's, an infantryman from World War II, once told me the joy of walking in the woods had been forever taken from him; at every turn on a country trail he could imagine where the snipers were located, just as they had been on Luzon. As I walked up the narrow stairs, I imagined gunmen with silencers around the corners of the land-ings. I took a deep breath.

Through the half-open door of Mohamed's office, I saw Frances Da-jani, who smiled and held out her hand. Her hair, which had been piled high the evening before, was collected in a bun at the back of her neck.

"Sit down," she said, "let's chat till the others come. I was sent over to hold the fort, to tell you they'd be late."

I selected one of the ten chairs placed with their backs to the book-lined walls. Frances sat in Mohamed's chair behind the desk, the one from which he conducted seminars for his graduate students. I repressed an urge to get up and close the door.

"So," I said, "tell me what's happening."

"Oh Bill, it's all coming apart. I hope we can put it back together again. I mean, our personal lives. It's all so scary."

"Tell me."

"Mohamed will tell you about the party last night and all that. What I should tell you is we're leaving. For the States. In three days, if the air-port's open. All of us. We'll stay with my parents a while, then go to Provo. Mohamed has a one-year contract at Utah." The words rushed out, then stopped just as suddenly. She looked at me and sighed.

"Are you glad?" I asked finally.

"Oh gosh." It was a cry from a tortured heart. She desperately wanted to stay, desperately wanted to go. "We just have to go now. Especially since last night. Mohamed's farewell gesture, the last thing he could do for Palestine. But the intrigue. You wouldn't believe. And the things he's said, publicly, ever since we decided to leave, things against the groups that aren't loyal. Everyone knows now that Mohamed's a loyalist to the PLO and Arafat. He's a target for the others, and we don't know who some of them are. We think Abu Mousa and his hardliners in Iraq have people here masquerading. We have to get out."

Yes, it had long since come to this, Palestinians killing Palestinians in a war fought underground. This woman could have left but her breeding told her to be true-blue. Now she was caught in the war's ambushes and booby-traps. Tears filled the dark eyes.

"What about the children? Where were they last night?"

"With friends. I'll pick them up later." She brushed away a couple of the tears. "I've been tired lately. It'll be all right after we leave. The nearer it gets, the more worried Mohamed gets, and the guiltier he feels about the sinking ship. So he made all those statements and offered to give that party for the cause. He's tired too."

She fiddled with paperclips on Mohamed's desk, rearranging them, hooking them together.

"Do you think we should stay? Should I persuade him to stay?" Her voice was low. She looked up from the desktop. "Perhaps you're the only one I can talk to who understands."

"Mohamed understands as well as I do," I said. "And I agree with him. Leave as soon as you can. The academic year is almost over. The sooner the better. Don't open up the question again, don't ask him to decide the same thing a second time. Just go."

"Yes," she said softly. She looked up again and gave me a smile, a social reflex to express her thanks. For several breaths we sat quietly, following separate lines of thought. I thought about shortening my stay in Beirut, getting back to the order and security of Jerusalem.

She asked about my wife and children in the tone of one being courteous, but I sensed she wanted to know. I gave her the latest news, and she said she was glad things went well for me. She stood up.

"I'll leave you here, I think. They should be along any minute. When do you leave?"

"In three days. Friday morning, same as you." But earlier if I could, I thought.

"Come for supper tomorrow night," she said. "Just a pick-up supper. You can see the kids."

I said it was no time for the Dajanis to have guests for supper, but she insisted. She said they'd "shoo me out" early. She kissed my cheek and left.

*   *   *

I did not have long to wait. Soon I heard footsteps in the corridor. Two people, no voices. The door swung wide. Abu Kerim came in first, and we embraced, patting each other on the back, murmuring the greetings we hadn't voiced at the party. Mohamed watched the reunion, smiling, and carefully closed the door. I understood we should keep our voices down.

"Well, well," said Abu Kerim, holding me by the shoulders at arm's length, "you look all right. Quite all right."

"And you? How is it with you? Health."

"Okay. I should get more exercise, but okay, basically okay." He took my question as seriously as it was meant. "Family?"

"Okay. Kids are fine. Cath knows something's up, but doesn't know what." It was all staccato shorthand. Our friendship started up again like warm well-made machinery. The two of us constituted half of our unbreakable group of four that would last until death. Mohamed watched the quick resumption of friendship with sympathy but worry made the lines on his face seem deeper than the night before. He pointed to the far corner of the office. The three of us sat down, looked at each other, then Abu Kerim wordlessly reached out a hand to each of us, like a silent secular grace to bless what we had to say.

"These are," he said, releasing our hands, "dangerous hours for all of us. We must say much to each other in a short time. Let us begin by apologizing to Bill about last night. Mohamed?"

The latter gave a quick nod. "Yes, we apologize for springing that on you. You reacted well, and by now you understand what was happening. All those factions – Lebanese, Palestinian, even Syrian. Things have moved fast here in Beirut. Thanks to Abu Kerim, the PLO can now stay in Ras Beirut, at more or less the level of an unofficial embassy. It took hours of negotiating, with the Shiite Amal, with the Druse, especially with the Falange. We kept the army till last. Even though Amal now runs West Beirut, we need an all-Beirut agreement because we don't know what will happen next."

A deft summary of what I had already inferred.

"Are we talking PLO or just Fatah?" I asked.

"Both. Abu Kerim will be Arafat's personal representative. He'll act in both capacities. The PLO factions in Damascus would accept this."

"And Syria?"

"Well, we expected them to kick up a big fuss with Amal and the Druse. But then something happened, we don't know what. We think the Assad brothers decided it would be smart to have a minor loyalist counterweight here in Beirut."

"How did you get people to talk to each other?"

"There's been a lull, as you know. The Green Line is now just a frontier, not a battleground. And it might get even better. Senior people from each side go back and forth, starting with social reasons but now they talk politics, try to find formulas. We had to get our agreement while the lull was on. Last night you saw the results."

He held up his hand. Footsteps sounded outside. We waited until we heard a door close down the corridor.

"And why your place, for God's sake?"

"A lot of reasons I won't bore you with. It turned out to be the only possible place."

"Guilt feelings?"

"Take my word for it. There was no other way."

Abu Kerim broke in. "He's right, Bill. No other way. Anyway, there's no time to go into it."

"All right," I went on, "another question. What do you offer? Why should any of them like you?" The only issue most Lebanese could agree on was dislike of Palestinians.

"Ah, the key question." Abu Kerim took over, pleased to give the answer, as if acknowledging authorship of a good book. "Neutrality, that's what we offer. Non-participation. Non-participation in Lebanese politics. We'll be on nobody's side. We don't have a militia any more, or at least we can make a good case we don't, so now they're all pleased to have the legitimate PLO here as a neutral. If any Palestinian militia controlled by Syrians tries to control some territory in the mountains, any Lebanese government can deny its legitimacy because of the loyalists down here in Beirut."

I nodded. Approvingly.

"Everybody's happy so far," he went on, "except of course for traitors. We cleared it with Tunis and Arafat." His eyes gave him away, I thought, just as they used to. He was stretched close to the limit. With Abu Kerim you could always tell from the eyes. One more small pull and ...

"So you sealed the deal last night. Now the real question. Why invite *me*?"

The other two glanced at each other. Abu Kerim answered.

"I asked Mohamed to ask you. For one thing, Maronites are always impressed by Americans. For another we had to tell you about this meeting today without putting anything on paper. As of now only the three of us plus Frances know about it."

"Come on, old friend."

"Yes, there are other reasons."

He got up, walked to the door, came back to his chair.

"This corner of the office, if we speak low, is secure. Mohamed and I tested it." He was stalling.

"You want *me* to tell *you* what the other reasons are?"

"Why not?" Abu Kerim gave a quick grin, a little like old times.

"One reason," I said, "has to be that a lot of people know about me and Abu Hisham. I assume the word has gotten around, a lot more than I thought. An anti-PLO plot? A plot to exclude the PLO? So I had to be paraded. Just in case your boys ever needed to know what I looked like."

"And another reason?"

"More crucially, to show we weren't close friends, just acquaintances from school."

"It was important." He sounded defensive. "Important for all our sakes. Listen, I don't want to run out of time. Let me tell you what I know, then you fill in." He glanced at Mohamed. "Mohamed knows what I know."

Abu Kerim got up again, paced the office, then remembered and came back to our corner. He ran his hand over the dark moustache.

"What I know is you've been approached to talk to Abu Hisham. By the Americans. To persuade him to represent Palestine in talks with the Israelis. Without PLO approval. True so far?"

"Yes. How did you know?"

"I can't tell you that. But it wasn't Abu Taleb. As far as I know, he knows nothing."

"Yes, he does. I told him." I paused. "Was it you who sent Nabil Farah to watch me?"

"Of course."

"Why?"

"Should be obvious. The word was out. You were going to be asked to see Abu Hisham. Up here we knew all about it. If we knew, others knew. I sent two people to keep an eye on you, people I could trust. I thought others would also send people. To scare you off or do you harm."

"Did those others kill Mousa Sabri?" I thought of the body, dead and lonely, propped against a tree.

"Yes, the one that was left. After Nabil caught them trying to kill you."

"And who were they?"

"Not sure. One of the Damascus factions. Probably PFLP-General Command. Gebril's outfit."

"And how come Farah knew where I lived but the other two didn't till later?"

"I told Farah, but the word around here was you had children at some American school. They started there."

"Did you," I asked, "tell Farah to check on me or protect me?"

"Both. I didn't mention being old friends. I said it would be bad for our moderate image if you were harmed. After the remaining Damascus boy killed Mousa, he left Egypt, so Farah left too."

I stared at the shelves behind Mohamed's desk. They were crammed with scholarly books in three languages. Could scholarship prevent killing?

"Who is Abu Jameel in Cairo?" I asked. The words I'd overheard at the Dajani apartment had lingered on.

"You should not know and you must not ask." His tone indicated that discussion about this would be a waste of time.

"All right, let's go back to last night. How can it be a secret we're good friends?"

"Ah," he said, the hand stroking the moustache again. "Sometimes, if you do something publicly enough, people come to believe. Last night was important, I mean aside from the parading. At the moment nobody knows we're close friends. Or so I think. I've been back over the times we met before in Beirut, even that time we sat outside at the coffee house in Rue Hamra. I don't think anybody focused. If they did, there's nothing that couldn't be explained. Just as a precaution, for years I've never mentioned anyone from Ramallah, especially Abu Hisham but also you and Abu Taleb, except to say, if required, I remember you and was acquainted."

I wanted to break in, to tell him I knew the rest, but he raised his hand.

"No, let me say it. If nobody knows we're close friends, it's easier for me to make moves that protect Abu Hisham, and now you. I won't get accused of conflict of interest. We don't know who the spies are. If the rebels got hold of the information we were old friends and passed it to the legitimate factions in Damascus, I'd be guilty by association, an old friend of someone working for the Americans to get Abu Hisham to talk to the Israelis. Then they'd find out Abu Hisham and I were old friends too. Then they'd put the word out it was a conspiracy. Then some of us would get killed."

"But a lot of people have to know about you and Abu Hisham." And you and me, I thought. I tried to keep fear out of my voice.

"No, they don't," he said. "and they won't unless there's a reason to believe it. Most of my colleagues are younger, and if they run across some older person who was at Ramallah when we were, I've worked out credible ways of denying the whole story. Don't forget, I haven't seen Abu Hisham since we were students, not even that time he was exiled." He looked at Mohamed, then back at me. "And who knows, sometime down the road that old friendship might be useful, providing no one knows about it until the clinching moment. And perhaps that moment will come sooner than we think."

"How come?"

"Things are changing, Fatah has changed. Arafat now thinks moderation is a good thing."

"And do you?"

"Its hour has almost come."

I looked at him hard. Had he just said something important? I wanted to ask a lot more, about where he stood, about Fatah, but there was no time. I came back to my own danger.

"Does Nabil Farah know we're old friends?"

"Not unless you told him last night when you talked in the dining room. But he could find out if he wanted to. He could find out about Abu Hisham and me if he wanted to. So could anybody. We just have to pretend, proceed as if we weren't friends and hope for the best. The important thing is not to give anybody a reason to inquire."

The dark eyes were at their most intense. "Mohamed and I had to decide whether we should brief you before the party. But how? Where? I told Mohamed it'd be better anyway to tell you nothing. If we told you about it, you'd worry, start working out your lies beforehand, and mess things up. But if you had to improvise, you'd do fine."

We remembered other times, close to smiling. It occurred to me he'd become less of a risk taker, more of an analyst. Cooler. But yes, stretched tight, very tight. As I was, I thought. I glanced at Mohamed, who sat unsmiling. His face held an expression of tense inquiry, a touch of anger.

"Why," he asked, "have you agreed to do this thing, to betray us? To reach an agreement without involving the PLO? Of course you are an American, we know that, and so perhaps we should expect nothing else. But I would have guessed otherwise about you. I ask this not because it will affect our friendship but I want to know."

Yet I knew an element of our friendship was at stake. Abu Kerim nodded as if the question were no surprise and reached out a hand to each of us.

"Mohamed asks a fair question, which I also ask," he said. The hands were withdrawn. The moustache was stroked again, a new habit. "But because I know Bill so well, perhaps I know some answers. If I guess right, Bill is caught by our politics and must find a way out without harm to himself. He's now an assassination target for hardliners, inside and outside the PLO, even inside Fatah, and it makes no difference whether he intends to intervene or not. Even if it were known he refused to intervene, he is still subject to the revenge of some perverted mind, a symbolic killing to show the United States it must pay attention to us. Am I near the truth, Bill?"

He spoke as if he had been on a pleasant stroll through part of my mind.

"Yes, as far as you go."

He looked at me blankly for a moment. I remembered the look. Behind the blank stare a new set of arguments was being prepared and tested.

"Ah yes," he said, "the ideological rationalization. Peace, compromise, non-violence. I should have remembered." He rubbed his eyes with both hands. "There is not the time to indulge ourselves in this old story. If we'd followed the advice of you and your father, there would be no PLO and no Palestine. Before Arafat, we could have sat with the Israelis and talked peace and practiced non-violence — and the Jews would have taken everything. But when we offer to talk from a position of greater strength, they refuse to talk. Why? Because they know they will refuse to compromise and they don't want the rest of the world to know."

"Why would it hurt to put your theories to the test?" I found myself leaning forward, speaking intently. "What do you lose by talking? There might be solutions you never imagined."

"Listen," he said impatiently, "we've been willing to talk. Everyone knows that, though apparently you don't. Tell that to the Israelis. The only people they're willing to talk to are people they can push around." He leaned back and let his breath out in a kind of half whistle. I felt intensely sorry for him. He had too little time, too much responsibility. The rubber band was stretching, stretching …

"Bill," he said, sounding patient, "you know and I know they couldn't push Abu Hisham around at the negotiating table. And we know he knows that Palestinians on the West Bank would insist on PLO approval. Then why would the Israelis agree to talk to Abu Hisham and not us? Why? Something's wrong."

"Listen," I said, "you're a politician. You understand that no Israeli government could talk to the PLO and stay in power. There's a reason why they'd agree to talk to Abu Hisham. It's an indirect way of talking to *you*."

"We're wasting time," he said. "For two reasons. First, if the Israelis are willing to talk to anybody, it's because they see an unfair advantage. Second, Abu Hisham will not agree to talk with them anyway. He is not crazy. He likes life."

"Sure, it's a risk. But the security in Jerusalem is good."

"Jerusalem is vulnerable, don't underestimate our factions. They can penetrate. Listen, some of them don't like what they perceive as treacherous behavior. Any communication with the enemy, short of dictating terms at the end of a successful war, is considered treason. Which means death. You know I don't hold with that; talking with the Israelis would not be treason, just misguided and stupid."

"Hence the attack last night? Am I a traitor or just a blundering American?"

"What attack last night?" Mohamed was staring.

"Bill was ambushed last night," said Abu Kerim. "My boys saved him. Yes, you're a blundering American for some, a traitor for others."

Mohamed let his breath out heavily, sat back in his chair, shook his head as if trying to shake something off.

"Listen," Abu Kerim said, "just so you understand the position, I have a question to ask."

"Go ahead."

"Suppose, just suppose, that I thought you or Abu Hisham or both could be successful in doing what you plan to try to do, what would be my only honorable course?"

"Kill us, I suppose."

"Yes, either that or kill myself or resign and go to work in Kuwait. What you should understand is this: I myself would have to face the problem of whether or not to have you killed. Others more so."

"Okay, I've received that message." My heart was pumping. "So now that you think Abu Hisham won't even consider what I suggest, I'm no longer a problem for you. But I am for others."

"Yes, lots of people." Abu Kerim had the look of a teacher going over old ground with a poor pupil. "Don't count on rationality. I've already explained this. Some of our people are almost paranoid from frustration. To kill a meddling American would be satisfying. So would killing a moderate like Abu Hisham."

"If it is known what I intend to do, then it is already known about Abu Hisham. So he's in the same danger."

Abu Kerim looked over at Mohamed and signaled him to respond, as if needing a respite from talk, as if he'd expended all his energy backing away from a black hole.

"Bill," said Mohamed, "we don't know who knows what. And Abu Hisham may have made some moves we don't know about." The lines on the tired face were deeper. "But the more the meddling, the greater the danger, just as a general proposition. You should leave Beirut as soon as possible. What are your plans?"

"I leave Friday."

"Are you really going to Jerusalem?"

"Yes. Frances asked me to come by for supper tomorrow night."

"God," said Abu Kerim.

"No," said Mohamed, "don't come. I'll explain and give her your love. We'll see you in the States."

"I presume," said Abu Kerim, "you'll see Abu Hisham."

Mohamed looked at him sharply.

"Yes, Mohamed, he has to. He's caught. Leave the Quaker talk aside for the moment. It's irrelevant. He's got to find some way of getting *out* of politics, so that all of us, I mean all of us, know he's no longer *in* politics, no longer a worthy object for symbolic murder."

"But why Abu Hisham?"

"For one thing, I know very well he intends to see him no matter what we say. Very stubborn he is, especially when things are glossed over with ideas about peace and conciliation." His glance at me was a mix of affection and exasperation. He had found the energy to pull himself back from the black hole, though the eyes still sent the same messages. "He won't take my word; he has to hear it from the horse's mouth. And I presume he's worked out a safe way of seeing him." He looked at me and added, "And please don't tell me about it."

Abu Kerim got up, paced around the office, sat down again.

"The real reason for going to Jerusalem is to find a way out," he said to me. "I understand why you had to come to Beirut. You had to know who was out to get you. Okay, now you know, more or less. And why. But for finding a way out, Beirut's too chaotic. Jerusalem's nearer the action. You may have to change jobs, go back to the States. Unless you can show us all you don't matter anymore."

"How do I do that?" I was groping for a plan.

"I don't know, I don't know. Stay alive until you see an opportunity. Then take a risk. Either that or get yourself and your family out of here. Fast."

"One question."

"Go ahead."

"What about my family? What are the odds?"

"Bill," said Abu Kerim, "I can't answer with certainty. If they get you with a bomb, they don't care who else they kill. But in my experience they leave families alone if they can. That's what I *think*."

He glanced at his watch. "Now I must go. One thing more, and it's important. You know I've had a lot of experience with intelligence services. I'm a professional. I'd never do what the CIA is doing now, asking you to intervene. You're *not* a professional. You may know more about the Near East than all of Washington, but you're not a professional."

"What are you getting at?"

"I'm saying that something's not right. I don't know what it is. Somebody may be playing games. Maybe with you, maybe with Abu Hisham. This is not normal behavior for any intelligence organization. Be very careful. Please."

He let out his breath.

"We've run out of time," he said. "I'll leave first and make my own way off the campus. Bill, you leave after five minutes by the north door of the building and out the medical gate. Mohamed, you wait for a bit, then go by the main gate."

He stretched out his hands again, held our hands in his, and switched to Arabic. "So, my friends, we may see each other again, though probably not. May the blessings of God be with you. May He shine upon you."

He held our hands an instant more, then stood up. He clasped Mohamed in a close embrace. When he turned to me, he shook his head to say he had no appropriate words; his embrace was strong. It was an emotional moment. He moved toward the office door, then turned back.

"Tell Abu Hisham I love him always," he spoke hoarsely.

*   *   *

Mohamed and I sat several moments without speaking. Then, touching my arm, he said he was sorry about the invitation to supper. I asked him to give his kids a big hug from me.

"We must take no chances," he said, "any of us. It's near the end now." He paused, making up his mind about something. "Bill, there's something I'd better tell you. Just in case. We think the Nicosia faction is out to get us. Maybe including you."

"Why?"

"Abu Kerim doesn't tell me everything. But I know he's decided to put his weight behind what's happening in Tunis. Apparently the moderates are making a move to take over."

"Tell me quickly." We were running out of time.

"That's about all I know. The hardliners, especially in Nicosia, have been indiscreet. There's a rumor out they have a high-up contact in the U.S. Arafat likes to be consulted and the hardliners didn't talk to him first."

"Why would hardliners want to target me?"

"They must know about Abu Hisham."

He had run out of information. We had time for a few words about his new job in the States. When I got up to go, I knew he wanted to say something else.

"That remark I made about betraying us. I'm sorry about that. I think I understand why you must proceed, and I'd forgotten about the non-violence your father used to talk about."

"Just so you understand that if I get people to talk to each other, I consider it not betrayal but the most loyal thing I can think of."

"Yes," he said, "I understand your position. I don't agree, of course. For me it is traitorous behavior. But you would expect me to disagree."

I nodded. We embraced, and I left him at his desk untangling the paper clips his wife had hooked together. I think he was pleased to have something to do with his hands.

*   *   *

The phone rang at first light, pulling me roughly out of a deep sleep. My watch showed 5:30 a.m. I'd spent the rest of the previous day seeing clients one after the other, compressing my schedule in order to leave Beirut as soon as possible.

It was the tall Palestinian economist I'd chatted with at Mohamed's big reception.

"Have you heard?" he said. He spoke in Arabic.

"No, what?" Suddenly I was wide awake.

"About last night."

"I heard nothing. What happened?"

"Your friend, your old friend from school. They killed him. Senseless, mindless."

"What old friend?"

"The unmarried one. Abu Kerim."

I tried to absorb the news. I felt short of breath, felt my heart moving into action. Perhaps it hadn't really happened.

"God," I said.

"Yes." He paused. "Very symbolic. They also killed the two guards." The line went silent a few moments. Then he spoke again.

"I'm afraid there's other bad news."

"Yes?" I held my breath.

"They bombed the Dajani flat."

"Christ."

"The whole family. No survivors."

"Christ."

"When are you leaving?" he asked.

"This afternoon. For Jerusalem."

"Leave now, right now. Museum crossing, then change taxis on the other side."

I hesitated but not for long.

"What about you?"

"I'll be here. We have to move ahead, find a new leader, take revenge."

I started to say something else, but he hung up. The light of the new day was stronger now. I began throwing things into my suitcase.

NINE

Jerusalem, May 1990

I had little to say to fellow passengers on the trip back to Jerusalem. In Damascus I scrutinized the square that serves as the transport hub, saw no person or thing out of the ordinary. Nonetheless, rather than taking a *servis*, I hired a taxi to get me quickly across the Jordan border, as if it were safer in Jordan. In Amman I shifted back to a *servis* headed for the Allenby Bridge and found I was glad to have fellow passengers again. My gut began to unknot. My mind kept trying to reject what had happened.

For the most part I stared out the window, conscious of what flickered by but not focusing. Questions fought for attention but my mind would not linger on them long enough. Why would they kill? What did it get them? Who were *they*? The candidates for evildoing equaled the number of the Eastern Mediterranean's intractable chauvinists, persons for whom murder was as normal as argument. Who stood to lose most from a PLO "embassy" in Beirut? I hoped that was the question, but deep down I think I knew it was not. The attack on me and the killing of Abu Kerim and the Dajanis had to be related. What could I have done to save their lives? Not go to Beirut?

Images of Abu Kerim from other years kept appearing. I saw him returning to the dorm from a night out in Jerusalem, the face young and happy and successful, to a barrage of hilariously ironic comments from the others. I saw him at fifteen years old, returning from a visit to Nablus.

177

He had just learned of his mother's inoperable cancer. Desperately cheerful, his eyes, as always, gave him away. Abu Hisham put his arms around him, providing a release, allowing him to sob.

As my taxi approached Amman, I became aware that tears were rolling down my cheeks, but I flicked them off quickly, almost guiltily. I had been taught not to cry. Later, near the Jordan River, the driver asked the passengers, all of whom were Palestinian except myself, if this was the first time they had come home within the year. Several had worked in the Gulf for half a decade. All listened as the driver told them what to expect on the Israeli side of the frontier. Put up with the body searches, he said, without complaint. Do not show disrespect when they paw through your luggage. Answer all the questions without trying to be tricky. Then things will go easier, he said.

Drained of energy, I had shied away from explaining why I knew Arabic, so we went through the charade of translating. The driver told the others I would have no trouble. They take the Americans, he said, and please them in every way they can.

A couple of returning Palestinians, speaking good English, tried to include me in their conversation from time to time, but I had allowed the exchanges to go dry. Now I had to respond. "The driver says you will have no trouble," said my translator, a neatly dressed man in his early thirties wearing horn-rimmed glasses. He was pleased to speak English and told me he worked as a teacher in Kuwait.

"Do you expect difficulties?" I asked.

"No, no." He hesitated, then decided to say more. "I've come home before, I know what to expect. The indignity. You see, the inspections are total, including the rectum" – he was proud to know the term – "and they leave the luggage disorganized, tear the parcels and presents apart so we can't put them back together. They don't want to encourage these visits. It's easier if you come in by air." He paused. "I have some twine in my pocket to do up the parcels again."

"Why should they be afraid of you?"

He shrugged. "I suppose they think we will hurt them someday, take revenge."

The Jordanian officials looked hard at my passport but found no Israeli stamps. Across the bridge, on the Israeli side, my fellow passengers were separated from me and herded into another building. An attractive Israeli woman interrogated me. She asked why I was coming to Israel. I said I was on business.

"Of course," I added, "I'm coming not only to Israel but also the Occupied Territories." Thus my anger struggled to express itself. Arriving at the third border of a long day, I felt testy and aggressive. And in Israel I could speak less carefully. She looked at me quickly, then smiled. The impertinent reminder that the two of us were at a frontier post legally on the West Bank, not Israel, led to more questions. When she asked where I would stay, I said the American Colony. She thought for a moment.

"Do you always stay in East Jerusalem when you come?"

"Yes."

"Why do you not stay in West Jerusalem? The hotels are nicer." She said it dead-pan but I sensed she was having fun. "Do you have friends in Jerusalem?"

"Yes, of course."

"Are they Americans or Israelis?"

"Both. And Palestinians also."

"You mean Arabs?" She laughed, delightedly, and if recent events had weighed less heavily, I might have grinned. Clearly she was not a hard-liner, for whom *Arab*, not *Palestinian*, was the proper term, implying that the local inhabitants could feel at home anywhere in the Arab world, that a Palestinian nationality did not exist.

"Excuse me for a minute." She smiled in a friendly way, shaking her head at me like a schoolmarm. My passport in hand, she went across the room to a man in his early forties. Glancing my way, he checked the passport. Then he retreated into a small cubicle, searched among papers on the desk, found a piece of paper he was looking for. I saw him frown as he read it.

He came over to where I was, a tall sturdy-looking man, exuding authority, with open necked blue shirt, dark trousers, sandals, and a diplomatic expression. He led me over the ground explored by the woman, but his sober manner did not invite impertinence. Like the woman, he eventually wanted to know about Palestinian friends.

"These friends, where did you meet them?"

How to answer? It was easier at the airport the time before. From somewhere I remembered a dictum asserting that if in due course the truth will be required, be truthful from the beginning. In any case I retained from years past what Sam Paul referred to jokingly as "a misguided respect for authority." I took the plunge.

"I met them when I was young but I have not kept in touch."

"Where was that?"

"In Ramallah. My father was a teacher at the American School there."

"Was your father the headmaster?"

"Yes." Did he know from what he had just read?

"How long did you live in Ramallah?"

"For many years, then I left for America, about twenty-five years ago."

"How often have you been to Israel since?"

"Twice only. Once on my honeymoon, about seventeen years ago. Once last month."

He went back to the Ramallah years and asked for dates and names and places. He seemed to know many of the answers already. Then he asked about Starr Johnson, about business contacts in Israel. I told him more than he wanted to know, then stopped when I realized this might signal my relief at leaving the subject of Ramallah.

At the luggage counter in another room an inspector asked me to identify my bag, then asked for my briefcase. She wore thick glasses on a round middle-aged face; her accent was heavily Yiddish. I eased myself down on a bench. I'd been awake a long time. My face felt grimy, and the May heat of the Jordan Valley was oppressive. Staring vacantly straight ahead, putting my mind into neutral, I avoided thinking about the night before. The woman in thick glasses started reading the papers in my briefcase. Happily the phone number I needed for "other business" was in my wallet. Glancing at a group of French tourists on the other side of the room, I saw that two of them also had briefcases, but these were opened only perfunctorily.

It took another thirty minutes to get through. When I finally emerged from the customs shed, some Palestinians came out of the building next door but not the group I'd arrived with; the latter would still be undergoing "inspection." I bought the last three seats in a waiting *servis* and we started up the long hill toward Jerusalem.

TEN

Jerusalem, May 1990

The pink stone on the lobby floor hadn't changed. The same young clerk welcomed me with a smile. I felt a surge of nostalgia, like seeing a cottage, once lived in, that now belongs to strangers, like looking at a once-loved crab apple tree now too small to climb.

The clerk handed me an envelope, called for the old man to show me upstairs. The envelope was addressed in a scrawl I didn't know, but excitement grew in me and I somehow knew who it was before I opened it. *Am in room 8. Come by when you can. B.* What was Barbara doing in Jerusalem?

I was taken to the room I had had before and waited impatiently as the old man satisfied himself the room was in order. When he left with a sweet smile, I went to the basin, gave my hands and face a quick wash. I knew where Room 8 was, just two rooms down the corridor, and though I thought quickly about Cath and the kids, about unknown forces threatening my life, what I wanted most at that moment was to have my arms around Barbara Corum.

The door opened to my knock and she stood there, in skirt and blouse but barefooted, looking at me, the dark hair framing the greenish eyes. Hands to cheeks in a gesture of feigned surprise, a mischievous smile on her face. Wordlessly she reached out and drew me into the room, closing the door with exaggerated quiet, then turned to snuggle against me with her arms around my neck.

182

We stood together a long while. When we took deep breaths at the same time, I felt her smile. "How nice, how very nice," she whispered, stroking my hair. Feeling me stiffen against her, she put her hands behind my hips. We kissed, a long quiet kiss.

When I spoke, it came out inanely. I'd travelled all day, been pushed and pulled, felt sweaty and smelly. Something, perhaps it was anger, was not far away, awaiting a small signal to emerge.

"I have to take a shower," I said.

She bent back, eyes staring a moment into mine, then giggled softly. Her eyes and hands went over my face, and the giggle changed to a seductive smile.

"You can take a shower later," she said.

*   *   *

We dozed off after we made love, arms around each other. After a while we woke up and began to talk. Hovering over me was the shadow of infidelity. It was dusk. Through the window, just outside, we heard a treeful of birds twittering as they settled down for the night.

Neither of us wanted to "talk business," at least not yet. No doubt we would have to do so soon, but tomorrow would come soon enough. For the moment I chose not to think about knives and guns and bombs. Nor about my family. But my mind kept disobeying its instructions. In any case we spoke of other things. The walls, she said, were thin, we should talk softly, just above a whisper. As we murmured to each other, caressing each other, the light faded and the bird chorus outside tapered off to the single notes that are final messages of some kind. She got up to put on the bathroom light, closing the door partially, and the room took on a shadowy intimacy, its furnishings magically assuming friendlier shapes. The desk and chair near the window looked over at us benignly, comfortably; the tall bureau with brass handles stood like a loyal sentinel against the wall.

In the half-light her face was subtly altered, shadows against the cheekbones transforming it. But her lips felt the same. I can't say what we talked about. Much of it I cannot remember, except that it seemed important at the time. More important were the messages behind the words, feelings I could not name because I didn't then admit the word *love* – was it loyalty to Cath? – into the private place where my feelings for Barbara were being defined. But the tenderness I felt for her surprised me and came at me in waves.

The words I do remember sound uninspired and banal in the telling, phrases that would be embarrassing to overhear. Yet for me, and I think for her, they came across as comforting, warm and cheering, countering the other feelings lurking inside me. And yes, they were loving; some of them admissions implying this was more than hedonism, assertions that implicated the heart, tentatively made lest they be sidestepped by the other or struck down as assuming too much too soon, signals of resistance to greater intimacy, an unspoken plea to keep the affair pleasurable, orderly, unentangled by personal commitment. But we did make commitments, not big ones, just small ones that slipped out, avowals that appeared casually in our murmurings.

"When you left Washington," she said, stroking my brow, my hip, "I told myself I must think about you professionally. But every time your name came up I thought of you lying next to me. I imagined people could see me breathing faster." At such a moment, either one of us could have put up a warning. I could have responded that I was glad she thought of me that way, or, in flippant cliché, that sex was a wonderful thing and, I hoped, here to stay. Practiced women-chasers, I supposed, would have done it this way. But I did nothing of the kind.

"Yes," I responded, "when I thought of you, it was the same." And I kissed her forehead, then her ear. I meant what I said and she knew it. Thus, little by little we lured each other along, not daring to think the affair was serious, hoping and fearing it was.

Was it then our affair became a love affair, or began to become one? I didn't think about it in such terms, let alone assume the responsibility that goes with a love affair, as I had from the beginning with Cath. But during that early evening in Jerusalem some watershed was crossed that committed me in ways I was not aware of. Perhaps it had much to do with the grim stresses I felt in the world outside the room, though from the moment of receiving Barbara's note I had sought to block these out. It had to do, also, with the tenderness I felt as I held her, as I brushed back the hair from her face and looked at her. At such moments she kissed me softly, gently, responding with the same tenderness. Inevitably, after darkness fell outside, I wanted her again, and she let her breath out in an anxious happy sound.

*   *   *

Later we realized we needed food. We should not, she said, be seen together in the dining room. I got up, slipped along to my room, showered and dressed, and went down to the lobby to get a taxi. The young man at the desk asked if I wanted dinner later on, and I said no. I took the taxi to a restaurant I remembered on Salah-id-Din Street. Though its name had changed, it still provided half-loaves of Arab bread filled with *kebab*, hot pickles, tomatoes, and fried eggplant; I bought more than we needed, plus three bottles of light beer, and after the ride back, walked as unobtrusively as possible through the archway and upstairs to number eight. I felt like a schoolboy avoiding the headmaster, but when I got to her door, it was like winning a treasure hunt.

She drew the blinds and moved the desk so that we could look at each other while we ate. She wore a long dark-blue dressing gown that I remembered from Washington; the dark hair was brushed back casually, increasing the intimacy, and her skin had the rosy hue that comes after making love. At intervals one of us put out a hand and the other squeezed it. We ate hungrily, smiling at each other.

Finally she put her hand purposefully onto mine, smiled ruefully, and sighed.

"Yes," I said.

"Shall I begin?"

"Please."

"You weren't surprised to see me?"

"Only at first."

From the beginning I had wondered at being sent off on my own to carry out a vague scheme hatched in Washington and casually embellished in Egypt. The only link I had to anyone official was a witless cable code worked out with Gav Middleton; I'd tell him our scheme had not worked, he'd cable back to come home or sit tight. But that was it. If it all seemed loose and unbusinesslike, Gav had not appeared to think so. Gav, of course, did what he was told.

So Blake sent Barbara. Of course. Blake had to know that my agenda and his differed markedly. For me simple survival took precedence, but Barbara would see that Blake's priorities were observed. Abu Kerim's warning that something was not right hovered somewhere nearby. I brushed it away.

"Blake knows the arrangements with Middleton," she said in crisp phrases, "but he always planned to have one of us on the spot. I mean one of the group that knows the whole story. Middleton knows a lot, but not all. Unexpected things happen, someone has to make decisions. And I'm the case officer so ..." Her tone changed, she fondled my hand. "I wasn't sorry to come."

"How much does Middleton really know?" I asked.

"Enough to do what he's supposed to do." She looked at me a long moment, then looked at her hands. "Maybe he knows more than I think. It's all up to Curtis Blake. He thinks Middleton is the best there is."

"And what are you supposed to be doing here in Jerusalem, at the American Colony?"

"I'm assigned to the Consulate General for temporary duty, as someone from the U.S.I.A., doing a study on reading habits. What publications should Washington make available and why." She smiled. "So if you've read any good books lately ..."

"Do you have an office at the Consulate, a secretary?"

"My office, as of two days ago, is next to the office of the Cultural Officer, a nice man who piles reading matter on my desk about reading habits. He knows reading habits don't interest me, but he doesn't know what I'm supposed to be doing."

"If I need to, can I call a secretary and get in touch?"

"Yes, but I do hope you'll find ways to communicate with me at the American Colony." She grinned impishly.

I took her hand in both of mine, and she brought her other hand onto the pile. "What did you tell the clerk when you left that note?"

"I told him I knew of you and asked him what you looked like. For public consumption we could meet for the first time at breakfast."

She was quiet, watching our four clasped hands.

"Life," she said, "can be so good at times, meeting you here, having this big chance."

"Chance at what?"

"Chance at bringing off the meeting with Yusuf Al-Khalil, or Abu Hisham as you call him. A chance at making a real difference. If I were in show business, I'd call it my big break, a special assignment, top secret." She looked up, saw my questioning expression, took a long breath. "Yes, I know. It's different for you, though only partly. For me it's ideological too, but more than that. I mean, there's no problem I'd rather help solve. Partly because I'm Jewish, partly because it's a senseless conflict. But you've got to understand I want to get ahead, to make it in this profession, that I'm excited by the chance to have people know I've done well." Her eyes held mine. She wanted a response.

"Of course," I said, "I'm ambitious too. Nothing wrong with that." Not the ambition but the reference to show business had caught me unprepared, turning death into mere drama. Was it only that morning Abu Kerim had died, leaving me dismembered? And the Dajanis whom I had come to value deeply. I wrenched my mind away from the children. Their children, my children.

Her eyes remained on mine. "I want to be as open with you as I'm allowed to be. It's difficult not to say everything. I have to be professional. There's not much I can't say. Just the same it's important to me to have you understand my position."

"Of course," I said.

"I mean, I don't want anything to come between us. I don't want you to get angry if I have to do things you disagree with."

"Why would our judgments be that different?"

She looked at me silently. Something was worrying her. Her eyes dropped to the four hands, still laced together.

"I don't know what I mean. I guess I'm scared about something but I'm not sure what. I want things to be right between us, especially after tonight. There are moments when I reach out and you're not there. I don't know where you are. As if you were on guard, holding something back, keeping yourself under control."

"I do want to reach out," I said earnestly. I disengaged one of my hands, stroked her cheek. "Maybe I don't know how. I'll try."

She looked at me but said nothing, and so I went on.

"You see, I want a settlement, probably more than I can explain, but I've got other things to worry about." I took a deep breath. "Such as staying alive, such as not letting harm come to Abu Hisham, and some others. Such as keeping my family safe. Your man Curtis Blake is crazy if he thinks there's no connection between his little scheme and my being followed in Cairo and almost killed. And having old friends murdered last night in Beirut. So I've got personal responsibilities here. That others don't have, including you."

"What old friends?" She broke in.

I shook my head, wanting suddenly to cry, not trusting myself to speak. Her hands tightened on mine.

"What old friends?" she asked again. She watched my face. "Was one of them someone you knew at Ramallah? Was it someone you call Abu Kerim?"

I nodded, the enormity of the loss suddenly hitting me like a falling oak. The hands gripped mine more fiercely.

"My love, I'm so sorry, so very very sorry." She began stroking one of my hands, like rubbing a magic lamp. Her voice was subdued. "I've never had a really close friend die. Not like that. And the others?"

"A professor and his family. Two children. Their apartment was bombed."

"Were they close friends too?" When I nodded again, she bowed her head, continued to stroke my hand. "I guess I've known from the beginning, in Washington, when you brought up being followed. I just didn't say it. Blake knows too. He says the fact you *think* there's a link means you have other priorities. He says he doesn't think there's a link."

"What do *you* think?"

"We have to assume there is."

"It couldn't be otherwise. Which is why Abu Kerim and the others are dead. And I worry a lot. You should know this." I took my hands away and sat back in my chair. Then I reached for her hands again, as if retracting a curt comment.

"As you say," I said, "especially after tonight."

We looked at each other for a long moment.

"That's not what I meant. I knew all that, about your political worries, about your family. I want to help." She'd kept her voice low but now it was sharper again, more searching. "It's something else, something that sometimes makes you stand away from me, hold me off. That's what I feel."

"I don't feel as if I hold you off."

She let out a long breath. Her eyes searched my face. "I don't know why I'm getting so intense. Maybe just normal paranoia. Anyway, there's much else to talk about. My paranoia will wear off. I promise."

Then we talked business. I reported my meeting with Abu Taleb's sister Ni'meh. I used no names, and Barbara asked for none. I spoke as openly as I could without revealing identities, answering only general questions about Ni'meh. I wished I could have mentioned Ni'meh's Bedouin origins. Had I felt free to provide details, could I have explained about Ni'meh? Could I have interpreted one civilization to another – and Ni'meh's nearly gone by, an ethnic remnant? I imagined the two women, the East Coast urbanite and the Bedouin sheikh's daughter, meeting and talking.

"When will you make the final plan for meeting Abu Hisham?"

"I'll know more day after tomorrow. The sister knows my schedule, knows I have ten days in Jerusalem if I need them. When I see her, she'll tell me what she and her brother have decided."

"Do you know the brother?"

"Yes, a trustworthy sort. I knew him long ago."

"So, already two more people are involved. How can you be sure they'll say nothing?"

"I can be sure." I paused. How could I be so sure? Behind this judgment, this certainty, lay a lifetime of relationships in a world of strict and honorable rules regarding intrigue. They would gladly betray the United States or any country in a good cause. They would never betray Abu Taleb. "It's a family thing. I'm a close friend, almost a part of the family."

"Is this a family you grew up with?"

"In a way. I promise you the security is good." I caressed one of her hands. "I mustn't tell you more."

"Of course not. I understand that." With one finger she drew pictures on my palm. "I remember you had three special friends at Ramallah. The one with the PLO is dead. Why was he killed?"

"Just an accident, in a way." I meant an accident of politics, in a place where the accident rate was high.

"How much did he know about our plan?" She asked as if she knew he'd known more than he should.

"He told *me* most of it."

"Would you have told him most of it if he hadn't?"

"Probably not most of it, but enough to keep my credibility in the face of what he already knew, enough to protect him, not enough to involve him and get him tarred with the same brush. Enough so he could protect me but not so much he would be honor-bound to turn me in." I looked down at our hands, still enlaced. "Not so much he'd be unable to disagree strongly that I should be killed."

"This was your friend?"

"Yes, he was my friend. He wouldn't have been if I'd told him lies or told him too much." I groped for the right words. "The important thing is to know what people don't want to hear."

"God."

"It depends less on beliefs than being friends." She was staring at me. "If you had to choose between the United States and someone you loved, which would you choose?"

She thought for a moment, shook her head, drew her hands from mine on the excuse of rearranging the folds of the blue dressing gown. I took my hands away too, leaning back on the straight chair.

"What did Abu Kerim think about our plan?" She had avoided my question about conflicting loyalties.

"He thought it would fail. He thought Abu Hisham would not agree. He thought there was something fishy about the plan, as if it was hiding something else."

"What did he mean?" She looked puzzled.

"He meant it was strange the CIA would ask me to do what I'm doing." I looked carefully but her face showed nothing.

"How did he find out about the plan? Did he tell you?"

"No, he said specifically he could not tell me."

From her face I could see I had given her things to think about. Not my simplistic attempts to describe the nature of Abu Kerim's and my friendship. This she doubtless discounted. But now she *knew* there'd been a leak. Speculation had become fact.

"And your friend in Cairo, the other close friend at Ramallah, how much does he know?"

I hesitated. Whatever I told her she had to report to Blake, which was the professional thing to do. Though she might suspect that Abu Taleb was helping me meet Abu Hisham, she could not be certain. Even if she speculated, only speculated, in a report to Blake, it might be leaked, and Abu Taleb and his family, targeted by hard-liners as traitors, would become objects of murderous indignation. So far, no one knew about Abu Taleb's involvement except, of course, his two full brothers and his sister. Unless the wrong person had seen us in the café in Heliopolis. In Beirut, no one, because they were all dead. Gav Middleton knew I was working through an "old Palestinian friend."

I'd dropped too many hints. Barbara watched me, waiting for an answer.

"Who do you mean?" I asked.

"I mean the one that was such a close friend, along with Abu Hisham and Abu Kerim."

"Oh, you mean Abu Taleb. He knows nothing at all. A literary type, something of a poet, sort of a professor." I veered away as quickly as I could. "As far as I know, only our mutual friend in Beirut knew most of the plan."

"The one who died last night?"

"Yes."

We fell silent. In a preoccupied way, she picked up waxy sandwich wrappings and placed them tidily in a plastic bag. We finished the beer. She looked up at me suddenly and smiled.

"You're a straight arrow and I love you for it."

"What's that all about?"

She got up and came round to the back of my chair, putting her arms around me tightly, kissing my ear.

"I want to tell you what I'm *not* doing tomorrow. I'm *not* mentioning the name Abu Taleb in any report and maybe getting him killed. I'm *not* even saying you're getting help from an old friend. And I'll do my best *not* to look in the Jerusalem English-language phonebook, which is at my bedside, to see if there is anyone named Abu Khayyal. Isn't that Abu Taleb's family name?"

I reached behind me and pulled her round onto my lap. I wanted to laugh with her but I was frightened at my own ineptness, at the way I had just endangered the lives of four Abu Khayyals. She put her fingers on my mouth and kissed my cheek.

"Don't worry," she said.

Relief flooded through me; for the moment the four were safe. But for how long?

"How could you know?" I asked.

"If I liked you less, you might have got away with it. Or if I hadn't just read all the material on Abu Taleb's family." Her face sobered, and her hand began stroking the back of my head. "I don't want his blood on my hands."

As she looked at me, her eyes kept watching my lips. We kissed gently and for a long time, and my hand began caressing her breasts and her belly. When she felt me grow hard under her, she regarded me in mock astonishment.

"Not again," she said, "not possible."

"Very possible."

"How nice, how very nice."

∗   ∗   ∗

We had fallen asleep. I awoke when she began stroking my brow and my hair. I knew I had to get back to my room.

"Don't leave. Not quite yet." She nestled in closer, breathing contentedly. We lay quietly in the semi-darkness, with an occasional caress or light kiss. The bathroom light shone steadily through the partially closed door.

"I don't feel you're holding me off now, not so much at least." Her voice was low, almost a whisper.

"I don't think I ever did."

"I doubt if you realize it."

"Nonsense." I ran my hand down her back.

"Well, there's a barrier. Or something. There are things you don't say because you think I wouldn't understand, things you leave out." She was silent a moment. "As if it were tiring to explain something. Like when you talk about the man in Beirut. Or your old friend in Cairo."

"Perhaps. I'll think about it." Cath felt the same thing, I thought. Then I quoted her almost verbatim, feeling like a plagiarist. "Maybe you mean I live in two worlds and it's difficult for me to go back and forth. A divided mind."

"Maybe," she said. The hand brushed the hair back from my brow again. In the dim light I could see the eyes looking into mine. "Does it have something to do with being Jewish?"

"Certainly not."

"Don't answer so quickly. Think a minute."

"I don't need to think a minute."

"You *should* think a minute. It's important." She started to say something else, then stopped, her eyes on my face all the while. "Listen to me, really listen to me. The Jewish thing is important. To me it's important."

I said nothing and kissed the tip of her nose. She kissed me back, making an exasperated sound.

"Here's something else," she said. "You talk about two worlds, about the difficulty getting back and forth. All right, that's possible. But what about taking people with you? Why not take *me* along? Do you think I'm so alien I couldn't appreciate that other world, feel what it feels, want what it wants? Why not see if I can come along, see if I can understand?"

Perhaps Cath had once felt the same. I think she had, though she never put it into words. Over the years, Cath and I had learned to by-pass many kinds of words and put ourselves on a single wave length. If Cath felt left out of part of my life, I think she was content this should be so, because she was queen of the part where I lived and worked and had a family. Or almost content. On one occasion, with a touch of resentment, she said I changed personality when I spoke Arabic. I became different, more talkative, more prone to laughter. Abu Taleb, she noted almost tartly, had the same personality in both languages.

Did I want to bar Barbara or Cath from my Palestinian world? If so, why? When I arrived at Swarthmore, I told other freshmen where I was from, where I went to school. The courteous indifference I evoked ate at my self-esteem. When in late-night bull sessions, trying to match intriguing stories from American suburban life, I recounted bits of personal history from Palestine, I was met not with disbelief but with signs that what I said was irrelevant. I became wary of talking about my upbringing, focused my energies on learning about life in America. After I met Cath, weeks passed before she began asking about my background. Only when we left for Saudi Arabia did I try consciously to introduce her to my past, staying at the American Colony, spending time in Ramallah, but it didn't work out the way I wanted. Instead, in the years that followed, we became normal American expatriates, conforming to the social patterns our fellow countrymen found congenial.

Perhaps this explained my friendship with Sam Paul. He could accompany me across the divide. But Barbara, I thought, was getting at something else.

"Listen," I said, "I don't find it easy to explain things like this. I don't *feel* I'm keeping you out of part of my life. We haven't talked about Cath, of course."

"We don't need to if you don't want to. I'm talking about you and me."

"It might have something to do with her, though. A feeling of guilt. On my part. Some notion I shouldn't like you as much as I do. Some idea I should be attached only to her."

"No," she said, more softly. "Don't think of it that way. Please. Let this be between you and me. Just you and me. No complications. Just a special bit of luck."

We lay together a few moments more. No complications, she said. I realized I was relieved to hear it, though I'd not yet thought about it. I kissed her lips, her cheek, her ear.

"Yes," I said, "a special bit of luck."

We made plans for the next day. She said she wanted me to come to dinner at her sister's place.

"Sister's place?" She had a sister? Here?

"Yes, sister's place." In the darkness she smiled at my astonishment. "She's lived here more than five years. She's a nice thing, and you'll be interested in her husband, a perfect example of a die-hard. Don't worry, you'll survive." She gave me a light kiss.

ELEVEN

Jerusalem, May 1990

I had another night of unsound sleep and worry, and in the morning I phoned Abdu in Cairo. I needed reassurance. When he heard my voice, he did not seem surprised. "My special people report nothing unusual," he said. "You seem to be the problem, not your family. How are things in Jerusalem?"

"Same as always."

"Remember," he reiterated firmly, yet sympathetically, "if you hear nothing from me, you don't have to worry." He wished me well in his formal way.

I felt better after this long-distance medication but of course my worries continued, though they were mitigated by memories of Barbara the night before. My business appointments went well that morning, resulting in almost a surge of new orders for Starr Johnson products. Clearly our part-time Greek agent had performed poorly. I phoned Cath on schedule after lunch. She sounded in good spirits.

"Paul has placed my piece in the New Yorker," she said almost excitedly.

I had to focus for a moment. Paul? Ah yes. Paul Taylor, her agent in Manhattan. "That's great," I said.

"He is still insisting I make a trip to New York," she said. "We can talk about it when you get back." It would, I thought, be a long talk, with many logistical and family complications to be worked out. Then we chatted about the kids and then about Jerusalem. I didn't mention my plans for the evening.

Barbara's sister and her husband lived on the other side of the city, in an apartment building off Ramban Street, overlooking Rehavia Park. The place exuded wealth, boasting reserved parking for tenants, uniformed doorman, well-kept hedge and flower bed in the half-moon formed by the drive, a thickly carpeted lobby. After looking at me long enough to let me know he had a decision to make, the doorman told me Dr. and Mrs. Cohen lived on the fifth floor. Arrival in an Arab taxi had not enhanced my standing.

The elevator went up smoothly. Ordinarily, I thought, I would have considered the day to have been one of the good ones. And now, in addition to the day's business successes, another guest at dinner would be a woman I wanted very much to see, with whom I would later make love. I was aware of Cairo nagging at me but at the moment it seemed far away.

But I had found Jerusalem disquieting while doing my business rounds. Walking about that morning on the Jewish side, I kept turning things over. Twice I imagined I saw the Dajani children at play. I wondered why an Israeli customs official would have my name on a piece of paper in his office. I spent time finding excuses to look over my shoulder, searching for oddities of pedestrian behavior that might mean I was being followed. By whom? Despite my respect for Israeli security, Abu Kerim's comment that "our factions can penetrate" would not leave me. At times I had the curious sensation my old friend was walking beside me, as if I could turn to him and comment on what I was seeing or fearing. The Jerusalem Post reported his murder in a lower corner of its front page, calling him a "prominent PLO official." No mention was made of the Dajanis. The apartment house where the Cohens lived seemed almost like a fortress, a welcoming refuge. Unpleasantness, I told myself, did not occur in sumptuous apartments on the Jewish side of town. I anticipated an evening free from fear at the home of Irving Cohen, M.D., as announced on a polished brass plate. He himself opened the door, a tall spare man with graying hair and neat gray moustache, in his fifties. Expensively dressed, or so I thought, because he wore a tailor-made shirt and a maroon smoking jacket belted with a gold-threaded maroon sash. His dark tie was silk, his black handmade shoes highly polished. His movements suggested a man in good physical condition.

"Mr. Hampton? I'm Dr. Cohen." His tone was brisk and not discourteous, a brusque formal manner that Barbara had sought to explain. He had been, she said, in the midst of a distinguished medical career in Manhattan when his daughter, working one summer on a kibbutz, had been killed in a terrorist raid. The killing, a watershed in the life style of the Cohens, had brought them to Israel to be "near the concerns of her spirit." Cohen's terse manner, once reserved for the hospital, became part of his life everywhere, and the younger Cohen emerged rarely. He used to be so different, she said.

Beyond Cohen was a foyer, then a big arch that gave onto a large, luxuriously furnished living room with picture windows on two sides. Several other guests chatted, drinks in hand, and Barbara was among them. From where I stood, I saw stunning views in the direction of the Knesset and the Hebrew University.

Barbara's sister Lois came to greet me, effusive rather than brisk, less elegantly dressed than her husband, yet tastefully adorned with diamonds at the neck and on the fingers. At least ten years older than Barbara, becoming slightly plump, but the same eyes and cheekbones. She looked more Jewish, in the American sense of "looking Jewish" I had learned at Swarthmore. She drew me into the living room, hand tucked around my arm. Barbara, looking strikingly beautiful, stood smiling at me.

Two men waited to say hello. The younger one, in his fifties like Dr. Cohen, was introduced as Moshe Feldman from the Ministry of Foreign Affairs, the other one, older by a decade, as Ehud Elath, a historian at the Hebrew University. A look at the dining room table, set up for dinner in a spacious corner, told me the party was complete.

Soon we took chairs at the table. Its rounded shape would compel a six-way conversation. A pleasant-looking maid, who Lois said was a "nice Sephardic girl from North Africa," brought platters of food. Feldman, with the polish of a senior bureaucrat, launched us all into courteous inquiries about each other. Dressed like a diplomat, slender except for a small pot belly, he had a clean-shaven face, dark eyes, thick dark hair graying at the edges. I had the impression of a person who misses little, whose mind has long insisted on inquiry, whose major amusement is to know.

"Barbara," he said, "tells us you live in Cairo and once lived in Ramallah. What an extraordinary background! Do tell us how things are going for our Egyptian allies." He said it not sarcastically but in a friendly way that seemed to regret the current strain between the two countries. When I protested I was a business man, not much given to political reflection, he said that was an excellent way to introduce a definitive statement. So we laughed and proceeded to talk about many things. Lois sat quietly, with a motherly air, as if such discussions were a game for men.

Ehud Elath, the older man from the Hebrew University, was short and had a round heavy face and white beard. He spoke gently. He had a different way of meeting me, somehow guarded, not looking me in the eye, responding to my comments by making remarks to others. Was it my foreignness? Something to do with being the non-Jew at a gathering in Israel? Then something changed. He began looking at me as if I had a right to be there. Did he need to know first whether life in the Arab world had set me against Israel? This was a question clearly on the mind of an Israeli businessman I had visited that morning.

The food, non-kosher, was excellent and the wine delicious. I was almost able to put my troubles aside and bask in an atmosphere created by civilized dining and affluence. We became a company of friends, thanks more to the skills of Feldman than those of our host. Elath overcame his shyness, if that is what it was. The conversation covered theatre in New York and London as well as the progress of cancer research, a topic that explained Irving Cohen's fame in medical circles. Eventually we talked about Palestinians and Jews.

*   *   *

If a conversation is long enough, I suppose certain topics have to arise. So it was that evening at the Cohens. We settled into a discussion of Palestinians and Jews as if coming home to sit in our favorite chairs. Each face around the table registered intense interest, except perhaps that of Lois Cohen, who had a cautious look.

The discussion started simply enough. Feldman claimed Israelis were out of touch with Palestinians, and Cohen denied it. We went on from there. As forecast by Barbara, Cohen played the role of die-hard. Like Curtis Blake, he abandoned positions with great reluctance; he had a formal style of delivery as if he were asking an intern to defend a diagnosis. Elath, for his part, mixed irony with dry professorial comment. He had a charming smile.

Feldman, whom I found puzzling, took strong positions but I felt he did not necessarily believe what he said. He came across as urbane, amusing, at times forcefully persuasive, but somehow manipulative. Barbara seemed wary as she listened to him. Was the real Feldman on display? At an early juncture Elath gave him a mocking look.

"Ah Moshe," he said. "Here we go again. Always the catalyst." The gentle voice of the older man had an edge.

So we proceeded to cover familiar political ground. At one point Feldman insisted we should not mince words just because Bill Hampton, a non-Jew, was listening. And indeed, nobody was mincing words. Among the three men – Cohen, Feldman and Elath – an atmosphere of clubby vitriol took over. We covered every aspect of the tricky and complicated and wide-ranging relations of Israelis, Palestinians, and other Arabs. As well as Americans, including American Jews of various persuasions.

I glanced occasionally at Barbara, realized she was hearing some of this for the first time. I allowed much of it to wash over me; I was bemused, partially distracted from my worries, anticipating Barbara's body later on. As if fearing others could read my thoughts, I straightened in my chair and began listening more carefully. Cohen was saying to Feldman: "You said earlier that Arafat's faction wants to talk. If Fatah or the PLO want to talk, it's because of hatred, it's by no means in order to make peace. They have some strategy in mind that aims at hurting us. Their hate is implacable. It's the most pronounced anti-Semitism in the world."

I came suddenly to attention.

"Surely," I said, implying that the phraseology was a slip of the tongue, "surely you don't mean anti-Semitism."

Cohen looked at me uncomprehendingly, anxious to brush aside this unexpected verbal obstacle. The others, except for Elath and perhaps Feldman, showed surprise. Lois looked uneasy.

"I don't understand," said Cohen.

"Just a minor point," I said. "I don't think Palestinians, not the ones I know anyway, have what you call anti-Semitic feelings."

"That makes no sense at all, Mr. Hampton." Cohen glanced around the table, as if apologizing for the necessity of speaking curtly.

"I would be interested," said Feldman, "to have Mr. Hampton explain what he means."

I wished I had not brought the matter up. Barbara watched me gravely, gave an almost imperceptible nod of encouragement. Last night she had said "the Jewish thing" was important.

"I have difficulty with words for things like this," I said, glancing at Cohen. "But I personally believe what I'm trying to say is important. I mean important for peace."

All eyes were fastened on me. Cohen's expression indicated he couldn't imagine what direction my remarks would take. Barbara, I thought, seemed tense.

"As you know, I was brought up in Ramallah, even went to school there. Palestinians, and most other Arabs for that matter, don't think about Jews the way Europeans and Americans do. Yes, at the moment many Palestinians hate the Israelis, and by extension they hate those who support them, especially Jews, but it's a political hate, not a social one."

"You mean we're all Semites together, or something like that?" asked Feldman with a smile.

"No, no, I'm talking about what in America gets called anti-Semitism and saying in that sense it doesn't exist among Palestinians."

"But that's preposterous," said Cohen. "Surely," he added. For courtesy's sake.

"I can only report my own experience."

"What in your experience would allow you to know what anti-Semitism was like or not like?" Cohen's tone, though brusque as always, was inoffensive. Even flattering in the sense I was now admitted into an inner circle where verbal thrust and insult were expressions of solidarity.

"When I went to the United States at age eighteen, I had anti-Semitism pushed at me for the first time. I'd had brushes with it before, from Americans and English I knew in Lebanon in the summertime, but I didn't recognize it then. And I never got any of it from my parents. They were Quakers of a special sort, strait-laced, sort of. I'm sure they knew about anti-Semitism but they never told me about it."

They had, I thought, wanted me uncontaminated by any prejudices that did not reflect their liberal convictions. In Philadelphia, where their notions of right and wrong had been worked out, I could have tested them, seen them in context, adjusted to other notions picked up from playmates. But in Ramallah the context was different; my playmates introduced me to an unrelated set of ideas about good and evil. Like apples and oranges. And among the oranges the idea of anti-Semitism never appeared. That was a surprise administered at college, in the United States.

"Fascinating," said Elath, nodding, "and quite possible. A special case. Please proceed, Mr. Hampton."

"Well, there's nothing to proceed with. That's it. At Swarthmore, at eighteen, when I realized there were feelings against Jews, I remember wondering what the Gentiles were angry about. What had the Jews done? Did they steal? Did they take land from the Gentiles? I couldn't ask about it without looking foolish. I realized little by little that the Jews hadn't done anything; it was a social thing. That it wouldn't go away if, say, the Jews made some kind of apology or retribution. So I heard words like 'kike' from otherwise decent classmates, with a tone of voice that made it all sort of dirty, and then references to Jewish habits from friends of my parents, at Sunday dinners."

In my freshman English class a nice-looking girl named Lucille sat next to me. From a couple of friends I came to understand she *looked* Jewish. So I began to examine the features of other students to see if I could tell Jew from Gentile the way Americans did. Or at least claimed. I could never do it well. Where I excelled, and where my American friends were hopelessly incompetent (not that they cared), was to know who was, say, Greek or Armenian. In Ramallah and the mountains of Lebanon we knew about Greeks and Armenians and our own kind of Jews.

"So?" said Elath gently. They watched me intently. Lois had lost her uneasy look.

"So, I guess that's my evidence, my experience. Nobody in Palestine taught me about anti-Semitism. They taught me about the political sins of Jews, taking the land, using their power, not allowing freedom of speech. How can I say this? It was like having a quarrel that arose from some infraction of the rules, some unfair act, and once one starts acting fairly again, the quarrel can be made up and forgotten." I hesitated. Barbara's expression was unreadable. "Only from Westernized Palestinians did I ever get a whiff of anti-Semitism, a kind of borrowing by upper-crust intellectuals. In my day at least, it had no effect on ordinary townsmen or villagers. Not ingrained like in Europe and America."

"But Mr. Hampton," said Cohen, picking words with precision, "while this is interesting, I'm not sure it's helpful. You say Palestinian feelings against Jews are different from those among Americans. The fact is, of course, Palestinians hate us a great deal more than Americans do."

"Irv, I can only presume you are purposely missing the point." Elath's quiet voice again had an edge. "I presume you wish to think that Palestinians are anti-Semites. It motivates you. What Mr. Hampton says is that all is not lost, that Jews can be forgiven, that Herzl's analysis of anti-Semitism in Europe does not apply here. We do not need to leave or be exterminated in order to be accepted. Here in the Eastern Mediterranean we need not be social pariahs. Is this what you are saying, Mr. Hampton?"

"No, you are saying more than I was. I simply wanted to contribute one social fact about Palestinians."

"Damn it, Ehud, damn it," said Cohen, bristling with assertions struggling to come out. "Jews can be forgiven, you say? What kind of nonsense is that? Whose fault do you think it all is? The aggressor race, the aggressor race. For God's sake."

"Cool down, Irv," said Elath. "I don't deny that the aggressor race, incidentally a term you should reject in the interests of science, is basically at fault. But the fact is, and I speak psychologically as well as socially, the *goyim* in the West, for reasons of their own, find it impossible to forgive us for being ourselves. No doubt that is their loss. And a great many of them feel guilty about it. But there it is. No matter what we do, rise to the top or fail miserably, they do not forgive us. They have this sickness. They forgive the Germans and the Japanese, they cannot forgive the Jews. They can't even tell us what we did that needs forgiveness. On the other hand, Orientals have made it economically in the United States, and they forgive them for being Orientals. I have no reason to believe the same will not happen one day with American blacks. But they don't forgive the Jews. Thank God I'm an Israeli."

There was a pause, then a different voice in a different mode.

"Do *you* forgive us, Bill?"

All of us looked at Barbara. No one could fail to know how personal the question was. Oblivious to the stares of others, she fixed her eyes on my face. Some powerful instinct told me I could not answer with a social put-off or light comment. I looked down at my empty coffee cup. No one spoke or moved.

"I'm not sure I understand this business about forgiveness." I kept my eyes on my coffee cup. If I returned her gaze, it would give everything away. "Yes, I've taken on some resentments against Israelis and Jews. I think I know the reasons. Political reasons."

I kept looking down, using my spoon to change the liquid patterns at the bottom of the cup. I felt no antipathy in the air, but I was being judged.

"You see," I said, "I react like a Palestinian in some ways. They are angry but as I said, they'd get over it if they thought justice were done, or their children's children would. It wouldn't linger on forever like anti-Semitism."

I put my hands down in my lap to indicate I'd finished talking. I glanced at Barbara, who was looking at me intently.

"I greatly fear," said Cohen, quickly, "you're living in a dream world, something you remember from your youth. My God they hate us, with the possible exception of the upper-class boys you went to school with. Which is not so different from going to an upper-class school in the States, with nice liberal kids who are taught not to hate Jews."

"I wasn't taught not to hate them, I wasn't taught anything at all."

Elath shook his head, not in disagreement but in discouragement. "I'm old and tired," he said, "and it's getting late. Irv, what if Mr. Hampton is right? Do we go on thinking we're going to be hated for the rest of time, a self-fulfilling prophecy?

"In the early days," Elath went on, "there were clear paths to take. It was easier then. I want to say one thing about anti-Semitism before I leave." He looked around the table. "I'm the only one, besides Mr. Hampton, who was born in these parts. I grew up mostly with Jews but I had Arab friends, a few of them. And I knew a lot of Arabs here and there. Our non-Jewish friend is right; there was no anti-Semitism or special hatred in those days. Suspicion, yes. Ethnic difference, yes. Rivalry, yes. But hatred, no. Insidious social ostracism, no. One other thing, and now I speak as a historian. Anti-Semitism is a Western and East European phenomenon, a special disease. Some non-Western cultures have similar problems but not with Jews. India has its Parsees, Egypt has its Copts, but it's the Western and East European tradition that carried the disease of anti-Semitism to the Americas, maybe Greece. Perhaps to Palestine one of these days if we're not careful."

Elath stopped. He looked weary. Cohen was yearning to respond, eager to reenter the fray. Lois looked at him beseechingly, reminding him he was the host. It came hard. Alive with disagreement and the joy of inquiry, his scientist's face had an unsatisfied look, like a hungry man who must stop eating too soon. We began to leave, reverting to social chatter and expressions of pleasure. Cohen, his formal manner front and center, thanked me for coming. It occurred to me suddenly, for no particular reason, that Cohen was a completely honest man.

Feldman, who had put the evening into motion and then to some degree sat back to watch it unfold, enlivened our final conversation with amusing remarks. He asked Cohen if he felt more Jewish or less so after our discussion. In the lobby he turned and, casually, asked if I was free for lunch the next day at the King David. I saw Barbara watching us. The doorman called a taxi for her and me, and when she gave instructions in halting Hebrew, the driver replied in English. He was not pleased at the prospect of going over to the Arab side late at night.

TWELVE

Jerusalem, May 1990

In her room our arms went around each other. We stood there, bodies close, until softly she said "come." The tenderness of what followed filled me with awe. I thought about my family, about danger, but only for a moment.

Later we talked, in the muted way that was now part of a special counterpoint, two soft voices like quiet harps, with overtones of enchantment at the candor with which we found ourselves speaking. Each phrase was like a caress. Under such circumstances what happens to substance? Are meanings distorted? Like a poet who writes to strains of moving music, does the poetry sound different the next day when the music is gone? That night we spoke of many things. Each new topic was brought up casually, each one involving our relationship in subtle ways. I felt relaxed and found myself, almost without worry, saying what came to mind.

At one point she talked about Feldman. "He makes me uneasy," she said.

"Why?" But I knew what she meant.

"I'm not sure what he does. He says he's at the Foreign Office, so I guess he works in that building. Whatever he does, it's low-profile. Did he say why he wanted to have lunch?"

"It seemed to be spur of the moment."

"I doubt it. He says what he plans to say." She was silent a moment. "I'll find out about him tomorrow."

"How?"

"Never mind. But don't forget we have an embassy in Tel Aviv."

"You think he has something in mind?"

"Maybe. Or maybe wants to pick your brains. If he's in one of the Israeli intelligence outfits, and something tells me he is, he may want to know more about you, do some probing."

"Why would he bother?"

She stroked the side of my face and my hair. "Because, my wonderful lover, he's paid to probe whenever something odd comes along." She kissed me for a long moment. "You're a friend of mine, he knows that. He knows we're both staying here. Probably he knows we're lovers, maybe he saw me looking at you; it doesn't take much to know. What else? Well, he undoubtedly knows from Irv I work for the government in Washington. So he wants to know more. So he has a chatty lunch to find out why I sleep so happily, so very happily, with a man brought up in Ramallah."

Another kiss, longer this time. "So be careful," she said. Her hands stroked the small of my back and my hips. I bent and kissed a nipple, caressed her belly. She made a husky sound in her throat.

Later, she asked if I agreed with Elath that anti-Semitism was a Western disease, not endemic outside the West and Eastern Europe. I said I didn't know; I knew only I had never encountered the disease in the Eastern Mediterranean. Nothing, I said, like Swarthmore.

"Swarthmore," she said. "It bugs me the way you talk about Swarthmore. I mean, it's the sort of place you think is pretty pure. Nice kids, no snide remarks."

"Well, Swarthmore's not bad. Everything's relative. Perhaps a Jew wouldn't notice it at Swarthmore. Those nice kids are more courteous."

"Don't worry, we always notice. And we notice when those nice kids bend over backwards, they're nice to you *because* you're Jewish. Embarrassing."

"How did your parents handle it?" I asked. "How did they keep you from getting hurt?"

"I think they were different, at least my father was. He was sort of like Elath, a gentle man, very quiet. But for him anti-Semitism wasn't a Gentile disease, more a curse for Jews, something you live with, cope with.

He didn't join Jewish organizations, and he went to the synagogue only enough so people would know he wasn't trying to hide. We'd have long talks at dinner, sitting around the table for hours, sometimes with another Jewish family we knew, but usually not, and we talked about everything under the sun. So whatever happened at school, and not much did but there were little things, we always had this kind of refuge, a friendly place to go. Every evening."

"No television?"

"Hardly ever. And we did our homework in the afternoons. One of the teachers complained to my mother I often seemed sleepy. My father laughed. I think he did it all for me, not Lois. He said most Jews learn to cope but I'd always find it hard."

I knew I should leave. So did she, but she snuggled against me and made a contented noise.

"Some Jews," she said, "never seem to worry. I'd have given anything to be like that."

"How did you feel about what I said about Palestinians tonight?"

"I don't know. I don't know enough Palestinians. Every once in a while, when I'm tired, some ancient thing reasserts itself and I feel Arabs hate Jews, that they aren't trustworthy. Deep down. Intellectually I know better, and I check myself whenever I make a professional decision, to see if I'm being fair to Arabs. Because, really, I know Palestinians are just as trustworthy as Israelis. Both come out smelling like faded roses. I guess I'd trust Elath any time, but I have to remind myself to trust Arafat."

"I hope you wouldn't trust Arafat. What about Elath's real counterpart, say a professor at Bir Zeit?" Ramallah's Bir Zeit was Palestine's foremost college.

"That's the trouble. I don't know a professor at Bir Zeit."

*   *   *

We had breakfast together in the dining room. When she came in, I rose with ostentatious formality and asked her to join me. Looking back, I cannot imagine that a spectator with a semi-discerning eye could fail to know we slept with each other. We kept talking in order to show we were acquaintances, not lovers. She said she'd be at the consulate most of the day; we'd meet that evening for dinner. She was excited I was about to take the first small step toward the meeting with Abu Hisham. I said I'd phone with a fake message to let her know about the visit to Ni'meh.

When I went to the desk with my key, the young man did not give me his usual smile. He put his hand on the key, kept it there for a moment, looked hard toward one of the overstuffed chairs in the lobby. Following his gaze, I saw a nondescript man in a dark suit reading a newspaper. Not the man who had followed me once before. As I turned back toward the desk, the young man flashed a piece of paper onto the counter. It said "Israeli." I nodded impersonally, proceeded on my way. Losing the man was not difficult. I don't think he knew I was aware of him. As before, I walked into the old city through the Damascus gate, slipped around a few corners, and left by Herod's Gate, waiting behind a building a few minutes to make sure I had shaken him. In Zahara Street the green paint on the gate of the villa seemed to have faded since the week before. The morning light made a difference. On this Jerusalem day the early sun bleached the colors applied by man, but persuaded flowers and greenery to rejoice. The garden inside reached upward, stretching its pinks and yellows and reds toward the blue above.

Ni'meh took me through the villa and back into the garden, to green chairs placed around a green table in an open space covered with pink-gray gravel. The sun felt good on my back. Ni'meh said we could go inside if it got too warm. The same heavy-breasted peasant girl brought us a tray with tea, English style.

"You never serve Bedouin coffee?" I asked, smiling.

"Sometimes for myself, after a meal." She took the question seriously, not socially. The dark eyes looked out solemnly from the slender Bedouin face, so delicately constructed one had the feeling it could be crushed like brittle pottery. She wore a dark skirt that came below the knees, a white blouse with long sleeves and high neck.

"I am pleased to see you," she said formally, speaking English, preventing familiarity. "I hope your trip to Beirut was successful."

"Yes, a good trip, thank you. From my point of view, that is. Business matters. Of course you know how bad things are."

"Of course." Her tone implied an acceptance of evil. "I was sorry to read about Abu Kerim."

We sipped our tea. "Very sorry," she added. We soaked in the morning sun. The silence, not uncomfortable, was broken by the buzzing of bees hovering over nearby azaleas. What evil, I asked myself, could enter this garden and survive? The sounds and smells triggered the memory of another garden, sun-drenched behind our Ramallah house, where as a twelve-year old I read stories about America, concocted my images of the Mississippi and the Great West, listened to the buzzing of other bees. In this Jerusalem garden could evil be contemplated? Perhaps Ni'meh thought so. The knowledge of something wrong touched her eyes.

"I have done what you asked. My brother Abdullah comes tomorrow evening from Gaza, and he could see you, he says, the day after tomorrow in the morning." She saw the disappointment on my face. "I told him you had only a few days. He said it would work out, that's all he said."

Frustration gnawed at me, but I had to stifle my impatience. I was frustrated by more than delay. Sitting in the quiet garden with the sun on my back, I knew suddenly I had to pull my life back together. It was being pulled apart, though so far I had felt little pain because Barbara's body next to mine killed the pain. This quiet place brushed at my instincts, alerted me of pain to come, told me to go home, leave my new-found love and Palestine and my boyhood and the tonic of politics and hopes of peace. Go home to Cairo, get on with the business of living.

Yet how could I go and stay alive? Did I want to? Ni'meh watched me thoughtfully.

"Is anything wrong? I think it is all right to wait for Abdullah. He seemed certain about it."

I said I was sure things would be fine. She poured me another cup of tea.

"I hope you will not worry. I can tell you are not used to these things, and I am very glad. When I was growing up, I never wanted to know about them, even if I had to carry messages. Abdullah was so different." She switched to Arabic, lowered her voice, glanced around the garden. "He always wanted to understand what was happening. He followed Abu Taleb around, asking him questions, trying to understand how things

worked. He loved dealing with political matters. He'd sit for hours negotiating some little matter with friends his own age, usually his cousins.
Once when he was sixteen, he spent three days reaching an agreement
with cousins on who would use a football my uncle had given the whole
family. They negotiated a complicated plan to share it. There was lots of
money to get other footballs, but the negotiating delighted them. My father and my uncles encouraged them."

She was pleased to remember those days. The slight smile of reminiscence was not unhappy. After she switched to Arabic, much like the
time of my last visit, I had the odd impression she became my sister, a
woman I was responsible for.

"Was Abdullah the closest to you?"

"Yes, the next oldest. He protected me. Now he's like a father to my
boys."

"I remember him well."

"He remembers you, of course. That was long ago. He remembers
you as different from the others, even if you spoke Arabic like us." The
lovely half-smile appeared as she thought back. "And before '67 to have
an American come across to Gaza, across Israel, was exciting. Even if it
was a time when the Israeli patrols didn't care much." She was remembering a scary trip I had taken as a school boy a long time ago.

"Yes, exciting. And frightening."

"Suppose the Israelis had caught you and the Bedouin you were with.
What then?"

"My father would have accepted it, put up with it, suffered it. My
mother too, because he would have expected her to. They were tough in
a way."

"Yes, Abu Taleb told us about them. He admired them. He said they
often seemed sad."

"Sad?" I had never thought of my parents that way.

"Perhaps I have it wrong. I do not always understand what he says."
She hesitated a moment. The sun, which was warmer now, produced tints
of color on the tightly pulled dark hair. "Not sad like me, from losing a
man. I think he meant sad with themselves, perhaps stern with themselves. I don't know."

"They didn't laugh much, that's true."

"Neither do you," she said. The melancholy look became more pronounced. "I would like to laugh the way I used to. Perhaps one day I will, when I get the boys married. But I don't feel it now. Please explain this to Abu Taleb when you see him."

I thought of Dr. Irving Cohen, over on the other side of town. Was it just the other side of town? Though an ethnic chasm stretched between Ni'meh's world and his, death had paid the same visit to each, squeezing out the juice and leaving both, like dry oranges, with little joy. "I'll tell him," I said, "perhaps next week. I'm glad about what you say. I remember you laughing when you were little."

We walked through the flowers and the brightness to the green gate. She held out her hand, man-fashion, to say goodbye.

"You were in Beirut when Abu Kerim was killed?"

"Yes."

"I suppose he too was seeking peace?" The irony was tinged with melancholy, the face sorrowful.

"He was a decent man," I said. "God have mercy on him." Sudden tears filled my eyes. She appeared not to notice. She just nodded, sighed, and used my name for the first time.

"Please, Bill, be careful. God be with you."

*　　　　　*　　　　　*

I went back to the American Colony to pick up my dark-suited follower, to make it appear he had lost me by accident. He was waiting in the same chair. I phoned Barbara at the consulate and asked her to have dinner with me, though later than planned, meaning progress was slow. Then I made off in a taxi to keep two business appointments. My follower had his own car.

When I arrived for lunch at the King David, Feldman was seated in the lobby, dressed less formally than the night before. Light-weight charcoal trousers, open shirt, charcoal jacket to keep warm in the air-conditioning. Downstairs, the non-kosher restaurant was half full, mostly

American tourists, many in shorts and sport shirts. The plush furnishings and décor, deep red and cream, jarred the eye.

"Last night was a pleasure," he said after we had ordered from the waitress, a plump dark-haired girl. "Irv and Lois add a touch of gracious living to my humdrum life, and when I say humdrum, I mean I don't have the money for gracious living. Hardly any of us do."

The smile, infectious, lit up the slender face. As at dinner the night before, I saw the energy in the brown eyes, the constant state of alert and analysis. We chatted on. He had met Irv Cohen at Harvard when both were students. Irv was quite different then, he said. Feldman's English, I noted, was almost perfect. Only a trace of something else, something European. I decided Feldman, trustworthy or not, was entertaining, likable.

"Last night," I said, "something Elath said suggested you came to Israel from abroad."

"Yes indeed." Again the engaging smile. "You mean you don't think I come from the Eastern seaboard of the United States? It's the damn diphthongs give me away. I keep putting one vowel instead of two. What's your guess on first language?"

"I don't know Europe that well. Maybe Czech."

"Interesting guess. Actually a trick question. My father was French, mother Czech, and mother's mother Slovak. A real mix. We survived the holocaust because at first we were in Vichy territory. Complicated story. We had a bit of luck. Then to Paris after the war."

"But why leave France?"

Feldman shrugged his shoulders in a Gallic way. A touch of France remained.

"Why not?" he responded. The plump waitress arrived with bread and beer. "Why not avoid anti-Semitism if one can? Your remarks last night were pertinent. And incidentally amusing, not because they were unserious, mind you, but because they got Irv so intrigued, so upset. What you said is good for several dinners, each as delicious as last night's." He glanced at the tables of American tourists. His face showed distaste. "I suppose most American Jews think anti-Semitism is worldwide. Like Cohen. Do you think Barbara agrees with him?" The question came casually. But the brown eyes studied my face. What did he already know?

"I don't know Barbara that well. Just a chance acquaintance from Washington I ran into at the American Colony. My good fortune." As I spoke, Feldman was busy with his soup, which had just arrived. Now his ears, rather than his eyes, were totally alert, I thought. "I've never discussed these matters with her, and of course she didn't say much last night."

"Yes, she was quiet, so I wondered," he said. "I met Lois only five years ago, when she and Irv moved here, but I gather the father and mother of the two girls were Zionists, faithful to Israel."

This was not what Barbara had said.

"Zionism," he said, "seems to run in families. Very hard not to have chauvinistic views on Israel deep down if your parents had them when you were growing up."

"People do change."

"Sometimes. But I didn't, not as far as gut convictions were concerned. I doubt if you did either." He smiled again. I felt he was about to change the subject, as if the present one had served its purpose. What purpose? I had protested too much. Did he now know I was Barbara's lover?

The main course arrived. Yes, I thought, he could be in intelligence or it could be as he said it was. He had not asked what Barbara's job was; presumably he knew the answer.

"I suppose," he said, pretending to shatter the illusion our meeting was a purely social affair, "I should tell you the real purpose of this lunch, or put another way, the means by which I'll put it on my expense account."

I protested it should be my lunch.

"No, today you're the guest of the Israeli government, a fact I suspect you'll find less than thrilling. Never mind. It won't be so bad." He examined the table to see if I had all I wanted. More beer? I indicated he had my complete attention.

"Well," he said, "one of my jobs at the ministry is to be staff person for a committee that worries about our relations with Arabs, and especially our near neighbors. We have our so-called experts. Someone on Syria, for instance, can always tell us the facts about Syria, who's doing what to whom in the military in Damascus, what the wheat crop will be if the weather holds. In general our information sources are good."

I nodded, wondering what came next. Most of us knew the Israelis had the facts of life across their frontiers well in hand.

"What we don't have is balanced information on the Palestinian communities in those countries and their effect on Palestinians inside our borders *and* in the occupied territories. Israelis in my view cannot be trusted, they color their information with either hate or excessive affection. Strange to relate, we have people who love all Palestinians no matter what."

I sat bemused, astonished at the familiar ring of his words. Was this a standard ploy for spooky bureaucrats like Feldman and Blake? What Blake had wanted, of course, was not only information on Palestine but cooperation.

"Of course," he said, "all my little experts try to *sound* balanced but each may be grinding a political or emotional axe, unbeknownst to me. So, quite frankly, you could be a help to me if you were willing."

"Of course I'm willing, since you're buying this fine lunch." I smiled, not meaning it, trying to keep things light. As so often in recent weeks I felt my gut beginning to tighten up. What was he after? The dining room, full now, contained tourists in all colors and states of dress. We could almost have been lunching at a resort hotel in New Jersey. At the next table sat a beautifully proportioned young woman in a yellow bathing suit, with a sweater over the shoulders. At another table, less like New Jersey, an American rabbi with skullcap was earning his livelihood by presiding over a table of elderly Brooklynites on pilgrimage, all chatting happily over non-kosher food.

"You know," I said, "I used to have close Palestinian connections. But that part of my life is long gone." I was proceeding cautiously.

"Listen," he said. "I don't want to make too big a thing of this. I just want to justify my expense account excesses." He looked around the dining room. "Good Lord, what a tourist trap. Food's good, otherwise dreadful."

"What could I tell you that you don't know much better than I?"

"Well, let's see." The plump waitress brought coffee, and Feldman put in a Spartan amount of sugar. "For instance, one question my committee wrestles with is the matter of alternatives to the PLO. Someday we'll have to talk to some Palestinian group. But talking with the PLO is now impossible, so our little committee has been asked to look around for alternatives. Just off the top of your head, do you have any ideas on what or who the alternative might be?"

He looked at me in friendly interested fashion, like a professor having a stimulating conversation at the faculty club. I remembered Barbara's comment that Feldman said only what he planned to say.

"No, no ideas at all." I wanted to sound as if it were the first time I'd thought about it. "I'd say probably there *is* no alternative. I don't remember running across a Palestinian who didn't want the PLO to negotiate for him. Has your committee come up with any notions?"

"Nothing much. One fellow endorses the Village Council idea, says we should give it another chance. When he says this, two other committee members burst into raucous laughter, as the phrase goes, and ask why Israel should trust Palestinian Quislings any more than Palestinians do."

"What about the West Bank mayors? And the mayor of Gaza?"

"Sounds good until you stop to think who they are. Most of them are strong PLO sympathizers and wouldn't move without a nod of approval."

The waitress brought more coffee. The crowd was thinning out.

"When you were at the Ramallah School," asked Feldman, "did you know a man named Yusuf Al-Khalil?"

Perhaps I should have anticipated the question, or something like it. My mind responded sluggishly, like a soldier deciding whether or not he's been hit by sniper fire.

"Yusuf Al-Khalil? Yes, I knew him at school. We called him Abu Hisham. I gather he's one of our distinguished alumni."

"Did you know him well?" He made it sound casual. Blake had worked up a remarkably good dossier on my life as a schoolboy; Feldman could have done the same.

"No, not well. But he was in my class. One of the leaders. Very nice fellow." I felt Feldman's gaze on my face. "Why do you ask?"

"As you say, not only a nice fellow but a leader. I hardly know him myself. In the nature of the case I can't chat with him. Perhaps you know he's the only man with enough prestige to carry the Palestinians with him if he negotiated, the only man who could unite the mayors and most of the nationalists and proceed without the PLO."

"I didn't realize he was that important."

"Oh yes. Definitely. And what is remarkable is he does it with a low profile. To the outside world, and to most Israelis, he's just an Arab lawyer with a shingle. But he knows excellent Hebrew. And he's got Israeli friends who are also lawyers. They work together to defend Palestinians who've had their land taken by the military or by illegal settlement. For just an Arab lawyer he has an extraordinary reputation. For honesty, for practical politics. And he may have a following, not disciples exactly but people who believe in him. A friend of mine thinks there's an organization."

"What kind of an organization?" This was highly interesting.

"I'm unable to say because I don't know much. This friend of mine, an acquaintance really, worries about such things. In strictest confidence I can tell you a bit. He says it has to be a small organization, otherwise we'd know more about it. About two years ago one of his people overheard two Palestinians talking near the Damascus Gate. Extraordinary luck, because they couldn't see him, he was behind some boxes. But that's what intelligence work is made of. Anyway, one said to the other something on the order of 'it would not help the *hai'a*.' On the face of it, nothing much. Our listener didn't know what the context was. The *hai'a*, or organization, was not any *hai'a* he recognized. But, most important, twice in the conversation the name Abu Hisham was mentioned."

Was this the nature of intelligence work? On this were momentous decisions based?

"Yes," he said, seeing my unbelieving look, "my reaction exactly. But apparently it's the follow-up makes the difference between good cops and investigative genius. Perhaps I could do the same if I had the manpower my friend has at his disposal. He set twenty men to work for three months listening for various things, including the word *hai'a*, especially if used in conjunction with the name Abu Hisham."

He hesitated a fraction of a second. I sat looking at him.

"Anyway," he went on, "in three months of listening in public places, markets, post office, tourist centers, big shops, and so on, his people reported five references to *hai'a* they didn't understand and in three instances in conjunction with the name Abu Hisham. Not much to go on, and there may be other Abu Hishams, but I respect my friend's instincts. He's convinced there's an organization."

"So what's been done about it?"

"Almost nothing. He couldn't justify further expense. The operation cost a great deal and his minister put his foot down. Told him to keep an eye out but otherwise forget it."

I sat back in my chair and looked at him. He smiled, and I smiled back. Why let me in on what must be classified material? Was he helping me, warning me, working on me in some way?

"Back to your original question," I said, needing something to say, "you say Yusuf Al-Khalil is a real possibility as an alternative. Did I understand you right?"

"Well, I mentioned his name because it's one of the alternatives we considered. Some corridor talk, especially around the PM's office, says it's worth a try. In the youthful bright set, ideas like this come and go, have their moments and disappear. My little committee is left with the residue."

"You mean the idea of Abu Hisham as an alternative is no longer possible?"

"Oh it could always be revived, especially if the PM himself made a casual remark about it to his secretary, who then whispered it to the bright young men." Feldman's respect for the bright young men seemed minimal.

"But is it a good idea, apart from what those young men are saying?" I wanted to pin him down to an opinion, to hear him say it was important, a good cause.

"No, definitely not. Not right now. Perhaps in five years, maybe a decade." Shifting to elaborate sarcasm he said that discussions with Palestinians right now would interfere with putting settlements into the occupied territories, actions crucial to creating better negotiating conditions.

I wanted him on my side. "Doesn't one have to try, have to make a move? The Israeli state of mind, how can it change if no one gives it a push, if no one forces people to re-think?"

He gave me a hard look. The real Feldman, I thought, was not far away. "My heart's in the same place as yours," he said. "But my time plan is more realistic. Both sides must be despairing, dead tired, before they're willing to talk. Ten years maybe? Right now our side thinks it can win. We think the proper application of force will produce the security needed by a Jewish state. No need yet for compromise. That's what we think."

He stared out the window at Jewish Jerusalem.

"Well, not all of us," he said, the real Feldman now in open view. "Since Lebanon, since the madmen in Likud got hold of us, lots of people have asked questions. Does force work? Has it served the interests of the Jewish state? The only answer possible, on the evidence from Lebanon, is a resounding no. But this hasn't sunk in with the voters. It'll take another glorious failure of force, maybe a war with Syria. Another victory turning into defeat."

We said nothing for a long moment. What messages was I supposed to receive? Negotiation now wouldn't work? And why me? Because, I supposed, he knew my real reasons for being in Jerusalem.

"Of course," said Feldman, his inner self disappearing again, "you Americans are the real imponderables."

Having delivered his messages, whatever they were, he was changing the subject. Presumably my responses, even if meant to deceive, had given him the answers he sought.

"It would interest me to know," I said, "how much pressure you get from the Americans about the PLO. About negotiating with them."

"There's always some."

"Yes, sure, but someone told me there'd been a lot lately." Reginald Hughes, my journalist friend whom I'd seen in Beirut at the Commodore, had said a lot more than that; he'd said the CIA could deliver an Israeli agreement to negotiate, that the CIA had said as much to Fatah.

Feldman became suddenly busy with the check. "Well," he said finally, "there's been a bit extra lately. It comes and goes. We have to resist, of course. We can't negotiate now with anyone. Maybe sometime with someone else. As I said."

"You mean someone like Abu Hisham?"

"Yes, in a few years. Someone like that. That's my personal hope. But the bright young men don't want to negotiate with anybody. Ever."

"Have you ever met a man named Curtis Blake?" I threw caution to the winds.

He stared for a moment. "Funny you should ask," he said. "There's a big-time Washington bureaucrat by that name who's been here several times recently, making the rounds. A pushy opinionated sort. Stupid in a special way. Obsessive. Do you know him personally?"

"Not really. I met him once in Washington at some cocktail party. He talked as if he knew a lot about Israel."

"He knows an odd assortment of people, Israelis and Palestinians, but not much about Israel. We don't take him seriously." Feldman spoke curtly. For an instant his slender face showed acute distaste.

I made a move to go. He made no further mention of helping with information on Palestinians. We exchanged pleasantries a few moments. As we walked into the lobby, I saw Feldman's eyes scan the assemblage. My dark-suited follower was seated in a chair, reading the Jerusalem Post. Perhaps Feldman focused on the man, but I could not be sure.

*　　　　*　　　　*

I wandered back through the old city, killing time, presuming my follower was behind me. Bright sun hit the shuttered houses and shop fronts, forming thin triangles of cool-looking shadow. The streets had emptied out; it was siesta time, late spring, hot and drowsy. Even my stomach muscles started to relax. No automobiles inside the old walls, just quiet. Looking to right and left, down passages no wider than two pairs of shoulders, I saw plants, patios, once a small fountain surrounded by beds of ferns and geraniums. The smells, brought out by the warmth of early afternoon, were familiar and comforting. As if I had come home on baking day.

More than killing time, strolls like this had become restorative. During my last stay I'd explored the old city whenever I found a spare half-hour, sauntering and remembering. Ten steps in, through the Damascus Gate, I entered a world I wanted back. Irrationally, I felt safe inside, strolling without looking over my shoulder.

On this day, as on other days, I wanted to be soothed by memories. Instead I found myself pondering and worrying. What about Feldman? My instincts assured me he was devious. At a relatively honest moment he had said the political climate had to change and that reconciliation would take five or ten years. Abu Kerim had said the Palestinian struggle had to go on until the PLO was recognized as the only legitimate negotiator. The positions were not inconsistent.

I had to talk to Abu Hisham, but I had to curb my impatience. The day after tomorrow seemed a long way off. Turning a corner into an empty street, I walked up toward Herod's Gate. Shuttered shops gave way to silent hospices with brass plates at the doors, spiritual embassies of the world's Christian sects, each seeking to outmaneuver the others for special privileges in their Holy City.

"You have the time?"

The voice seemed to come from nowhere. Looking around quickly I saw a Palestinian peasant, his hand pointing to my wristwatch. He must have emerged from a narrow passage on my right. Unshaven, dressed traditionally in *galabiya* and headpiece. He looked at me with a stupid expression.

I looked at my watch, glanced up in time to see the stupid look turn vicious. His arm went suddenly into motion and hit hard on my shoulder, then on my neck. I went down, slumping against the front wall of a house on the narrow street, holding up my arms to ward off blows. Three men in peasant garb suddenly surrounded me, kicking at me with polished brown shoes. They muttered Arabic expressions such as "God give me strength" and "This for the Arab nation." I saw the flash of a knife, and someone said: "Put it into him."

Desperately I kicked at the oncoming blade. A whistle blew. The knife clattered to the ground, and the three men ran off down a side alley, shoes clacking on cobblestone. From up the street sprinted two Israeli police, machine pistols ready to fire. The attackers had disappeared. Bending over me, a policeman asked something in Hebrew.

"I speak English," I said in a whisper. I said it again louder. It hurt my ribs when I talked.

"How badly are you hurt?" His English was good. Both men looked spruce, efficient.

"Not sure yet." I started to get up. I felt dizzy. The English-speaker put out a hand to help me.

"How do you feel now?"

"All right, I think. Ribs hurt. Neck, shoulder, not so good."

"Shall we get you to a hospital?"

What I wanted was to get to the American Colony and lie down, without any police complications or inquiries.

"I think I'm all right." I felt I could manage. No bones broken. The rib problem would go away.

"May we see your papers?"

I produced my passport, told them where I was staying, explained my business in Israel. I stood unsteadily, but my voice came through stronger now; I was getting used to the aches. I said I needed a rest, that was all.

"Do you have an idea why these men attacked you?" The English-speaker, I noticed, was a sergeant.

"No. Perhaps they wanted money." We both knew such an explanation bordered on absurdity. Old-fashioned robbers waste no time kicking and flashing knives. The sergeant picked up the knife, which had a finely honed slender blade and bone handle.

"Palestinian," he said. "Why would Palestinians wish to kill you?"

"I don't know. Perhaps they didn't. Probably a mistake."

"Did you recognize any of them?"

"No. Just Palestinians in the usual *galabiya*. One was a peasant. Maybe the others."

The sergeant stared at me. A handsome dark-haired man with a neatly trimmed moustache, slender but compact. I shouldn't have used the word *galabiya* or shown myself able to distinguish a peasant from a townsman. The interest of the Israeli police could make things difficult, even impossible.

"Well," I said, "I really don't know anything about it. Those clothes they wear, aren't they called *galabiyas*?"

"Yes." The sergeant frowned slightly. "Did the men say anything while they were beating you?"

"Only some words I didn't understand."

The sergeant's face showed nothing. Pulling a notebook out of a pocket, he began writing. He asked his companion something in Hebrew, and the man responded with a grin. He wrote some more, then put the notebook away.

"Mr. Hampton, I have to make a full report on this. The more information we have, the better. If you remember anything helpful, I'd appreciate hearing. Here is the number where I can be reached. Ask for Daoud."

He handed me a slip of paper. I said I'd get in touch if I remembered anything, and he nodded his thanks.

"Also," he said, drily, "if you happen to think why anyone wants to kill you, it would help us find the men who tried. I think you realize you were lucky we happened along."

Looking at the deserted street, I said I did. They offered to arrange a ride to the hotel, but I declined, saying the walk would help work out the stiffness. Sergeant Daoud seemed to agree. They walked with me as far as Herod's Gate and saw me out into the human traffic on Suleiman Street.

Walking slowly to the hotel, I felt my bruised body would recover. I thought guiltily, happily, I'd be able to sleep with Barbara that night. My neck began to stiffen up.

Then I stopped. Suddenly I knew that Israelis, not Palestinians, had attacked me. They made one small slip, which started a line of thought. One of them had said "Put it into him" and in Arabic the word "put" has a hard "h." Like the cab driver who had brought me from the airport, the man said it the way Oriental Jews and Greeks often do, with a special guttural sound that is a source of Arab jokes. A working shibboleth for modern Palestine.

So the whole thing was a fake. The attack, the rescue, the knife. If I were to be stabbed, they would stab me as soon as possible, not after a round of chopping and kicking and muttering in Arabic. After the whistle sounded, with ample time to do the job, they let the Palestinian knife fell to the ground. They wanted to be sure I saw it.

In fact they had staged the event with skill and had improvised with speed and efficiency. How did they know I was wandering through the old city? They couldn't have known my route beforehand; I hadn't known it myself when I started out. And the implications? If Sergeant Daoud had connections with Feldman, he had to know I understood the Arabic of my assailants. If the connections involved my dark-suited follower, who had disappeared, the situation probably remained the same. My lie would confirm, if further confirmation were needed, that I was playing some game.

*   *   *

Filling the bathtub almost full, I made the water as hot as I thought I could stand. My body yearned to submerge quickly but the process took five minutes. Then the heat wrapped itself around me and soaked in. I got my bruised neck under water. My muscles began to relax.

But which Israelis, for God's sake? Feldman, that likable lunch partner? Someone else? If someone was trying to scare me off, why bother if, as Feldman implied, Blake's plot was bound to fail?

Now I was muttering to myself. Too simple, I said, try something else. Someone in the Israeli government wanted to negotiate with Abu Hisham, and someone else (Feldman, say) was against it. Perhaps because it would fail and be an embarrassment to the government. Or it faced the government with choices it could not afford to face. Such as giving up the West Bank in return for a peace settlement. Such as a Palestinian state.

I kept emptying the tub halfway and refilling with hotter water. I felt better, well enough to keep a business appointment, and finally heaved myself out. Without the hot water I felt shaky. Putting on socks produced sudden pain. But moving carefully, I could perform the usual routines. I couldn't turn my head, I had to turn my shoulders. The right side of my neck had a bruise the size and color of an inkwell. My face was unmarked.

Ehud Elath, professor of history, was seated near the main entrance. He looked up with a smile.

"Greetings," he said. "I wondered if I'd see you here. I'm waiting to meet an academic friend but I'm a bit early. I enjoyed our conversation last night."

Was it only last night?

"Do sit down for a minute, keep me company." The gentle voice and manner were the same. "Better still, since it looks as if I've got more than a half-hour, let me treat you to something by the pool."

I thought I detected a note of entreaty. Glancing at my watch, I decided to telephone and delay my appointment. I saw no sign of the Israeli plainclothesman. It crossed my mind that last night's dinner party was lingering on. I wondered if "an academic friend" existed.

We sat at a table in the glassed-in cafeteria by the pool. Three teenagers, shouting at each other in accents from the American South, played tag in and out of the water. We ordered lemonade from a sleepy waitress. I felt a slight awkwardness.

"Do you often come to this side of town?" My bruised body sought a comfortable position on the plastic chair.

"Yes, I make a point of it. I suppose to prove I'm a friend of all the world, like Kipling's Kim." He paused, then smiled. "And how was your lunch with Moshe?" He must, I surmised, have overheard Feldman's quiet suggestion the night before.

"It was a nice occasion," I said, looking at him pleasantly, wondering what came next. If he had something he wanted to say, how to help him say it? In the bright daylight the signs of age showed on his face. Through the white beard I saw that the flesh sagged and hung off the cheekbones, and the ears had a long and rubbery look. Before being plump, I thought, he was thin. I imagined him as a slender young scholar, not a guru with a following, yet much-loved by a few students. The previous evening I had understood he was a prestigious academic.

"Ah that fellow. Moshe is such good company. I suppose he picked your brains and got you to tell him Palestinian secrets. Or was he circumspect?"

"We chatted about everything, including Palestinians." I thought I might do some digging. "He seemed interested in the question of alternatives to the PLO, someone else to negotiate with. He wondered if I had any notions."

Elath gave a professorial smile. "You mean, he didn't come up with notions of his own?"

"He talked about Village Councils and what a poor idea that was. Then he mentioned the name of a man I knew slightly years ago in Ramallah, a lawyer named Yusuf Al-Khalil. He said this man was the sort the Israeli government could eventually deal with."

"You mean as a negotiator for all Palestinians?"

"That's what he implied, as a possibility only. I think he was playing around with ideas." I tried to be casual.

"I've known Moshe for years, and we are good friends, but in so many ways he will always be an acquaintance. With friends, one knows what they are thinking. Not with Moshe." I felt he was getting close to the message he wanted to deliver.

"How long have you known Moshe?" I asked.

"Perhaps twenty years. I've always found him charming and intelligent. And through him I met Irv and Lois Cohen, for which I must be forever grateful. When my wife died, the Cohens took care of me."

He scratched the side of his jaw under the beard, then went on. "You see, we can disagree with Irv with total honesty. He remains steadfast in friendship. But Moshe? One never knows. He's a very important man, one of Israel's key bureaucrats, much more powerful than most people realize. But much as I like him, I have to say he can be unprincipled. Yes, that is what I have to say. Unprincipled."

He said it as if getting a heavy burden off his back. He looked at me steadily. I opened my mouth to make an acknowledging remark but he held up his hand.

"Moshe Feldman, you see, is a nationalist, an ardent one but highly specialized, in the Darwinian sense. He does not believe in force; he believes in brains. The real Moshe? Hard to say. Probably he'd love to control the West Bank without the help of the Israeli Defense Forces. What he says is what the situation calls for, not what he believes. If he likes you and you are not an antagonist, you would never notice anything but charm."

The steady gaze continued for a moment more. Then he sat back in his chair. The gentle smile reappeared. We sipped our lemonades.

"You see," he said, "I felt I should tell you to be careful of Moshe."

I stared. "But why should I worry about such a thing? I'm grateful to you, of course, but I really have no reason to ..."

He interrupted quickly. "Yes, yes, you are right, of course you have no reason to worry about him. It's just that I ... You see, Irv told me Moshe asked to meet you."

"Why would that be?"

"I really don't know. He told Irv you were a friend of Barbara's and would be an interesting person to talk to. Before the dinner party, had you ever heard the name Moshe Feldman?"

"No," I said. "This is all very curious."

"I thought so too."

He drained his lemonade and stood up, looking tired around the eyes. He said he had students waiting for him at the university. As we shook hands he gave a sudden elfin grin, saying that his "academic friend" was apparently unable to make the appointment.

∗   ∗   ∗

We made love before dinner. She drew her breath in quickly when she saw the black-and-blue bruises on my neck and ribs. I said I'd tell her about it later. I think she wanted to talk but I said I wanted to make love before doing anything else. Perhaps it was a way of by-passing anger and fear. She insisted on getting on top and kept her weight off my body. Her breasts rubbed lightly against my chest. She would bend her head and kiss me tenderly in the rhythm of love-making, then when our passion mounted, I held her down against me, the ache of my ribs a sort of tribute.

"I love you," I said. "Very very much." As I said it, I felt guilty but somehow liberated. "Yes, I love you," I said again, and I liked the sound of it and I knew it was true. Now I could tell her why I loved her, the extraordinary things about her, the tenderness, the honesty in her eyes, the compassion. Had I said such things to Cath? Yes, but long ago. When I made love to Cath these days, it was more physical, less openhearted; with Cath I was silently intent on the mechanics, keeping thoughts to myself, whispering no endearments, seemingly unmoved.

We lay side by side. Putting her hand over my mouth to stop the flow of happy words, she held me tight, saying she loved me too. "Very much," she said. She kissed me again and again, on the cheek, the ear, the mouth. "You love me for myself, for who I am ..." She said she was fulfilled by this thought. She said she felt transported when we made love, as with no one else before. We did not talk about the future. That is, what we were to become to each other.

Finally we had to talk about the events of the day, and I reported on the visit to Ni'meh, my Israeli follower, the Feldman lunch, the fake murder attempt and Sergeant Daoud's miraculous intervention, the "chance meeting" with Elath. First she wanted to know how badly I was hurt, then with gentle questions had me fill in the details she needed. During the silences between questions, her embrace would tighten suddenly, involuntarily. Eventually I said I was hungry, and so, smiling, she helped me on with shoes and socks, saying she had to keep me in the very best physical condition. We made our way to a restaurant on Asfahani Street to eat *kufta* and *kabab*.

Every so often her eyes focused not on me but on the wall beyond. Out came another question, seeking another detail about the day's events. I found myself answering in a way that would protect her from a reality I did not wish us to contemplate on this particular evening. But she did not allow it, continuing each line of questioning until reality surfaced.

"I found out a bit about Feldman," she said. "He's very powerful, apparently the key bureaucrat handling relations between the PM and the intelligence services."

"Elath also said he was very powerful. Why would he pay so much attention to me?"

"That's the question." She was quiet a moment. "I shouldn't tell you this. Each time Blake comes out here, he spends a long time alone with Feldman. Our man in Tel Aviv is not sure what they talk about and is peeved he is not asked to come along. He was surprised I didn't know about Feldman."

"Blake didn't brief you on him?"

"No. Very odd. I wasn't even given his name. Why not? Of course Blake's a great actor, and if he wanted to conceal something, he'd have no trouble. None of us would dare query him on something like that, he takes it out personally on people who get uppity, but why not brief me on someone that important? It would be the proper thing to do. Why not tell Rosberg?"

"You sure he didn't tell Rosberg?"

"Absolutely." She looked at the wall again. "I shouldn't be telling you any of this."

We walked back arm in arm. I did not think we were being followed and said so. She said she'd already checked. She asked how my ribs felt.

"Why would someone think I'd be scared off by Palestinians?" I asked.

"For some reason someone's reminding you about Palestinians. Maybe someone thinks you're not stubborn. Or maybe they know you are."

We said goodnight in the lobby for the benefit of the nightman at the desk.

THIRTEEN

Jerusalem, May 1990

In the morning the young man who went to the Ramallah School watched me from the desk. A taxi as usual? Turning to the switchboard, he plugged in a line. Barbara, impatient that the next step was twenty-four hours away, was passing the time in her room with a good book. I didn't see the dark-suited plainclothesman. In two minutes the taxi arrived, an old well-polished Ford with an outsize luggage rack. The driver, older than the Ford by five decades, wore a dark jacket and open blue shirt. He welcomed me without leaving the front seat, made no attempt to speak English. Giving an address on the Jewish side, I edged my aching ribs into the car. When I heard a car start up down the street, I assumed my Israeli follower was on the job.

"A delightful day," said the driver, struggling to put the car in gear. Yes, I thought, the sky pure blue, that special Jerusalem blue, and the trees making patterns of sun and shadow on the quiet street.

The driver went on in Arabic, a Bedouin dialect that pleased the ear, commenting on the weather of the previous winter and the winter before that. An old man happy with a listener. I took in little that he said; my mind was elsewhere. Suddenly I heard something familiar, a name I knew. I came alert.

"Excuse me, what did you say?"

"I said, Abu Hisham wants to see you. He asked me to bring you." His eyes watched me in the mirror. The old taxi suddenly speeded up, turned two corners, then stopped abruptly. A man dressed in jacket and tie sprinted to open the door of the Ford, sat quickly beside me. The taxi took off in a rush. The man turned and smiled.

"Please do not worry," he said in English. "Abu Hisham said to tell you it is a long time since 'omelettes of fluffy lust.' He said you'd recognize that phrase." The man smiled again. He had the manners and speech of Palestinian upper crust; his dark hair, thin enough to see his scalp, lay flat on top of a square face that was dark along the jaw despite a recent shave. I started to speak, to protest, to think about jumping from the fast-moving taxi; my bruised body cringed from another beating. The man kept smiling anxiously, the phrase he used began to sink in. Omelettes of fluffy lust, he'd said.

I too began to smile, incredulous and delighted. The phrase came from a poem by e e cummings, to whom a young English teacher, just out of Haverford, had introduced us. Abu Taleb had taken the collected poems from the library and we had them in our room a month. Sitting absorbed, he would suddenly lift his arm and quote passages, usually selected for graphic descriptions of the sex act, and one hilarious evening he gave us the phrase that became a password among us. We began using expressions such as "How fluffy!" and "What an omelette!"

The memories brought an involuntary chuckle. My companion sat back relieved. Our ancient taxi was now moving very fast, cutting corners one after the other. At each turn we held on to ancient straps.

"Sometime Abu Hisham will explain the special magic of that phrase," said the man beside me. "If you are such old friends, why the rigmarole? But I do what I'm told."

"What is your name?" I braced myself as we turned yet another corner. If the Israeli was still trying to follow, he would by this time know he'd failed.

My companion laughed in an embarrassed way. "No name at the moment. Abu Nothing, I guess." His accent had a trace of Scotland, perhaps an instructor or a nanny from Edinburgh years back. "Abu Hisham will ask you to forget you've seen me."

The old Ford made one more turn, then swung quickly into a gravel lane whose entrance was almost obscured by large oleanders. We were still in East Jerusalem, but I could not have found the lane again. The car brushed rapidly against the oleanders for fifty yards, then entered a garage and braked to a quick stop. Immediately someone shut the doors behind us.

In the semi-darkness I saw a small boy locking the garage. At the other end a door, open a crack, through which I saw foliage. My companion hustled me through the door saying he was sorry to rush me. Quickly we moved onto a path hidden from view by more oleanders, almost a jungle trail, and through another door set into a concrete wall. I thought we had walked along the edge of a large garden but I couldn't be sure.

Beyond this door came another dark room with the smell of a garage, and beyond that yet another. In the second one stood a small delivery truck, and my companion pointed to the back of it. I understood I was to get in.

"I apologize," he said. "We cannot be too careful. You'll have a ride in complete darkness for a while, but your old friend is waiting for you at the other end. Good luck." He smiled again, shook my hand, closed the doors. The truck moved off. I never got a glimpse of the driver.

In the next half-hour I lost my bearings completely. Several times the truck stopped for short periods, then took off quickly. After many corners, I gave up trying to figure directions and distances. Just before the last stop we went onto a gravel road. Then I heard the closing of more garage doors.

He opened the back door of the delivery truck and peered in. We stared at each other, then started to laugh.

"What an omelette," he said.

The laughter turned into broad grins.

*   *   *

The room was small and square, unlit except for a casement window that looked out on a sunlit garden with red and yellow rose bushes in front of a high stucco wall. We sat in armchairs, a prayer rug stretched between us, a coffee table within reach. The window curtains were gray, in tasteful contrast to a floor of red tile. Against the wall stood a stack of folding chairs. Abu Hisham had closed the door in from the garage. Another door, I guessed, led to the main parts of a large silent house.

We had talked for two hours, as if in a hurry to get everything said. If Abu Hisham had special messages for me, we had not reached the appropriate moment for delivering them. We covered other things first: Abu Kerim, the Dajanis, health, wives, children, the personal hopes and disappointments of two decades. Reminded by a word or a random thought of things we wanted to mention, we checked items off on unwritten agendas, aware of the totality of what ultimately had to be said. A smile signaled remembrance of past dialogue or episode or phrase; the other would grin in response. As with the other two, the language was the conversational shorthand of Ramallah. A word or a gesture sufficed for a paragraph of thought or feeling.

He looked much the same. A bit fleshier around the clean-shaven face, a bit paunchier around the gut, a full head of dark hair. The light brown eyes were steady and alert, though they seemed more deeply set because the circles surrounding them were heavily wrinkled. His gaze was still direct, whether listening or talking. The arms revealed by the short-sleeved navy-blue shirt were still muscular, the tall body still graceful. The marks of leadership, of being somebody, showed on his face, in the way he carried himself. This had always been true.

Once he got up to make Turkish coffee on a ring fed by bottled gas on the tile floor. He sat on his haunches, like a villager, as he guided the ritual bubbling of the brew. Yet he was as far from being a villager as any Palestinian I knew – born a landowning aristocrat, member of a Jerusalem family whose influence stretched centuries back, a townsman in every way. A few generations ago, at the right moment, neither too soon nor too late to be considered odd, the family had switched with the times, shifting to Western dress, Western bathrooms and toilets, Western education for children. When he was growing up, Abu Hisham spoke Arabic with his mother and English only with his father. His great grandfather had spoken Turkish, using Arabic for the servants.

I think Gav Middleton's phrase "old buddies" implies less in America. At Ramallah the four of us constituted a *shirka*, which meant a close-knit group presenting a common front to the outside world, a partnership whose members consulted each other first, an alliance not formed against anybody or anything, yet breakable only under dramatic pressures. Something like a marriage. And not uncommon. Abu Hisham and I were back on that intimate footing the minute I stepped out of the truck.

I noticed nothing similar at Swarthmore, where the notion of unthinking support for someone else was confined to having a girlfriend, a part-time partnership for purposes such as sex or campus events. In a sense Cath and I followed that road, though we became closer than most campus twosomes. Almost a *shirka*. Among the men the competition for individual success never cooled, or so it seemed to me, and after a few months in America I expected less from friendship. Thus did my Americanization proceed.

So the reunion with Abu Hisham brought a moment of happiness. Partly because I had not seen him for so long, also because he was always important to me, as he was to Abu Kerim. Abu Taleb, bolstered by a separate and powerful Bedouin tradition, may somehow have been less dependent on Abu Hisham's good opinion, but nonetheless a closeness had always been there. Thus in that small room in Jerusalem the smiles that kept appearing on our faces reflected not amusement but the healing re-awareness of buddyship, Arab style, the rush of feeling arising from the reminder we'd always be on the same side.

*   *   *

We talked first about Abu Kerim. Not the details of the shooting and the circumstances, those came later, just the blank space, the void. The feeling of not having him around. Abu Hisham said finally he supposed it was bound to happen sooner or later.

"I feel responsible," I said.

"Why?" He looked at me carefully.

"We'll get into that when we talk about the Washington business."

He nodded, accepting my agenda. "Just the same, as a general proposition people make their own choices. He selected his way of life, not you. He lived in his particular world for a long time. He could have gotten out."

"Yes, but he could still be in it and alive. Same with the Dajanis."

"Look, he's gone," he said. "I feel responsible too, not for the killing, not directly. But somehow, somehow I should have gotten him out of Beirut, off to the Gulf, out of things. In Beirut you have to lose. Eventually." His eyes filled with tears, but the direct gaze did not waver. "It's too loose, too easy for killers."

"I'd like to kill someone but I don't know who to kill."

The gaze intensified. "It would do no good, and if you did, you'd never be able to forget. You're tough and resilient, but killing is something you couldn't handle. I doubt if you've changed."

"Maybe not."

But for a moment I was seduced by the pleasant thought of counter-attack, of inflicting lethal damage on someone else.

*   *   *

The hardest part was telling me about the accident, the death of his son. He asked if I'd heard about it, and I nodded.

"It was my fault, my fault," he said. "Poor little boy, such a little fellow, very decent. I shouldn't have allowed him out on that busy street, at least I should have had someone with him. I was busy with something. It was so quick. A big truck, Palestinian driver from Jericho. No sense."

"The others?"

"Azizeh thinks it was her fault. So she keeps telling me. Because she knows I blame myself. The other two kids seem okay. Five years ago now. They haven't forgotten but maybe the memories are less acute."

He looked away. "Sometimes it's hard to figure one's priorities. What should I have been busy about when it happened? Looking after my son, looking after my career, looking after Palestine, or what? The truck crushed his skull, you know, just crushed it."

"How does Azizeh cope?"

"She manages. It's tough on her. She's a brave woman."

"I was sorry to meet her only that one time." I wanted to change the subject.

"Yes," he said gratefully, "a tricky time. The one time I was allowed out of Israel, expelled by courtesy of the government, there you were in Jerusalem." He sat a moment saying nothing, forcing himself to forget the truck and the crunch of the small skull. Then, as if telling me to take his mind off unpleasant memories, he asked about Cath. Not the usual information. He meant, *What was she really like?*

"Well, she looks like a Nordic goddess, I guess." I was proud to say this. "Lots of energy. Very competent. And very stalwart, very steadfast. I mean, she puts up with a lot."

"A lot of what? You?" A smile.

"Well, partly me. She says I can't relax, let it all out." I grinned. "Also there's my choice of places to live. She likes Cairo better than Jidda."

"You mean she'd rather live in Pennsylvania." He paused. "Still, Cairo's not a bad place. God, I'd give a lot for a holiday there. Even Jidda. Either one. I asked the government for a trip to Egypt last year. They turned me down within twenty-four hours. You and I and Abu Taleb, long evenings in a Cairo café. Pretty special. And for a while it'd be nice not to be followed all the time."

"All the time?"

"Almost. Right now they only think they know where I am. At least I hope so."

"Who follows you?"

"I've stopped trying to work it out. Sometimes a Palestinian hardliner. Various lesser Israelis. Only thing I'm sure of is the Israelis don't all work for the same boss."

"Why you especially?"

"Why not?" He looked amused. "Maybe they know you're a friend of mine. After all, the Israelis have apparently got someone following you too. Or did. Whoever it was, my boys confused him this morning."

He got up to make more coffee, an intermission before the "business" part of our conversation. But he had something else on his mind. With the next question he had his back to me, granting me a moment free from the steady gaze as I sought an answer.

"What about the brunette woman, the one at the hotel?" His voice was gentle, sympathetic. He was not judging me. He only wanted to know.

I stared out the window at the red and yellow roses. He finished pouring coffee into the small cups but waited with his back to me. What about her, indeed? If we were reporting on the important happenings of our lives, I had to tell him about Barbara Corum, but I was ashamed to let him know of my faithlessness to Cath.

"She works for the American government," I said finally. "It's part of why I came to Jerusalem."

"I know all that." His information network was apparently functioning well. He turned and handed me my cup. His face showed compassion. "I meant, what is she to you?"

I had known he meant exactly that. He looked into his Turkish coffee as if absorbed. To save me the awkwardness of answering right away, he went on talking.

"You and I have known each other a long time," he said. "I was worried more than twenty years might change you or change things between us. That was stupid. You are the same, harder, more sophisticated perhaps, a few American additions, but really the same. For you to have an affair would not be easy. I could never imagine you making love casually."

I forced a smile, though I did not feel like smiling. "You mean I'm not like Abu Kerim."

"That is certain." He followed my lead for the moment. "For Abu Kerim women were convenient receptacles. Whenever a woman was unwilling, he wasted no time, moved on to another. His only real love affair was Palestine. Or the creation of Palestine. Like an orgasm. What happens afterward? What kind of society will Palestine have? He never thought that far ahead."

He went to the window, coffee cup in hand, and looked intently at the roses. "The rest of us have families. We have to look ahead. If Palestine exists again, what kind of life will there be for our children? Just to have Palestine again, is it worth it? Do we need a certain kind of Palestine?"

"I have not looked ahead. I do not know whether it is worth it, and I do not know what it means for my children." He knew I was not talking about Palestine. The image of the two children in Cairo was suddenly before me. Cath was with them.

"You are in love with two women?"

"I guess so." Then in a surge of sudden knowledge about myself, I said, "Yes, I am."

"With you it could not be otherwise, I suppose." He smiled. "Now if it were me, I'd have a discreet affair and then forget it. Azizeh would never know. Is that not possible?"

I shook my head.

*   *   *

Later.

"What did you mean when you said you knew all that, all that about the American government?"

"I meant I knew why you came to Jerusalem. Getting me to negotiate with the Israelis."

"How did you know about Barbara Corum?"

"You mean, how did I know she worked for the Americans or how did I know you were having an affair?"

"Both. And it's not an affair." The choice of words made it tawdry.

"Sorry. You're right, it can't be an affair. Whatever you call it, it's not hard to know when people are in love. Even when they pretend to be strangers at breakfast." He smiled gently at the disbelief on my face. "Jerusalem is a small town, almost as small as in our Ramallah days. Provincial, I suppose. At least on this side of town. The word gets around fast if you listen for it."

I thought of Moshe Feldman, his confidential reporting about Israeli plainclothesmen who listened for clues about an unknown *hai'a*.

"Yes, but how do you listen for it?" I asked. "Do you have a group that listens and then lets you know?"

He looked at me intently, faint surprise on his face.

"Have you heard about something like that?"

"I had lunch yesterday with an Israeli named Feldman. He said an organization probably existed but was still unidentified. And associated with the word *hai'a* and the name Abu Hisham."

"Ah, Moshe Feldman." He looked relieved. "A mysterious fellow. We've never met, but he sends me messages. He must have known you'd be seeing me. Did he say so?"

"He asked if I knew you. I said I knew you from Ramallah but not well."

"Then he knows why you're here. But who doesn't? Anyway, it's nice of him to send the message."

"What's the message?"

"Hard to know exactly. Maybe he's saying keep out of things, especially the thing you came about, and don't give Israel any trouble. Maybe he's cautioning us both."

"Why should he send you messages?"

"I can only assume he thinks I might be useful sometime. Beyond that I don't know. He may be telling me to be careful. I've got a lot of theories, some complicated. The simplest one is he does not, under any circumstances, want the government to be faced with talking to Palestinians. Talk means compromise, perhaps even territorial compromise."

"He talked about negotiating with someone like you but said it could only happen after a few years."

"Interesting. Another message."

"I think he meant it. Perhaps he wants you to know this."

"Perhaps. I keep a mental list of his messages. What's your hunch?"

"He's a devious fellow, but just the same I think he has you in mind as a negotiator. Though not now. Sometime down the road."

"That fits with other things I've been picking up." He paused. "If true, it could change matters a bit."

We were quiet a moment.

"The key, of course, is the occupied territories," he said.

"You mean, if Israel keeps them, she eventually has more Palestinians than Jews."

"Right. So we must have the foresight to stick where we are. Maybe people like Feldman think, or did think, they can trick us into leaving. For Jordan, for instance. Then they won't have to worry about population statistics and being outvoted. Only then can they afford to be a democracy. This is the real battle."

*　　　　　*　　　　　*

Finally we began discussing "my project," known to me as "Blake's plot." It seemed like moving to the periphery of things; what was central had gone before, the fine-tuning of a relationship that had been proceeding at long distance for too long. Abu Hisham, as we talked, had settled farther back into his armchair and now had his feet up, arms around knees, in a posture of years ago. But the steady gaze persisted. I sat sideways, legs dangling over an upholstered arm.

Blake and his machinations were clearly at the heart of the matter. My life being in danger, or so I believed, I had to find a way to cope with personal peril. And why had so many other people had to die? For God's sake, why? I counted on Abu Hisham to find a way out. I asked again how he knew Barbara was part of what was happening. He hesitated, like someone reluctant to leave a warm fireplace and face the winter outside.

"Yes," he said finally. He gave a sigh, shifted in his chair, dropped his feet to the floor. "I suppose we should begin on all that. Shall I start?"

He knew a lot about Blake's plot, a surprising amount if one included the informed guesswork. And why not? A story known in Beirut is surely known in Jerusalem. If only Blake's statement were true, I thought yet again, that no one knew the story except Blake and Barbara and Rosberg and me. I could have paid a social call on Abu Hisham and his family. Or could I? Anyway, someone had blabbed, and now we were all maneuvering and manipulating, and some of us dying, in the name of Israel or Palestine or peace. And was it Feldman's Israel or Sharon's? Abu Hisham's Palestine or that of an extremist?

His voice changed gear. It had been relaxed, almost in schoolboy mode; now it took on authority, the voice of someone used to burdens and to taking charge. Behind the voice I heard something else, akin to discouragement or tiredness, yet mixed with doggedness, as if it were immoral not to carry on. Did he also yearn for freedom from worry?

He did not know the names of the CIA players in the story, except that Barbara was part of it. But without knowing the name Blake, he knew what was concocted and why. When he heard I'd been asked to contact him, he'd guessed I would say yes in memory of my father. He knew I was almost killed in Cairo. I told him about the attempt in Beirut.

"Later," he said, "when we know all the facts available to the two of us, we can discuss the scheme itself. Whether it has any merit, I mean. I think not. At least I can find none so far. A silly death-dealing notion by a silly bureaucrat. But later I will listen to what you have to say."

His words thudded against my hopes, my dream of peace. We sat silently as I absorbed his pessimism. Reluctantly, I agreed to lay out the facts first. I cast about for things I wanted to know. Not difficult to find.

"How did you know about the Cairo business?"

"PLO sources."

"Abu Kerim?"

"No, precisely not." He smiled without humor. "Abu Kerim and I haven't communicated directly for years. We had an understanding. I have other PLO sources."

"Where are they?"

"Lots of places. The word gets around. They have a man in Washington, one in Cairo."

"Who's the man in Cairo?"

"Someone codenamed Abu Jameel. He's the principal one. I know nothing about him. No one does."

Suddenly I felt compelled to talk about the Dajanis.

"They were such decent people. She didn't have to stay. And the kids, they were ..." I had no words for what they were.

"Yes, I know." He gave a cheerless nod.

"I never met Frances," he said, after a pause. "A fine lady, I understand. What a waste."

The horror of the early-morning phone call hit me again.

"The boys standing guard on Abu Kerim," he said, "were both sons of friends. What I don't understand ..." He broke off, looked out the casement window at the roses. "It doesn't make sense. Why was the party for the agreement held at Mohamed's place? Anyone against the agreement, an important thing like validating the return of Fatah and the PLO to Beirut, would use his place as a symbol. As something to get blown up."

"I don't know why. I've thought about it. Frances said Mohamed was determined to make a last gesture and insisted. Someone had to do it, he told her. Then Mohamed and Abu Kerim both said there was no other way. Absolutely no other way, but they didn't explain.

"I think," I added carefully, "the whole thing has something to do with me."

He gazed at me, absorbing what I said, unbelieving. Perhaps he re-membered that I said I wanted to kill somebody.

"Are you saying you were there the night the agreement was reached? Was that the night they tried to kill you?"

I nodded. He shook his head in reluctant understanding, then pursed his lips in a soundless whistle. "Oh my," he said. And then, "Curse their fathers," this in Arabic, meant for the human race generally. I explained the theatrics, the pretenses we had sought to establish at the party and then recounted the meeting the next day in Mohamed's office. Neither of us spoke for several moments.

"Some unfriendly Palestinian at the party," he said, "had to know you were involved with the CIA plot, and in spite of all your play-acting, some-one had to know you and Abu Kerim were close friends. Hence the killing and the attempt to kill you. Your presence at Mohamed's party could even have meant that the agreement reached at the party was connected to the CIA in some way. And therefore a sell-out to the forces of evil. Who knows who tried to kill the three of you? There are more than a few can-didates wandering about."

"Abu Kerim thought there was something fishy," I said.

"How was that?

"He said it was strange the CIA would give me such a job."

He frowned and looked away.

"Well," he said after a while, "maybe, maybe not. Americans can get idealistic notions and plow ahead, but I confess the same thought had crossed my mind. Abu Kerim knew about such matters. More than I."

We sat quietly, reflecting. I was facing implications I did not want to face.

"I shouldn't have gone to Beirut."

"You *had* to go to Beirut. You had to know what was happening, to look after yourself. Whether or not your presence was responsible for the killings. Those are the rules of the game. Also, Abu Kerim was already marked. Clearly someone knew about the four of us."

I felt as if a recent meal were churning my stomach. "Someone knew about the *shirka* at Ramallah," I said. "So whoever it is knows about Abu Kerim and you. And so on. About you and me, me and Abu Taleb ..."

The briskness of the response did not disguise its fatalism. "Yes, if someone knew about you and Abu Kerim, then he knew the rest. Or it is highly probable." He made a helpless motion with his hands. "The conclusion is, old friendship is a liability. We're floundering around, messing things up."

He began to pace the floor. "So our job is to know what happened, then calm things down. What about Nabil Farah? Did he give no sign that he knew you knew who he was?"

"Not that I could see."

"Was my name mentioned when you talked with him?"

"No. I told him only I was an acquaintance of Abu Kerim and Mohamed."

"I think," he said, "that Abu Kerim trusted Nabil for certain things. Such as protecting you in Cairo. Personally I do not trust him. I knew him when he was much younger, a passionate sort, controlled but dedicated, given to ..." He broke off, frowning.

"Given to what?"

He did not really hear the question. Eyes fixed in the direction of the roses, his mind had veered onto another track. I repeated my question.

"Oh," he said, "I was going to say given to reckless action or something like that. What I mean is violence."

*   *   *

When I told my side of the story, I left out details only when I thought them irrelevant. I had nothing to hide, he knew about Barbara. I began with Pinstripe and went on from there. He listened intently. When

I finished, he asked for more on the Washington sessions, more on the CIA reaction when I told them I was being followed.

"They tried to persuade me it was for some other reason. It had to be, they said. They said the security was total."

"Dear God, total." He gave a dry laugh, put his feet back onto the armchair. "In fact, they had to know there was a leak. Why didn't they call it off right then? Too bullheaded to admit anything? Or just hoping something might work out?"

"I can't answer that. The man Blake who runs the show is hard to read."

"And Barbara, what does she think?" His voice was gentle.

"She has to know, know there's been a leak, I mean." I thought of a moment when she caught her breath and held me close. "She says her boss is persuaded otherwise."

There was much she could not tell me, I supposed; she was loyal to the organization. Some information could not be voiced, even if understood between us by the special channels lovers have. In this, our love affair was no different from others, except that in ours, lives were at stake, some already sacrificed. In ours, the plot had been written and directed by someone else.

"It occurs to me Abu Kerim was right," he said.

"Right about what?"

"Right about something being fishy. The CIA business is strange."

He looked hard at the wall for a moment.

"Please forgive me but I must ask another question." Again the gentle voice, but this time with an edge. "Could Barbara have been a leak?"

"God no!" I burst out. It was suddenly important to tell him about Barbara, the kind of person she was, her integrity, her decency. He listened gravely.

"Yes, you are in love. Again I'm sorry, but one cannot be too careful." He shrugged, fixed me with the steady gaze, gave a neutral smile. "If she loves you, why is she insisting on endangering you? Not that it matters too much. The word's out. Always was."

"But how did the word get out? Where was the leak? Or were there several of them?"

"One's enough," he said tersely. "Information goes back and forth, gets everywhere. Easily." His voice betrayed an acceptance of the reality of mixed motives, of dishonor, of treason. "Sometimes for money, sometimes old loyalties that everyone's forgotten about, sometimes by accident. As you well know, if someone out here wants information, he can usually arrange to get it."

"And in this case?" I wanted to direct my anger at someone specific.

"You mean, how might it have happened? Hard to know. The two most likely places to look are Washington and Jerusalem. But it could happen in Cairo or Beirut."

He stood up, thrust a hand into his pocket, and pulled out a fistful of coins, which he proceeded to arrange in different ways in the palm of his hand. He paced the room, seemingly intent on the coins. When he spoke again, his voice was cheerless, determinedly neutral as if listing his own sins.

"When it comes to passing information, it's cleaner when it happens between sides, usually a matter of money, professional information gatherers. No convictions about right and wrong get in the way. But between factions of one side only, the Palestinian side, not so clean. Or maybe I mean not so simple. It finally comes down too often to passionate murder, to killing other Palestinians. Many of them not involved. Just Palestinians."

He was telling me nothing new. I sat quietly, waiting for the self-wounding admissions to stop. Was it not possible to persuade this man to negotiate, if only to help his people heal, to become whole again?

"It's the same as in any small community," he went on. "Any Palestinian working in Kuwait knows exactly what's going on in the rest of the diaspora. And information gets passed not for money but for ideology. The art at which we have all become adept is turning loyalty into disloyalty. Persuading a man to betray his cousin."

He stood up, stared at the coins in his hand, put them impatiently back into his pocket.

"Hard to think," he said, "that in the politics of Palestine anyone might turn against you or inform on you. In the name of his particular

Palestine. It wasn't always like that but now it is, and it haunts me, especially at night when I want to sleep. The consolation is that it's as hard to be a turncoat or a plant in a small tight community like Palestine as anywhere in the world. I trust the people I work with, so far ... But yes, I find myself doing character analysis of each one in the early morning when I want to stay asleep."

"What do you mean, the people you work with? What is this *hai'a* I heard about from Feldman?"

"Nothing complicated, just one or two people I trust, like the fellow who brought you here this morning."

"It has to be more than one or two people."

"Maybe so, but you don't need to know about it. At the moment it's irrelevant."

*   *   *

Later.

"But why not, damn it? You have to talk to make peace. If you don't talk, just sit and hate, nothing happens. You don't get to know the other side is human. Christ, the peoples want peace. If leaders like you don't lead the way, the whole thing is hopeless."

He was on his feet again, staring at the roses.

"It's good to listen to you," he said.

"But you think I'm wrong."

"Not wrong. Tactically wrong."

"How so?" I wanted something to argue against.

"No, first let me say something else. The fact is the whole plan to have me negotiate with the Israelis was doomed from the beginning. Even if you're right, which I don't admit, even if it were a good idea to talk to the Israelis now, it wouldn't make any difference. As things stand."

"As what things stand?"

"I'm talking about the leak. Whatever I might do would be discredited before I began. Do you think the Palestinian public would listen to anyone who is reputed to be in league with the United States? Perhaps the leak is confined to relatively few for the moment, but it was enough to kill Abu

Kerim and the Dajanis, and my God it would be general knowledge within a few days. The Arab press and radio would carve me into little pieces. I'd be known forever as Uncle Sam's stooge. And not incidentally, my life would be worth very little."

"Yes, but given the leak, you're already branded as Uncle Sam's stooge. Isn't your life in the same danger right now?"

"Perhaps, but for me they have no proof, I haven't been caught red-handed talking to you. I haven't negotiated with any Israelis. I'm still clean. You're an ignorant American bumbler, and this is an image you may have to cultivate to stay alive, someone who tried to talk to me but wasn't able to." He looked out the window, smiled slightly. "Trouble is, not enough people believe the bumbler image yet. For some reason, the notion is if you can talk to me, you can persuade me to be an American stooge. So I've let the word get around I don't want to see you."

"How many people believe that?"

"Not enough, but it's better than a few days ago."

"And if you were caught talking to me?"

"Then, as I said, my life would be worth little. I can't be sure but I think they wouldn't harm Azizeh and the children. And if by some miracle I stayed alive, any influence the Israelis or the Americans think I have would disappear overnight." He thought for a minute. "In point of fact, it would be smarter of them to discredit me than to kill me."

"All the same," I said, not giving up, "surely without dialogue there can never be peace. These pacifist truisms are right. One can be too sophisticated to believe them, and then opportunities get lost."

"Of course."

"What do you mean, 'of course'? You're saying no. Or you say tactically wrong. Whatever that means." Even to myself I sounded testy.

"That's right, tactically wrong. What I mean is timing. Suppose right now everything worked out so that I sat down to negotiate the future of Palestine with the Israelis. For one thing it's so unlikely it hardly bears thinking about. But leave that aside. Let's suppose it worked out. What do you think would result?"

"Who knows? And that's the point." I was on familiar ground, my father's ground. "You can start only by talking and exploring what you have in common. You don't know the direction the talks will take. Perhaps both sides have peace as an objective at the beginning, perhaps not. Never mind. The crucial thing is the process, it leads to understanding where you agree and disagree, and inevitably, if the talks go on, it leads to a sympathy for the other side that didn't exist before."

"You know I don't disagree with any of that ..." He saw I was about to speak and held up his hand. "No, let me finish. When the time is ripe, I hope what you talk about will happen. But you have to understand it may not be in my lifetime. The fact is, now there is no middle ground. We agree on nothing. Neither side has despaired. Each thinks it can win. Win? No one can win. You know that and so do I. But damn few others do, and so the only one winning now is Mr. Death."

"You sound like Feldman," I said.

"Yes, I've received his new message. The one he sent me by way of you. He's saying he wants to negotiate. But eventually. Perhaps it's true. My guess is I'll be getting other messages along the same lines."

"Listen," he went on, "I agree that the way to locate middle ground is to talk. Truisms, sure. Well, I believe in them too. But today no one *wants* to find middle ground. Both sides say let those other bastards sweat. If a few oddballs negotiated some kind of peace, no one would accept the results." He gave a short mirthless laugh. "And can you imagine the kind of compromises reached if one of the negotiators was under the military control of the other? No mystery why the Israelis let my name drop. Why not? Fun and games."

"So you do nothing?"

"We wait. That's not nothing, it's something, and it's hard."

"Just that, wait?"

"No, not just that. Call it active waiting. Preparing for the time when both sides have nothing left but the possibility of compromise."

$$* \qquad * \qquad *$$

The sun reached its high. How long had we talked? Long enough to become familiar with the detail of the picture framed by the casement window, the red and yellow roses straining upward, petals opened wide to the nourishing warmth. An angular crack like an international boundary streaked down the stucco wall behind. Restless, I stood up and wandered over to the window. A tiny vegetable garden of tomatoes, cucumbers, and onions occupied the distance between the wall and the house. After a few yards in either direction the wall made right-angle turns and disappeared. At a corner was a toolshed made with sheets of corrugated iron, filled with flower pots and white sacks.

I turned back to the relative darkness of the room. Abu Hisham watched me from his chair, his legs folded up into it, chin almost on his knees.

"Sorry," he said.

"No, no, it's your life, your country." I looked down at the vegetable garden; someone had recently thinned the onions. "I hoped to be able to do something, to contribute to something good."

"I know."

We sat silently.

"Of course," he said, "it's your country too. As we both know. You'll never escape entirely."

"Abu Kerim was right," I said. "He said you wouldn't have anything to do with the idea."

I watched the roses, uncertain about my feelings. Like an athlete told he could not play in the big game, I felt let down, deeply disappointed. And what a game, the biggest I could think of, launching peace. Immensely satisfying. I'd have been filled with pride, almost exalted, atoning for unidentified sins, paying solemn tribute to a memory. Now I couldn't be a hero. Just another plodding businessman in Cairo, missing an opportunity to serve.

Yet for an irrational minute, I also felt relieved, as if I no longer had anything to fear. I felt it in my body, a relaxing inside the rib cage, a lifting of the spirit. I could take deep easy breaths, and part of me felt out of the woods, over the last obstacle, free to plod. A minute of misleading psychological magic.

"Are you or aren't you, then, with the PLO?" I asked.

"*With* the PLO, you ask." He smiled. "I like the way you put the question. Yes, I'm with them, of course I'm with them, in the sense that so many relatives and friends are involved, that their goals are the same as mine. But I'm not with them on methods. They've led us into deep trouble. Just bumbling along. Leaving the field to new forces, like Muslim fundamentalists. Arafat can't take tough decisions because he fears losing support. So now he's losing everybody. And there's no one to take his place."

"Could Abu Kerim have taken his place?"

He was quiet a moment. "He didn't have the name. Oh, he was well-known all right but not in the way he'd need to be. And the Damascus factions would have killed him if they could arrange it without suspicion. Arafat survives because he's a fuzzy thinker, dishonest with himself. He talks himself into new points of view as demanded by circumstances, he even keeps the Fatah rebels in Syria hoping for a reconciliation. Then as soon as he has them off balance, he makes yet another statement that brings his moderates into line."

He looked out the window. "Abu Kerim wasn't fuzzy enough. Too self-critical. And if he had all that responsibility, he'd crack. He wasn't like you. You've got a tough core."

"But I can't believe your aims are really the same as the PLO's."

"You're right, not always. We need one man, one vote. At its best moments the PLO, or Arafat's boys anyway, believe this too. But if they were the security forces of the new Palestinian state, would they support the government no matter what? Would they tolerate a government they didn't like? Hard to know. Fatah's a political movement, not just an armed force."

There was something else I needed to know.

"Tell me about this *hai'a*." My voice said I wanted a real answer.

He gave a wry smile, put his hands back to back, laced the fingers together, and stretched. He used to do this in Ramallah when he was thinking what to say next.

"Do you have to know? Would it help you personally?"

"Maybe not. But I'd like to know."

He stared solemnly at me. "With most people I would lie about it," he said. "Instead of telling you anything, let me ask a couple of questions. Let me say first a lot of personal liberty is at stake, perhaps a few lives."

"You mean jail?"

He nodded. "Either that or murder. So let me ask this: if you wanted to create climates of opinion in which negotiations could take place, what would you do?"

"Okay. Persuade people."

"And given the fact that extremism thrives these days, where and how would you start? How would you organize without getting killed?"

I thought a minute. How *would* one organize without getting killed? With a single breach of security, one became a symbol to be destroyed. Like Abu Kerim and the Dajanis.

"How many people in the organization?"

"I didn't say there was an organization. Please remember. But there are almost eighty people I can count on."

"That's not many."

"Quite enough. A lot more than Abu Nidal, our big-time well-known terrorist operating out of Iraq, can count on. His inner circle is less than a couple of dozen. He may claim to have five hundred followers but he can't trust them."

"Am I a person you can count on?"

"You always have been. But you can't be active now. Maybe you never can. Give it a year or two, then see. By then you should be out of danger. Out of sight."

The feeling inside the rib cage returned. The irrational minute was over.

"Why that long?" I asked.

"You have to be careful, very careful. You're known as an old hand that people listen to. As long as a few extremists consider you a threat, you're in danger."

"But it's over. I'm out of it." But I had already understood I wasn't out of it.

"How can we let them know it's over?" I asked. I hoped my voice betrayed no fear. In the business world I'd sit down to have a drink with an adversary, smooth things over with a chat. A lunch at the Nile Hilton, say, as with Sam Paul.

"We can let them know," he said. "That's easy. But the real question is, will they believe us." But he spoke with his mind on something else, putting his feet on the floor and sitting straight. "Ironic you should be in greater danger than I am at this moment." As he spoke, he gazed at me without focusing. I waited. The tightness in the chest increased in anticipation of his next words.

But when the words came out, they provided no escape. Abu Hisham, it seemed, was working something out in his head. Then he acted like a coach making certain the team has its signals straight. "Now let's see, yes, I told Abu Taleb's brother not to come over from Gaza. And I've told his sister Ni'meh about this. You stay on a few days, be a businessman as ostentatiously as possible. Don't go near Ni'meh. Don't go near the American consulate. If you must see the American woman, be as discreet as possible. And tell her as little as you can. I need to think a bit more," he said, his manner becoming brisker, more cheerful. "What can we do to get us both free and clear? Perhaps not much, but who knows, perhaps we can discredit people who want to discredit you and me."

He glanced at his watch, said we'd soon have to get back to the real world. "Stop worrying," he said. "I'll be in touch about another meeting."

"How will you be in touch?"

"You'll know." He stood up, pulled out the coins one last time and studied them. "I said you hadn't changed much, but it now occurs to me you've changed more than I first thought. In the old days you were never willing to be devious or violent, not even for a good cause. Such as saving your own life." He smiled at me anxiously, then changed the subject. "Incidentally, the day man at the desk, the young man who went to Ramallah, you can trust him."

I was glad to hear there was someone he thought I could trust. He put a hand on my shoulder.

"Just in case we don't see each other for a while, this has meant a lot to me. Thank God you still combine integrity and compassion. God, suppose it had …" He broke off.

"I thought we were meeting again," I said.

"Sure. I was speaking just in case. You never know."

FOURTEEN

Jerusalem and Ramallah, May 1990

I was delivered back to the American Colony the same way, except on the last lap my nameless escort did not suddenly appear. The old driver chatted about the weather, said he thought a certain gentleman was a fine gentleman. The trip seemed shorter on the way back.

What now? I had to readjust. From the beginning, it seemed, Blake's leaked plot had never had a chance, though a few short hours ago I had still dreamed that Abu Hisham, leak or no leak, could be convinced to attempt nothing less than "a historic breakthrough for peace." I could dream no longer. He would never agree to have his name put forward as a negotiator.

But the plot refused to die, because some of those involved, some of the more passionate ones, did not believe it was dead. A persistence of irrational belief that sustained small groups in need of a reason for being. The plot, created by intrigue for a purpose no longer relevant, was now an evil spirit careening around on its own, flitting out of control, killing here and there.

I felt jilted. I'd counted on Abu Hisham to extricate me from the web Blake had spun (and would now presumably abandon, leaving me enmeshed). All I had to cling to was my old friend's intent to "be in touch about another meeting." His initiative, not mine. Not "active waiting," just waiting.

What would Barbara say? I remembered that she'd thought of Blake's plot as a "big chance," a triumph if she pulled it off. Pull it off? After knowing about the leak, how could any of us – Barbara, myself, Blake, Rosberg – imagine it could be pulled off? I'd lived in the Near East, I should have known better. But as with the others, perhaps, I'd been beguiled by the glamor. Hampton, the Peacemaker, the Great Conciliator …

When the cab drew up at the hotel, the old driver told me to wait. He got out stiffly and came round to let me out, no longer in a chatty mood. He spoke softly, avuncularly.

"Always be careful getting out of cars, especially at a place where you're expected back."

He held the door open. Involuntarily I looked around, though I was uncertain what I looked for. A sharpshooter from the hedges across the street? A rifle pointing at me from a window? I smiled my thanks. The driver's heavily lined face was impassive, the drooping gray mustache stained at the ends with yellowish cigarette tints. The bloodshot eyes held mine for an instant. He did not smile back but like an old soldier stood at attention until I left. The familiar Israeli plainclothesman sat in the lobby.

The young man at the desk handed me two telephone messages and an envelope. The messages involved the business appointments I'd made and missed. The envelope contained a note from Barbara saying she'd gone to the consulate. But when I phoned the secretary assigned to her, I was told she hadn't been in. I had the same answer in the afternoon.

*   *   *

Late afternoon, after my business appointments, I got back to the hotel. Barbara's room key was gone from the rack. His face expressionless, the young man behind the desk handed me two more envelopes. The first came from Reginald Hughes, the British journalist I had seen in Beirut; he wanted me to save lunch the next day. The second had to be from Abu Hisham. An anonymous brown envelope with nothing on the outside.

I looked about and sat down in a corner of the lobby, disguising the agitation I felt by settling in my seat before opening the envelope. The letter, which was typed, had no salutation, nothing to connect it with anything.

The person I trust can find a car. Drive alone starting 8:15 pm tomorrow to the 5-km marker on the road to Ramallah, first left on gravel road up the hill to house on top. Sit on veranda, wait quietly. Destroy this.

I glanced at the desk. Bent over the hotel register the young man was studying the entries. I got up, approached the desk, and smiled at the man Abu Hisham said he trusted. He looked up.

"Can I do something for you, Mr. Hampton?"

So he arranged for a car at minimal cost and said he'd have the keys when he came on in the morning. Neither of us mentioned Hertz or Avis.

Now impatient, I went up to my room, threw my briefcase on the bed, and washed the grime off my face. Then I darted down the hall and tapped lightly on her door. She was in her blue dressing gown. We wrapped ourselves in each other's arms. As her body leaned contentedly against mine, I said I had news. I felt her go tense. I think she had been expecting to make love.

"News? What news?" I knew she'd have preferred to close off the outside world for a spell. But I also knew she'd want *this* news, and anyway I needed to share the excitement of seeing Abu Hisham after so many years, to let her know how it was. To make certain she grasped his reasoning. When she understood what was coming, she drew her breath in sharply and sat down on one of the straight chairs.

Sitting on the edge of the bed, I began the tale of my meeting with Abu Hisham, happily disregarding his counsel to tell her as little as possible. I left out what he had said about the *hai'a* and the eighty people he could trust. As she listened, she got up restlessly, hands thrust deep into the pockets of the dressing gown, wandered about the small room, then leaned against the wall near the window, watching me gravely. When I came to Abu Hisham's adamant refusal to consider Blake's scheme, her face grew unhappy. She interrupted sharply.

"But did you tell him about the potential, the real possibility of a breakthrough? Did he understand about that?"

"Yes, he did understand. I explained but he had already understood." Her face was showing blighted hope. "He believes the time isn't ripe, the two sides aren't yet desperate enough to negotiate in good faith. He hopes that will change but doesn't expect it to happen soon. He wants what we want, but he says that to try now would delay things, not help them."

"But a *breakthrough*..." She used the word as if it were capitalized, as if its very use was a conclusive argument. "A breakthrough needs courage. One has to take risks at great moments of history. How can he be so certain it would delay things? You thought it might work. You were excited about it. Now you're backing off."

"No, I'm reporting Abu Hisham's reasoning."

"His reasoning seems to have influenced your point of view."

The conversation was moving in the wrong direction.

"I tried to persuade him." I wanted her to like Abu Hisham. "Barbara, he knows a lot about how such things work. More than I do. We have to listen to what he says."

"Yes, but his advice is not to go ahead." Intensely disappointed, adjusting to defeat, she gazed at the floor. A vision of peace, and of personal success, was fading.

"You see, even if he thought the timing was right, he would say no because of the leak. He'd have to." Again I felt anger. The leak, the damn leak ...

She leaned back, looked at me with an odd expression. "Ah yes, the leak. We come back to that. How much did he already know?"

"Almost everything. No details, but nothing he needed to know that he didn't already know."

"Did you tell him whatever he asked?"

"There was no reason not to. He's already told my family friend from Gaza there's no reason to have a meeting." What else should I tell her? I felt her eyes fixed on my face and shifted position awkwardly. "He asked about *you*."

"You mean you told him about me?"

"He knew you worked for the CIA. What he asked was about our personal relationship. Whether I love you."

"What did you say?"

"I said yes. Yes, I do." I smiled, and she came over and sat next to me on the bed. I wanted to explain. "My dear, he and I were finding out about each other, what happened during all those years, how we felt about things. Not politics. The important things, personal things."

She stroked my hair, stood up from the bed, and wandered about the room again, locking and unlocking her fingers in a series of folding stretching gestures. Her eyes searched mine; they had an unsettled look. Perhaps anxious. She made a face.

"Damn, damn, damn."

"You understand what Abu Hisham is saying?"

"Yes, but he ought to take a few risks."

"With his life, his family?"

"Ah, yes. We come back to the leak."

*   *   *

I hadn't yet told her about the following night's meeting with Abu Hisham. I had wondered whether I should. But when the moment came, I did not hesitate. I felt responsible for her disappointment.

At first she looked as if she had heard me wrong.

"What?"

I handed her the note in the brown envelope. Professional excitement crept back into her face. Words spilled out.

"But this is good. Tomorrow night. Why didn't you tell me before? Who's this person he trusts? Bill, we have to handle this right. Perhaps he'll change his mind after all." False hopes, but nothing would dampen them. She kept talking about "another effort," about "chances at breakthroughs," about "place in history." Her spirits lifted dramatically.

"Listen," I said, taking a deep breath, "I'm sure he won't change his mind. He's doing this to help me. He knows I'm scared. He wants to get me off the hook. Somehow."

She looked at me steadily for a moment. Her face showed impatience, then concern, then something I could not read.

"How much danger are you really in?" Was she implying that the danger might be less than I thought?

"I don't really know. People tell me to be careful. They explain I'm a target because other people think I can talk Abu Hisham into negotiating. Or because I'm a meddling American. They don't know I'm opting out."

"Don't say that. You mustn't opt out. Listen, the other times, when you were attacked, it wasn't real, was it? Wasn't it just for show, to scare you off?"

"Maybe. When the Israeli cops supposedly came to the rescue, that was a fake. But the Cairo thing was real. If I hadn't moved when I did, the bullet would have hit me in the gut. I'd be dead if it weren't for Pinstripe." I paused. "I guess you should know they tried to kill me in Beirut. Some Palestinians shot at me from a car. It was close. After that, they killed Abu Kerim and his guards. And bombed the apartment of my friend and killed him and his family. All that was real."

She stared at me a long moment, then sat beside me wordlessly, put her arms around me, leaned her head on my shoulder.

"I didn't know all that," she said softly.

"In short," I said, "I don't like getting beaten up and shot at, and I'm scared about having it happen again, even if no one means to kill me."

She cupped my face in her hands, kissed me, and said fiercely. "I don't mean it that way. Anyway, I think the worst is over. We're on the last lap."

"I think you're hoping against hope."

"One possibility occurs to me, and I think I should mention it just in case it might be true." She spoke with care. "Is it possible Abu Hisham is telling you to be careful for reasons of his own? I mean, if you're worried about danger, are you more pliable, more suggestible? More likely to agree with him?"

The suggestion was distasteful.

"Let me see if I can say it right," I said. "I said I was scared, though I'm not sure exactly what being scared feels like. I've never experienced this before, I mean the possibility of being killed. My muscles tense up, and I get a feeling in the chest. The feeling's been building up fast since Beirut but it's been there all along, since Cairo, before I went to Washington. So Abu Hisham is not responsible. He isn't trying to make me more suggestible."

Her arms remained tight around me.

"It can't go on," I said. "What's the next step?"

The words triggered a memory. Years ago in Ramallah, my father and mother and brother and I, the four of us in front of a fireplace in late summer, security and love intertwined, my brother and I reveling in the occasion. I was eleven. My mother sat on the sofa between John and me, her strong angular face softened by the firelight, dark hair pulled back into a bun. She gave me a squeeze, my father looked at her in surprise. "Bill," said my mother, "works on problems till they're solved. He takes them one step at a time."

Now I heard myself saying to Barbara, "The next step is the car. That's all fixed."

"Who's the man he trusts?"

"Do you need to know?" The young man at the desk came too close to Abu Hisham's *hai'a.*

She looked at me curiously, and an amused look appeared. "I guess not. Bill, you're beginning to sound like Blake. And incidentally, you may be scared but you never act that way."

Her hands moved about my body, and we began to make love. Even as I cupped her breasts and began a long kiss, I remember thinking she hadn't given up. As our passion mounted, the tightness in the chest changed to an excitingly tender reaching out of the heart, a surging sense of belonging to this woman. By agreement with myself, I blocked Cath from my thoughts.

*   *   *

I felt Barbara smile.

"Did you tell him how we made love? A conversation like the old days at school?"

"Good Lord, no."

"Did you compare Jewish lovemaking with Palestinian lovemaking?"

I got up on my elbow and looked at her.

"May I ask what you think you're getting at?" I also smiled, but here again was the business about being Jewish, some force from the West I knew about but didn't deal with easily.

"I'm not sure what I'm getting at," she said languidly after a long caress. "Not sure at all. Gentiles usually ..." She broke off. Now it was her turn to get up on her elbow and look at me.

"Gentiles usually what?"

"Well, the Gentiles I know care about it, about my being Jewish. It's almost a way, yes almost a way we have of reaching out to each other." Another smile began. "Do I really mean that? Yes, I think I do. But with you, what is it, I don't have that, well, comfort ... No, not that. What do I mean? I don't have that bond. You don't sympathize about being Jewish."

"But I do."

"Yes, you do. But it's sort of an exercise." She snuggled against me. "In fact you treat me like a Gentile."

*   *   *

Later.

"You know," she said, "sometimes you're almost innocent, sometimes tricky. I can't always trust you."

"Do you trust me now?"

"Perhaps." She was quiet, started to say something else, stopped, then began again. "Sometimes you act as if your big love affair is with him, that Palestinian, not me. Yes, I love you. So much I'm scared. And I know you love me, I couldn't be wrong about that. We never mention your wife. I know I agreed to that, but doesn't she ever want to know who you really are? What you love? Is it glory? Honor? Success? You never say."

Cath once told me she wanted to pound me with her fists because she wanted to know who I was. When I asked what it was she wanted to know, she turned away with an exasperated look and asked me to get angry once in a while. "Maybe," I said to Barbara, "I don't know who I really am."

"I think you do," she said, stroking my brow. "I've been in love before but it wasn't like this. You can upset me and I'm not sure why."

*   *   *

"Why," I asked ponderously at breakfast, "would a British journalist pick up a story that the CIA could deliver an Israeli agreement to negotiate with the PLO?"

"A journalist?" Her tone said journalists were an unreliable breed.

"The fellow I'm having lunch with today. I saw him in Beirut. He talked about a reliable PLO source. The source said Fatah had a highly placed friend in the CIA."

She gazed at me warily for a long moment. She had not yet had coffee, and we had had too little sleep.

"I suppose Fatah often feeds journalists that kind of story," she said.

"Can you imagine the story being true?"

"Anything's possible," she said, "but it seems damn unlikely."

"The phraseology's so much the same. Strange. Blake told me he could *deliver an Israeli agreement*. Then this source says the same for Fatah."

The coffee arrived and she reached for it eagerly. She asked about something else.

∗   ∗   ∗

Later that morning when I passed the desk, the young Palestinian handed me the keys to a car. An old Ford, he said, but in fine running order, light blue, parked just outside. Pausing, he looked at me with a friendly air and said:

"I'm sorry to hear about your back problem, Mr. Hampton, but I'm sure Dr. Homsy will be able to help."

I stared, not understanding. He smiled engagingly and turned to answer the phone. Standing at the desk, I waited to ask what he meant, but somehow, all at once, I knew the conversation had ended. He'd told me something I wasn't meant to grasp right away. When he finished the phone call, he went to his chair and busied himself in paperwork. So I drifted away from the desk, stowing his words into my mind: a back problem, a Dr. Homsy.

I was restless and jittery. I tried to read in the lobby but couldn't manage. I would have liked to pay a call on Ni'meh Abu Khayyal and listen to the bees in the garden on Zahara Street, but for her that spelled danger, perhaps death. Hampton had become special poison. My Israeli follower was nowhere in sight.

Reginald Hughes had said a quick lunch. We met by the hotel's pool. As always he looked British, though the blazer had given way to something cooler, a light tan jacket also tailored in England. Neatly turned out, dark hair in place, trousers in press, tie snugly knotted. A handsome fellow, I thought. I envied him, a free spirit roaming the area, his only responsibility to observe and write. No family (at least he never mentioned one), no involvements, no danger.

I was pleased to see him. The morning had passed slowly, the afternoon promised more of the same. I needed to be doing something beyond waiting restlessly to see Abu Hisham. Barbara had left after breakfast for the consulate, looking anxious, saying she would be back long before 8:15 when I was due to leave for the road to Ramallah. As instructed by Abu Hisham.

Reginald and I chatted about local politics. Then like a good journalist he began picking my brains. He had heard all sorts of rumors that some persons on the Palestinian side might be willing to talk peace, some of them non-PLO, but he had no names. He wanted names, names of Palestinians he might arrange to meet, names he might include in his next story.

"Listen," I said, marveling at what seemed to be an extraordinary naiveté, "when you ask for names you are asking a pretty direct question. The answer could be dangerous. Some radical would think the fellow you name was a traitor and kill him. Even if it was just a rumor."

"You mean I'm endangering the lives of others just to get a good story?"

"Maybe you are."

"But in fact I know the dangers," he said. "And it's only with you I've been direct."

"Perhaps with others you have to be more indirect than you think." I tried a smile and thought briefly about asking him not to mention the name Bill Hampton. "So indirect, I suppose, that you won't have a story."

*   *   *

Barbara came back from the consulate about seven. She had an air of suppressed excitement, suppressed because she tried not to talk about Abu Hisham and the road to Ramallah. Neither of us wanted to make love. We sat in the bar, not saying much, occasionally smiling at each other.

At one juncture she said he must see how important it was. She resisted using the word *breakthrough*. I repeated she must have no hope he'd change his mind. She did not ask about my lunch with Hughes. A couple of times she excused herself to make phone calls. When I left, I had the feeling she was relieved not to have to make further conversation, but I may have been projecting my own tensions, which knotted my stomach. She came out with me to the car and asked again where it came from, but I forced a smile and said I'd tell her another time. As I drove off, I looked back to wave. Her slender face had a look I did not recognize.

I left the hotel at exactly 8:15, headed in toward the city, and made several turns. I waited around a corner a few minutes but no one seemed to be following me.

The light had only begun to fade when I finally started north toward Ramallah. The sun had come close to the hills and the parking lights of oncoming cars were switching on. The red roofs of Arab Jerusalem gave way to the white high-rises of the new Jewish perimeter, and then I broke through into the occupied zone and back into my boyhood. Red roofs again. Then villages.

Though lanterns still flickered from a few village doorways, electric lights shone from many windows. It was 1990 now, my boyhood fairyland had changed. Modern two-story houses, some split-level, appeared on the high ground away from the road, probably built by Palestinians with money from the Gulf. On the left I saw a Jewish settlement. Here and there, a giant crane stood guard beside a half-finished building. If I knew every turn in the road from long ago, the view to either side had become foreign. Alien trees, alien truck gardens, alien hedges went past the car window. Even the olive groves seemed different, though the sight of them reminded me of happy times long ago when our family helped at harvest time.

I glanced at the dashboard to check how far north I'd come, then the four-kilometer marker flashed by on the right. Dusk had arrived, and I turned the car lights on full. Gentle hills rose on either side, separated from the road by small fields. I could live here happily, I thought. Living with whom? Working at what? I concentrated on the road, searching for the five-kilometer marker.

It came soon. I turned sharply onto the gravel road that led away to the left a few yards beyond. The road wound up a gentle slope through fruit trees. Half a kilometer away, at the top, I could discern a house against the sky's waning light. At each curve the headlights lit up the red soil and white rock that stretched between the trees.

The road ended in a wide deserted parking space below the house. Turning off the headlights, I got out of the car. A truck rumbled by on the main road way down the hill but otherwise the quiet was absolute. The only light came from a half moon in the east. Reminiscent of a Swiss chalet, the house had a wide veranda around three sides, its front section looking down imperially onto the parking space. Within a few feet of the car a long steep staircase led upward to the veranda.

When I reached the top of the stairs, the house seemed empty. A door and four windows, all dark and unshuttered, one of them open a crack, gave onto the veranda. In front of the windows stood three armchairs grouped in friendly fashion, looking out across the valley. As my eyes got used to the darkness, I made out the shapes of the hills on the other side and the patches of trees on the slopes. A kilometer up the valley, looking north, a lamppost left a puddle of light at the center of a small village.

The instructions had said to wait. So I sat down in one of the armchairs, my back to the door, looking at the view, wondering what would happen. The quiet was absorbing. Once I thought I heard a noise below the house in the orchard, but after listening hard I decided it was my imagination, or perhaps a bird arriving late at the roost. In ordinary circumstances my mind would have drifted pleasantly, but events had left me too alert, too tense. Every so often I needed to take deeper breaths.

My eyes scouted each set of headlights in the valley below, waiting for a car to turn into the gravel road.

Finally a car made the turn. Its lights cut jerkily into the darkness of the orchard as it handled the curves. Almost smiling as I anticipated the meeting, I sat waiting. The car drew up near mine in the parking space and the headlights went out. A man emerged, waved at me, and began to climb the stairs to where I was seated.

"Welcome, welcome," he said in Arabic.

The man came slowly up the steps to the veranda and held out his hand. It was not Abu Hisham. He had the same build, and in the moonlight at ten yards I might have mistaken the face. But not at two yards. Unthinkingly I took the outstretched hand. Because it was there.

Then it all happened. A gun went off at the north corner of the veranda. A voice shouted "traitor" in Arabic. The man whose hand I'd taken fell down, clasping his right shoulder. The assailant, gun in hand, ran toward us from the veranda corner, stopped, held the gun on the fallen man at pointblank range. But he hesitated.

He never pulled the trigger. A burst of heavy fire from one of the windows dropped him to his knees, like a buck dying gracefully, and his gun clattered onto the veranda. Out of the door charged two more men, the second racing to the north end of the veranda with a machine pistol. "Stop!" he shouted in Arabic, firing another burst off the veranda into the orchard at someone I could not see.

The first man from inside knelt down by our felled assailant, who was clearly dying. Blood oozed from the right side of his chest. Three yards away the fake Abu Hisham struggled to a sitting position, leaned against the railing and made moaning sounds. I stood fixed to the spot I had occupied when the action started thirty seconds before. As if by moving I'd turn the bloodletting into reality.

I looked down. Pinstripe. It was Pinstripe who lay dying on the veranda. Kneeling beside him was Sergeant Daoud, the Israeli policeman who had pretended to rescue me in the Old City. For reasons I do not understand, I felt no surprise that either should be part of this violence.

I knelt down too. Pinstripe was dressed in jacket and trousers of dark blue denim. Well-cut, I thought mindlessly. The blood was oozing fast, his eyes were cloudy. But he recognized me. When he spoke, I could hear a lot of pain.

"So, we meet again." He smiled in a twisted way. "And so it wasn't your old friend, after all. Just a doctor, just a doctor. Not a traitor. Not like Abu Kerim and Mohamed."

"You son of a bitch," I said.

"Perhaps ... but Abu Kerim, yes, a traitor."

I said nothing, just waited. The man with the machine pistol came back from the end of the veranda and said something in Hebrew to Daoud. Daoud spoke gently, urgently to Pinstripe. In English.

"The three others got away. So that's okay." He made his voice cozy, conspiratorial. "That's right, isn't it? Three others?"

"You speak ... English ... like a Jew." The words came harder now. Though he was close to the end, I imagined I saw an amused look. With difficulty he turned his head slightly and looked at me, almost speculatively. "I would have ... killed you too ... I liked you ..."

His eyes closed. I turned away. The flowing blood sickened me. I did not want to watch him die.

Daoud looked at me stonily. "This terrorist seems to know you. Mr. Hampton, isn't it?"

I nodded. Pinstripe had died. "Why did you have to kill him?" I asked. "Why?"

The man who looked like Abu Hisham cradled his arm and watched from where he sat against the railing. Now he spoke quickly. "Ah, Mr. Hampton, so it is you. What a terrible thing, what a terrible thing."

"And who are you?" cut in Daoud. He spoke in English, his voice no longer gentle. Like a policeman.

"I am Dr. Homsy. Raouf Homsy. This is my home."

Sergeant Daoud stared hard at Homsy. His face had the look of one reassembling the facts. He turned to me. Still ungently.

"And why are *you* here, Mr. Hampton?"

Homsy stanched his wound clumsily, listening intently for what I would say. The blood continued to flow, but I answered as instructed by the young man at the hotel.

"I had an appointment to see Dr. Homsy about my back."

Daoud looked down at Pinstripe, felt his neck in final confirmation, then stood up. Blood was seeping into the wood of the veranda, staining it unevenly.

"Very clever. Yes, very clever." The Israeli sergeant's face showed controlled anger. He shouted something in Hebrew into the house. Out came a third man, armed not with a gun but with a flash camera. Daoud pointed to the dead man, and the photographer took pictures.

"Let me see your papers," said Daoud roughly to Homsy. The doctor, grimacing, struggled to his feet and brought out his papers with his left hand. Daoud looked at them, then made an uncaring gesture to the man with the camera to bind Homsy's wound. First aid equipment appeared out of a large leather camera bag; inside I saw a high-fidelity tape recorder.

"Don't think you've been clever," said Daoud tightly, shifting contemptuously to Arabic. "Now I know who you are. We will watch you. Very carefully."

"I don't understand," said Homsy, responding in educated English. "What have I done? I demand to speak to the authorities. I agreed to see a Mr. Hampton here in my private clinic, and then you kill a man on my veranda. Who are you? Why should you be watching me?"

"I'll watch whoever I choose to watch. Wherever terrorists and pigs are concerned." Daoud could no longer control his anger. He stepped close to Homsy and with the flat of his hand hit him a sudden hard blow on the side of the face. "Why did this man want to kill you? Answer me. I saved your life. Do you recognize that?"

"I don't thank you for it. I have no idea what you're doing here or who you are or anything about this dead man. I am an ordinary doctor trying to do his job. I've never been in trouble with the authorities, if you are indeed one of them. May I see your identification, sir?" The man with the camera was dusting powder on Homsy's wound; the bleeding was minor. Blood had also appeared at the corner of Homsy's lip, but the man paid no attention to it. The camera bag gaped open; the tape recorder inside was Starr Johnson's top of the line.

"You'll see nothing." Another hard blow to the face by Daoud, his expression showing hate. The man with the camera went on dressing the wound, adjusting to his patient's sudden lurch. "Next time, my tricky friend, I won't save your fucking life." He held Homsy's papers for a moment, then with a decisive motion put them in his pocket. He scribbled an address on a card, handed it to Homsy. "Pick your papers up tomorrow morning at ten o'clock. You will come into Jerusalem for an official interrogation."

"I cannot come at ten o'clock. I'm a busy man. I have many patients at the hospital. People depend on me." He implied that no one, by contrast, depended on Daoud, but we all knew Homsy knew he had to go.

"If you fail to appear, you'll be arrested for endangering the security of the state." Once again Daoud stepped close and dealt him yet another blow, this time on the other side of the face. As Homsy staggered to one side, Daoud bit off each word. "In the meantime we will take your car. You'll find it in Jerusalem when you come. I advise you not to object in any way."

Daoud gave an order in Hebrew to the camera man, who held out his hand to Homsy for the keys. Homsy made a surly gesture indicating the keys were in the car. His nose bled; his jaw had begun to swell.

"What about this body lying here?"

"It will be picked up later on. Don't move it or touch it."

"And how do you expect me to get to Jerusalem without a car?"

Daoud laughed unpleasantly. "I'm sure you and Mr. Hampton can figure something out."

He signaled me to come with him to the end of the veranda out of earshot.

"You realize," he said, "I could make a lot of trouble for you. I could keep you in Israel for days. I could have you arrested. Your interference in our internal affairs has been unpardonable. I don't want to be unpleasant, I just want cooperation. You understand?"

"No, I don't understand anything. I don't know what is happening. I advise you not to hit me."

Daoud sighed, unsympathetically. "Listen, Hampton, please be sure I understand why you say you cannot understand. What I'm doing is telling you to keep your mouth shut about what went on tonight. I can make difficulties for you, yes, but especially I can make difficulties for friends of yours here. Difficulties you'd choose not to be responsible for. Now do you understand?"

"Listen, Daoud," I said, now enraged, "I don't know what kind of game you're playing, but I'm tired of getting pushed around. By you and everybody else. So don't give me a hard time. I can make trouble for you too. First you have fake Arabs attack me in the Old City, then you barge in here, make mysterious threats, and cuff my doctor around. Well, fuck you."

"What do you mean, fake Arabs?"

"You know goddamned well what I mean. You and whoever you work for can go to hell. Any more trouble for me or my doctor and I go straight to the world press."

Daoud's face showed cold fury. He wanted to hit me, but instead he wheeled away without answering. From up the valley in the direction of the distant village came the sound of gunfire. Then silence. Then gunfire again. Daoud listened attentively, grunted in satisfaction.

"Bastards," he said.

The man with the machine pistol suddenly began firing off the veranda into the orchard. He pointed at a spot below the veranda, then down the hill. I saw a shadowy figure running through the orchard, zigzagging professionally. At Daoud's command the other two clattered down the steep stairs to Homsy's car. Daoud turned to Homsy and me, his face hard as flint.

"I advise you not to push your luck."

He took the steps two at a time and jumped into the car, which leapt forward onto the gravel curves.

*   *   *

From the veranda we watched them go down the hill and turn north in the direction of the shooting. The car stopped a half-kilometer up the main road, where they picked up another car and raced on. Putting fingers to his lips, then to his ear, Homsy pointed toward the walls of the house.

So we played charades, saying what we thought we might have said if we had been what we pretended to be. If Daoud had planted a listening device, he cannot have thought our talk was natural. Homsy closed and locked the window through which Pinstripe had been killed, then locked the front door, looking at me wryly as if to say locking a house did not mean it was secure. Pinstripe's corpse lay in the middle of the veranda, face toward the dark sky, like a Hindu prepared for cremation. I avoided looking at him. When Homsy got into the car, I saw him wince in pain. His face had blotches of dark red.

He leaned forward toward the dashboard and turned on the radio. The third movement of Mozart's forty-first, played by the Israeli Philharmonic, flooded the car. "Now we can talk," he said.

That the Mozart soothed the pain, I doubt, but it permitted answers to questions I found difficult to contain. I was angry at the world. The violence had my mind in turmoil.

"You see," he said, "there were five of them. I happen to know. From the sound of things, two will get away, back across."

"Back across to where?"

"Syria, I suppose. A good supposition. Farah had definitely gone over, perhaps a while ago." I'd almost forgotten Pinstripe's real name.

"You mean, no longer with . . ?"

"Yes, no longer with what you might call the Beirut group. Now, of course, he's no longer with anybody at all." For a long moment he looked out the car window at the moon, as if in silent prayer. "And I should tell you I know about *you*. You and a friend of yours were fifth formers my first year at Ramallah. I admired you from afar."

Turning left toward Ramallah, I glanced at Homsy. He would not, I thought, understand my anger. I did not understand it myself. Homsy seemed to be a down-to-earth sort, not given to smiles, not one to dramatize a situation or make light of it. Did he not find casual murder unnerving? In the darkened car, with only the dashboard and the half-moon for illumination, the resemblance to Abu Hisham would have fooled many.

"Are you related to Abu Hisham?" I wanted some answers.

"No names, please. I try to make a habit of no names. But no, not related. In fact, not at all. I'm a Christian. The only connection, quite ungenetic, is our fathers were close friends." He paused to listen to the

Mozart, now at a glorious climax. "The irony is that Farah – I don't mind using *his* name – is a cousin of mine. I'm sorry he lost his life. I knew him long ago when he was younger and happier. Before the troubles."

"Did he recognize you? Is that why he didn't shoot?"

"I think so. At least, he knew it wasn't our mutual friend. But I will assume he knew who I was. That way I can remember him with greater charity."

"He knew you were a doctor. He said so."

"Yes, I thought I heard him say that. I'm glad."

"I once talked with him. I thought we could become friends … Of course, he was a son of a bitch. He killed friends of mine."

"I know. Your classmates. In Beirut." He paused an instant, then went on. "With the extremists you never know. They can be your friend but they can kill you in the name of something-or-other. To them this is not abnormal behavior."

He moved carefully in his seat, using his left hand to shift his right arm to a more comfortable position.

"I think tonight's affair went well." He spoke as if discussing a patient with a close relative. The formality of his speech suggested honesty, though judging by recent events he could be successfully deceptive. Was I cut from the same cloth?

"What about tonight's affair, for God's sake?" I burst out. "What about it?"

He was looking straight ahead at the bends in the road but at the angry sound of my voice, he looked uneasily at my face. We saw the lights of Ramallah in the far distance. "I cannot tell you much. I too would like to know. I did what I was told." His manner became almost soothing, as if he were worried about a younger friend.

"You could easily have been killed. So could I. What about that?" The fury inside me would remain for a long time. This I knew.

"Yes," he responded. "We could have been killed. But the risks of death were less than you might think. The first shot, if it came, would be at me, and after that it would be known I was not Abu Hisham. Sorry, I mean our mutual friend. Which would stop the shooting, we thought. Maybe not. If Farah hit me in the head I'd die, but he shot for the body.

To get an easy hit, then follow up. He didn't know the Israelis were inside. A better shot would have hit the vest."

"What vest?"

"The bullet-proof vest I'm wearing. Very hot. I'll be glad to get it off."

I drove automatically, my mind seeking comfort but finding only jagged surfaces. Once again, I was acting in *someone else's* scenario.

"What good would it do for Farah to kill Abu Hisham and me?"

"Yes, what good would it do? None at all, I suppose. But several people thought it would. I've wondered about that. But there's too much I don't know."

We were silent a moment. All at once I understood some of it, but I didn't know how much Homsy wanted to know. Hadn't Reginald Hughes, my journalist friend, talked at lunch about getting a great story? About someone like Abu Hisham plotting to negotiate with the Israelis, plotting in secret with an American, and (for an added bit of spice) killed as a traitor while plotting. Breaking the story, Reginald had said, would destroy the possibility envisioned by the story.

"What if it had really been Abu Hisham?" I asked urgently, still angrily, ignoring the directive not to use names. "What would have happened?"

"I don't know. Once again, I know very little. But those extremists, clearly they thought it was worth a lot of effort." A grunt of pain escaped him as he moved in his seat. "The same goes for the Israeli extremists. I will be interrogated tomorrow and will know nothing at all. Of course."

Then I thought about the Beirut press, informed in detail by Pinstripe and his friends; it would have had a field day, assassinating Abu Hisham's family honor in the process. I would be painted as an American agent, a mole in the Arab midst, a man using the accident of upbringing to betray those by whom he'd been nurtured.

And the Israelis? The same notion, though principally with camera and tape recorder, fewer bullets. In what guise would they have leaked their evidence to the media? An American plot uncovered, with me as a pro-Arab fascist? Abu Hisham described as a Jew-hater, a PLO plant who would negotiate as a moderate and then destroy the Jewish state? A discreet leak to journalist Hughes and others about the evening's discoveries?

But which Israelis? Which Palestinians? I thought sourly about Israeli and Palestinian extremists, natural bedmates, washing each other's sheets, members of Intransigents United whose worldwide purpose is to foster intransigence in others ...

"What now?" I said. "What's the result?"

"I really don't know."

We entered Ramallah. I felt a sudden urge to talk about the town, to keep my frayed mind away from jagged surfaces. Questions formed in my mind, and I came close to voicing them. But Homsy, I thought, was not the sort to indulge in nostalgia, if that was what it was.

"What will Daoud ask you tomorrow?"

"Ah, so you know his name." Homsy shook his head. "Don't tell me more. I know who Daoud is, that is enough."

"Who is he?"

"Anti-terrorism. Hardliner of the worst sort."

I thought for a moment.

"Do you know a man named Feldman?"

"Of course. A different sort altogether. Not like Daoud, who is known for interrogation techniques. Daoud calls himself a sergeant but he's a lot more than that. With me he'll have to keep the violence to a minimum. Or so I hope. The drawback is I'll have a file all my own from now on."

"Did some of the people with Farah get away?"

"You'll know tomorrow, maybe the day after." The streetlamps of Ramallah lit up his face, and despite the puffiness around the jaw, I could see lines of tension. "To the press they will announce a certain number of infiltrators were shot at the border. Sometimes they use names, sometimes not."

We stopped at the main door of the hospital, and with his left arm he reached out and took my hand. "If we meet again, it will be a long time from now." He sighed, opened the car door, eased himself out.

He peered in for a final word. "Are your mother and father still living?"

"No, they died some years ago."

"I'm sorry. They were kind to me." He hesitated, then decided to go on. "Your mother once held me when I cried; I was very homesick."

Saluting awkwardly, he turned into the hospital door. I sat a moment before moving off. Had my mother held me when I cried? I knew she loved me but I couldn't remember if she held me when I cried.

FIFTEEN

Jerusalem, May 1990

I remember little about the darkened countryside during my trip back to Jerusalem, the curves in the road, the outskirts of the city. The car set its own fast pace, like a horse hurrying back to the stable. They'd put up three roadblocks on the way back, and at each one it seemed to be the car, not me, that stopped testily. My mind was elsewhere. Or almost. I do remember thinking the Israeli soldiers expected me. After a look at my passport they waved me on.

Leaks, two of them. Blake's plot was the big one. Who had made Blake's plot public enough to be lethal? Who had decided that William Hampton and friends were expendable? I could not undo what had been done, but by God I wanted the name of the squealer. The anger I felt, deep enough to make me grip the wheel and curse, may have come from witnessing a killing up close. My psyche had been left unsettled, exposed.

And the other leak, the recent one about the meeting on the Ramallah road? Who knew about that? A double leak, actually; two sources operating independently, resulting in plural deaths. Someone told Pinstripe's group, whichever it was, and someone told Daoud. By God I would find the sources. Only a few people, after all, knew about the meeting. So I told myself, until I remembered that Blake's plot had been in the same category. Only "a few people" had known. According to Blake.

My mind was jumping about. I sternly instructed myself to reason. Two sets of people had been tricked into coming, both expecting to find

Abu Hisham and an American in secret and guilty conclave. Instead they found an American on a legitimate visit to a doctor for a bad back.

That Abu Hisham had purposefully arranged for Pinstripe and his group to learn about the meeting as if by accident, I had no doubt. But why the elaborate drama? How did it help? Those who had come to find Abu Hisham would know it was a trick; the striking resemblance to Homsy could not be a coincidence. Ironic, Abu Hisham had said, that I was in more danger than he. Was he taking me off the hook? Somewhere in the Palestinian labyrinth, thanks to chancy stagecraft on the road to Ramallah, perhaps a tiny alleyway had opened, a way out. Where was it?

The car sped along, past the five-kilometer marker. I glanced up the hill at Homsy's house but no lights showed. Presumably the body still lay in state, face to the sky. What way out? My mind stumbled from one possibility to the next. I talked to myself, aloud, as if talking would improve my reasoning. Who was Abu Hisham protecting me from? Palestinians, of course. Which ones? Any one of several varieties of Damascus-based hardliner.

The headlights picked up the four-kilometer marker. The Palestinian who fled down the hill after the events on the veranda would, if he survived Daoud's manhunt, tell Damascus what had happened, and if he did not survive, the basic information would be reported by the others. Did the hardliners now think they had less to gain by killing me? In order to discredit Abu Hisham, they had wanted to kill us both in each other's company.

That's it, I said exultantly in a ringing voice. Abu Hisham has, by God, announced to Damascus the skirmish is over, he's on to the scheme, the scheme has aborted. If they still looked for ways to discredit him, involving Hampton would waste their time. Hampton, I shouted, is useful no longer because they know Abu Hisham won't go near him. All starkly illustrated on the Ramallah Road, acted out for the benefit of those who receive messages with difficulty. The American, Damascus will now know directly, has become unusable.

But then, what about Cairo? Why had Pinstripe saved my life when I was attacked in the hallway of my office? Had he not yet become a traitor to Abu Kerim? Yes, he had; he was already a traitor. On this I trusted my instincts.

I tried out various combinations, like a crossword puzzle, but using humans not letters to fill the spaces and match the clues. Above the sound of the motor and the noise of the wind I gave utterance to my arguments as if debating with a blockhead.

Not until I asked how Pinstripe could serve two masters, yet do the same job, did his part of the puzzle get filled in. Keep tabs on Hampton, Pinstripe was told by two groups. And protect him. The reasons differed but the end result did not. On behalf of both I was kept safe by the same man. Abu Kerim had two reasons; one was for the consumption of colleagues, the other for old times' sake. And the Damascus group (whichever one it was) wanted me safe to play a later role in the exposure and discrediting of Abu Hisham. To them this was a game of paramount importance, an intricate cat-and-mouse game, which had finally failed on the road to Ramallah. For his part in all this, Pinstripe was rewarded by death.

As for those who tried to kill me in that dark hallway in Cairo and on a dark street in Beirut, who could know? Did it even matter much, providing news of the histrionics on Homsy's veranda spread quickly? Doubtless yet another faction, operating from Damascus, more hotheaded, less devious. A faction that felt it should kill me on the basis of a leaked rumor. Abu Mousa's Fatah rebels? Abu Nidal? Abu Abbas? A pick-up group of five with funding from Libya?

Would they now leave me alone?

Like a riddle after you're told the answer, the answers seemed obvious. I took a deep breath. I could feel my gut unknotting. *But I continued to see the guns pouring lead into Pinstripe from the veranda window.*

*   *   *

The two-kilometer marker went by. How much would I give to revise the thoughts that went through my head from then on? Because I had to ask myself about the Israelis. Who told *them* about the meeting?

Who were the people who knew? Abu Hisham and Homsy and pre-sumably a few more of their *hai'a*. Plus Barbara and myself and maybe a back-up at the consulate. No reason for any of us to inform Daoud or any other Israeli. My heart beat faster before I knew why. The car reached the Jewish high-rises on the city's perimeter. Barbara. My God, Barbara. It couldn't be. I loved her, yearned for her. But she fit the puzzle's spaces and clues. She was *Jewish*. By her own admission she didn't trust Abu Hisham, speaking of an ancient Jewish feeling that prevented it. She was dismayed about our earlier secret meeting but delighted when another was arranged. Knowing the time and place, and in league with certain Israeli allies, she could assist in discrediting Abu Hisham. (I thought of Daoud's man with the camera bag and tape recorder.) Yes, she had to discredit him. Of course. He represented a middle way that made Israel's national ambitions more difficult to reach. Israeli success depended on Palestinian intransigence. Barbara knew that.

Where had she been that day when I tried to get her at the consulate? What about those phone calls before I left for the Ramallah road? If they were social, she would have told me about them. Abu Hisham had implied that my love for her blinded my judgment. Feldman had spoken about the Zionism of her parents, how hard it was to escape the prejudices inculcated at an early age. Had she had a hand in arranging the dinner party at her sister's? Probably.

This would explain the big leak, the Washington one, how Blake's plot became known. Barbara could now return to Washington and report the plot a failure, through no fault of her own. And to her Israeli friends and allies, I thought bitterly, she could report a success. Or a partial success. Abu Hisham would not embarrass them, and the image of Palestinian unreasonableness would remain undisturbed. Even without the discrediting of Abu Hisham, she had done a good job for her fellow Jews.

The lead poured out of the window. I saw the blood oozing out of the blue denim suit.

The car took me down the Nablus Road toward the hotel. There flicked across my mind the memory of my father telling me never to make judgments when I was angry and unnerved. Or perhaps he used the word distraught. So, grimly, I went over it all again. It made more sense the second time around, but I felt sick. My face burned and my chest felt constricted. What now?

God, what now?

The car stopped where it had been parked. Thank God I hadn't told her who arranged for it. I slammed the door and made for the lobby.

*   *   *

I went straight to her room, knocked, pushed open the door. She was sitting by the bed in the blue dressing gown, reading by the bedside lamp. When she looked at my face, she had to know something was drastically wrong. She stood up, hands to her cheeks.

"What happened?"

"Yes, what happened," I said mechanically. I had not thought how to proceed, how to get her to tell the truth. I stood a moment looking at her, avoiding the moves that would have brought her into my arms. She waited for a clue, hands clasped.

After a pause I began reciting the bare facts of the evening, my voice at a monotone. As if I were reading a statement at a meeting. Reactions flickered across her face: disappointment, puzzlement, relief, something akin to maternal concern when I mentioned the violence and potential violence. I turned and stared out the window to escape her gaze.

When I finished the story, she wanted to ask questions. But I cut her off with questions of my own. I could see her blurred reflection in the window. The bedside lamp shone on the blue dressing gown.

"How long have you known Feldman?" I asked.

"I didn't know him before the dinner party." Her tone was studiedly impersonal, as if she thought it best for my anguish to work itself out in this way. "I had heard about him often from my sister and brother-in-law."

"And who suggested the dinner party to your sister and brother-in-law?"

"I don't know. I told my sister there was someone I wanted her to meet. I don't know how it worked out after that."

"Didn't your sister tell you Feldman suggested the party?"

"No. If he suggested it, it only fit in with plans she already had. To have you and me." The words came out glibly.

"What about your parents? Did they know Feldman when he was at Harvard?" I had to find the connection.

"I don't think so. That was before Irv met Lois."

I turned toward her. She was looking at me strangely. Her tone had become less neutral.

"You said your parents were serious Zionists?" She hadn't said that. It was Feldman.

"No, my mother was thoughtlessly Zionist, my father wasn't especially interested in Israel. I told you that." Her voice was sharp.

Who had lured her into treason? When?

"And whom do you know in the Israeli government?" I turned blunt and clumsy. "Who are your counterparts? Who do you talk to?"

She had paused after each question, but the pause lasted longer this time. When she spoke, her voice had more of an edge.

"Why are you asking me these things? You know I can't tell you that."

"Answer as best you can," I said stubbornly, insistently. The connection had to be somewhere. She had betrayed me, told Daoud or his ilk about the meeting, set violence in motion. She moved the bedside chair forward and stood behind it, hands on the back. Putting a barrier between us. I yearned for her.

When she said nothing, I went on to other questions. Doggedly, no strategy, just questions. "When did you first talk to Daoud?"

"I've never talked to him."

"What did the CIA tell you to do about Feldman?"

"Nothing. We've already talked about that"

I pressed on. I couldn't control the compulsion to lash out, to hammer away until she admitted her guilt, her betrayal.

Somewhere in the back of my consciousness a voice asked me what I was doing. To her. To me.

"Where were you the day you said you were at the consulate but you really weren't there?"

She stared at me, mouth slightly open. Her face had the look of one unable to absorb what was happening. I plunged on.

"Whom did you make the phone calls to just before I left for the Ramallah road?"

I heard a quick intake of breath as the full horror finally broke over her. She was breathing fast. "Oh God," she said, "oh God, oh God." She began to cry softly, hands gripping the back of the chair, tears spilling onto her cheeks. Yet she stood erect, looking at me unashamed, like a child whose pride will not permit defeat.

I stayed paralyzed against the wall, my arms folded as though locked. If I moved, what had happened would become true, my vile behavior would become part of our private record, and that would be the end of it. Tell her you love her, said some inner voice, tell her. Please stop crying, said the voice, say everything is all right. But the time for that had gone by.

I could not look at the hopelessness in her face, and so I stared at the far corner of the room that had been our haven. Gradually despair took over my body and released it from immobility. My arms unfolded themselves; my hands went into my jacket pockets. Suddenly I sobbed, a single sob I did not expect. I took a deep careful breath, looked at her again. The soft crying had ceased.

"I trusted you," she said. "I trusted you, you did not trust me." Tears welled again. The look in her face reached toward me like a pair of arms.

Could she be innocent? If she was, what I'd done was somehow irreversible. It was anyway. If in fact she had betrayed me, I thought, I'd be better able to face the soul-wrenching impact of the last few minutes.

"For your sake," she continued, then stopped to bring her voice under control. She remained behind the chair, hands still gripping the back as if for support. The light from the bedside lamp caught the angles of her face. "For your sake I suppressed my doubts. About your middle ground. In the end I believed in what you said. I loved you. We were together, working for something good, something decent."

Her hands continued to grip the back of the chair. My eyes were fixed on the bedside lamp. She looked at me and kept looking at me.

"I will not answer your questions, I will not dignify them." Using an ancient defense she emptied her face of all expression. "You seem to be in the grip of ideas about my loyalty, about me. About me being an Israeli spy. A traitor. That's what you thought, isn't it? Some kind of traitor?"

I did not answer. I kept staring at the bedside lamp.

"Haven't you found out what I really am?" she said. "Or was I just a little company for the road, a nice time in bed." No accusation, no irony, but as if she were asking herself about Bill Hampton.

"No," she said, "I know it wasn't that."

She waited for me to speak, then went on. "And who fed you these ideas? I wonder. Was it *them*?" She looked down at her hands. "Yes, I said *them*. Them. I mean those faceless Arabs you were teaching me not to fear. What did they tell you? That I was Jewish, couldn't be trusted? Once a Jew, always a Jew? A Jew can't be a good American?"

Silence fell. My stomach remained tight. I forgot to breathe, then exhaled carefully so that no noise would interrupt the stillness.

"When you left for the Ramallah road," she spoke in a low self-questioning tone, "we were in love. When you left, I remember thinking you were ... I didn't have inner forebodings anymore, maybe one or two judgments down deep but nothing that would get in the way. I felt liberated, wonderfully happy."

Another silence, not so long.

"How long might we have stayed in love? You'd never break up your family. That was okay. What we had was precious, very special. It could have remained in memory, maybe a lucky meeting from time to time, I don't know. Whether I remarried or not. That's what I thought ..." She sat down heavily on the edge of the bed, hands clasped and arms down between her legs, head bowed.

"Please say something," she said.

The moment for truth had come. I was wrong. I think I already knew I was wrong. Intuitively. And suddenly, as the mud of my roiled psyche began to settle, I knew also that Abu Hisham himself would have arranged to inform Israeli extremists as well as Palestinian ones. That's the way he'd have arranged it. That way it made sense. That way it ...

I cleared my throat. "You see, I was just wrong. That's it. Terribly wrong." I looked at her bowed head, suddenly wanting to weep.

"Wrong," I said again, gaining courage from the repetition. I took a deep breath. "I have no excuses. It's the atmosphere, the tension, the strain. When I thought about it, it was clear. It had to be you. But it wasn't. Now I know. I was thinking like a Palestinian or an Israeli. It gets to you. I was scared, pushed, there was violence, somebody was killed. Can you understand?"

The figure in the chair made no sound, no move.

"It was the violence," I said desperately.

"Could you ever forgive me?" I asked.

The question fell quietly into the silence. I knew the answer. On the surface of things, forgiving comes easy, a formula, a few words. But, as with the old maxim, the heart forgives only if it forgets.

"Please answer." What I wanted at this point I don't know. Absolution of some kind? Something definite, however negative? She sat there, looking down, saying nothing. Finally her head shook slowly, tiredly. She spoke without looking up.

"Yes, I can forgive. I'm trying to understand, I'll go on trying. If I can understand …" I leaned forward to catch her words. "You say you were acting like a Palestinian or an Israeli, but that's not true. You were acting like an American." She shook her head again. "Would you have been suspicious of me if I hadn't been Jewish? No, you wouldn't. It's my Jewishness. Always that. It never leaves me. I'm so sick of it."

Her head remained bowed, her voice low.

"I can't be a patriot without having it thrown in my face. The people I work with, it's always there, at the back of their minds. Something in their eyes. Should this Jew be working on Middle Eastern stuff? Divided loyalties? And so on. And on and on. They never say anything. They lie in wait for signs of bias. That's what I'm sick of …"

She paused, then went on. "Signs of bias … I bend over backward to discount my biases. What about the Wasps? Do they do that?"

She looked up, her face beyond hope.

"Now everything's changed. I found you, now I've lost you." I wanted to say she hadn't lost me, but I knew what she meant. She kept looking at me, examining my face.

"You were something new, you didn't care what I was." She stopped a moment. "No, not that exactly. Somehow … with you, my being Jewish was just a fact. Not an obstacle. Just an irrelevant fact. For you I was just a human being. Not a Jewish human being. I felt so wonderfully alive, so free."

She looked at her hands, toyed with the belt of her dressing gown, then spoke so softly I almost did not hear. "You were free of that subtle thing, that thing the others can never forget. They're always aware. Some days you think they've forgotten, but they're always aware."

We fell silent. I came over and sat on the bed, next to the chair, not too near, thinking about the if-onlys of the last few hours. "Perhaps …" I began, but she shook her head and cut me off with a tiny gesture of the hand.

"It can't be the same again," she said. Looking at my face, she put her hand up and gave my brow a short stroke. "I'm so sorry, so very sorry. Dear Bill. It can't be the same. You understand. Anybody else but you, any other thing between us, maybe we … If you'd been less important … But you lifted me up and let me crash."

She began to cry once more. I took her hands in mine and held them a while. As she cried, one of her hands rubbed one of mine in an automatic way. I stared at the floor.

"My father told me once I wasn't tough enough to be a Jew," she said, "I should be more like my sister, he said." She continued to cry. I put my arm around her gently and stroked her back.

"Please hold me," she said.

She drew me down onto the bed, keeping her arms around me and burying her face in my shoulder. I stroked and patted her back through the rough texture of the blue dressing gown. The tears stopped but her face was still wet against my neck. Every so often I kissed the top of her head, and eventually she responded with a tiny kiss below the ear.

"Come," she said, and as if by plan we took off our clothes and got under the sheet. When we made love, it came out fiercer, less tender. I think we both sought release from pain. For me at least, the pain persisted. In the drowsy moments afterward, she sobbed once or twice, then slept.

*　　　　　*　　　　　*

I glanced at my watch, knew it was time to return to my room. Her hand caressed my face to let me know she was awake.

"Stay a few minutes," she whispered, "then say goodbye."

"Goodbye?"

"I don't want to face you at breakfast downstairs, trying to think of things to say." The tight feeling told me she planned to leave.

"Can't you stay a day or two? Isn't it all right between us?"

She stayed silent a while. Her hand stroked my back.

"Yes, it's all right. But it's different, much different. I need to get away from here, stay at my sister's place, do cables for Washington."

She moved in against me and we held each other tight a long moment. I wanted to avoid saying goodbye.

"But we must see each other again. Very soon. I mean, I love you, very much. So …"

A finger came to my lips. "Dear Bill, I'll always love you. But now I have to be by myself for a while. I have to adjust. I have to come to my senses, get on with my life. Cope with the reality of things. So let me leave easily. Please."

"You see," she said. "I've been living in an unreal world." Her eyes betrayed a desire to weep, but she kept herself under control. Or almost. "I do know you'd never leave your wife and family. That's true, isn't it?"

She wanted some kind of final confirmation.

"Bill, that's true, isn't it?"

Was it true? Yes, of course it was. But did this mean that we should break things off, stop seeing each other, be lovers no longer?

"Yes," I said, "that's always been true. Can't we go on as we have?"

"No, we really can't. I have to get on with my life – without dreaming about you, without hoping to see you all the time. I need to go back to Washington, live my life the way my friends do. I can't live two lives at once." She kissed my cheek.

I was reluctant to understand, but suddenly I accepted what I knew to be true. Our love affair couldn't go on this way – despite deep love and longing. Had we been different kinds of people, perhaps … But we were what we were.

We were both quiet for several moments. Finally I cleared my throat and spoke huskily.

"But when shall I see you again?"

"Perhaps next time you're in Washington. You know where I am." There was a long pause, then a careful intake of breath. "I'll expect you when I see you."

"Will you go right back to Washington?"

"As soon as I get my cables sent and all that. I'll give them the complete story," she said. Then she added, "Except for our affair."

An affair, not a love affair.

"Was it just an affair?"

She took in her breath quickly.

"I didn't mean it that way." She kissed my neck, my cheek. I felt I was being comforted. "You must know you'll always be very dear to me."

"Will you marry that other fellow in Washington?"

"Perhaps. Perhaps not. I'll have to see how things are."

Another silence.

"Maybe I've changed," she said. "But I'll always love you. I want you to know that."

"Is the fellow in Washington like all the *goyim*? Is he always aware?"

She put her face back against my neck but she didn't cry.

"Yes," she said finally, "he's always aware. But he's sorry. And I can handle it."

*   *   *

In the morning I phoned down for a cab to take me to Lod airport. When I came down an hour later, bags in hand, the young man at the desk smiled and said someone was waiting to see me. I turned and saw Professor Ehud Elath seated in the far corner of the lobby.

"I understood you were leaving," he said in his gentle voice, "and I wanted to say goodbye."

In the end, just as if he had not planned it, he had my bags put in his tiny car and we set off for Lod. He drove carefully and slowly. That was fine, I did not feel rushed. My plane was not scheduled to leave until early afternoon; I preferred sitting in a departure lounge to staring out the window of a hotel room.

We said little as he negotiated his way out of Jerusalem and started down the hill. The sky was wonderfully blue. Trucks and taxis zipped by us, and far below I could see more of them crossing the plain. In the distance, despite the haze, I glimpsed the darker blue of the Mediterranean. My mind, seeking rest, began to wander ...

I heard Elath's gentle voice and came to attention. "Sorry," I said. "Didn't quite catch that."

He smiled. "I think your thoughts were someplace else. Nothing important. I said only I'm sorry you're leaving. But of course you've finished what you had to do. Your computers and so on."

"It's been very pleasant. Very pleasant."

A friendly little man. I valued the ride and the company. I did not think we had much to talk about. At the speed he drove his little car, the airport needed an hour or more.

"I'm glad it was pleasant." He frowned as an impatient taxi overtook us in too short a stretch of road. "Sometimes, of course, one wants a bit of excitement, not just pleasantness."

We lapsed into silence a few minutes, then he spoke again.

"It was good that Barbara Corum brought you to that dinner party. A very nice woman." We were coming down the steep part of the hill, and he drove with dangerous caution. "Is she still in Jerusalem?"

"Yes, I think she is. At her sister's place."

"I thought she told me she was staying at the American Colony."

"She was, she moved out this morning." It came out more curt than intended.

"Oh I see, I see." But clearly he didn't see as well as he wanted. "I hope all is well between you."

I took my eyes off the road and stared at him. What did he know about Barbara and me? He turned and looked at me an instant, then went back to the business of driving.

"You see," he said, "I know a bit about what happened last night. On the road to Ramallah, I mean."

Startled, speechless, I continued to stare.

"I was worried about what you would think," he said. "You see, I was asked to let certain government people know about the meeting. In an indirect way. So I did. But I thought, that is, I was afraid you might have thought it was someone else. Perhaps you thought it was, uh, Barbara Corum."

I remained silent because I was uncertain how to reply. Elath gazed stolidly ahead, and I had the impression he was embarrassed. Perhaps deciding I needed more time, he spoke again.

"When one deals with extremists, one can get excited, nervous. This is no disgrace. Under such circumstances, I for one jump to, uh, unwarranted conclusions."

Something clicked in my mind. *Extremists,* not an everyday word, expressed a point of view. Dr. Homsy had used it, so had Abu Hisham. Suddenly I had questions.

"Who told you I was leaving this morning? Who told you about the road to Ramallah?"

He seemed to blush under the white beard, though the morning sun behind us made it hard to tell. I saw a tiny smile.

"Well, you see, we have a few friends in common. I mean in addition to Irv Cohen and Moshe Feldman. Perhaps you think I learned from Moshe? No, that would be looking in the wrong kind of place. Would it be a doctor who lives on the road to Ramallah? That would be a better guess. Would it be someone who quotes the poetry of e e cummings and talks about fluffy lust? That would be a good guess too."

He braked to avoid hitting a slow-moving oil truck that appeared suddenly coming uphill. My feet pressed against the floorboards. But my mind was circling, hovering, looking for a place to land. A place with a different landscape, different formations than I was used to. As the oil truck roared by, my feet relaxed. I expelled a lungful of breath in a kind of half whistle that could have been taken as gratitude that my life had been spared. Elath knew better.

"Yes," he said, "it rearranges things a bit. You see, a friend of ours thought you ought to know. The involvement with Jews, I mean. He said I could tell you. He said it was the greatest secret of all and that you would keep the faith, even with a very old friend you both have. In Cairo, I think he said."

"Yes," I said woodenly, "Cairo. Right."

Neither of us spoke for a minute, each staring down the road ahead. I should have known, I thought yet again, and if I had, would Barbara and I still be at the American Colony? Perhaps, but now the water had gone its unmerry way under the bridge. Elath glanced over, his face anxious.

"Would it have been better if you had known I told the security people?"

I sat quietly a moment. This brave and gentle man, part of an organization some of his fellow countrymen would judge treasonous, hoped, so it seemed, that Barbara and I were still lovers, that by some fluke of timing our love affair had not been seriously threatened or radically changed.

"You are really asking about Barbara Corum and me?"

He sighed. "Yes, but it is a selfish question. I do not need to know. I blame myself."

"Could you have told me before if you'd wanted to?"

"No, not really, I suppose. It was discussed, of course, but judged to be dangerous. You would not have acted naturally." He sighed again. "Do you think that is true?"

"If I'd known, I might be dead."

"That's true, that's true … I'm very sorry, so very sorry. A lovely woman. Perhaps things will work out."

It hurt to think about what might have been. Though from the beginning Barbara and I had never had an open road ahead. *Illi fat mat*, the Arabs say, what has gone by has died. The road ahead had always had unforeseen curves, I thought, though maybe not discernible at first. Cath says I have a way of forgetting the unpleasantnesses of life. Sometimes perhaps. Not this time.

"Who was it then?" I asked harshly, knowing he'd know what I meant.

"You mean the leak, of course. The one out of Washington."

"Yes."

"If I knew I'd probably tell you. If you knew, would you forgive?"

"It would be very difficult," I said. "When you say you don't know, how can I know you're telling the truth?"

"I can't help you there." The gentle voice turned melancholy. "You are right. There are few ways of knowing about new friends."

He drove in silence across the plain.

"If you do find out, perhaps you'll be less angry," he said.

"Perhaps."

"Anger turns into sorrow, sorrow for others. Sometimes."

"Perhaps," I said again. I looked for a way to change the subject. "Do you think the Ramallah business will do any good?"

"We think it went off well. You are safer now than you were a day ago. And the position of our mutual friend is better."

"Do you think Moshe Feldman knows about your connections with our mutual friend?"

"No, definitely." An amused look came over his face. "If he did, he would send messages, the way he did with you."

I saw him glance at the rear-view mirror, and on impulse I turned in my seat to look back. A hundred yards behind us came a Jerusalem taxi, proceeding at the same pace as the cautious Elath, a single passenger in the back. A guardian? I could not make out the faces.

"Yes," said Elath, smiling, "you've been a strain on our meager resources. But it was a pleasure to have you here."

A mile from the airport he stopped in back of yet another taxi that waited at the side of the highway. The guardian taxi had disappeared. Clearly part of a careful surveillance plan. Bag and briefcase at the ready, I got out quickly, said goodbye.

The new driver said not a word, just took me through the airport check post and left me in front of the main lounge. I knew he would not accept a tip.

SIXTEEN

Cairo, June 1990

At first my homecoming seemed better than I deserved. From Cairo's hot dusty airport I phoned Cath to say I was a limousine ride away. She drew her breath in quickly, perhaps anxiously. I heard the kids in the background. At supper she sat quietly while the children reported. I was thrown back into family life like laundry on wash day. The kids were full of news about life in suburban Maadi, about the American School. Sarah had a new Japanese friend. Larry had won his 100-meter event at the school's annual track meet.

"Larry has a girlfriend." said his younger sister, almost impishly, "He danced with her twice at the dance last Saturday." She was delighted to hand on this piece of gossip. Larry blushed, denied any special attachment to someone named Deborah. I moved quickly to defend my teenage son. "Sometimes you have to dance twice with someone," I said. "Sometimes there are social reasons." For a fleeting moment I thought about "dancing twice" with Barbara Corum but turned my mind back quickly to life in Cairo.

Sarah was intrigued by the notion of social reasons for doing things. So we went on from there in our family tradition of discussion and intellectual adventure. All of us joined in, including Cath. Each kid, I thought suddenly, had an unshakable belief that yesterday was "super" and tomorrow would be the same. The enthusiasm, the gift for life they both possessed moved in on me, filled the room, left me aching for something

I couldn't name. I came embarrassingly close to tears, yet enchanted by what they told me. Cath watched me gently and with a look of inquiry, as if something remained unsettled.

The kids finally left the table, Sarah because it was her bedtime, Larry because he had homework. As she always did, Cath went along to Sarah's room to watch over bedtime routines and listen to prayers. In a few minutes Larry returned, glanced down the corridor, sat down again at the table with an intent look.

"Dad," he said. "I thought I ought to tell you that something's bothering Mom. I asked her about it the other day but she says everything is fine. But sometimes she looks off as if she's thinking about something private, not like her at all." He sat back and raised both arms in a gesture of uncertainty.

"I'm glad you told me," I said. "I'll give her a chance to tell me about it." I was suddenly proud of him. To change the subject I asked him to tell me a bit more about what was going on at the American School in Maadi. We talked a bit about getting into the right college and then into the right medical school. When he left the table again to study in his room, he seemed satisfied that his father would handle his mother's problem, whatever it was.

When Cath reappeared, she looked composed, ready to exchange the usual end-of-journey reports. I touched only on the events of a standard business trip – except for the murder of Abu Kerim and the Dajanis, which she had seen in the Herald Trib. I hesitated about what else to tell her and when, so I put off the decision. When she asked about Abu Hisham in Jerusalem, I said I'd phoned, had a short conversation, been unable to meet. The outright lies came less easily than leaving things out, so I left out many things. For the moment Jerusalem and Beirut seemed remote.

Yet I sensed a residue from the violence, a slow burn deep down anxious to emerge. Though my father and mother had taught me that killing others was one of the ultimate sins, I realized I was getting savory tastes of what the sweetness of revenge might be like. Her eyes had shown horror when I spoke about Abu Kerim and the others. She knew what violence did to my psyche and she put her cheek against mine in ritual sympathy. Then energetically yet soothingly, as if the world's evil were elsewhere, she told me about Cairo during my absence. As I listened, the relaxation I felt in my body told me the old life was at work, restorative, loosening the grip of what would be good to forget.

The hospitality of our Cairo community had been bountiful, even exhausting, she said. "Abdu phoned every two days from Interior to say hello. He kept asking if I was all right. And Mary" – this was Sam Paul's wife – "phoned from time to time, though last week she went home on a leave to show baby James to her parents. Then Abu Taleb phoned twice from Heliopolis." She paused. "So it seems they all had a special reason for phoning, for checking on me. And before you left, you were worried about something, but you didn't tell me what it was." She gave the special smile and waited for an answer. The blue eyes did not leave my face.

I couldn't tell her now. It was not yet over. The slow burn confirmed this. And I would never tell her all of it. But I had to say something. I hesitated, uncomfortably.

"All right, you needn't answer," she said, speaking before I had a chance to lie. The blue eyes were still fastened on me, though the smile had disappeared. "I don't need protecting, do I?"

"No, no."

"Is it anything to do with Abu Kerim? Or that time you said you fell in the lobby of the office building?"

"Can I tell you some other time?"

"You must tell me soon. Please. It can't go on this way. I've a right to know, don't I? I know when things are wrong. I know something's very wrong."

"I promise I'll tell when I can." But perplexity and hurt showed in her face. "Things are all right," I said. "I just can't tell you yet."

She resolutely changed the subject, telling me her agent Paul Taylor continued to insist that she pay a visit to New York. "I think he's right. I should meet the writing crowd there, talk about the direction of things. Now that the New Yorker is going to publish my article, he says several influential people want to meet me."

"How long would you be?" I asked.

"Perhaps a couple of weeks. Would that be too long?"

"Certainly not," I said. "I'll arrange not to be away." I decided this was a good moment to plunge. "Larry says you're preoccupied with something."

She stared at me for an instant. Then she smiled. "Ah, sweet Larry. Yes, I think he's been keeping watch on me lately. When I think I'm by myself, I wonder about all sorts of things, and I think one time before supper he caught me doing just that. The darling boy asked me if I was all right, if everything was okay."

"And is everything okay?"

"Yes, I think so. I worry about what you might call my writing career. But that's going well right now, thanks in large part to Paul. And I find myself worrying about you, when you're away, whom you're seeing, all that. You're an attractive man, and other women would be intrigued, I think. But the main thing is I know you love me and you love the kids. That's the main thing."

Yes, I thought, that was the main thing. I smiled, she smiled back.

After we got into bed, I felt guilty as I entered her but also excited and loving. Had the style of our lovemaking changed? Less successful perhaps, more ritualistic, something to be gone through at homecoming. But, yes, loving. I thought wonderingly about the flexibility of the male, able to shift bedmates without trauma. One had only to put up with guilt. There came the unwanted image of Barbara in the hotel room, standing tall behind the chair, crying softly, saying "oh God."

*   *   *

Two evenings after my return we went out to Maadi to another garden party, a big one given by the deputy at the German Embassy. I was glad to go if only to divert my mind from the anger that kept arriving uninvited. I needed soothing moments. Early June had bestowed its special blessing on Maadi's flowers, especially the roses, lit here and there by garden lamps with shades like coolie hats. The perfume of expensively dressed women in cool evening dress blended not unpleasantly with the reassuring, though faint, smell of the bug-killing chemicals that make such parties civilized.

Among the men was Gav Middleton. He saw me immediately and signaled with his head toward the far end of the garden. Cath was soon surrounded by friends. Gav and I, as planned, drifted out of the crowd toward a distant table with two chairs. He turned his big body, looked over at me, and shook his head.

"Sorry," he said. I thought about dead friends, including (strangely) Pinstripe. The anger surged suddenly.

"Shit, we're all sorry." I stopped for a moment thinking to get the anger under control, then plunged ahead. "And angry. And we were all stupid. Has Barbara Corum written a report?"

"I can't let you see it. You know all of it anyway."

Not all of it, I thought. Or maybe I did know all of it. The name of the leaker would be missing.

"Quite a goddamned charade," I said.

"I want you to believe we weren't playing games." He looked down at his huge hands. "We're not unprincipled. I promise you by and large we do our best."

"Shit."

"Honest to God. I wasn't in on all of it the way Blake and Rosberg and Corum were. But to get a settlement is in the American interest. Anyone would agree with that. Nothing to be ashamed of, for chrissake."

He stopped, uncertain how to defend his organization. Perhaps he wondered if an appeal to patriotism cut any ice with Bill Hampton.

"I don't know Blake well," he went on, "but I know Rosberg and Barbara were for a settlement for its own sake." Perhaps Middleton didn't know Blake well, but Blake, according to Barbara, knew Middleton well enough to consider him "the best there is."

"I've got nothing against a settlement, whatever the screwed-up motivation," I said. "I don't like being expendable."

"What do you mean?"

"My life's worth more to me than the success of American policy. CIA policy, to be more exact. That's what I mean."

The heavy shoulders shifted awkwardly. He said nothing for a while, then put the subject back to where it had been.

"Listen, it was a chance that looked good. Your old friend, what does Barbara call him, Abu Hisham, he'd trust you if you said the Israelis would agree. But then the whole fucking thing got out of hand. You understand I couldn't say anything. I knew we were in big trouble when you found you were being followed."

"You couldn't say anything? Fuck you all. Big trouble for a friend, like getting killed, and you couldn't say anything?" But Gav obeyed orders in the American interest. A principle of his life.

"We couldn't call it off," he said. "We'd gone too far to stop. Everything was in motion. The thing had a life of its own. And hell, you might bring it off. There was a reasonable chance. Depending on secrecy."

"Christ, secrecy."

He flushed. "Yeah, well, sure. There was a leak. That's not what I'm talking about. I mean secrecy later on, post-leak secrecy. Secrecy at the level of nobody knowing you'd see Abu Hisham, how you'd see him, pretending you wouldn't see him. We wanted to discredit the original leak. Get it forgotten about as just another rumor. We'd keep you out of danger by making it just another rumor."

"Hocus-pocus," I said. "What bullshit. Keep me out of danger? I was saved in Cairo by a terrorist, saved in Beirut thanks to an old friend." I didn't mention being guarded in Israel, though perhaps it was only on the way to the airport.

"Do you realize my job is in jeopardy?" I asked.

"How so?"

"How do you think I can go back to Beirut or Jerusalem with makeshift terrorist groups out to kill me?"

"Bill, these things always die down. I promise you."

"Tell that to the boys in Damascus and Baghdad." I felt pushed around, irked, badly done by. But to go on giving Gav a hard time? The generals in Washington gave the orders, not a foot soldier like Gav. In this case the general was Curtis Blake, an unprincipled bastard. The remark about hardliners in Damascus and Baghdad brought another flush to Middleton's face.

"Listen, Gav," I said, relenting. "It wouldn't have made a difference if you *had* called it all off. It was too late by then. You get me?"

He smiled thinly. "Yes, the goddamned leak." He pursed his lips, sat back heavily in his chair, apparently wondering how to proceed.

"And what do you think now?" he asked finally. "Think anything's changed?"

"You mean the charade that was staged on the Ramallah road?" I gave a short laugh. "Maybe I'm safer. I'll know it didn't work when they nail me. It wasn't in time to save others."

"Barbara says Abu Hisham arranged the charade, as you call it." He looked at the crowd drinking cheerfully at the other end of the garden. No one made a move in our direction. "He must have had help."

"Just the doctor, as far as I know."

I wasn't about to explain to Gav the intricacies of what had happened on the Ramallah road, what I now understood about it, the elaborate planning done by Abu Hisham to steer the hardliners into other directions, away from him and me. Not to mention his ultra-skillful and indirect manipulation of hardliners of the Israeli security forces. Quickly I took another tack because Gav wanted to focus on things I wanted to avoid.

"There's something I'd like to know, not that it makes any difference now, but I'd like to know." I saw Cath glance our way from the other end of the garden. People were being herded to a long table near yellow roses; behind the table Nubians wearing red tarbooshes spooned out platefuls of food. Middleton was listening carefully.

"Did you really, I mean *really*, have the Israelis lined up to accept Abu Hisham as a negotiator?"

He didn't answer for a while, stared musingly at the glittering international crowd. I saw him bite his lip.

"I guess you've paid your dues." He sighed. "You understand Blake would carve me up if it gets out ... I'm not especially proud of this."

We sat silently as he worked something out in his mind.

"Barbara doesn't know this yet," he said. "But probably we couldn't have delivered on that one. After you left for Jerusalem, I woke up one morning and I knew, don't ask me how, I knew the Israelis would never have agreed. How could Blake have had a guarantee? How could he deliver? All that paranoia inside the Israeli government. Blake told us he'd fixed it at the highest level. I don't believe it. It couldn't be true."

He chewed his lip a bit more and seemed to take a decision to proceed. "My Tel Aviv counterpart was down here last week. Nice guy, known him a long time. So I asked him in a roundabout way. As far as he knows after some casual research, there was never any deal between Blake and the Israelis, just some exploratory conversations that my colleague wasn't even in on."

"Jesus," I said.

"Yeah, not so good."

"That son of a bitch."

"Listen," he said, "I know what Blake wanted, and maybe it was the right thing to do."

"Some people got killed. Might have been more. He murdered ten of us at least."

"Ten of who?"

"Ten of us humans," I said.

He stared a moment. He didn't want to talk specifics about murder. "Blake's no murderer. It's whoever leaked the scheme. And it wasn't on purpose."

"Ah, accidental death."

"Look at it this way," he said. "Blake wanted Abu Hisham as bait, to present the Israelis with an honest-to-God alternative to the PLO, then to put pressure on them. Threaten to expose them if they refused to negotiate with Abu Hisham."

"Did Rosberg know Blake couldn't deliver?"

"I guess he must have, but maybe he didn't." A long pause. "Incidentally I hear he's left the Agency, gone off to teach at Boston University."

I pondered this bit of information. "I suppose it was an offer he couldn't turn down," I said drily. Middleton looked at me sharply, but he didn't want to talk about it. I pushed on with my queries.

"And these so-called exploratory conversations, who were they with? Which Israeli did Blake talk to? Who brought up the name of Abu Hisham?"

I thought I knew the answer already.

"My friend from Tel Aviv didn't give any names." But he spoke evasively.

"Was it someone named Feldman?"

"I don't know," he said. "Blake talked a lot with someone named Feldman but it might have been someone else."

We got up and walked over to the buffet table near the yellow roses, where the servants waited patiently. We were the last to be served.

"We haven't talked about the big question," I said.

"Yes, I know. The damn leak." Middleton spoke somberly, plate of food in hand. "I've probably said too much already. Look, I can't tell you about the leak. Partly because I don't know, and what I do know I can't tell you."

"Come on, Gav. I need to know. Names."

"No, you don't need to know. It's over now."

"Not for me," I said heatedly. "Not for me." Without further comment in either direction, we strode off to join our wives at separate tables.

✳   ✳   ✳

I spent a while sorting out my life, catching up on business matters, becoming a Cairene again. Cath seemed content to have our family routines back to normal, though I caught her looking at me questioningly at odd moments. As if she felt something wasn't right. Things weren't right for me, of course, given my angry preoccupations. But the kids seemed happy, though Larry looked at me from time to time as if seeking information about his mother's state of mind.

As soon as I could, I made my way out to Heliopolis, plowing along behind endless lines of polluting traffic, snarling at drivers driven to a frenzy of impatience by the heat of early summer. Seated in Abu Taleb's café over Stella beer, I was able to lean back and tell him the story as if chatting about old times, and with a smile he congratulated me for my improved ability to handle intrigue and deceit. I did not mention the love affair. We talked a lot about Abu Kerim.

"Poor bastard," he said. "He didn't live to see Palestine again."

"If it weren't for me, he and the Dajanis would probably be alive."

"Don't hang that on yourself. You had to do what you did. And there may be other reasons. He'd have been killed sooner or later anyway. And if the CIA knew about Ramallah, plenty of others did."

"That's what Abu Hisham said."

"As for Mohamed Dajani, he seems to have had a death wish."

"No, if it hadn't been for me, he might have got away with it."

"I think that Quaker school left you both with a permanent guilt complex." He took a swallow of beer.

"A pity about our little plot," he went on, looking out at the dirty street. "It would have been nice to sit again in my orange grove and tell my children how things were. On the other hand I never thought anything would come of it. Too many cooks. Just something you had to do anyway, because you were in trouble."

He signaled the waiter, ordered more beer, said we ought to celebrate.

"What are we celebrating?"

"We are celebrating your return to this lousy shitty city."

"I find it good. Some days anyway. Cairo, I mean."

"Like a safe haven?"

"Sort of."

"You can have it." The slender Bedouin face held a look of distaste. The beer arrived with frosted glasses and felt wonderfully cool. Content with each other's company, we watched the café crowd for a while. The morning clientele, half of them Palestinians with little to do but sit and talk, filled most of the tables.

"Well, you'll have to take care," he said, "but I think our old friend did pretty well. That business on the road to Ramallah. Shrewd. You're a lot safer now, maybe he is too, but keep your eyes open. Not that you won't." He paused, looking at me with mock criticism. "You've changed. In the last couple of months I find you much more Palestinian. A pleasure."

I laughed. And marveled that I could laugh. It had something to do with old friendship, which seemed to keep the anger below the surface. "Don't worry, my eyes will be open. As to whether I'm safe or not, check the morning papers. Incidentally, if they know about me, they know about you."

"Yes, I've thought about that," he said. "We better telephone each other, not see each other, until we see how things work out."

"There's quite a bit to do yet."

"You could stay out of it. But if you can't, I'd be glad to help."

I thought about the tall economist's final comment in Beirut. "I've got revenge in mind," I said. "Fuck 'em all."

"Yes, why not. Time for the *shirka* to make a move."

"I'm dead serious."

"Yes," he said, "I know you are. As I said, I'd be glad to help. Get him within range and I'd be glad to do the actual killing."

"I'd love to do it myself, but damn it I just can't. My damn upbringing."

"Yes, I know." He smiled suddenly, remembering my story about Jerusalem. "The part I like best is that part about omelettes of fluffy lust."

*   *   *

That evening Cath and I went over to Abdu's place and sat on their terrace, looking out over the city and the river from Zamalek's northern tip. As usual, visiting him and his wife reminded me that everything about them was Egyptian upper-class, except perhaps their friendship with foreigners like Cath and me. When the two women went inside after dinner, he looked at me, amused in his formal way, and asked about my Palestinian friends.

"They seem to be behaving themselves. Thank you for looking after my family."

"That was nothing, really nothing."

"I'll always be grateful."

"By the way," he said, "I was told the other day by my friend who worries about such things that your mysterious follower was killed in a border skirmish. His name was Farah. Another person was killed with him."

So three got away. He looked at me for a moment, then smiled. With Abdu, curiosity never seemed to win out over courtesy.

"Bill, I don't need to know anything about your recent visits to Lebanon and Israel. I'm glad things are all right now. Or I hope they are. Have you told Cath about it?"

"Not yet."

He nodded with the conviction of one who believes that wives need not be told everything.

∗   ∗   ∗

When the letter arrived, I was watching the river from the terrace. Mohamed, our ancient *bawwab*, brought a dirty envelope to the door, reporting with disapproval that someone in scruffy country dress had delivered it. Cath and the kids had gone to the back of the apartment.

The letter, badly typed, had no signature.

Dear old friend:

Naturally I must write to explain. It was all a minor skirmish in the struggle for peace but it was important to both of us.

Was it worth it? If human life has value, then it wasn't. I continue to think with horror about all the deaths. But from one point of view I'm glad. You and I reestablished ourselves and put ourselves back where we were. I have few real friends. Those I have left, two from Ramallah and three from AUB, I want to keep.

Yet so much has happened to each of us. I lost a son. You have had your sorrows. We've lived complicated lives. When we will meet again, I do not know. Very soon, I hope, because there will always be much to talk about. Speaking realistically, probably not for quite a while, which would be best for us both. But things change; who knows what will happen?

You will have understood most of what recently occurred. Never, of course, did I intend to come to the meeting, which was carefully compromised to deal with extremists of two nationalities. Yet the meeting had to take place so that you and I would be seen, clearly seen, to be no longer a part of the little game we were all playing. The drama, I hope, did what words would never have accomplished.

From your point of view things have gone well, though I understand you will, like me, be disturbed by the killings, including the killing of a dedicated extremist. But you can now return to your life almost as it was before. I say almost, because you will always *have to be on guard. Who knows what mad extremist may get you in mind, if he is reminded? <u>The trick will be not to remind anyone.</u>*

Which leads to the problem of how to conduct your business in Lebanon and Israel. I've been thinking about this. For Lebanon, unless things change radically, I urge you not to stay in Beirut, go only to Jounieh (capital of the new Maronite kingdom!) and have people come see you. If you must, make quick trips down to East Beirut, but I don't advise it. Never go to West Beirut. As for Israel, come only to Tel Aviv and if you have people in Jerusalem you must contact, spend company money on telephone calls. The situation here will soon get worse. The intifada is losing steam. Frustration is everywhere more apparent. The fundamentalists are gaining ground every day. Palestinians are beginning to kill other Palestinians, more than before. I'm using my influence to stop the killing but feel helpless.

The only encouraging note is your country, which seems to be pushing us all toward negotiation — not like the mad all-or-nothing scheme you and I have just coped with. No plots, no tricks, just a long slow road. The extremists, of course, will do a lot of killing in order to wreck the process, but finally we must succeed, though doubtless there will be many ups and downs before success actually arrives. So I'm glad the effort to discredit me failed. Perhaps this will turn out to be important in five years or ten. Or twenty. Our unesteemed leader, believe it or not, has been in touch. Apparently there's a major shift to moderation that would include myself. The PLO may even administer the occupied territories eventually! Unwittingly you probably had something to do with this.

Please extend brotherly greetings to our friend in Cairo. I miss you both, more than I can say. As for our other friend from the stricken land to the north, I miss him terribly. But he would not want us to weep for him. May we all meet one day in Jerusalem.

I put the letter down and watched the river again. The evening breeze from the Mediterranean ruffled the water and played tricks with the lights from the other side. My eyes fell on the low wall along the riverbank, which was where it all began, but Pinstripe had gone. Picking the letter up, I tore it into small bits.

In a while Cath came to join me. We sat silently a while. Then she put her hand on mine.

"It's hard seeing you this way," she said.

"What way?"

"Your eyes are different. Sad. Angry. Even the kids have noticed. Sarah asked why."

"I don't know why. I didn't know I looked like that." I forced myself to smile and then by some magic felt better. She watched the smile, gave my hand a pat, got up. She came back with a bottle of white wine and two glasses.

"Don't be sad and angry," she said, hoisting her glass. I felt she was making a determined effort. "We have a lot, don't we?"

"Yes, we do. I think we do." Touching her glass with mine, I took a deep breath. "I have to tell you a long story."

I left out only the love affair. Why load my guilt onto her? I told myself it was cowardly to make myself feel better by making her feel worse. So I told myself. When I'd finished, she fell silent a while. Then she leaned over and put her cheek against mine.

"God," she said. She looked at the river for a few long moments. "It had to be something like that. Poor Abu Kerim. And all the rest."

"Yes, all of them."

Again she was quiet. "Why didn't you tell me before?" she said finally. "You thought I'd be frightened?"

I nodded. "Frightened for the kids, for me. There was nothing we could do except hope it would go away. Or go to the States."

"Has it gone away?"

"Not entirely, not for me. There's no danger for you or the kids. So I think."

"How much danger for you?"

"Less every day. Abu Hisham thinks I have to be careful not to remind people, but the danger's almost over."

I did not add that a yearning for revenge, a yearning to kill, remained embedded in my psyche. What would my father have said?

She watched the river again. "Do you think I should get the kids out of here?"

"I think we have to proceed with our lives. You'll take them to Pennsylvania this summer anyway, then we'll see. If I think there's the slightest danger for them or you, you'll have to stay for a year."

"Without you?"

"Look, it won't come to that. If it did, I'd visit you often. A year at the outside. You have your writing to do."

She nodded, as if a diagnosis had been confirmed. "Yes," she said, "you couldn't leave."

Later she asked about Barbara.

"The CIA woman in Jerusalem, what was she like?"

"A nice person. Very competent."

"Attractive?"

"I suppose some would think so."

"Did you like her a lot?"

"She was a good colleague, kept her balance."

The blue eyes looked into mine, then searched my face as if it had a message on it. When she put her hand on mine, I had the feeling I was being consoled.

*   *   *

They say old routines have a healing effect. Perhaps, perhaps not. With Laila's help I dug into the mountain of Starr Johnson paper that had accumulated at my office. I played rounds of golf with various friends and found my game temporarily improved. Middleton phoned a few times about playing a round, but I said I was busy and so he stopped phoning. For the moment he reminded me too much of the recent past.

I wondered if I still looked angry. I preferred not to show it. I sensed the presence of anger, somewhere nearby, but the feeling that had now become easiest to identify was a restless feeling of unfinished business, a feeling that someone should pay. Heavily.

Adjusting to the story I told her, Cath spoke as if things were back to normal. One Saturday evening we celebrated Larry's birthday, just the four of us, and played hearts using the family rules; laughter and contentment filled the living room. But somehow, I think, Cath knew about Barbara. The blue eyes now shifted away and did not gaze straight into mine. She seemed less eager to make love, doing it more because it was the thing to do.

*   *   *

Next morning my vindictive thoughts came into better focus, as if I'd twisted the right knob on a new camera. Laila brought in a letter from David Rosberg. He had, he said, been thrust back into academic life quite unexpectedly but was enjoying himself. His new job included arranging a lecture series on the Middle East during the coming academic year. He hoped very much I would agree to speak. Then he added another paragraph in longhand.

Sometime I hope we can talk but for now I am most anxious you should know I have been completely sincere in our recent dealings. I highly value our association and its original purpose.

I sat at my desk staring at the letter, unsurprised, my intuitions confirmed.

*   *   *

The crucial bits of information were provided by Sam Paul. He had left for a business trip to the Emirates the day before I came back from mine. I had been home a full week by the time we met for lunch. We sat in a shady corner away from the Hilton swimming pool. The sky was washed light blue by the midday sun, which had chased others inside to air-conditioned territory. We sat in shirt sleeves enjoying the heat and the solitude. Our waiter stayed indoors, coming out only on signal.

We had business to go over, and we dispensed with that first. Then he asked if I was still being followed, if I had had further difficulties.

"No, all seems quiet on that front. No difficulties." I covered a yawn; we'd consumed a lot of kebab and beer. "Be sure and tell Mary thanks for phoning Cath while I was away."

He made a deprecatory gesture. "She was glad to do it. You never know what these Palestinians are up to."

"When do Mary and James get back from the States?"

"Oh, I thought you'd probably heard. Mary and the baby aren't coming back. She's been transferred."

"What?" I was astounded.

"Well, it was decided only a few days ago, and after a long talk on the phone we decided to do it this way. Save wear and tear on farewell parties, which I don't like much. And as you know, I've thought I should get back to the States a while. We both think James should have some years there."

I stared at him. He had never mentioned a desire to return to America, Mary seemed happy, the baby appeared to thrive. Sam smiled at me.

"Yes," he said, "it's very sudden. But they had this slot in Washington open, quite a promotion, and they asked if she minded going right away."

I found it hard to adjust. "But... so you'll be going? Soon? What the hell, Sam? Is it a good idea to go back now?"

"Yeah, I think it is. The firm wants me back, happy to have me, they say. And the more I think about it, the more I like the prospect."

The trouble was I thought he didn't like the prospect. Something in the eyes.

I asked him the usual questions, when was he going, how could I help, where would he work. As we talked, other things fell into place. Mary Hashwa, Lebanese origin, married Sam Paul, also Lebanese origin, and worked at the embassy. In the political section? Yes, but the political section headed up by Gav Middleton, station chief for the CIA.

Abu Hisham had told me something about PLO sources in Cairo. And what had I overheard at that gathering in Beirut, the party at the Dajani apartment? Just before Abu Kerim let everyone know I knew Arabic? Someone mentioned Cairo and asked about ... who was it?

"You know," I said quietly, "only the other day I learned you also used the name Jameel for your son James. So you would be Abu Jameel, I suppose."

Sam sat immobile for a while, not looking at me, watching nothing.

"Oh," he said finally, "so you know about that."

I nodded, my eyes fixed on his face.

"I'd have told you sometime," he said. Then words came tumbling out. "You know I meant you no harm, I did all I could to keep you from it. I pointed out Farah that day when we were having lunch, remember, and you focused on him. I wanted Middleton to know you knew you were being followed, so he'd call the whole thing off. I want you to believe that."

"It's okay, I believe it."

"Once these things get started …"

"I know. They get all out of hand."

"Listen, I'm glad you know. Makes it easier. You think I'm Lebanese. Not really. My parents were from Ramallah. My dad was a nationalist, had close friends on the Arab Higher Committee." He spoke with pride. "We came to the States when I was a young kid, changed our name."

"And Mary?"

"She was born in Lebanon. Her parents were Palestinian."

"How come she doesn't speak much Arabic?"

"She does, reads and writes it. They told her not to let on."

"She got the information from Middleton's office, about Abu Hisham and me, about what the CIA had in mind, and you passed it on?"

He nodded.

"And when you passed it on, what did you think would happen?"

"I didn't think much about it, just did the proper thing, passed it on. Personally I thought it was a bonehead idea, bound to fail."

"Well, fuck you." I let out a long breath.

"Listen, Bill, I tried to stop it but I couldn't. I had to do what I'm supposed to do."

"And what are you supposed to do? Kill your friends? Bounce babies off the sidewalk? Be a spy for the PLO?"

"A spy? What do you mean a spy? I don't get paid." He looked at me crossly. "Unlike twenty-five thousand others in the U.S. from Ramallah, I'm unwilling to be an armchair Arab. I'm a patriot for two countries, just like American Jews."

"Come on, Sam, don't go off half-cocked."

"What do you mean, half-cocked? You know and I know it's all un-fair, it's evil, a screaming injustice. Christ, the Jews nibble away at our country, taking the land bit by bit, putting their goddamned colonies in the occupied territories, stealing the rest and calling it Israel. And you know what? They do it because they're stronger, more willing to kill. And because America helps them. Does America help Palestine? Never. Not once."

I wanted to speak, to vent my own anger, but he did not permit it. He waved a forefinger.

"I don't work for pay," he said. "I'm a successful businessman. Just like any ardent American Zionist, I work at what I believe in, because I believe in it. If American Zionists can support their murderous thieving agents in Israel, I can support the PLO, which murders less and, God knows, hasn't been able to steal a fucking thing."

He stopped, exhaled heavily. My eyes followed someone diving into the pool, but my mind was wandering around in a jungle I'd just glimpsed once again.

"What will happen to Mary?" I asked.

With an embarrassed look Sam shifted in his chair.

"Sorry to blow off, it's the unfairness of it." He calmed down. "Mary? Nothing much will happen. So I gather. The Agency is pretty angry at the moment. They know she was the leak. My guess is they'll keep her in a harmless slot in Washington for a while, then ease her out."

"How did they know it was her?"

"They had to know, finally, once the thing got so big. She reads most of the traffic, does the decoding." The sardonic look appeared. "Not any more, of course."

He went on. "She wants to quit anyway, now that we have James. She wants another baby. I've been asked to work in New York and I'll go as soon as she gets the best deal she can on severance pay."

He stopped, then said with a shrug. "Point of fact, Washington can't be too hard on her. Not all her fault, in a way. The message about you came in at her level. So she decoded it. But it should have been eyes-only for Middleton. She was surprised. So was Middleton." A hard look came into his face. "They can't be hard on her. All she says is, what's best for America in the long run is justice for Palestinians, just like Zionists in the government say what's best for America is what's best for Israel."

What had he said? It should have arrived eyes-only for Middleton. It should have but it didn't. So the real leak, then, was not Mary. It was someone who knew that Mary, like Sam, almost automatically passed things on. I began fitting all this startling new information into what I knew. If I found out, Ehud Elath had said, I might be less angry. Anger becomes sorrow, he said.

"Sam," I said, "because of you and Mary some people are dead, what about that?"

"It's a risk we all take," said Sam. Then, with a glance at his watch, he shifted back to unfinished business matters.

SEVENTEEN

Cairo, Summer 1990

After three days I phoned Gav and told him I had to see him. The story line had lost some of its blur. Sam Paul had been orchestrated, his passion for Palestine set to music and exploited. Snatches of conversation in five cities had been coming back to me. I might have missed on some details, but the general picture was clear enough. At first I thought I had to be wrong, as I had been so very wrong on the road back from Ramallah, but in the cool light of a few days' reflection, what I was seeing had to be right. So I thought.

We met at the race track at the Gezira Club and trudged around. I dispensed with the usual courtesies.

"I know about Mary Paul," I said evenly.

"Listen, Bill, I can't talk about any of that."

"All right, I'll talk to the local press about it. I mean the guys from the New York Times and the Washington Post." My anger was close to the surface.

"Come on, Bill."

"I'm dead serious, I don't advise you to call my bluff." We trudged a few steps in silence. He must have heard the anger. "I know Mary leaked the whole thing about me and Abu Hisham. Sam Paul relayed it to the PLO. From there it went everywhere."

"If you know all that, why ask me?" The big hands went into the pockets of his jacket, as if seeking something to do.

"Because there's something I don't understand. Why would Mary decode a top-secret message like that one? Wouldn't you do it by yourself ordinarily?" I spoke peremptorily.

"Just routine."

"Routine, routine. Bullshit. You know goddamned well it's not routine. You know goddamned well someone screwed up at the Washington end and didn't mark that message eyes-only for you."

He stopped and looked at me hard. Then he turned and we trudged on again.

"What does all this matter now?" he said.

"Shouldn't a message like that one be eyes-only for Middleton? Shouldn't it, Gav? Or do you think I'm really and truly stupid?"

He seemed to be deciding something.

"It was a terrible mistake," he said.

So I had one confirmation. I needed one more.

"Who authorizes the level for a message like that? Who says it should go routine or eyes-only Middleton?"

"Bill, it was a mistake."

"You mean a competent Washington bureaucrat like Blake would let a message like that go out at the wrong level? Come on, Gav. You mean Blake would okay the message, put his signature on it without checking the destination?"

"We all make mistakes sometime."

So there it was. Blake had authorized the message. Not yet the complete confirmation I wanted, but enough for the moment.

"Gav, I want to tell you a story." I pointed him to a shaded bench near the race course. It was a long story but I made it short. As short as I could. He had to know most of it anyway.

He had an uncomfortable look. The shoulders of the big body shifted forward awkwardly. He sat down heavily and looked straight ahead. Sitting beside him, I reflected for a moment on evil, on how you define it. At the beginning I kept my voice quiet, conversational.

"Once upon a time there was a powerful high-level bureaucrat in Washington who wanted a settlement between Israel and Palestine. He worked hard at it. Maybe for many years. Pride deeply involved. He had what he thought were logical solutions, blueprints for peace, at the ready, but he couldn't get people to negotiate. Not Israelis, not the PLO, not his own government. His particular obsession was to be the hero, the person to get things started. But finally what obsessed him was that he was blocked at every turn."

Was this evil? Not so far.

"Of course the key to the story isn't politics. Not in the usual sense. The key is the kind of man he is."

Where does evil start? From within, they say.

"So what do I know about Blake?" I asked. "That's where the story begins. Gav, you've told me more than you realize. So have others. If I don't know what he was like thirty years ago, I know what he's become. More than a natural hardliner. Stubborn and opinionated. Not the kind to be confused by the facts or to let them get in the way. Fixed ideas triumph over facts whenever convenient. Inflexibility of a brilliant sort. I know you agree about this, Gav."

As I spoke, I could almost hear Blake at the meetings in New York and Washington. Gav had crossed his legs, staring straight ahead at nothing.

"Blake's other things too. He wants success at all costs. Though he seldom shows it, he's hard-driving and vindictive, also manipulative. Wants to win every race, no matter what happens to anybody else. Or so it seems. Inside the CIA, people who've tried to cross him know he never forgives being crossed. I know you know all this, Gav."

Middleton hadn't moved. His face was unreadable.

"Okay so far, Gav?"

"You're way off base, Bill."

'You mean my description of his character is wrong?"

He looked away. I paused to give him the opportunity to disagree, but he said nothing. In his pocket he found a bunch of keys and began to finger them like prayer beads.

"Maybe he was flexible when he was younger," I said. "But in recent years he seems to have adopted a particular approach toward Israel and Palestine, toward getting them to negotiate. An approach embedded in his brain as the only way to go. In a way it's hard to blame him. He had to listen for years to the so-called experts in Washington, all the lobbyists, all the academics. Pretty exasperating claptrap."

"And what was this 'only way to go'? It was lean on people, push hard, threaten, force people to negotiate, manipulate them, force them to agree. I think he just plain enjoyed the use of power. Trouble is, like anybody else, Israelis and Palestinians don't like being pushed around."

"So?" His voice had an impatient edge.

"So instead of plugging away quietly like the rest of us, he got angry. A powerful influential Washington bureaucrat, obsessed about getting nowhere. Blocked by people he couldn't manipulate."

I took a long breath and soldiered on.

"And then one day, lo and behold, a year or two ago Fatah began making noises about negotiating, not public noises, just hints here and there. Especially a conservative faction in Nicosia. The Israelis, of course, refused to talk publicly about negotiating, even though some ultra-secret talks were apparently taking place. And your friends at the State Department acted sensibly, they sat back and relaxed, waited for better openings. In fact, from fellow bureaucrats they knew that new openings might be on the way. But Blake was impatient. Here was a big chance, it might not come again. He plunged in, got in touch with the hardliners in Nicosia, lied to them that he could guarantee an Israeli agreement to negotiate if Fatah would play ball and recognize Israel.

"Why did he contact the hardliners, the group the Israelis liked least? Not so much because he was a natural hardliner himself. More because he knew the hardliners were losing ground in Fatah politics and would be more likely to agree, would be pleased to be singled out and fight Blake's battle for him inside Fatah. Always providing the whole thing was confidential. It seems the Nicosia hardliners thought it was worth the risk."

Middleton continued to stare straight ahead.

"Remember to interrupt, Gav, whenever you disagree."

He kept staring straight ahead.

"And Blake must have thought it was worth a shot, even though Israeli cooperation was unlikely. But then, as always, along came that flawed approach to what makes humans do what they do – use pressure, then things work out. Unrelenting pressure on each side. This was the way to get a public agreement to talk. Maybe nothing wrong here either, providing you're willing to back off when nothing happens. But not Blake. No backing off. Not with his pride and inflexibility. Not at this moment of opportunity. His compulsions, let's face it, were not too far from a kind of madness, though on the surface I'm sure he seemed perfectly normal and rational.

"So in Washington he became identified with this ultra-hard line. What was his dream? One bright day, sometime in the future, the settlement he engineered would be the jewel in his crown. This was the footnote he wanted in the history books ..."

I took another long breath, kept my eyes on his face.

"So his obsession told him to act now, no matter what. If he'd bothered to hear what he was doubtless told, he'd have heard Fatah was in a delicate state of transition. Factions were jockeying, cousins were killing cousins, the hardliners were having a tough time. Not the time, for God's sake, when anyone in Fatah could make big decisions."

I tried to maintain the tone I started with. A confidential tone, as if imparting gossip to a friend.

"But the Israelis, not the hardliners in Nicosia, were the real key – and they were not cooperating. Why should they? Blake thought they would if he pushed them. If they would agree, he could swing Fatah faction by faction, using the Nicosia group as his leverage. But how could he have thought the Israelis would knuckle under to pressure when they had nothing to gain? Israel knows very well how Washington works, has people in place who tell them what's happening.

"And the Israelis sure as hell knew what was happening at State. Because that was something else. Those bastards over at State also wanted their names in history books, working indirectly, more flexibly, more, yes, intelligently. And the Israelis seemed to be listening to them, listening to new and different notions about peace talks. All very secret. My guess is this infuriated Blake. After the years of work he'd put in, the clarity with which he saw the problem, how could those bastards at State think they could muscle in and louse things up for him? So now he's in even more of a hurry than before. Pressure on the Israelis. Pressure, pressure. The

Israelis have to agree, as soon as possible. Publicly, of course. Just to show everybody Blake's in charge."

"Listen, Bill ..." But he said it as if he thought he ought to be saying something. I waited but nothing further came out. I was filling gaps with guesses. If he wanted to disagree, I wanted to let him.

"So what then, Gav? It's all hard to believe, almost incredible, but it seems to be true. Blake made a few trips to Israel, all within the last year. He was getting jumpy, more compulsive. Felt time was running out, needed quick progress, enough to show his approach was working. He talked to a lot of people in Israel: politicians, counterparts in Israeli intelligence, a powerful man in the PM's office named Feldman. To most of the meetings, as you damn well know, he didn't take along his local station chief, because he wanted to be free to report his conversations any way he liked. Got that? *Any way he liked.*

"And if none of the people he talked to were cooperative, that didn't make him stop and think. Incredible, right? But true. Behind him, of course, he felt the hot breath of those bastards at State, those adversaries."

A special stillness on Middleton's face gave him away. He was listening – with great care.

"What did make him stop and think was Feldman. He realized Feldman was the key person. When it came to deciding when to negotiate, under what terms, Feldman's view would prevail. *Feldman mattered.*

"So now let's imagine how it went between Blake and Feldman at their meeting or meetings. All by themselves, remember. And the crucial backdrop? They didn't like each other at all. Both stubborn men, both insisting on winning any skirmish, and Blake, at least, vindictive as hell. The result? Blake couldn't get Feldman to do what he wanted. For his part, Feldman found Blake pushy, and in view of what he knew about Washington, about Fatah and its factions, he found him a waste of time. It's a good bet Feldman couldn't disguise his exasperation."

No need to explain to Gav how the meetings (which Feldman agreed to because Blake had high-level clout in Washington) might have gone. But I told him anyway. Blake says the PLO is the only organization that can negotiate credibly with Israel, and here's a unique opportunity. Feldman says no, there are better people to talk to or better times to talk, and in any case not for several years. Blake threatens political pressure, such as influencing annual defense allocations for instance, and Feldman asks, studiedly courteous, if the State Department can be brought in on the discussions. When Blake says there's no one but the PLO to talk to right now, Feldman says oh yes there is, someone, say, like Abu Hisham. Maybe he means it, maybe he just wants to get Blake off his back and out of his office. The best hope, says Feldman, would be Abu Hisham or maybe he says someone of this sort.

Blake, of course, can't shake Feldman. I could imagine them sitting together in private conclave, Feldman just talking and smiling, and of course disagreeing.

I realized my voice had risen a step.

"Bill, knock it off. For chrissake."

"You mean I've got the story wrong?"

"Look, it's doing no one any good. It's all guesswork. Sure you're right to be angry, but you're going off the deep end."

"And just what have I said that was guesswork? Tell me where I've guessed wrong. Go ahead."

He pursed his lips, as if to say he wouldn't know where to begin. I waited a moment, then proceeded.

"Okay, here's more guesswork. Stop me any time. Given the kind of man Blake was, what would you think he'd do? He's mad as hell, frustrated, but holding course no matter what, determined to show that bastard Feldman who was boss. That he, Blake, had to be reckoned with. What would he do?"

I tried to keep my voice in neutral. Middleton's face had taken on a frown. He kept looking at the keys, turning them over in his hands.

"You'll find some of this hard to believe, Gav. You and I don't think the way he does. But I think in the end you'll agree. After all, you've known Blake pretty well. Ruthless, vengeful. So what would he do? What did he do?

"Well, I don't know all the things he did. For sure and certain he kept looking for ways to get Feldman under control. To make clear to Feldman that Blake's was the only way to go. Maybe you guys have books on that. Maybe one of the things is to cut off the other guy's options, or show him you could if you wanted to. But we both know one of the things he decided on, don't we? No guesswork necessary. He decided to discredit Abu Hisham. Destroy his reputation in his own community. The obvious thing. Then Abu Hisham would be out of the ball game, and Feldman would get the message he mustn't mess with Blake. Maybe Abu Hisham was only a minor nuisance, but Blake could use him to show his power. So, as a matter of everyday routine, just everyday routine, Gav, Blake makes a move. He moves to eliminate Abu Hisham as a negotiating option. Just as if Feldman had been serious in bringing up his name. Not that Blake spent a lot of time on it. Like squashing an insect.

"What other options did he casually destroy in his fight with Feldman? God knows. But we have to believe what he tried to do to Abu Hisham, don't we? What's tough to believe is how his mind worked, an obsessed mind, casually making a plan to destroy someone else, a way of passing the time of day."

I paused as some club members strolled by. Middleton sat stolidly beside me. The frown had disappeared as if under instruction, the face studiedly vacant again.

"Is it fun working for a man like Blake, Gav? Barbara Corum said Blake thinks you're the best in the business. Has it been fun persuading him how good you are?"

I might have been interested in a response, but he treated it like the rhetorical question it really was. My voice went up another notch.

"You know what really gets me? For Blake the discrediting of Abu Hisham was just routine, minor routine, no fuss. One day he learns from his station chief in Cairo that one of the code clerks married an American businessman with strong PLO connections and was probably passing information. Perfect. So he makes the moves that will destroy Abu Hisham's honor. If it works, fine. If not, he'll think of something else. No big deal."

Middleton's face had a different look now. As if hoping what he expected next would go away.

"Sound crazy, Gav? What I'll do, says Blake to himself, I'll just pretend I want to have Abu Hisham negotiate. I'll pretend Feldman suggested it as an immediate possibility. I'll get his old friend Hampton – how did he know about me, Gav? – and make him feel important, tell him he can change the course of history. Feed him all that Quaker mush. And it won't take much of my time. All Hampton has to do, I'll say, is persuade Abu Hisham to agree. I'll tell Hampton we can deliver an Israeli agreement and Hampton will get all excited. Perfect."

For a moment I fell silent, watching some kids play soccer on an adjacent field. Like the game of nations, the play was hard, aggressive. Middleton knew the story I was telling him, how could he not know it? Stage one of Blake's plan was easy. Not understanding the implications, Mary Paul, by way of Sam, routinely spreads the word that Hampton will talk to Abu Hisham on behalf of the United States. The word is electrifying. If Mary Paul doesn't spread it, Blake can arrange for someone else. As soon as Israeli intelligence, Palestinian extremists, or anyone else with an interest hears about this American plot and Abu Hisham's collaboration, they start arranging for his exposure. Or my death. Preferably both.

Then stage two. Let nature take its course. All Hampton has to do is meet Abu Hisham. He doesn't even have to talk to him. One or the other of Abu Hisham's natural enemies, extremist or otherwise, will learn about the meeting and arrange to catch the two of them together. A superb proof of treason, because the rumor of treason, circulating by happenstance via Mary and Sam Paul, is then shown to be true. The discredit is total. Abu Hisham is destroyed.

I waited for a comment but none came. I heard my voice harden.

"When you thought all that was going to happen, Gav, did you feel good about it? Was it in the American interest?" I paused a moment. "No comments? Want to correct my story?"

"Bill …"

"Hampton's a dumb shit," I said, suddenly savage, "the perfect non-professional to louse things up. He'll just go charging ahead with a message about peace and conciliation, louse things up for his old buddy Abu Hisham. Very convenient. Did you agree with Blake about what a dumb shit Hampton was?"

"Goddamn it, Bill, lay off."

"How about it, Gav? Does the whole thing sound too stupidly piddling for the American government?"

Middleton let his breath out audibly, as if tired of all the nonsense he was hearing. But I knew he was acting, and he knew I knew.

"So Blake collects a couple of idealistic colleagues with no field experience and persuades them this is it, a fucking breakthrough. He manipulates them, Gav." I was biting off my words. "Makes them think they're in on a great moment in history. He tells them it's top secret, they're the only ones to know the whole story. He lies to them about his talks with Feldman. Doesn't consult any of his station chiefs. God no, they know too much. Or did he consult you, Gav? He says he cleared it with the director and his deputy, and that's all. So the two idealists, ripe for the plucking, are flattered. One of them thinks this is her big break in the Agency. Both are decent people, wanting to do the right thing …

"That's another thing gnaws at me, Gav. Both decent people. If exploiting them was in the American interest, I suppose it was okay. Is that what Blake would think?"

Barbara. Hurt would come her way soon, or perhaps it already had. Like a knee in the gut.

"So what happens? That's where you come in, right, Gav?" I was looking straight at him now, my voice intent. "The long message arrives, approved for routine decoding, as if by accident. Soon Mary, then the PLO and everyone else are in the know. If ten people get killed, never mind. If a rumor gets around and Hampton gets killed, who gives a shit? If a station chief gets his friend killed, who cares? Right, Gav?"

"For chrissake, Bill."

"Ah, so it was for Christ you did it." I added elaborate sarcasm to cold anger. "I knew it was some big fucking goddamned cause. It had to be big, not a piddling thing, otherwise you wouldn't have sacrificed any lives. Right?"

"Listen, Bill, I didn't do anything like that. You have to know that."

"If it wasn't you engineered the leak, it had to be Blake. So I'm asking you, who was it, Gav?"

He looked stonily at the keys. He wasn't going to lie, but he wasn't going to talk. I switched to Reginald Hughes' story from Nicosia.

"And at the same time you were dealing with the Fatah hardliners in Cyprus, telling them you could deliver an Israeli agreement to negotiate. Don't think I don't know all about that. It was you, wasn't it? Wasn't it?"

"I didn't have a goddamned thing to do with that. Listen, Bill, I played it straight as I could. You have to believe me."

"But you knew Blake was talking in two directions, talking to Fatah at the same time, didn't you? You said you weren't playing games. That's bullshit, isn't it, Gav?"

"Listen, Bill ..."

"You knew something was fishy, didn't you, Gav? You knew about talking to the PLO. You knew why Blake, fucker Blake, sent the message for Mary Paul instead of you. That's right, isn't it?"

There was a pause. I sat and waited, my eyes on his face. Just waited. Waited until there was a response. A long interval ensued. Then he started to say something and stopped. Then another long interval. "For two days," he said at last, "I thought it was a mistake." He crossed his legs the other way, put the keys in his pocket, and examined his big hands. He went on examining them for a while, then cleared his throat and looked away.

"Shit," he said. We both stared into space for a long minute.

"Don't worry," I said finally, "the thing failed. Abu Hisham's still in place. And things are changing. In five years or ten, he'll be there. He and Feldman. Blake can roast in hell."

Yet another interval. Was he asking himself how he should have handled things? Then he shook his head and let his breath out slowly. After a bit we got up from the bench. He said we should play a round one day soon.

*   *   *

Cath and the kids went to Warren for the hot-weather break, and I decided not to join them for my usual three weeks in August. I told Cath I had too much to do. For some reason not clear to me, I felt strongly I had to be in Cairo during the hot dry summer. With the family away, I was free to be angry.

The three of them left two days after my conversation with Middleton. I could not bring myself to tell Cath right away about Middleton's perfidy. For the moment her powers of adjustment had been stretched far enough. I would, I decided, tell her in the fall; by then anger might become sorrow. Perhaps. At the airport Larry shook my hand as if he were an older relative, then changed his mind and gave me a hug. Sarah clung to me and said she'd see me soon, and I clasped her tightly. When it came time to embrace Cath, she held me close for an instant only. Her eyes had an uncertain look and shifted away from mine. The children at that moment needed no attention, but she pretended they did.

During the next week I brooded about things. My golf game went sour because I couldn't concentrate on the ball. One afternoon, without company, I walked several times around the race course, staring straight ahead. In the evenings I sat on the terrace, staring at the river. I felt lonely but made no attempt to see anyone, because in addition to the loneliness my anger was working on me like a virus, and it seemed to arrive often, anywhere I happened to be. At the office Laila began treating me carefully. I had to watch what I said; I had taken to using strong language as if it came naturally. Only memories of a hotel room in Jerusalem put me in a different mood.

Slowly I began to forgive Middleton, as I had Sam Paul. Just cogs. Increasingly I thought about Blake, and increasingly the thought of him made me yearn to lash out, to kill. Blake, the casual destroyer. Blake, the engineer of pointless death … The trouble was, I couldn't kill or cause to be killed.

But the thought of revenge did not go away. I phoned Abu Taleb and said I had to talk. We arranged to switch to public telephones, and in a long conversation in verbal shorthand that no chance listener would understand, we fixed a meeting. In indirect and oblique language he said the safest place was the zoo in Giza. The zoo in Giza? Yes, the zoo in Giza.

"I have no friends or enemies who would imagine I was interested in going to the zoo," he said. Thus one afternoon, using roundabout routes and checking for followers, we arrived at almost the same time and sat down back-to-back on separate benches across from the elephants. I told him my recent thoughts.

"Very Quakerly," he said after listening to my scheme. "I'd be delighted to be of assistance."

"Without you it wouldn't work."

"Don't be modest. In the last months you've developed noticeably. But I see a problem. It's called credibility."

"Yes, I've thought about that. What can I do beyond better acting?"

"The answer is, you don't go to Middleton. We make him come to you."

"But that would take a long time."

"Not as long as you think. Listen, Bill, you've got to be prepared to spend the time to do this right. Like a work of art. Once the story is planted, it'll take four to six weeks to get back to us. Then we're on the way."

He turned on his bench, looked at me, and smiled. The smile had the quality of tempered steel. He, too, wanted revenge. The *shirka* was making a move.

"One other thing," he said. "You're going to have to re-create your great friendship with Middleton. Throw him off the track. It shouldn't be difficult for a devious fellow like you."

*   *   *

So I rang Middleton and suggested a round of golf. If he was surprised, it didn't come out over the phone. As we walked round the course, we chatted pleasantly. Reestablishing our relationship came more easily than I had thought, perhaps because my rage was now directed elsewhere. I had, in fact, forgiven him. We joined his wife for lunch afterward. I liked having someone to eat with. And so the long summer involved more golf games and social occasions. While I could never forget the part Gav had played, some special grace allowed me to overlook it.

The memory of Barbara, however, was difficult, very difficult, to overlook. In the evenings on the veranda, I found myself resolutely thinking of other things to think about. It was not easy. But I knew it had to be done. As the lonely days went by, I found the memories of Jerusalem were receding a bit. Partly, perhaps, because the Zamalek apartment kept reminding me of Cath and the kids. And I could always allow my anger to surge, blotting out much else.

One day in the office Laila brought in an unopened envelope – clearly personal, unrelated to business or government. Unlike the envelopes she usually opened on my behalf. I knew who it was from and tore it open as soon as Laila left the room. It was handwritten without salutation or signature.

Just a note to let you know I am adjusting to life and to DC. It would be good one day, not too soon, to compare notes.

∗   ∗   ∗

Reginald Hughes came through Cairo in mid-July. As planned with Abu Taleb, I saw more of Hughes than I usually did on such visits, arranging to have him invited to two useful receptions and hosting him at the Yacht Club on his last night. He seemed pleased. Perhaps, now that he could associate me with the Levant as well as Egypt, I had double value. Over coffee I asked if he had anything further on the Fatah story from Nicosia.

"You mean the CIA man who could deliver an Israeli agreement to negotiate? A month ago I was told Fatah was in a critical state of flux, whatever that means."

"What *does* it mean?" I asked.

"My guy seemed to be implying a major shift to the left, dropping some hardliners. Naturally, on such rumors I wait for one solid bit of evidence." He paused, as if deciding whether to tell me more. "Listen, you should know that Arafat's apparently been turned. Why he's suddenly become a moderate, I don't know. My guy says it's partly because of that story about the link with the CIA."

"You mean the CIA story is true?"

"Whether true or not. Rumor is truth. Like that business about the Israelis negotiating with a non-PLO Palestinian. Haven't heard a thing recently." He looked at me sharply. "Have you?"

"No," I said, "but speaking of rumors, I heard an odd one the other day. I'll have to trust you to treat it confidentially. Not unrelated to what you were saying. I gather some high-up CIA fellow who talked to Fatah has got himself tagged as an enemy of the radicals in Damascus. Someone said he'd been put on a hit list."

Hughes' eyes lit up. He peppered me with questions I pretended I couldn't answer. I tried not to show how much I was relishing the occasion. Who was the CIA man? he asked. By chance someone named Blake, Curtis Blake?

This I neither confirmed nor denied.

"Of course," he said, "it stands to reason one of these days one of the radical Palestinian groups will want to do some symbolic killing inside the U.S. Especially as long as the Americans play footsie with the moderates. I don't know how much you know about this fellow Blake, but he'd be ideal for them. Well-known, and so on."

I left it at that.

*   *   *

Abu Taleb phoned a few days later to suggest a conversation. So we switched to public telephones and he reported in special shorthand that the same story, though with more details, could now be said to have put down strong roots in fertile Palestinian soil. The story, he assured me, would develop a happy life of its own, delighting its narrators, gathering substance as it spread. He grunted his approval when he heard about Hughes; the latter would soon be asking his usual sources about it, including PLO people of assorted shades as well as station chiefs in East Beirut, Tel Aviv, and Cyprus. The story would then grow inside the journalistic community, which would finally consider it almost authentic, though unfortunately not publishable.

*   *   *

In mid-August Abu Taleb reported the story had come back to him with a neat embellishment. The faction that had put Blake on its hit list, it was said, already had three men in place in the Washington area.

In late August I was able to report the same after Sam Paul and I had our final lunch by the Hilton pool. Mary Paul, finally reaching agreement on severance pay, had arranged to join him in New York. Looking at him across the table, I realized I'd miss him, not just for business reasons but also personally. Sam was Sam. Did he know I'd forgiven him? He doubtless thought there was nothing to forgive.

"Have you been able to forget about last spring, or do you keep looking over your shoulder?" he asked.

"I haven't worried about it," I said diplomatically, if untruthfully.

"Well, I think you're in the clear. I've heard nothing about you." This good news, I thought, came from a reliable source. He took a swallow of his beer. "You know, I did the best I could."

"Sure."

"By the way, somebody else may be in trouble," he said. "You must know the name Curtis Blake. One of the big shots in Mary's outfit. It seems he's been put on a hit list, a political target. They need publicity inside the U.S. and they've already got men in place."

"Which outfit is it?"

"I don't know. One of the radical ones. This guy Blake is known to be Fatah's friend in Washington. Sounds like PFLP-General Command. Gebril's group."

Satisfying. Also soothing.

$$*\qquad\qquad*\qquad\qquad*$$

Cath and Larry and Sarah returned in mid-September. The kids interrupted each other to tell me about the fabulous summer in a small cottage near Cath's parents. I knew most of it because I had been in frequent touch by phone, but the two happy faces brought temporary deliverance from my vindictive preoccupations. Cath seemed content to be back, and I found I was deeply pleased to have her once again in the same place. When we made love that night, it turned out satisfactory, even exciting. An improvement, I thought, over times when she made love in order not to explain why she'd rather not make love.

*　　　　　*　　　　　*

Not until October did Middleton tell me he had to see me urgently. He did not suggest golf; he said he wanted advice. We met at the Gezira Club in the morning and ordered coffee. No one sat within earshot.

"Bill, I've had a disturbing query from Washington. Actually it came in about a week ago and I've been sitting on it, wondering what I ought to do. You're the only person around who can help. And you've always been absolutely straight."

Ah yes, that was me. Bill Hampton, a straight arrow.

"How can I help, Gav?"

"I've always said there's no one knows as much about Palestinian politics as you. The problem is Palestinian, very Palestinian. Blake wants your reaction. In spite of that business last spring, you should know he respects you a lot and believes you know what you're talking about."

There I was again. Hampton, straight, foursquare.

"Bill, an odd bit of information has been picked up by several of our people in the area. It sounds pretty authentic, and that's the problem. It seems one of the radical factions has been looking for someone to kill in the United States and has picked Blake as the logical target. Big name, strategically placed, key supporter of hardliners in Fatah, and so on. Ring a bell?"

I hesitated before replying, expelling breath audibly.

"Yes," I said, "it rings a bell, though I didn't know Blake was the target. I've had it from several sources." I had to say this right. How would Reginald Hughes have put it? "I guess I should say one of those sources has never let me down. Not once in fifteen years. "

"What exactly have you heard?"

"Pretty much what you say. A distinguished American to be killed by one of the factions. They have their killers in place, disguised in various ways. They already know a lot about the target. They've scouted his movements."

"Who's the good source you're talking about?"

"Gav, I can't tell you any of my sources."

"All right, but which faction are we talking about? You can tell me that."

"No, I can't. I've got a lot to lose on this one, Gav. If it got out I told you, they'd trace it to my source and there'd be hell to pay."

"Bill, I've got to have the name of the outfit. It won't get out, I promise you. I can guarantee you."

I thought about the security guarantees Blake had once given. And the changes since – the changes in my outlook on things. For a long moment I pretended to consider the matter.

"All right," I said finally, "but remember, top secret, no leaks, no slips." When he nodded, I told him it was PFLP-General Command. "Gebril's outfit in Damascus," I said. I thought it was the best one to choose.

"Christ. You sure?"

"Yes, I am." I paused. "Sorry to be the bearer of bad news, but it's better to know what you're up against. They've been looking for a suitable symbolic hit for some time, something to consolidate their political position among the radical groups. There's never been a major killing in the U.S."

"What should we do? What should Blake do?"

"Well, he's got to take care, watch himself carefully. These guys play for keeps. Especially Gebril."

"Yes, but …"

"Listen, Gav, I can tell you what I know from out here, but I don't know how you work things in Washington. I think you'd better tell Blake to get help. Bodyguards, I mean. That's my recommendation at this stage. Beyond that, hard to say." Then I quoted Abu Kerim. "The usual pattern for these guys is, they don't go after families, but they include families if they have to. If they have to use bombs, I mean. If they're using rifles, I don't think the families have to worry."

"Christ."

"Gav, I didn't know it was Blake. You'd probably better move pretty fast if you want him to survive. I don't know their timetable but it's probably within the next several months. That's what I understand."

When we parted company, I knew the story had been swallowed. Middleton thanked me and said Blake would be grateful for my counsel.

Ah yes, there was Bill Hampton again: a wise counselor, a decent caring fellow.

$$* \qquad * \qquad *$$

That afternoon I reported to Abu Taleb by public telephone. Now the son of a bitch can begin to sweat, I said.

"Yes, we can relax a few weeks. Then we'll do some more planting." Abu Taleb, a perfectionist in these matters, wanted to keep the story healthy and happy. Soon he would be providing some spurious clues about the identity of the killers. In a few months, yet another set of clues on the specifics of assassination would be put into the soil and begin to grow.

"Join me long distance at sundown," he said. He switched to Bedouin dialect. "We'll drink to Abu Kerim. May he rest in greater peace. He and those others."

I wondered if Blake would dig for further corroboration. Probably not, because Middleton and the other minions would persuade him. But if he did, he would be dipping into a world whose manipulation Abu Taleb and I knew more about than he did. Even if he had all the rumors carefully analyzed for the possibility of falsehood, he'd never be fully convinced they weren't for real. And as Abu Taleb had pointed out, there was always the remote possibility that Gebril himself might take the rumors seriously, might feel pressured to make them come true. In that case, I asked Abu Taleb, would I be a murderer?

"No," he had said crisply, "you wouldn't be, though you'd probably think you were."

$$* \qquad * \qquad *$$

Later I sat on the terrace looking at the Nile and the early evening stars. The breeze from the Mediterranean, one of Cairo's summer rewards, had taken on the tang of autumn. The bushes by the river, always green, had lost their freshness. I felt no triumph, and I wondered why. What I felt was inner disquiet. And self-disgust. Yet surely Blake merited the moments of fear I was meting out. I presumed he had a wife and I wondered if he'd tell her; he'd have to explain the bodyguards. If I found myself wavering or feeling sorry for him in the months to come, I had only to remember those on the list: Abu Kerim, Mohamed and Frances and the children, (oddly as always) Pinstripe, all the rest.

Cath showed up with a wine bottle and two glasses. We sat there saying nothing, looking out at the evening. I realized suddenly I wanted to cry.

"Don't worry," she said in a firm voice. "Just don't worry."

I turned to look at her. She was not looking at me, just watched the river and sipped her wine. Though I did not know what she meant, the sound of her voice comforted me. Not so long ago, I thought, the blue eyes would have been fixed on my face.

Each wrapped in thought, we cradled our wine glasses and went on looking out. I glanced at her again, felt a surge of love, then looked at one of the bright stars and silently asked somebody to make me steadfast "as thou art." I needed time, I thought. Time to get used to something new I could not identify. Then my mind shifted to the past, which I found difficult to shake. I thought briefly about my other love, a woman in a Jerusalem hotel room yearning to be fair, and as so often, I went over the roster of the dead. I lifted my glass and drank to Abu Kerim.

The river flowed calmly by. At the moment I did not find human nature, including mine, pleasant to contemplate, and so I tried to focus on an imaginary place I could sometimes see, a patch of middle ground where I could build a house, grow olives, and sit in the sun under the blue sky.